Chaos

By Jamie Shaw

Chaos
Riot
Mayhem

Chaos

JAMIE SHAW

AVONIMPULSE
An Imprint of HarperCollinsPublishers

Excerpt from *Chasing Jillian* copyright © 2015 by Julie Revell Benjamin.
Excerpt from *Easy Target* copyright © 2015 by Kay Thomas.
Excerpt from *Dirty Thoughts* copyright © 2015 by Megan Erickson.
Excerpt from *Last First Kiss* copyright © 2015 by Lia Riley.

EPub Edition JULY 2015 ISBN: 9780062379702

Print Edition ISBN: 9780062379696

AM 10 9 8 7 6 5 4 3 2

For every reader who falls in love with Shawn.

Prologue

Nearly Six Years Earlier

"YOU'RE SURE YOU want to do this?" my twin brother, Kaleb, asks with his arms crossed firmly over his lanky chest. His bottom lip twists into a knot that he sucks between his teeth, and I roll my eyes.

"How many times are you going to ask me that?" One of my legs is already dangling out my second-story bedroom window, my weighted combat boot stretching my leg toward the grass. I've snuck out of my house a million times—to play flashlight tag, to spy on my brothers, to steal some desperately needed alone time—but never have I felt as nervous as I do tonight.

Or as desperate.

"How many times do I need to before you realize this is CRAZY?" Kaleb whisper-yells, casting a nervous glance over his shoulder. Our parents are sleeping, and for tonight to go as planned, I need to keep it that way. When he returns his gaze to me, he has the decency to look guilty for almost ratting me out.

"This is my last chance, Kale," my quiet voice pleads, but my twin remains unfazed.

"Your last chance to *what*, Kit? What are you going to do? Confess your eternal love just so he can break your heart just like every other girl those guys ever come into contact with?"

I sigh and throw a second long leg over the windowsill, staring out at the clouds rolling over the crescent face of the moon. "Just…" Another heavy sigh escapes me. "If Mom and Dad wake up, just cover for me, okay?"

When I look over my shoulder, Kale is shaking his head.

"Please?"

He meets me at the window. "No. If you're going, I'm coming with you."

"You don't—"

"I'm coming with you or you're not going." My brother's eyes mirror my own—dark and determined, a brown so dark they're almost black. I know the look he's wearing, and I know there's no point in arguing with it. "Your call, Kit."

"Party boy," I tease, and before he can push me out the window, I jump.

"So what's your plan?" he asks after hitting the ground after me and breaking into a sprint at my side.

"Bryce is going to take us."

When Kale starts laughing, I flash him a smug smile, and we both hop into our parents' SUV to begin our wait.

Adam Everest is throwing a party tonight bigger than he's ever thrown. He and the rest of his band all graduated this morning, and rumor is they're all moving away to Mayfield soon. My brother Bryce would have graduated too if he hadn't gotten suspended for vandalizing the principal's car as part of a senior prank. Our parents grounded him for life—or at least until he moves out— but if I know Bryce at all, that isn't going to stop him from making an appearance at the party of the year.

"You sure he's coming?" Kale asks. He taps nervous fingers on the passenger-side armrest, and I point my chin toward the front door. Our third-oldest brother steps onto the porch, sporting that midnight-black hair that all of us Larson kids are known for. He shuts the front door quietly behind him, shoots nervous glances both ways, and jogs toward our parents' Durango, slowing when I give him a little wave from the driver's seat.

"What the fuck, Kit?" he asks after swinging my door wide open, letting in a gust of late spring air. He shoots an angry glance at Kale, but Kale just shrugs a bony shoulder.

"We're coming too," I say.

Bryce's head shakes sternly from side to side. He learned to give orders as star quarterback of our football team, but he's apparently been hit in the skull one too many times to remember I don't take them.

"No fucking way," he says, but when I rest my hand on the horn, he tenses. I'm the baby of the family, but having grown up with Kale, Bryce, and two other older brothers, I know how to play dirty.

"Yes fucking way."

"Is she kidding?" Bryce asks Kale, and Kale lifts an eyebrow.

"Does she *look* like she's kidding?"

Bryce sneers at our brother before gluing his eyes back to my weaponized hand and asking me, "Why do you even want to come?"

"Because I do."

Impatient as always, he throws his aggression back at Kale. "Why does she want to come?"

"Because she does," Kale echoes, and Bryce bristles when he realizes we're doing the twin thing. I could argue that the sky is neon pink right now, and Kale would have my back.

"You're seriously going to make me take you?" Bryce complains. "You're fucking *freshmen*. It's embarrassing."

Kale mutters something about us technically being sophomores now, but it's lost under the snark in my voice. "Like we'd want to hang out with you anyway."

In my frustration, I accidentally push too hard on the horn, and an impossibly short, impossibly loud beep silences the crickets around us. All three of us are frozen in place, with wide obsidian eyes, and hearts that are racing so fast, I'm surprised Bryce doesn't piss his pants. Silence stretches in the space between our getaway car and our six-bedroom house, and when no lights come on, a collective sigh of relief fills the air.

"Sorry," I offer, and Bryce laughs as he rakes his hand nervously over his short-cropped hair.

"You're a pain in my fucking ass, Kit." He offers me a hand and yanks me out of the car. "Get in the back. And don't blame me if Mom and Dad ground you 'til you're forty."

THE RIDE TO Adam's place takes forever and no time at all. When my brother parks in a long line of cars on the street, shuts the ignition off, and turns to me, I'm pretty damn sure this is the dumbest idea I've ever had. I've lost count of how many telephone poles and streetlights have separated me from home.

"Okay, listen," Bryce orders with his eyes flitting between Kale and me, "if the cops break this thing up, I'll meet you at the big oak by the lake, okay?"

"Wait, what?" Kale says, like it just occurred to him that we'd be at a party with underage drinking and a record breaking number of noise ordinance violations.

"Okay," I agree for both of us, and Bryce studies my twin for a moment longer before letting out a resigned breath and climbing out of the car. I climb out too, wait for Kale to appear at my side, and follow Bryce toward the sound of music threatening to crack the asphalt under our feet. The party is already in full swing, with kids swarming all over the huge yard like ants harvesting red Solo cups. Bryce walks right into the mayhem inside the front door, and when he disappears, Kale and I share a glance before making our way in after him.

Inside Adam's foyer, my eyes travel up and up to a chandelier that casts harsh white light over what is most definitely a million freaking bodies crammed into the space. I maneuver my way through a sea of shoulders and elbows, through hallways and overstuffed rooms, to get to the back patio door, the music in my ears growing louder and louder with every single step I take. By the time Kale and I emerge outside, it's beating on my eardrums, pulsing in my veins. A massive pool flooded with half-naked high schoolers stands between me and where Adam Everest is belting lyrics into his microphone. Joel Gibbon plays the bass to Adam's left. The new guy, Cody something, plays rhythm guitar next to Joel. Mike Madden beats on the drums at the back.

But all of them are just blurred shapes in my peripheral vision.

Shawn Scarlett stands to Adam's right, his talented fingers shredding lead guitar, his messy black hair wild over deep green eyes locked on the vibrating strings. Heat dances up the back of my neck, and Kale mutters, "He's not even the hottest one."

I ignore him and command my feet to move, carrying me around the pool to where a huge crowd is gathered to watch the band. In my combat boots, torn-up jeans, and loose tank top, I'm severely overdressed standing behind bikini-clad cheerleaders who wouldn't know the difference between a Fender and a Gibson even if I smashed both over their bleach-stained heads.

The song ends with me standing on my tippy-toes trying to see over bouncing hair, and I turn on Kale with a huff when the band thanks the crowd and starts packing up their stuff.

"Can we go home now?" Kale asks.

I shake my head.

"Why not? The show's over."

"That's not why I came."

Kale's gaze burrows under my skin, digging deep until he's swimming in my brainwaves. "You're seriously going to try to talk to him?"

I nod as we walk away from the crowd.

"And say what?"

"I haven't figured that out yet."

"Kit," Kale cautions, his navy blue Chuck Taylors slowing to a stop, "what do you expect to happen?" He looks at me with sad dark eyes, and I wish we were standing closer to the pool so I could push him in and wipe that expression off his face.

"I don't expect anything."

"Then why bother?"

"Because I have to, Kale. I just have to talk to him, even if it's just to tell him how much he changed my life, okay?"

Kale sighs, and we both let the conversation go. He knows that Shawn is more than just a teenage crush to me. The first time I ever saw him play guitar was at a school talent show when we were both still in junior high. I was in fifth grade, he was in eighth, and he and Adam put on an acoustic performance that gave me goose bumps from my fingers to my toes. They both sat on stools with guitars on their laps, with Adam singing lead vocals and Shawn singing backup, but the way Shawn's fingers danced over the strings, and the way he lost himself in the music—he took me with him, and I got lost too. I convinced my parents to buy me a used guitar the following week, and I started taking lessons. Now my favorite thing to do will forever be linked with the person who taught me to love it, the person I fell in love with that day in the junior high gym.

Love, as much as I hate to admit it. The kind that makes me ache. The kind that would probably be better kept secret since I know it will only break my heart.

I know I'm fucked, and yet an undeniable part of me still needs him to know what he did for me, even if I don't tell him what he *is* to me.

With my body on auto-walk and my mind a million miles away, Kale and I find Solo cups in the kitchen and head toward the keg out back, my thoughts slowly drifting back to the present. I've had beer with my brothers before, but I've never operated a keg, so I watch a few people fill their cups before me to make sure I don't make myself look like an idiot when it's my turn at the tap. I pick it up with twitchy fingers, fill my cup and Kale's, and then wander Adam's property while my brother and I begin our underage drinking. Adam's yard is big enough to be a public park, surrounded by a wrought-iron fence that protects the pool, a few large oaks, and enough teenagers to fill the school gym. I spare a glance at my twin and follow his gaze to a group of guys laughing by the side of the pool.

"He's cute," I offer, nodding my head toward the one that Kale is now pretending not to have been staring at, a cute tan boy in Hawaiian board shorts and flip-flops.

"He is," Kale challenges with feigned indifference. "You should go talk to him."

I give my twin a look, he gives me one back, and I say, "Don't you ever want a boyfriend?"

"You do realize Bryce is still hanging around here somewhere, right?"

I scoff. "So?"

Kale gives me a look that says it all, and I try not to let him see how much his refusal bothers me. It's not that I don't love being the one who keeps his secrets—it's just that I hate that this is one he feels needs to be kept.

"So if Shawn isn't the hottest one," I say to change the subject, "who is?"

"Are you blind?" Kale asks while pushing his face close to mine to inspect the black around my pupils. I use my free hand to push his forehead away.

"They're all pretty cute."

A girl nearby screams bloody murder as the boy in board shorts picks her up and jumps in the pool. Kale watches them and sighs.

"So which one?" I ask again to distract him.

"Mount Everest."

I chuckle. "You're only saying that because Adam is a man-whore. He's the only one you could probably convince to switch teams."

"Maybe," Kale says with a tinge of sadness in his voice, and I frown before taking his cup to the keg to refill it. I'm squeezing the tap when he elbows me in the arm.

I look up to see Shawn Scarlett and Adam Everest—walking toward the keg, toward *me*.

There are two ways this can go. I can pretend to be confident, offer to pour their beers for them, smile and start a normal conversation so I can say what I need to say, or—nope! I drop the tap, nearly twist my ankles in a supersonic twirl, and bite my lip all the way to a secluded spot that doesn't feel nearly secluded enough.

"What the hell was that?" Kale asks breathlessly from behind me.

"I think I'm having an allergic reaction." My palms are sweating, my throat is closing, my heart is pounding a mile a minute.

Kale laughs and pushes me. I'm stumbling forward when he says, "I did *not* come all this way to watch you turn into some kind of girl."

With my lip pinned between my teeth again, I glance back toward the direction we came and see Shawn and Adam, beers in hand, slip inside the house through the patio door.

"What am I supposed to say?" I ask.

"Whatever you need to."

Kale circles behind me and nudges me toward the door again, and I continue walking forward in a daze, my feet eating the long distance step by step by step. I don't even realize that my twin hasn't followed me until I turn around and see he's not there. My Solo cup is empty, but I cling to it like it's a security blanket, avoiding eye contact with everyone around me and pretending I know where I'm going. I navigate a narrow path through a few familiar faces from school, but not many seem to recognize me, and the ones that do just kind of raise an eyebrow before going back to ignoring me.

Everyone from school knows my older brothers. *Everyone.* Bryce was on the football team before he decided getting into trouble was more important than a scholarship. Mason, two years older than Bryce, is infamous for breaking the school's record for number of suspensions. And Ryan, a year and a half older than Mason, was a record-shattering track star back in his day and remains a legend. All of them straddle this weird line between treating me like one of the guys and acting like I'm coated in porcelain.

I find myself looking for Bryce, desperate for a familiar face, when I spot Shawn instead. He's sitting in the middle of the couch in the living room, Joel Gibbon on one side and some chick I instantly hate on the other. I'm frozen in place when some idiot slams into me from behind.

"Hey!" I shout over the music, whirling around as the jerk leans on me to steady himself.

"Shit! I'm—" Bryce's eyes lock with mine, and he starts laughing, wrapping his hands around my shoulders to steady himself in earnest now. "Kit! I forgot you were here!" He beams like a happy lush, and I scowl at him. "Where's Kale?"

"By the keg out back," I say, crossing my arms over my chest instead of helping my drunk-ass older brother stay on his feet.

His brows turn in with confusion as he finally finds his balance. "What're you doing in here by yourself?"

"Needed to pee," I lie with practiced ease.

"Oh, want me to take you to the bathroom?"

I'm about to chew him out for treating me like a baby, when one of his on-again, off-again girlfriends sidles up next to him and asks him to get her a beer.

"I think I can find my way to the bathroom, Bryce," I scoff, and he studies me through a glassed-over gaze before agreeing.

"Okay." He eyes me some more and then unties the oversized flannel from around my waist and manhandles my arms into it. He pulls it closed over my chest and nods to himself like he's just safeguarded national security. "Okay, don't get into trouble, Kit."

I roll my eyes and take my flannel back off as soon as he walks away, but then I regret dismissing him so quickly when I find myself standing alone in a crowded room. I root myself to a spot by a massive gas fireplace and pretend to drink an empty beer while trying not to look awkward, which is probably useless considering I'm spying on Shawn from afar like a freaking creeper.

What the hell was I thinking coming here tonight? He's surrounded. He's *always* surrounded. He's amazing and popular and way out of my league. The blonde sitting beside him looks like she was born to be a cutout advertisement propped in front of Abercrombie & Fitch. She's hot and girly and probably smells like fucking daffodils and…is standing up to leave.

The spot next to Shawn opens up, and before I can chicken out, I rush across the room and dive ass-first into it.

The cushion collapses beneath my sudden weight, and Shawn turns his head to check out the idiot who nearly slammed right into him. I should probably introduce myself, disclose my affinity for stalking and ass-diving, but instead I keep my mouth shut and force a nervous smile. A moment passes where I'm certain he's going to ask who the hell I am and what the hell I'm doing hijacking the seat beside him, but then his mouth just curves into a nice smile and he goes back to talking with the guys on his other side.

Oh God. Now what? Now I'm just sitting awkwardly beside him for no apparent reason, and blondie is going to be back any second and order me to move, and then what? Then my shot is gone. Then I jumped out of my bedroom window for no freaking reason.

"Hey," I say, tapping Shawn on the shoulder and trying not to do something humiliating like stutter or, you know, throw up all over him.

God, his T-shirt is so soft. Like seriously downy-soft. And warm. And—

"Hey," he says back, something between confusion and interest shading the way he looks at me. His eyes, glassy from drinks he's had, are a deep, deep green, and staring into them is like crossing the border into an enchanted forest at midnight. Terrifying and exhilarating. Like getting lost in a place that could swallow you whole.

"You sounded really good tonight," I offer, and Shawn smiles wider, giving the butterflies in my stomach a little puff of confidence.

"Thanks." He starts to turn away again, but I speak up to keep his attention.

"The riff you did in your last song," I blurt, blushing when he turns back toward me, "it's amazing. I can never quite get that one."

"You play?" Shawn's entire body shifts in my direction, his knees coming to rest against mine. Both of us have worn-through shreds at the knees, and I swear my skin tingles where his brushes against mine. He gives me his complete attention, and it's like every light in the room focuses its heat on me, like every word I say is being documented for the record.

A shadow falls over me, and the Abercrombie model from before glowers down at me, all blonde hair and demon eyes. "You're in my seat."

Shawn's hand lands on my knee to keep me from moving. "You play?" he asks again.

My eyes are glued to his hand—his *hand* on my *knee*—when Demon Eyes whines, "Shawn, she's in my seat."

"So find a new one," he counters, casting her a glance before returning his attention to me. When she finally walks away, my cheeks are candy apples that have been left out in the sun too long.

Shawn stares at me expectantly, and I stare back at him for a loserly amount of time before remembering I'm supposed to be answering a question. "Yeah," I finally say, my heart cartwheeling in my chest at the feel of his heavy hand still resting on my knee. "I watched you…at a middle school talent show"—*please don't throw up, please don't throw up, please don't throw up*—"a few years ago, and"—*oh God, am I really doing this?*—"and it made me want to learn to play. Because you were so good. I mean, you ARE so good. Still, I mean"—*train wreck, train wreck, train wreck!*—"You're still really, really good…"

My attempt to salvage my heartfelt reasons is rewarded with a warm smile that makes all the embarrassment worth it. "You started playing because of me?"

"Yeah," I say, swallowing hard and resisting the urge to squeeze my eyes shut while I wait for his reaction.

"Really?" Shawn asks, and before I know what he's doing, he removes his fingers from my knee to take my hands in his. He studies the calluses on the pads of my fingers, rubbing his thumbs over them and melting me from the inside out. "You any good?"

A cocky smile curves his lips when he lifts his gaze, and I confess, "Not as good as you."

His smile softens, and he releases my hands. "You've been to a few of our shows, right? Normally wear glasses?"

Is that *me*? The girl in the freaking glasses? I've screamed from the front row for more than a few of the band's shows at the local rec center, but I never thought Shawn noticed me. And now when I think about how dorky I probably looked with my thick, square frames…I'm not so sure I'm glad he did. "Yeah. I just got contacts last month—"

"They look good," he says, and the blush that's been creeping across my cheeks blooms to epic proportions. I can feel the heat in my face, my neck, my *bones*. "You have pretty eyes."

"Thanks."

Shawn smiles, and I smile back, but before either of us can say another word, Joel is pushing at his arm to get his attention. He's shouting and laughing about some joke Adam told, and Shawn shifts away from me to rejoin their conversation.

And just like that, the moment is over and I didn't say anything even close to what I came here to say. I didn't say thank you or tell him that he changed my life or express anything even *remotely* meaningful.

"Hey, Shawn," I start, tapping at his shoulder again when Joel's laughter dies down.

Shawn turns a curious gaze on me. "Yeah?"

"I actually wanted to ask you something."

He turns his body back toward me, and I realize I have no fucking clue what to say next. *I actually wanted to ask you something?* Of all the things that could have come out of my mouth, *that's* what my brain settled on? The desperate, girly part of me that I don't like to acknowledge wants to tell him that I love him and beg him not to move away. But then I'd have to go drown myself in the pool.

"Oh yeah?" Shawn asks me over the music someone just turned up, and to stall for time, I lean toward his ear. He leans forward to meet me, and as I breathe in the scent of his shower-fresh cologne, my mind goes completely blank. I've lost the ability to form words, even simple ones like *thank you*. He's moving away soon, and I'm blowing my last chance to tell him how I feel. With my cheek next to his, I turn my face, and then Shawn's eyes are right in front of mine and our noses are practically brushing and his lips are centimeters away—and my brain says *fuck it*. And I lean forward.

And I kiss him.

Not quickly, not slowly. With my eyes closed, I press a warm kiss against his soft bottom lip, which tastes like a million different things. Like beer, like a dream, like the way the clouds swept across the moon tonight. My brain is flickering between wanting to melt into him and needing to jerk away when Shawn makes the decision for me.

When his lips open to mine and he deepens the kiss, my heart kicks against my ribs and my trembling hands anchor themselves to his sides. His fingers bury in the thick of my hair, pulling me closer, and I'm far too lost to ever want to be found. I fist my hands in the loose fabric of his T-shirt, and Shawn breaks his lips from mine to purr low in my ear, "Come with me."

Before I know it, my hand is in his and I'm following him through the crowd. Up the stairs. Down a hall. Into a dark bedroom. The door closes behind us, and in the faint moonlight casting a soft glow throughout the room, those delicious lips claim mine again.

"What's your name?" Shawn asks between kisses, his talented mouth dropping to my neck.

I think I might answer him if I could actually remember. Instead, I'm drunk on his lips and every spot they're touching, on his hands and the way they're charting forbidden territory across my skin. His touch sends shivers dancing over my goose bumps—and then heat, a fire licking over my neck, my arms, my heart.

"It doesn't matter," I pant, and a soft chuckle sounds against my neck before Shawn straightens and gives me a smile that turns my knees to gelatin. He tugs at the knot of my flannel shirt and lets it fall to the floor between us.

Then his fingers hook into my tank top and tug it over my head.

I've made out with guys before. I've passed first base and have lingered at second. But when Shawn tugs me toward the bed and lays me down on top of it, I know I'm being drafted into another league—one that I'm probably not ready for but will try to be good at anyway.

Because it's him. Because it's Shawn. Because even though I didn't come here for this tonight, now I think I'll die if I leave without it.

With my body sunken into covers that aren't mine, I pull him down on top of me so I can feel his lips again, moaning when every inch of his body molds itself against the dips and planes of mine. My fingers slide beneath his worn-soft T-shirt, and together, we tug it over his head.

"Shawn," I moan as I kiss him, the hardness inside his jeans sending me over the edge. I say his name just to make this real, to convince myself I'm not dreaming.

"Fuck," he breathes, and he separates our bodies only enough to unbutton his fly as he's kissing me. He unbuttons mine right after, and I wiggle out of my jeans and panties as he kicks out of his jeans and boxers. A foil wrapper is between his teeth a second later, and then he's rolling a condom over himself and I'm sneaking a peek down below and biting my lip between my teeth.

Everything is moving in fast motion, so fast that my brain keeps shouting, *this isn't really happening*. Shawn is a sweet dream kneeling between my legs, and when my gaze travels back up to his face, he's smirking at me. "This has got to go," he says, plucking at my bra strap, and I arch my back to unclasp it.

He removes the last item of clothing I'm wearing from my shoulders, and then his eyes are drinking me in and I'm shivering under his gaze. His calloused palm cups the ample swell of my breast, and he massages it gently before flicking his thumb across my nipple the way he would flick the tuned string of a guitar. I gasp at the sensation that ambushes every nerve ending in my body, and Shawn's eyes lock with mine again. He holds my gaze as he positions himself between my legs. As he eases forward, I feel pressure, then pushing and stretching that make my eyes squeeze shut. My fingers sink into his back, pulling him as tight as I can get him, and my chin anchors in the warm crook of his neck.

"Are you okay?" he asks, and I lie by raking a hand into his hair and sucking his earlobe between my lips. He doesn't know he's taking my virginity—because he doesn't *need* to know, because I don't *want* him to know.

What would he think? Would he stop?

He starts moving again, slowly, and I command my body to relax, to loosen for him so it doesn't hurt as much. This wasn't quite how I envisioned my first time. I imagined scented candles and music and...for the guy to at least know my name.

Oh my God, my virginity is being taken by a guy who *doesn't even know my name.*

"Kit," I blurt, and Shawn continues moving in and out of me as he pants, "Huh?"

"My name," I answer with my eyes still squeezed shut. I turn my face into the heat of his skin and fill my head with his scent, needing to remind myself that candles and music don't matter because it's Shawn, and that was always something too perfect to even dream of.

"Kit," he says, and when he pushes into me this time, my toes curl and a breathy moan drifts from my lips. He pulls away from my vise-grip hold to kiss me, and my body responds to him, adjusting to the increasing tempo of his thrusts.

His tongue is between my lips, his hips are between my thighs, and his body is in my hands—but it's me who is lost to him. I'm *his*, silently begging for more and more as he gives himself to me in the darkness of a stranger's room. When his body spasms and he collapses on top of me, I hold him close, allowing my hands to memorize the planes of his back and the way his sweat-dampened hair curls against the top of his neck.

I want to kiss him again, but now that what we did is over, I don't know if I should. With my fingers in his hair, I fight with myself too long and lose the battle when Shawn pushes off of me and begins gathering his clothes. He tosses me mine with a tired smile on his face, and I try to remind myself I should be happy. Even if I never see him again, at least I had tonight.

"Do you see my phone anywhere?" he asks, and I search the sheets around me to find it. He flips on the light switch, and I thank God when I don't see any blood anywhere. We're in Adam's room, judging by the band posters and lyrics scrawled on the walls, and I find

Shawn's phone in black satin sheets and hand it to him, ignoring the pain that throbs down below with each little movement I make. If he knew it was my first time, he probably would have been gentler. But if he knew it was my first time, he probably wouldn't have done it at all.

Realization hits me like a wrecking ball to my gut—because I *know* he's never going to talk to me after this. He's going to leave, going to move a hundred miles away, and my heart is going to break worse than it would have if I had just let him go.

"What's your number?" he asks, and I stare up at him. He's holding his phone in his hand, waiting for me to answer him, and the wrecking ball explodes into a thousand butterflies that flutter over my skin and tickle at my cheeks.

I get my hopes up before I can help it, rattling off numbers as Shawn enters them into his phone. When he's finished, I slide my last article of clothing over my head and eagerly take the hand he offers. He helps me up and then chuckles, pocketing his phone and saying, "Here." His fingers lift to comb through my hair, but he quickly gives up and simply smooths it out, finishing the job by tucking a long strand behind my ear.

"Better?" I ask, and he smiles before giving me an unexpected kiss that leaves me wanting to do more of what we just did on the bed, throbbing pain be damned.

The moment ends when he reaches for the knob and opens the door, and then we're walking into the hall and his arm is draping over my shoulder. In front of everyone. I contain a squeal and play it cool, smiling like I belong here at Adam's party. Like I'm not just some nerdy freshman who used to wear thick glasses. Like Shawn Scarlett's arm draped possessively over my shoulder is no big deal. Like he didn't just take my virginity and make my entire life. Like him asking for my number, giving me a kiss, and putting his arm around me doesn't make my heart want to explode in my chest. Like I'm not hopelessly in love with him.

"What the fuck are you doing, man?" a familiar voice asks when we reach the living room, and every hair on my body stands on end as Shawn and I turn and see my brothers approaching us from the crowd. Bryce's tone is light and amused, which tells me he has no idea we just came from upstairs. He laughs when I blush under his gaze. "Dude, that's my *sister*," he tells Shawn, and then he turns his attention to me. "Is this why you wanted to come here tonight?"

Oh God, oh God, oh God.

"You're his sister?" Shawn asks me, and I see it happen—the moment when he recognizes me as a Larson, when he realizes I'm the little sister of Bryce, Ryan, and worst of all, Mason.

"Yeah," Bryce answers for me, "and she's *fifteen*, man."

I barely have time to catch the mortified look Shawn gives me, but it embeds itself in my memory forever. His arm drops from my shoulder even before someone outside yells, "COPS!"

Red and blue lights flash through the windows, followed by sirens that trigger a stampede. Bryce grabs me by the arm and tugs me away from Shawn, and Shawn drifts farther and farther away in the chaos, staring after me in that way that breaks my heart. Like what we did was a mistake and all I am is a regret.

He moves away. He doesn't call.

He forgets, but I never do.

Chapter One

"THAT WAS A hundred years ago, Kale!" I shout at my closed bedroom door as I wiggle into a pair of skintight jeans. I hop backward, backward, backward—until I'm nearly tripping over the combat boots lying in the middle of my childhood room.

"So why are you going to this audition?"

I barely manage to do a quick twist-and-turn to land on my bed instead of my ass, my furrowed brow directed at the ceiling as I finish yanking my pants up. "Because!"

Unsatisfied, Kale growls at me from the other side of my closed door. "Is it because you still like him?"

"I don't even KNOW him!" I shout at a white swirl on the ceiling, kicking my legs out and fighting against the taut denim as I stride to my closed door. I grab the knob and throw it open. "And he probably doesn't even remember me!"

Kale's scowl is replaced by a big set of widening eyes as he takes in my outfit—tight, black, shredded-to-hell jeans paired with a loose black tank top that doesn't do much to cover the lacy bra I'm wearing. The black fabric matches my wristbands and the parts of my hair that aren't highlighted blue. I turn away from Kale to grab my boots.

"*That* is what you're wearing?"

I snatch up the boots and do a showman's twirl before plopping down on the edge of my bed. "I look hot, don't I?"

Kale's face contorts like the time I convinced him a Sour Patch Kid was just a Swedish Fish coated in sugar. "You're my *sister*."

"But I'm hot," I counter with a confident smirk, and Kale huffs out a breath as I finish tying my boots.

"You're lucky Mason isn't home. He'd never let you leave the house."

Freaking Mason. I roll my eyes.

I've been back home for only a few months—since December, when I decided that getting a bachelor's degree in music theory wasn't worth an extra year of nothing but general education requirements—but I'm already ready to do a kamikaze leap out of the nest again. Having a hyperactive roommate was nothing compared to my overprotective parents and even more overprotective older brothers. Pair that with Kale, who always knows what I'm thinking even when I'd rather keep it to myself, and I'm pretty sure I need to figure out what the hell I'm doing with my life or accept that eventually the white coats will need to drive out to retrieve me.

"Well, Mason isn't home. And neither is Mom or Dad. So are you going to tell me how I look or not?" I stand back up and prop my hands on my hips, wishing my brother and I still stood eye to eye. A growth spurt in high school gained him a few inches over me, and now he's almost as tall as the rest of our brothers, even if he is a whole lot lankier. At five foot eight, I have to tilt my chin to glare at him.

Sounding thoroughly unhappy about it, Kale says, "You look amazing."

A smile cracks across my face a moment before I grab my guitar case from where it's propped against the wall. As I walk through the house, Kale trails after me.

"What's the point in dressing up for him?" he asks with the echo of our footsteps following us down the hall.

"Who says it's for him?"

"Kit," Kale complains, and I stop walking. At the top of the stairs, I turn and face him.

"Kale, you know this is what I want to do with my life. I've wanted to be in a big-name band since middle school. And Shawn is an amazing guitarist. And so is Joel. And Adam is an amazing singer, and Mike is an amazing drummer…This is my chance to be *amazing*. Can't you just be supportive?"

My twin braces his hands on my shoulders, and I have to wonder if it's to comfort me or because he's considering pushing me down the stairs. "You know I support you," he says. "Just…" He twists his lip between his teeth, chewing it cherry red before releasing it. "Do you have to be amazing with *him*? He's an asshole."

It's not like I can't understand why Kale is worried. He knew how much I liked Shawn before that party, and that night, he squeezed every last detail out of me. He knew I gave Shawn my virginity, so he knew why I cried myself to sleep for the next few weeks when Shawn never called.

"Maybe he's a different person now," I reason, but Kale's dark eyes remain skeptical as ever.

"Maybe he's not."

"Even if he isn't, *I'm* a different person now. I'm not the same nerd I was in high school."

I start down the stairs, but Kale stays on my heels, yapping at me like a nippy dog. "You're wearing the same boots."

"These boots are killer," I say—which should be obvious, but apparently needs to be said.

"Just do me a favor?"

At the front door, I turn around and begin backing onto the porch. "What favor?"

"If he hurts you again, use those boots to get revenge where it counts."

I laugh and take a big step forward to squeeze my brother in a hug. "Promise. Love you, Kale. I'll call you when it's over."

With a big sigh, he hugs me back. And then he lets me go.

It takes me an hour to drive to Mayfield. An hour of drumming my fingers against my Jeep's steering wheel and blasting the music so loud that I can't hear myself think. My GPS interrupts the eardrum massacre to give me directions to a club called Mayhem, and I park in the side parking lot of a massive square of a building.

With my Jeep in a spot and my ignition turned off, I drum on my steering wheel a few more times before smacking the heel of my palm against my glove compartment. It pops open, a hairbrush spills out, and I use it to tame my wind-tangled locks.

Earlier this week, the name of Shawn's band—The Last Ones to Know—popped up on one of my favorite bands' websites. I blinked once, twice, and then pushed my nose toward the screen to make sure I wasn't seeing things.

They were looking for a new rhythm guitarist. After doing a little digging, I found out that their old one, Cody, got kicked out of the band. The website didn't say why, and I didn't care. There was an opening, and everything in me told me to send an email to the email address listed at the bottom of the online flyer.

I typed the email in a daze—as if my guitar-loving fingers wanted to be in the band even more than my spaced-out brain did. I wrote that I had been in a band in college but that we broke up to go our separate ways, I sent a YouTube link to one of our songs, I asked for an audition, and I signed my name.

Less than half an hour later, I received a reply overflowing with exclamation points and an audition time, and I wasn't sure if I should smile or cry. It was a chance to make all my dreams come true. But in order to do that, I'd have to face the dream that had already been crushed.

These past six years, I've tried not to think about it. I've tried to erase his face from my mind. But that day, with that email in front of me, it all came back in a rush.

Green eyes. Messy black hair. An intoxicating scent that seemed to linger on my skin for days, weeks.

I give my head a little shake to clear Shawn from my mind. Then I finish brushing my hair and take one last glance in my rearview mirror. Satisfied I don't look nearly as messy as I feel, I hop onto the asphalt and haul my guitar case from the backseat.

Now or never.

After a deep breath of city air, I begin making my way around the concrete fortress casting shadow over the parking lot. Unforgiving rays of afternoon sunshine wrap themselves around my neck and send beads of sweat trickling between my shoulder blades. My combat boots hit the sidewalk step by heavy step, and I force them to keep lifting and falling, lifting and falling. It isn't until I'm at a massive set of double doors that I finally stop long enough to let myself think.

I raise my hand. I lower it. I raise it again. I flex my fingers.

I take a deep breath.

I knock.

During the seconds that tick away between my knock and the door opening, I think about grabbing my guitar case from where it's propped against the wall and high-tailing it back to my Jeep. I think about who will open the door. I think about Kale and wonder what in the hell I'm doing.

But then the door is swinging open and I'm stuck on the threshold of a decision that could make my life or ruin it.

Long dark chocolate hair. Fierce brown eyes. A piercing gaze that smacks me right in the face. The girl—who I'm guessing is the one who responded to my email and signed her name "Dee"—trails her eyes all the way down to my boots and then back up again. "The band isn't here to sign shit or take pictures," she says.

Apparently, I've offended her just by breathing. "Okay?" My eyebrow lifts from the sheer gust of hostility she throws at me, and I resist the urge to glance over my shoulder to make sure I'm in the right place. "I'm not here for autographs or pictures…"

"Great." She begins closing the door in my face, but I slap my hand against it before she can shut me out.

"Are you Dee?" I ask, and the girl's glare hardens with either recognition or irritation. Maybe both. She's so focused on trying to murder me with her eyes that she doesn't even notice when a blonde-haired girl pops up behind her. With nothing to lose, I wedge my combat boot against the door and hold out my hand. "I'm Kit. We spoke over email?"

"*You're* Kit?" the blonde asks, and the brown-haired girl that I'm assuming is Dee slowly offers up her hand.

"Oh, sorry," I say with an apologetic laugh, realizing why the girls are acting like I'm some kind of groupie. Probably because I look like one, with my barely there top and my spider-leg mascara. "Yeah. I have four older brothers who thought Katrina was too girly of a name."

The running joke is that I didn't even *know* my name was Katrina until grade school—but it isn't a joke, because I'm pretty sure I really didn't. The boys boycotted the name my mom had insisted on, and eventually she gave up the good fight. It was Kit from the day I was born, and the only people who call me Katrina are people who don't really know me.

"And you're here to audition?" the blonde asks.

I pull my guitar case from where it's propped against the wall and give them a big smile. "I hope so. It *is* okay that I'm a girl, right?"

"Yeah," the blonde rushes to say, but Dee still has her eyes narrowed with skepticism.

Having been the only girl in an all-guy band in college, I'm used to it, so I'm not surprised when she says, "That depends…Are you a girl who can play the guitar?"

"I think so," I deadpan. "I mean, it's difficult since my vagina is constantly getting in the way, but I've learned to manage it just like any other handicap." I pause for dramatic effect, my expression somber when I add, "Sadly, I don't get special parking."

A long moment of silence passes where I'm sure my brand of humor is lost on the two chicks in front of me, but then Dee bursts out laughing and they both lead me inside.

On our walk through a short hallway, the blonde apologizes for the rude welcome and tells me her name is Rowan, and then we turn into the cavernous space that is Mayhem. A massive bar lines one wall, a stage lines the other, and in the middle of the room sits a row of card tables and six foldout chairs—like some kind of make-shift setup for the judges of *American Idol.*

I cross the club to lean my guitar against the stage and, in an attempt to convince myself Shawn isn't about to magically appear at any freaking moment, I say, "So it's just going to be us?"

"No—" Dee starts, but she's barely gotten the word out before a back door opens and bright afternoon sunlight spills onto the floor, paving the way for all four remaining members of The Last Ones to Know.

Joel Gibbon enters first, his blond hair giving him away. In high school, it was a gelled mess that stood up all over the place; now it's a disciplined Mohawk that cuts a line down the center of his head. He's followed by Mike Madden, who looks the same and yet somehow more manly, like he grew into himself. Adam Everest walks in next, looking even hotter than he did six years ago. His hair is still long and untamed, his jeans still look like they got into a fight with a paper shredder and lost, and his wrists are still adorned with stacks of mismatched brace-lets. The blonde girl walks to meet him, and I feel sorry for the way she's going to feel when Adam decides to stop calling.

And then, I get my first glimpse of Shawn Scarlett just before the door closes behind him. My eyes fight to adjust back to the dim lighting, and when it does, he's all I can see. He has that same dark hair, that same scruffy jaw, that same look about him that makes it hard for me to breathe.

"Guys, this is Kit," Dee says while Shawn continues stealing the breath from my lungs. "She's up next."

They all look me over as they gather close, with only Adam and Joel managing to contain their ogling. When I see the way Shawn is raking his eyes over me, a satisfied smile sneaks onto my face. After six years of not being able to forget him, this single moment is making it all worthwhile. Whether he remembers me or not, he's staring at me like I'm the hottest chick he's ever seen.

These pants were *so* worth it.

"We thought you were a dude," Joel says, wrapping his arm around Dee's shoulder and giving me an excuse to play it cool.

"Yeah," I say, withdrawing my gaze from Shawn even though I can feel his green eyes still tracing over the curves of my exposed skin. "I gathered that when your girlfriend tried to close the door in my face."

"Have we met before?" Shawn asks, and a laugh almost bubbles out of me. Have we *met*? Yeah, I guess you could call it that.

He's staring at me with a slight squint to his enchanted forest eyes, but I refuse to let them charm me. Instead, I meet them with a smirk and say, "We went to the same school."

"What year were you?"

"Three under you."

"Didn't you used to come to our shows?" Mike asks, but I stare at Shawn for a moment longer, waiting to see if my smile, my eyes, or my voice jog his memory. The rejected teenage girl in me wants to claw his face off for forgetting me, but rationally, I know he's given me the upper hand in a game I wasn't aware I'd be playing. One I'm making up the rules for as I go along.

When Shawn stares and stares and still can't place me, I turn to Mike and answer, "Sometimes."

As the guys continue asking me questions—have I been in a band before, were we any good, why'd we break up—and I continue giving them answers—in college, we could have been better, because they wanted nine-to-five jobs—I wonder what would happen if Shawn *would* remember me. Would I be happy? Would he laugh it off? Would he apologize for breaking my teenage heart?

Any apology now would be too little, too late. It'd be meaningless—and so infuriating that I'd have to use my combat boots to do just what Kale told me to.

"And you're sure this is what you want to do with your life?" Mike asks me, and I nod.

"More than anything."

Satisfied, Mike turns to Shawn. "Anything to add? Or should we have her play?"

Shawn, who hasn't said another word since asking me what year I was, rubs the back of his neck and nods. "Sure. Let her play."

Taking my dismissal for what it is, I walk away and grab my guitar, sliding it onto the stage before hoisting myself up behind it. I force Shawn from my mind and get set up in record time, strapping my Fender around my neck and stepping up to the mic. As I adjust it to fit my height, the guys are all sitting at the tables, laughing and carrying on. All of them but Shawn, who is too bored with my audition to laugh along with the rest of them.

"What do you want me to play?" I ask, ignoring the way he's staring at the table in front of him like it's far more interesting than anything I could possibly do onstage.

"Your favorite song!" Adam shouts, and the butterflies in my stomach fade away as I concentrate on the music in my head. I think about my options for a moment before chuckling under my breath and stepping back. As soon as I position my fingers and pluck the E string, all six *American Idol* judges start to groan and I can't help laughing.

"Just kidding!" I say into the microphone, knowing they must have heard "Seven Nation Army" by the White Stripes a hundred times by now by amateur guitarists. When I step away from the mic again, I smile down at my guitar, thinking about it for another brief moment before I begin playing "Vices" by Brand New. My fingers slide over the strings, the harshness of my chords assaulting the very foundation of the building we're in and reminding me how much I've missed being onstage. With my old band, I played small venues to small crowds, but a stage is a stage, and a show is a show. Performing is in my blood now—like being A positive or B negative. I couldn't forget what it feels like if I tried.

When Adam's hand lifts, I reluctantly stop playing.

"Do you write your own stuff?" he asks before my heart can sink too far. When I nod, he asks me to play something, and I play one of the new untitled songs I've been working on just because it's the freshest on my fingers.

Again, I don't get far into it before he stops me.

I wait for him to tell me I suck and order me to leave, but then the guys share a few words and all stand in unison, their chairs screeching against the floor as they get slid back. When Shawn, Adam, Joel, and Mike walk toward the stage, my heart beats hard, climbing inch by inch into my throat. I try to play it cool as Mike sits at the drums, as Joel and Shawn collect their guitars and hook them up, as Adam takes his place at the mic.

Adam names one of their songs and asks me if I know it, and I nod in a daze. My chin is still moving when Adam's thumb goes up and Mike's drumsticks tap together. Three taps, and then I'm swept up in a performance with The Last Ones to freaking Know.

We play bits and pieces of a few songs, and I'm feeling really, *really* good about my audition, when Adam gives me a big smile and says, "Okay. I think that's good. Have we heard enough?"

He glances at Mike and Joel, who are both smiling equally wide and nodding, and then he looks at Shawn, who nods too, with no light in his eyes whatsoever. No smile, either—not a small one, not a forced one, just nothing. He doesn't even try.

"Yeah," Shawn says, turning that unfazed expression on me. "Thanks for coming. We'll give you a call."

I stare at him blankly, not giving myself permission to speak or think or feel—not with him standing in front of me, staring at me like I'm nothing. I politely thank the guys, and then I gather my things.

I leave knowing I'll never hear from them again.

Because I know what it means when Shawn Scarlett says he's going to give you a call.

Chapter Two

"FIND FROYO," I order my phone on the way out of Mayhem's parking lot. I'm not going to cry. Not going to cry.
Not going to shed a single goddamn tear.

I am, however, going to drown myself in the biggest
bucket of frozen yogurt I can find.

"Sorry, I do not understand," the robotic voice of my
phone says back to me syllable by syllable, and I growl at
it sitting down in my cup holder before repeating myself.

"Find fro-zen yo-gurt."

"Can you repeat that?"

"FOR GOD'S SAKE, HELP ME OUT HERE."

"Say that again?"

"I WILL END YOU."

"That's not nice."

I'm about to pick my bitch phone up and pitch it
out the window, when the damn thing starts ringing.
Unknown number. Seeing an opportunity to take my

frustration out on an unsuspecting telemarketer, I whip my Jeep into a gas station and answer it. "Yeah?"

"Kit?"

I pull my phone away from my ear to stare at the number again before answering. "Yes?"

"Hey. It's Dee."

My heart launches into my throat, and I barely manage a pathetic, "Oh…hey."

"Hey, I just wanted to let you know that we all freaking loved you!"

"You did?"

"Yeah, you got the job!"

"I did?"

"Yeah!"

"Seriously?"

Dee laughs, and I silently thank God I didn't chuck my phone into a pothole. "Yeah, you were awesome. Seriously, you blew it out of the water. I only have one last question before we make it official-official."

Yeeeah, because that doesn't sound ominous at all. "Okay?"

"Which of the guys do you think is the hottest?"

I glance around the gas station for some kind of candid camera. "You're joking, right?"

"Nope, simple question. You could bang one, who do you choose? Adam and Shawn are pretty hot, but Joel is hotter, right?"

It's a trap. It's a giant deadly trap with flashing neon signs, because from my time in Mayhem, I could tell Adam was with Rowan and Joel was with Dee…sooo…I really have no idea what the hell is going on. "None of the above?"

"Aw, come on," Dee coaxes. "I'm just curious, honest. No one is even around me right now, and I swear I won't tell."

Never in my life have I been a girl's kind of girl. I've never kissed and bragged. I've never squealed over boys. And I've certainly never told an absolute stranger about my high school crush on Shawn Scarlett, so I'm not going to start spilling my guts now, right after that crush rose from the dead and pushed its dirty zombie fingers up and out of my chest.

"Dee, honestly…if I'm going to be in the band, those guys are going to be like my brothers. It doesn't matter how hot they are because I don't need that kind of drama."

And that's the God's-honest truth. Shawn is hot, but he seems to follow that unspoken rule that the hotter a guy is, the stronger his asshole gene is. I wouldn't sleep with him again if he begged me.

"RIGHT ANSWER!" Dee shouts, and I flinch at the excitement in her voice. "That was perfect! You're in!"

"What if I had said Adam?" I ask, because I never know when to keep my mouth shut.

"You'd be out," she answers, like it's no big deal.

"What if I'd said Joel?"

"Just be glad you didn't." She finishes with a little laugh that sounds downright evil, and I make a mental note: *don't get on the crazy chick's bad side.* "So look," she continues, "your first band practice won't be this coming weekend because it's Easter, but I'm thinking maybe next weekend. One of the guys will give you a call when they get their shit figured out, 'kay?"

I agree in a daze, and the call ends with Dee asking me where I live and suggesting maybe I find a place closer to town. Then I'm just driving toward home, wondering how I should feel.

It's done now. I did it. I landed a coveted guitarist position with The Last Ones to Know. The opportunity of a lifetime. And my job is going to entail practicing with Shawn. Performing with Shawn. Writing music with Shawn. Touring with Shawn...

"Kit?" my mom says at the dinner table, and my head snaps up so fast, I nearly bite my tongue clean off.

"Huh?"

"You've barely touched your chili," she notes from her seat at my right, at the end opposite my dad. "What's going on with you?"

"I got a job today."

I answer with a forced smile, keeping Shawn's name buried down deep. Sunday nights are family dinner nights, and I typically eat just as much and just as fast as my two-hundred-plus pound brothers—but tonight my stomach is in knots, and Shawn Scarlett's name is written all over every single one of them.

My mom's mouth crinkles at the corners. She's built like a ballerina, with soft brown eyes and fuzzy brunette hair, and those brown eyes light up when she says, "That's wonderful! Doing what?"

When she sets her silverware down and gives me her undivided attention, I lose the good fight and divert my eyes to my dad. "It's in Mayfield. I'm thinking of moving there."

My brothers and I inherited our mother's lean frame and smooth features, but our father's dark hair, dark eyes, and height. He's a big man with a way about him that just makes you want to spill your guts, so when he sets his silverware down too, I know I'm in trouble.

"What job'd ya get, hun?"

Great, it's like he and my mom are tag-teaming me and I'm on my own in the ring.

"Probably a stripper," Bryce throws in, which is *so* the opposite of helping. I swear he stopped maturing at the same time he stopped growing. If the past six years have taught me anything, it's that Bryce will forever be an eighteen-year-old trapped in a grown man's body.

I kick him hard under the table without ever breaking eye contact with my dad, and Bryce does just what I expect him to.

"FUCK, Kit! What the fuck! That fucking—"

My mom starts screaming about his language while Kale, Ryan, and Mason all snicker under their breath. I interrupt the chaos to finally answer my dad.

"I auditioned for a guitarist position in a new band, and I got it."

My mom stops in the middle of telling Bryce to watch his "darn mouth" to stare at me, a frown hiding behind her guarded expression.

"Another band?" my dad asks, but before I can answer, Ryan pushes me down the rabbit hole.

"Isn't that where that band you guys went to high school with went?" he asks. "Mayfield?"

Adam, Shawn, Joel—those names were infamous within the hallways of our school. With the exception of Mike, the guys were all players, with well-earned reputations that I have no doubt my brothers would remember. Because who could forget the whispers, the rumors, the long lines of batting eyelashes that followed them wherever they went?

I shrug my shoulders as fast as they can possibly shrug, but Mason's fork clanks onto his plate before I can change the subject. "You're not in a band with *those* douchebags, are you?"

"I don't even know what you're talking about."

I lie to prevent my brothers from going all vigilante on my ass and demanding I quit the band, but when Mason's eyes narrow, I realize the mistake I've made.

"Oh, come on, Kit," Ryan says with his mouth half-full. "You used to love them, remember?"

Mason's eyes are dark slits when he says. "What's the name of the band you joined?"

"They're still really small," I lie.

"So they don't have a name?"

With my brothers calling me out and a spoon in my hand, the first name that comes to mind is—

"The Murderspoons," I answer, mentally berating myself for my complete lack of originality—and then praising it when Mason merely lifts a silent eyebrow.

"And what are the guys' names?" he continues, interrupting my sigh of relief before it can even begin.

"Bill, Ty…" I take a big bite of spicy chili to buy myself some time. "Paul…and…" I choke into my hand while drowning out of water. No name is coming to the top of my head, not even to the tip of my tongue—none, nada, zero, zilch, oh God. I'm so fucked.

"And Mike," Kale finishes for me, and I nod vigorously because Mike Madden's name is just generic enough to work.

"And Mike," I agree, and then I turn to my dad before Mason can ask me anymore valid questions that I might just have to commit fratricide over. "They're still building their fan base, but they're really good, and I think it's worth going after."

"Kit," my mom says from the other end of the table, in that soft voice that means she knows I'm not going to like what she has to say next, "wouldn't you rather be a music teacher or something? Maybe give guitar lessons to kids? My friend Laura's husband does that, and he makes some decent money…"

"Come on, Mom," I plead, not wanting to rehash a conversation we've had a thousand times before.

"How are you going to afford to move?" Bryce asks, and I rub at a pain that's rooting in my temple.

"I have some money saved up from working while I was in school. It's not much, but it'll last a little while."

"So this band," Mason says, "they're all guys?"

My parents and each one of my brothers lock their sights on me, and I roll my eyes and sigh. "No, Mason, Paul is a girl's name now. Are you serious?"

My dad: "Can't you find a band with girls?"

Mason: "I want to meet them."

My mom: "Why do you have to move to Mayfield?"

Bryce mumbles something about Mason and him needing to make a trip there, Kale and Ryan nod vigorously while insisting they're going to come along, and then I'm standing up before I know it. My wooden chair scrapes against the hardwood floor, dousing the torches of the rapidly forming pitchfork mob.

"Okay, guys?" I stare pointedly across the table at my brothers, especially the three oldest ones who should know better than to think I need protecting. "Seriously, a 'congratulations' would have been nice at *any* point in this conversation."

"Kit—" my mom begins, but I just shake my head.

"I'm getting a headache. We can talk about this later, but it's my decision and I just wanted everyone to know."

I give my parents one more pleading look before turning around to leave, but Kale's voice is the one that swims after me.

"Congratulations, Kit."

IN THE SILENCE of my own room, I collapse on my bed and wonder which one of the boys is going to come up first. Normally, I'd think it'd be Kale, but this day has been anything *but* normal, and frankly, Kale doesn't seem too happy with me right now. Maybe it'll be Bryce, if only just to ask me if I'm going to eat the rest of my garlic bread or if he can have it. Or Mason, to tell me I shouldn't act like a baby if I don't want to be treated like one.

When someone knocks on the door and Ryan walks in, I'm almost thankful.

"Hey," he says, sitting on the edge of the bed and patting my knee.

"Hey."

Ryan's usually perfectly styled bangs tumble over his forehead, a sign he probably has a haircut scheduled for tomorrow, if not for later today. "We just worry about you, you know."

"Yeah, well, stop," I say, sitting up and pulling my knees to my chest. My boots dig into my comforter, my expression more unyielding than I feel. "I'm not a baby anymore. I can make my own decisions."

"You've been making your own decisions since you *were* a baby, Kit," Ryan says with a warm laugh. "Maybe that's *why* we worry so much. Ever think about that?"

I give him a look, he flicks me in the forehead, and I can't help laughing. Our parents had us all close together, so even though Kale and I are twenty-one, Bryce is twenty-four, Mason is twenty-six, and Ryan is twenty-seven, not one of us knows how to act our age around each other. I don't usually consider it a bad thing until it's four against one and I'm on the losing side of an argument.

"Doesn't it matter if I'm happy though?" I ask, and Ryan scoffs.

"Of course it does."

"So then why does Mom keep insisting I be a music teacher?"

"Because Mom is crazy," he answers matter-of-factly, and I find myself chuckling again.

Ryan scoots back on my bed until his back is against the wall, and he sits like that in silence until I say, "Giving this band a shot means a lot to me, and I don't need you guys messing that up, okay? This is what I want to do with my life, Ry. You *know* that. This town has always been too small for me."

"I think the whole *world* is too small for you."

"That's not necessarily a bad thing though."

My challenge brings a small smile to his lips. "Didn't say it was." He slaps my knee and stands up, pausing only when he's at my door. "Just promise me there's nothing to worry about? I'll work on the guys and keep Mason on his leash."

"There's nothing to worry about," I echo, and I can tell Ryan doesn't believe me, but he knows there aren't interrogation lights in the world hot enough to make me spill my guts—not with four bossy brothers who have spent my whole life showing me the consequences of telling them anything they don't want to hear.

"And you're going to let me help you move?"

I give him a sincere smile. "Sure, Ry. You can help me move."

Chapter Three

When I move into my new apartment a few days after Easter, all four of my brothers *and* my dad help move me into the new place. I insist it's overkill and my mom silently agrees, but the men insist on meeting my new landlord—a sweet old lady who's renting me out the finished space over her garage—and they don't complain when she feeds them cookies and milk and croons about how handsome they all are.

My first band practice with the guys is the following week, and if I rated it on a scale of piece of cake to zombie apocalypse, I'm pretty sure everyone in the band would be eating each other's faces.

"Kit," Shawn says in that voice he's been using to criticize me all damn afternoon, "seriously, how many times is it going to take you to get this song?"

In Mike's garage on the outskirts of the city, I resist the urge to go full-on rock star and smash my guitar against the floor. I applied to be the band's guitarist, not Shawn's personal punching bag, but from the moment we started practice, he's been taking my confidence and beating it up. My molars are grinding, the noise scratching at my eardrums, and I sound like one of my brothers when I growl, "Really?" I glance at Joel out of the corner of my eye and then glare back at Shawn. His words sting, but I bite. "*I* am the person you're going to bitch out right now?"

"You miss your mark at the same spot every single time."

"Your bass player is fucking hungover as shit!" I bark, the echo of my insult lost to the noise-cancelling equipment mounted on the walls. With dark circles under his eyes and his Mohawk lying in a matted mess on top of his head, Joel looks like he's been binge drinking all damn week and picked a shitty time to stop. "How the hell am I supposed to keep a rhythm when he's all over the damn place?"

Shawn blanches, and Mike twirls a drumstick between his fingers. "She's not wrong."

"She's right," Joel interjects before anyone can defend him. He unstraps the Fender from around his neck and sets it on a stand at the side of the garage.

"You're fine," Shawn assures him, turning those laser-cut emerald eyes on me again. "Don't lash out at him just because you can't do your job."

"Whoa," Adam says, but I'm already throwing my guitar pick at Shawn like it's a ninja throwing star and storming out of Mike's garage. I push the door open so hard that when it slams against the side of Mike's house, I'm surprised the tiny thing doesn't go toppling over.

I don't know why I ever thought joining Shawn's band would be a good idea. He was an asshole back in high school, he's an asshole now, and if the house *did* fucking topple over, I'm not sure I'd waste my energy digging him out.

"Kit!"

I ignore his stupid voice and continue walking, each stomp of my combat boots pulverizing the gravel of Mike's driveway into dust. The wind blows my hair back, transforming me into one very pissed off avenging angel who isn't going to waste her time avenging a goddamn thing. After two weeks of not being able to sleep because I was *so* anxious, of not being able to eat because I was *so* nervous, Shawn has made it a point to make me feel even smaller than the fifteen-year-old girl I was the first time I talked to him. And I am *not* that fucking small.

I lay my guitar in the back of my Jeep, climb into the driver's seat, and slam my key into the ignition.

Fuck going back to get my guitar case. I'd rather buy a new one.

When Shawn launches onto the running board beside me and clings to the roll bars above my head, I refuse to let him crowd me. I have a Taser in my glove compartment, and he has ten seconds before we both learn how it works.

Ten...nine...

"I'm sorry," he pants. "I didn't mean...to be so..."

"Such an ass?" I snap, forgoing the Taser when he offers his agreement.

"Yeah."

I narrow my eyes into pinprick black holes. "Too late."

"Huh?"

The afternoon sun casts a blinding halo all around him as I squint up at his stupidly gorgeous face. "I don't accept your apology. Now get the hell off my Jeep."

When he doesn't budge, I spin in my seat, lean back, and plant my combat boot firmly against his irritatingly flat chest. I give him a quick push with all intentions of knocking him on his ass, but Shawn reaches out for balance just as he begins to fall. His long fingers wrap tightly around my calf—around my barely there skull-print leggings and the suddenly burning-hot skin beneath.

And then I'm just there, leaning back in the driver's seat, with my trembling leg captured in Shawn Scarlett's hand. His green eyes crawl slowly up the length of my thigh, the flat of my stomach, the curve of my neck.

"What am I supposed to do with this?" he questions, his eyes full of fire that's giving me seriously bad ideas. Every part of my body is begging him to prop the leg he's holding onto his shoulder, and then take the other and do the same. And when his grip slides up to my ankle, it's like his hand is reading my mind.

My toes curl in my boots. My lungs stop working.

"You're *supposed* to get the fuck off my Jeep," I manage to growl, startling him with a forceful kick that knocks him the rest of the way to the ground.

When I spin around, I'm livid—and I'm not even sure which I'm angrier about: the fact that he's being an ass-hole, or the fact that he didn't throw himself on top of me instead of falling off my Jeep. Six fucking years, and it still only took one touch from him—one look, one tiny graze of his fingers—to make my entire body feel like it was ready to melt at his command.

I twist my key in the ignition, the hum of my engine drowning out the heartbeat drumming in my ears. But it's too late for an escape, because Shawn is already sprinting around my Jeep and launching himself into my passenger seat.

"What do you think you're doing?" I growl as he shifts on the worn leather to face me.

"Can you just hear me out?"

"I think I heard you plenty in there." I nod toward Mike's garage and tighten my fingers around the steering wheel. All fucking day, he hasn't had a single decent thing to say. *Kit, you missed your mark. Kit, are you even listening? Kit, it's no wonder I never called you after I took your virginity, because you can't do a damn thing right.*

Okay…he didn't really say that last bit. But he didn't need to, because I heard it every time he looked at me like I was some amateur imposter who had never played a guitar in her life.

"You made it pretty damn clear you think I'm terrible," I snap, and Shawn opens his mouth to reply, but I'm far from finished. "Actually, no, you know what? You made it pretty damn clear you didn't want me in this band from day one. So whatever, you got your fucking wish. I don't need this shit. I'm out. You—"

"You're amazing," Shawn blurts, and every word I'd planned to heave at him gets stuck in the back of my throat. His green eyes are sincere when he says, "You're amazing, okay?"

Six years ago, I might have fallen for a line as simple as that. Now? I shift toward him to show him *just* how unfazed I am. "Then why do you keep giving me so much shit?"

He looks more than a little uncomfortable as he scratches the hair at the base of his scalp. "I don't know…"

He *doesn't know*? Doesn't *know*?

All the insults I'd lost come back in such a rush, I'm not sure which to settle on. *Fuck off. Get bent. Kiss my ass.*

"I didn't trust you," Shawn adds, and my eyebrows slam together.

"You didn't *trust* me?"

"I thought maybe…" He shakes his head and stares down at the console between us. "I'm not sure what I thought."

I'm so angry, the hair on my arms is standing up. "What, because I'm a girl or something?"

Dee thought I was a groupie when she opened the door of Mayhem before my audition, and I guess Shawn did too. And why, just because I'm hot? Just because I have boobs and a fucking vagina? His eyes flash back up to mine.

"Huh?" His head starts shaking back and forth, the crease between his eyebrows digging deeper and deeper. "*What*? No!"

"Then *why*, Shawn?"

He stares at me for a long moment, but my gaze is as hard as his is soft. Finally, he nods and says, "Yeah, fine…It was because you're a girl, okay…but I said I'm sorry."

"It's about time," I mutter under my breath.

"Huh?"

"Nothing." My teeth snap back together after I bark at him like a temperamental pit bull. "Why are you still here?"

Adam pokes his head out of the garage, takes one look at Shawn and me sitting in my Jeep, and disappears back inside. The chilled April air is wrapping itself around me, sending a trickle of goose bumps up the back of my neck, but even though I have a hoodie in the back, I'd sooner freeze to death than get it. As far as Shawn needs to know, I'm indestructible. Impenetrable. Even the cold can't touch me.

"Look," he says, immune to the cold in his black T-shirt and jeans, "I said I'm sorry, and I meant it. You *were* off your marks today, but I was a jerk."

I cross my arms tightly over my chest. "I was off because Joel—"

"Joel just got dumped by his girlfriend," Shawn interrupts. "And he's spent the last week and a half putting himself through hell because he doesn't know how to handle having his heart broken like that."

The explanation hits so close to home, I immediately feel like a bitch for lashing out at Joel in the garage. The guy looks like a mess because he probably *is* a mess. But at least he's up and dressed and attempting to function, which is more than I would have been able to say for myself six years ago…"I didn't know—"

"It's fine," Shawn insists, his expression full of as much regret as mine. "We should've given you a heads-up or something. You're one of us now."

Another grass-scented breeze lifts my hair away from my pierced right ear, and I slide a hand up my neck to warm the cold metal. "One of you?"

Shawn's gaze tracks my hand before slowly swinging to meet my eyes. "Unless you still want out…"

"DID YOU KISS and make up?" Adam teases as soon as we reenter the warmth of Mike's garage. All six foot three of him is sprawled out on the dusty garage floor, like he was going to literally pass away from boredom if we took even two seconds longer before coming back inside.

Shawn helps him up—and then knocks him a step back with a hard punch to the arm. Which is good, considering I'm too busy blushing fire-engine red to form a snarky reply.

"Shut the hell up," Shawn scolds while Adam laughs and rubs his arm. Mike chuckles at them while I turn to Joel.

"Hey…I'm sorry for being such a bitch."

He gives me a small shake of his head, his sad blue eyes making me feel even worse than I already did. "Don't be."

I frown at him, but he simply replies with a weak smile and tosses me my guitar pick. I catch it and, knowing he doesn't want to talk about it, turn to Adam and Mike next. "Sorry I acted like such a girl."

"*You?*" Adam says while he continues rubbing his bruised arm. "Shawn was the one whining all morning."

He smiles and jumps away from the look Shawn gives him, and Mike interrupts the impending violence to ask if we can get started.

Shawn is already strapping his guitar back around his neck, but I don't bother following his lead. Instead, I shake my head. "I don't learn like this. I can *write* songs like this, but I can't *learn* them without seeing them written first. And I'm guessing none of you write music—"

"I can," Adam offers, stepping into the open doorway of the garage and lighting a cigarette.

His back is to us when I say, "You can?"

"I got the same degree you said you were going to school for. So yeah." He turns around and blows smoke out of the side of his mouth so that it doesn't drift inside. "And Shawn can help you practice. Which we can do at our place."

Our place? He told me earlier that he and Shawn are roomies, so...*Shawn's* place?

My voice almost squeaks when I say, "Your place?"

"Yeah," Adam answers, oblivious to the frantic beats my heart is skipping. He looks around the room at Joel, at Mike, at Shawn. "Who's coming?"

THE ENTIRE WAY to Adam and Shawn's apartment, it's easier to pretend I'm just on a casual drive. Just driving for no reason to no place in particular—definitely not to Shawn Scarlett's apartment six years after I let him inside me and never heard from him again.

The drive is too short, the parking lot is too empty, and even though my legs feel like soggy noodles, they carry me from my Jeep *way* too quickly.

The sound of my boots echoes off the floor in the arched-ceilinged lobby of his apartment building, and the entire elevator ride up to the fourth floor, all I can think is, *God, how many girls must Shawn have brought back here? What kinds of things has he done in this elevator? How many groupies since he decided I wasn't special enough to remember?*

When I enter apartment 4E, I almost expect to see panties hanging off of lampshades and a pile of naked girls passed out on the couch. Instead, I find Adam's girlfriend, Rowan, doing homework at a breakfast bar with a half-empty mocha and a can of whipped cream on the counter in front of her.

The walls are a pale gray except for a spot where someone has written in bright blue marker, DON'T COLOR ON THE WALLS! Guitar stands with Fenders line one side of the living room, stretching all the way to a massive entertainment system that screams "rock star bachelor pad."

"It needs to be tuned," Shawn says when he catches me running my fingers across the head of one of his Telecasters. Thinline. Three-color sunburst. Stunning.

I pull my hand away.

"Sorry," I say as he studies me. "I have one of these on my wish list…"

"You have a wish list?"

"Like twenty guitars long," I explain. "But I'd have to sell my right arm to afford most of them." I wiggle my fingers in the air. "And then what would be the point?"

The look on Shawn's face transforms into a wide smile, and I'm about to smile back at him, when kissy noises interrupt us from across the room. Adam has his arms wrapped around Rowan's shoulders, and he's smothering her with sloppy kisses while she laughs and wriggles all over her stool. She threatens to squirt him with whipped cream, he makes a sound that says he'd like that, and Shawn and I swap uncomfortable glances before moving to the couch and recliner at the far side of the room.

With Adam distracted, it's just the two of us. Mike opted to stay back at his place, and Joel took off in a beater Oldsmobile as soon as we got back, which sentenced me to the most awkward non-date ever.

"Is he actually going to get any work done?" I ask just for the sake of saying something, and Shawn casts Adam another look before rolling his eyes at the kissy sounds coming from that side of the room.

"When he feels like it, maybe. It'd be faster if we just did it ourselves. If I play it, can you write it?"

I nod, and Shawn disappears into a room off the living room, leaving me with nothing to do except twiddle my thumbs and pretend not to hear the noises coming from the breakfast bar. If those two start going at it, I swear to God—

A gorgeous acoustic Fender exits Shawn's room, and I forget all about everything that isn't the beautiful black instrument in his hands. It's vintage, and probably worth more than my Jeep, all smooth lines and polished wood.

"That guitar is beautiful," I breathe, the awe in my voice making Shawn smile as he sits down and props it on his lap. My fingertips long to feel the hum of the strings, and I rub my hands over my knees to distract my anxious fingers.

"It's a '54. Bought it at a thrift store."

That guitar belongs in a museum. Or in my lap. Not in a hand-me-down thrift store. "How good of friends would we have to be for you to let me play it?"

Shawn smirks as he tunes the strings. "I've never even let Adam play this guitar."

Judging by the way Adam haphazardly swung his mic around during practice this morning, I'm guessing that's been a good call. "What would I have to do for you? To get you to let me play it?"

There are moments in life—moments when your foot defies all rules of physics and manages to implant itself wholly and completely in your mouth. When Shawn looks at me like I just offered to put his dick in my mouth instead of my own foot—like he's surprised I'd be so forward—I realize this is one of those moments.

"That…that did not come out right."

My cheeks are stained red—I can tell, because my whole face is one giant freaking raging bonfire—and Shawn is graceful enough to not say a word…which triggers my say-exactly-what's-on-my-mind disorder and leads to an epic fucking disaster.

"I wasn't offering to give you a blowjob or anything."

Shawn's eyes dart back up to mine, and now both of us are just sitting there looking absolutely mortified.

"I mean, when I asked what I could do for you…I didn't mean I'd do *anything*, not like…*that*…I just"—I lift my hands and bury them in my hair—"keep talking. I just keep talking."

Shawn stares at me for a moment—like I just escaped from a mental ward—and I stare back at him—like he's right. And then, his face softens and he lets out a chuckle that breaks the awkward silence between us.

"God," I say after a chuckle bursts free of me too. Did I seriously just say the word *blowjob*? To *Shawn*?

Yes, I seriously just talked about giving Shawn Scarlett a blowjob. To Shawn Scarlett.

"Are you nervous or something?" he asks with an amused smile on his face.

"Why would I be nervous?" I untangle my fingers from my hair and curl them around my knees to stop myself from fidgeting.

"Because I'm insanely talented?" He gives me a smirk that makes me want to start talking about blowjobs again, or kissing at the very least, because God knows I'm thinking about it. Instead, I manage to smirk right back at him.

"You only think you're talented because you haven't heard me play that guitar yet."

"You haven't put a good trade on the table yet," he challenges with a suggestive smile.

My heartbeat kicks up a gear, his smile widens, and I realize belatedly that we are *flirting*.

In an instant, I wipe the smile from my face and clear my throat. "Do you have something for me to write with?"

Shawn's smile slowly fades into nothing but a curious spark that glints in his eye, and he goes back to tuning his guitar. "Yeah…I'll get Peach to get you something in a minute."

I sit farther back against the couch to put a few extra inches of distance between us, resisting the pull he still has over me. I didn't expect it to be this strong—not after this long, not after what he did to me.

It's like the best and worst form of nostalgia. It feels like being a teenager. Like feeling my heart beat for the first time.

Like being in love.

"Peach," Shawn shouts when he's almost finished tuning his guitar. "Can we have some paper and something to write with?"

He roots a guitar pick from his pocket, and Rowan escapes Adam by hopping off of her stool with a handful of papers and a pencil. She sets them on the coffee table in front of me and plops down on the cushion at my side as Adam resigns himself to rooting through the fridge.

"What are you guys doing?"

I gather up the papers and pencil while Shawn answers for both of us. "Kit needs to write out the music."

"Just the old songs," I correct, clarity finally reentering my cloudy head. Not being alone with Shawn means I can finally think again, can finally *breathe* again. "If I write my parts myself, I'll have them memorized, but if I'm trying to memorize someone else's—"

"Here," Adam interrupts, handing me a beer before setting another on the table for Shawn and collapsing into the armchair across from him.

Good. Shawn and me plus two extra people. A group. I can deal with a group. Groups are good.

"Oh," Rowan answers, looking around like she's just beginning to come out of her homework-induced stupor. Her blonde hair is up in a messy bun, and even though I don't remember her wearing glasses the last time I saw her, they're sliding down her nose today. "Hey, where's Joel? Didn't he make it to practice?"

Adam and Shawn explain that he took off as soon as we got back, but I zone out, mesmerized as I watch as Shawn's fingers continue working their magic. I've never gotten to admire his hands this closely before, so even though I know I shouldn't, I lose myself in the way they move, the way they fine-tune the guitar like it's an extension of his own body. They twist a spell into the pegs, bringing the ancient instrument back to life.

"Ready?" he asks, and I jab the point of my pencil against the paper to pretend like I was paying attention. To the paper. Not to his hands. Definitely not to his hands.

I nod.

Shawn plays slowly enough for me to watch his strings and hear each one, naming the chords as he plays them, and eventually, Rowan and Adam leave us alone in the living room. But I'm too distracted to mind—by the sounds coming from the beautiful Fender, by the notes born of Shawn's trained fingers.

"Would you mind if I made some changes?" I ask when we get to a song that doesn't sound quite as magical as the others.

"You don't like that one?" he asks.

"It's not bad…" I'm hesitant to say more, but Shawn just grins.

"Cody wrote that one. It sounds like shit to me too. What do you have in mind?"

"Not sure yet." I tap my pencil against my lips. Notes are running through my head, but I can't pick out the right one until I hear them first. I need my guitar, and I stand up to get it, but I don't get even half a step away from the couch before Shawn thrusts out the neck of his Fender, like…

"Are you letting me play your guitar…?" I ask.

His fingers dance on the neck like he's not sure, and they're still dancing when he nods. "Maybe. I haven't decided yet."

I reach out and gently take it from him before he can change his mind, settling back on the couch and taking a deep breath. Shawn watches me like I'm cradling his firstborn child, and I treasure the guitar like I am. I hold it softly, and strum my first string carefully. And then, with green eyes on me, I close my eyes and just *play*. I let the music consume me, carrying me to someplace outside Shawn's apartment, outside myself. I try riff after riff, tweaking the notes as I go until I find something that feels right, something that feels perfect.

"Here," I say, abruptly thrusting Shawn's guitar back at him. I rush to get mine and then order him to play lead. He plays his part, I play mine, and together, we're flawless. The sound is amazing, and by the time I stop playing, I'm sporting an ear-to-ear smile on my face. "Magic."

"Perfect," he agrees, staring at me like I'm the one who's magic and not the other way around.

It's a look that makes me nervous, so I do what I always do when I'm uncomfortable—I forget how to be a girl, and I become one of the guys instead. "Still think you're so awesome?" I challenge.

When Shawn laughs, I enjoy the sound too much to care about the way my cheeks are melting off or the way my heart is pounding behind my ribs. We continue going like that, song after song, until it's just Shawn playing and me listening. I want to close my eyes, but I can't—partly because Shawn might think it's weird, and partly because I can't stop staring at him. It feels like he doesn't even know I'm here, and yet somehow is playing just for me. The songs become *my* songs, *my* serenades. I watch him unabashed, the papers on my lap long forgotten by both of us, and even when his eyes periodically find mine, I don't look away.

My fingers yearn to touch something—maybe his guitar…maybe his hands…maybe his lips.

"I'm still working on it," he says of the song he's currently playing, his words slowing when we both realize I'm watching each one come out of his mouth.

"Awesome," I say in a rush, standing up so quickly that half of the papers on my lap end up spilling onto the floor. "Shit."

Shawn and I knock knees bending down to pick them up, get awkward when we make eye contact on the floor, and nearly jump out of our skin when Rowan pops up out of nowhere to ask if I'd like to stay for dinner.

"I, er—" I'm trying to get my wobbly knees to work and am bumbling like an idiot while Shawn stands beside me watching me go up in flames. I know why the hell *I'm* dropping papers and bumping knees, but what the heck is *his* excuse?

"Sweet," Rowan says with a bright smile. "I'm making, um...ADAM!"

"What?" he yells from somewhere down the hall.

Shawn's hand finds mine to give me the rest of the papers I dropped, and I nearly drop them all over again. I don't thank him, because my voice isn't working. I can't even make freaking eye contact.

"What do you want for dinner?" Rowan yells.

"Order something!"

"I should go," I mutter, taking a step back and banging the backs of my traitorous legs against the coffee table. I decide to stop moving so I don't end up falling flat on my face and needing Shawn to carry me all the way to the hospital.

Yes, because in my fantasyland right now, ambulances don't exist and Shawn is obviously the only doctor I need.

Fucking hell.

I am *not* this awkward girl. I had boyfriends in high school and boyfriends in college. One-night stands and semi-long relationships and casual dates and week-long flings. But not one of those guys ever took my number and didn't call me or made me want to Taser him or made me trip over tables or made my heart pound in my chest like it does every time I lock eyes with Shawn Scarlett.

Rowan just shakes her head. "Nope. We're ordering something to celebrate your initiation into the band, so you're pretty much obligated to stay. What do you want to eat?"

When Adam pops out of the bedroom and suggests pizza, Rowan volunteers him and herself to go pick it up, adamant that Shawn and I should stay behind so we can finish working.

"We already finished," I insist, but she just holds up her hand, smiles, and closes the door between us.

Abandoned alone in the living room with Shawn again, I take a minute before turning around. What the hell am I supposed to do now? Shawn and I have nothing to do, nothing to say, and Rowan literally shut us in here together and *smiled* while doing it. I take a deep breath and finally turn to face Shawn. "How mad would she be if I left before she got back?"

He scratches a hand through his hair, his vintage band T-shirt pulling taut over his chest. "Why do you need to leave?"

"I don't…"

"Then stay."

I should run. I should tell him no, and I should run far, far away. I shouldn't look back.

I shouldn't be here flirting with him, staring at his hands and his eyes and his lips. I should remember the way he made me feel when he said he'd call and then never did.

But my brain is having trouble remembering *any* of those things, so instead, I reluctantly sit back down on the couch. I take a long sip of my beer. I stare at Shawn's guitar. I take another sip of beer.

When I finish one, he offers me another, and the first conversation starts awkwardly but continues easily. Shawn and I talk about guitars and equipment. We talk about our favorite bands, the best shows we've ever been to, crazy shit we've done at concerts. Two more beers, and I can't stop laughing.

"And then Adam just showed back up with no pants," Shawn says through his laughter, "and I was so fucking drunk, I fell over from laughing so hard and busted my damn lip open."

Giggling like crazy, I wipe away my tears. "That's nothing. When I was eighteen, I went to see The Used, and Bert had the crowd do a wall of death—"

"Oh no," Shawn says even before I can finish.

I nod and hold out my left arm. "I broke my arm in three freaking places."

Shawn nearly coughs out his beer. "You seriously broke your arm?"

"My band had to cancel shows for two entire months," I explain, bending my elbow while remembering how much it sucked to be stuck in a cast. Shawn grins at me, and I laugh before adding, "My brothers freaked the hell out, so I had to make up some bullshit lie about slipping on a patch of ice—in *August*."

They had correctly assumed I broke it by doing something stupid—like slamming arm-first into a thoroughly inebriated Incredible Hulk—but I scrambled to say whatever it took to keep them from volunteering Mason to move in with me in my dorm.

"Why?" Shawn asks, and when I take another swig of my beer and lift my eyebrow, he clarifies, "Why'd you have to lie about it?"

I swallow the amber liquid down my throat and shrug. "Do you remember my brothers? Bryce was in your grade, Mason was two above you, and Ryan was one above him."

Shawn circles his thumb over the lip of his beer bottle. "Sort of. Don't you also have another brother?"

"Who, Kale?" I ask with more than a little surprise in my voice. He can remember *Kale*, but not *me*? "Yeah..." I answer, trying not to let it bother me. The numbness taking root in the tips of my fingers helps. "We're twins."

When Shawn says nothing else, I finish, "Anyway, they're all just kind of...protective. Overprotective."

"What would've happened if you told them the truth?"

I'm guessing I'd still have Mason as a babysitter to this day, because if there's one thing I've learned from being in a big family, it's *don't bring shit up unless you want to spend the rest of your life talking about it.*

"Who knows?" I answer as the front door of the apartment swings open and Adam carries Rowan in on his back. She's balancing a pizza box on his head with a slice already hanging from her mouth, and I watch them even though my face is still turned toward Shawn. "I'm used to lying. It's easier than fighting with them."

The entire couch stirs when Adam drops Rowan onto the cushion next to me.

"Fighting with who?" she asks.

"My brothers," I answer while Adam flips open the pizza box and both boys grab a slice. "I was just telling Shawn they can be kind of overprotective."

Rowan chuckles and finishes swallowing a bite of pizza. "What do they think of you being in a band with these guys?"

She points a thumb at Adam and a pointer finger at Shawn, and I just sit there, eyes stuck open, mouth clamped shut.

Rowan narrows her eyes. "They *do* know you're in a band with them, right?"

"Yeah," I lie to the sweet blonde girl in front of me. "Of course." I grab a slice of pizza to buy myself some chewing time, but it does nothing to distract Rowan.

"And they're cool with it?"

Shawn and Adam are both waiting for my response, so I flick another lie off the tip of my tongue. "They know this is a big dream of mine, so they're super supportive."

I consider the fact that my pants don't burst into flames a good sign, and Rowan's appeased smile is a bonus. She grins at me, Adam spins on the recliner until his legs are dangling over one of the arms, and Shawn just stares at me like he can read my mind.

"That's cool," Rowan says, oblivious to my paranoia about Shawn's potential telepathy. "You should invite them to Mayhem sometime."

"Yeah," I reply, not adding the rest of what I'm thinking.

Yeah, and while I'm at it, I should prepare myself to be tossed over Mason's shoulder kicking and screaming while Bryce restrains my hands to keep me from clawing Mason's useless ears off. Then Ryan can interrogate the guys about their intentions while Kale starts the getaway car.

"Maybe," I finish with a saccharine smile.

Rowan's questions about my brothers keep coming one after another. How old are they? What are their names? What do they do? Were they friends with the guys in the band back in high school? Why not?

"I'm kind of the black sheep of the family," I divulge, setting my crumb-filled napkin on the table. "The rest of my family is very…"

I'm trying to figure out how to finish that sentence when Adam volunteers, "Football." He's completely hanging off of the recliner now, his head smashed on the floor and his legs tangled on the seat. He's writing upside down in a mini-notebook, with a breadstick balancing like a bridge between his chest and his chin.

I chuckle and agree, "Yeah, they're very football."

My brothers aren't like me, with my blue highlights and nose piercing. They're not like Adam, with his black fingernails and stacks of bracelets. And they're not like Shawn, with his quiet genius and vintage clothes.

"So what made you different?" Rowan asks with genuine interest. "Why'd you pick up the guitar?"

My eyes were already on Shawn, and they stick there, remembering the first time I saw him perform, the way he played the strings of my heart with each and every note he struck. I had goose bumps and butterflies, and I'm not sure if they were all for Shawn or all for the guitar or all for both, but my fingers itched to touch those strings, and all of me longed to feel Shawn Scarlett.

"I was a big fan of the band in middle school," I confess when I finally manage to tear my dark eyes from Shawn's green ones. "They made me want to play, and the guitar just kind of…spoke to me."

"Oh wow," Rowan says. "So Shawn inspired you to play?"

"Hey," Adam protests from the floor. "How do you know it was Shawn?"

"Well, it couldn't have been Cody. But I guess it could have been Joel…"

"I played back then too," Adam complains, throwing a chunk of breadstick at Rowan.

She catches it in midair and pops it in her mouth, and I interrupt their flirty teasing by admitting, "It was Shawn…I'd never heard anyone play like him."

"You should've said something!" Rowan exclaims, and I manage not to argue that I *did* say something. I poured my heart out and was rewarded with having it stomped on.

"Yeah."

"They could've gotten rid of Cody so much earlier," she continues, like she's a million miles away. Her half-eaten slice of pizza gets discarded in the box, her voice somber when she adds, "Things could have been so different."

"Maybe," I agree, wondering how different they could have been if I hadn't gone to Adam's party that night.

I still would've cried myself to sleep, I always would have wondered what could have been, and I would have lost my virginity to someone who wasn't Shawn Scarlett…

I eat my fill of pizza, using silent moments to wonder if I would change anything, even if I could. Would I stay home that night? Would I give that night up?

Long after pizza, when Rowan finally runs out of questions and the sun has hidden behind the moon, I announce it's time for me to head home, and Rowan insists Shawn walk me to my Jeep. The walk is quiet, without even music from the elevator to pierce the silence, until I'm sitting in my driver's seat and Shawn is standing by my side. The parking lot lights cast harsh shadow over the planes of his face and stubble on his chin, and he parts his soft lips to say, "Sorry about Peach giving you the third degree."

The night smells like city air and Shawn's cologne, and I long to melt into him. To tell him it doesn't matter if he broke my heart that night six years ago, because I wouldn't change a thing. I wouldn't have wanted my first to be anyone but him.

"Shawn," I start, staring up into those dark green of his eyes. He's close enough to touch, and yet he's untouchable.

I should hate him.

I don't.

"Yeah?"

I don't know what I had planned to say...

Why didn't you call me?

Would you still be able to forget me?

Why couldn't you just love me?

"If I call you to run music stuff by you," I say, "will you pick up the phone?"

Rowan gave me all the guys' numbers tonight, insisting that they were idiots for not exchanging them earlier. The only number I had was Dee's, and Rowan's blue eyes dimmed when she told me that Dee has gone AWOL.

Shawn's eyebrows turn in. "Why wouldn't I pick up the phone?"

When my worried expression doesn't change, his softens.

"Yeah, Kit…I'll pick up."

"You sure?"

"I promise."

THAT NIGHT, WHEN I'm home alone in my own bed, I remember the way I practically begged him to answer my call and groan. My face is buried in my overstuffed pillow, and it's not enough to get his scent out of my nose or his voice out of my head.

Just because I wouldn't change what happened that night doesn't mean I want to do it all over. I don't want to fall for him again—not when the ground comes so quick, and not when it hurts so damn much.

I fell for Shawn Scarlett once.

And once was more than enough.

Chapter Four

THE NEXT FEW days are spent practicing music, listening to music, writing music, and doing whatever I can to go back to being the person I was before I reconnected with Shawn Scarlett.

Tough. Independent. Indestructible.

My hours are spent with a guitar pick between my fingers or between my lips, and food becomes an annoyance that nags at my stomach during songs and between songs and after songs. I live off of peanut butter crackers and coffee, and when I run out of the latter on Wednesday morning, I'm forced to change into real clothes and venture out of my apartment. In a black thermal, a tattered black skirt, a pair of star-print knee-high socks, and my trusty combat boots, I sit in my Jeep arguing with my phone until it gives me directions to the closest coffee shop: a Starbucks near the local college campus—one with no freaking drive-thru.

I somehow manage to keep my eyes open during the drive, and after reluctantly climbing out of my Jeep and into the real world, I cross the weather-beaten parking lot. Inside, I find myself in a mishmash of polo-wearing college kids who make me look like a neon blue sharpie in a box of ballpoint pens. Some of the guys stare at me like I'm contagious, and some stare at me like they want to catch whatever I've got, but most just stare at me like I'm a foreign food they want to taste but are too intimidated to try.

I scan customers gathered at tables and cozied on couches in the corner before my gaze drifts to the front of the line, where one guy is pulling at another guy's shoulder to get him to place his order, but the latter is too busy smiling at me like I'm an adorable kitten with a "Free to a Good Home" sign hovering above my head.

He's wearing pink Chucks, long cargo shorts, and a Strawberry Shortcake T-shirt that looks like it's legitimately scratch-and-sniff. Dark shades are pushed up into a thick lick of ombré hair, making the guy look just as out of place as I do.

When he smiles at me, I furrow my brows at him, and he turns around and places his order.

There's this weird dude staring at me in a Starbucks, I text Kale while I wait for my turn.

Oh, look who's alive.

If he murders me, bury me in my boots.

Those boots have probably melded to your feet. We'd never get them off.

Good!

"Miss?"

"Oh, uh." I pocket my phone and scan the board behind the barista's head. "A caramel mocha, please. Extra salt. Extra espresso." I glance around for Mr. Short-cake, but all that's left is polo, polo, polo.

I hold back a laugh when I realize that if I called out "Marco" right now, every single guy in this entire joint would need to call back to me. And judging by the way a few of them are beginning to ogle, they wouldn't mind if I felt around for them with my eyes closed.

I ignore the unwanted attention and move to the end of the bar to wait for my drink, pulling out my phone again.

Sorry I missed family dinner Sunday.

Where were you?

The writing cave. I'll make it up to you.

Better make it up to Bryce and Mason too. All they did the whole time was whine about how they've been replaced.

Considering I haven't seen much of Adam, Joel, or Mike, and Shawn is so *not* ever going to be like a brother to me, they have nothing to worry about.

Did you tell them to stop being girls?

I have the bruises on my arms to prove it.

I smile and pocket my phone again when the barista slides my drink over. It smells like heaven, and I risk burning the roof of my mouth to take a long sip. Of course, it burns the shit out of me, but the caramel flavor on my tongue is worth it, and I'm still sipping as I toss my straw paper in the trash. I'm five steps from the door when a college guy in a red polo shirt abruptly stands to get it for me, but I hurry my pace and escape outside before he can get to it. I'm chuckling under my breath when a voice from behind me nearly makes me drop my drink.

"Hey. Kit, right?" Mr. Shortcake pushes away from the wall as I finish spinning on my heel.

"How do you know my name?" I walk backward while simultaneously giving him my attention and scanning the area around us for anyone I might know. Either I'm in a practical joke or I *am* a practical joke, because I have no idea who this guy is—or why he's looking at me and talking to me like he's my biggest fan.

"I also know that you have three—no, *four* brothers, and that you grew up in Downingtown, and..." He closes his eyes and waves a hand around me, like he's reading my aura or something. "And you just joined a band."

When I stop walking, he opens one eye and smiles at me.

My voice is defensive when I say, "How do you know all that?"

"I can read fortunes."

His smile grows wider, and skepticism drips from my voice when I say, "Uh-huh." I take another sip of my drink to demonstrate just how unimpressed I am by his bullshit. "What's my fortune, then?"

He takes a sip of his coffee to mirror me, smacking his lips when he's through. "Ah, that's an easy one." He pauses for dramatic effect and then grins and says, "We're going to be best friends. Well, second-best friends, actually, or...third-best friends, but...semantics, Kit-Kat, that's not important."

"Who are you again?" I ask, and Mr. Shortcake sticks out his hand, chuckling when I make no attempt to shake it.

"If I told you I was Rowan and Dee's friend, would that help?"

I stare, and he smiles.

"I'm Leti."

"Leti?"

His hand drops to his side, and he raises a dissatisfied eyebrow. "You mean the girls didn't tell you about their big gay best friend?"

"No?"

"Seriously?" When my expression doesn't change, he pouts and flips his shades down over his eyes. "Well, that's just disappointing."

Leti talks, and talks, and talks—and somehow, within five minutes, convinces me to walk with him to campus. He insists it's so he can show me around, and I say five, maybe ten words total.

"And this," he says, gesturing to an auditorium in Jackson Hall, "is where Ro-cone met Adam. But more importantly, where she met *me*." He flashes me a bright smile and pushes his shades back up into his hair. "We used to spend entire classes swooning over the back of his head." He reminisces for a moment before resuming our walk and adding, "But I'm guessing he's not your type."

"What makes you say that?" I share looks with a snotty girl who apparently doesn't approve of combat boots or pink Chucks, celebrating a small victory when she looks away first.

Leti turns around and starts walking backward, pretending to read my aura with his hand again. "Your type is…tall, thin, but with…black hair. Green eyes." When he stops walking, I stop too. He closes his eyes in mock concentration. "Name starts wiiith…"

When he peeks an eye open and flat out says, "Shawn," I put on the best audition for "deer in headlights" anyone has ever seen. I stare, stare, contemplate running away with my arms flailing, stare some more, and then force my lips to curl up in a slow, amused smile.

"Nice try."

Leti's thick lashes drop over narrowed eyes, the corner of his mouth pulling up in a skeptical smirk. "You know, it's not very nice to keep secrets from your new best friend."

Satisfied I've neither confirmed nor denied his suspicion—and barely resisting the urge to shake him violently while demanding to know what ungodly black magic he used to find out about my lingering crush on Shawn—I walk past him with no idea where I'm going. "I thought you said we were third-best friends."

Pink Chucks rush to fall in step beside me. "What if I told you a secret about me?"

I shield my eyes from the sun as I gaze over at him, and then I chuckle. "You don't have any secrets."

His outfit, his hair, his smile—it all screams that he has nothing to hide, and that even if he did, he wouldn't hide it. He grins at my assessment. "Touché. But *you* have a ton."

I share none of them as we continue walking—not about my present crush, not about my past crush, not about losing my virginity in an upstairs bedroom at Adam's senior party. If I had a girlfriend, I might call her up and spill my guts, but instead, all I really have is an overbearing twin brother and a guy in neon Chucks who I've known for all of twenty minutes.

Eventually, the latter admits defeat, switching to conversations about the town and the school and a hundred other safe subjects.

"Have you been to Mayhem yet?" he asks from his place across the table from me at the college's closest café. We're sharing a large order of French toast bites while we wait for Rowan to get out of class.

I shake my head. "Just for my audition. Rowan invited me this past weekend, but I turned her down."

She said everyone would be there, and I told her I couldn't go because I promised my brothers I'd go home for the weekend. But really, I'd just had my fill of Shawn. I was pretty sure any more would kill me. Or turn me into a fiending addict.

"Probably for the best," Leti comments while he checks out a Polo who just walked through the door. "We weren't there long. It turned into a dram-o-rama."

"What kind of drama?"

He gradually gives me his attention. "I didn't ask. Just another chapter in the ongoing Dee-and-Joel saga."

I frown, remembering what a mess Joel was at the last practice. "He seems pretty wrecked."

Leti just shakes his head. "I don't get those two. Never have, never will. What about you, Kitten? Ever been smitten?"

I nod enthusiastically with my mouth full of bready, cinnamonny goo. "Mhm. He was gorgeous. Put together like you wouldn't believe. And old-fashioned too. They don't make them like him anymore."

Leti eyes me for a long while, his golden irises getting clearer and clearer. "You're talking about a guitar, aren't you?"

When I burst out laughing, he laughs too, and we're still chuckling when Rowan slides onto the stool next to him, her head swiveling back and forth between us.

"What are we laughing about? And um…?" She gestures to me, him, me, him. "When did you two *meet*? And suddenly become best friends?"

"Third-best friends," I correct, and Leti laughs some more.

"We ran into each other at Starbucks this morning," he says, "and it was third-best friends at first sight." With his chin on his hand, he swoons at me, and Rowan unapologetically steals one of our French toast bites.

"Weird. How'd you know who she was?"

"How could I *not* know who she was?" Leti asks. "You said she looked like a rock star. And"—he uses a cinnamon-covered pointer finger to gesture from my head to my toes—"I've never seen a more rocking-looking rock star in my life."

I remember the way he smiled at me in line, the way he approached me outside, the way he knew everything about me…including about my crush on Shawn.

"Did you tell Leti I had a crush on Shawn?" I blurt, and Rowan's blue eyes flash wide. I knew it couldn't have been Shawn, because Shawn doesn't remember. And the guys in the band are *guys*—they wouldn't notice, much less gossip. That left *a girl*. That left *Rowan*.

Leti yelps when she kicks him under the table.

"I just said you two acted weird around each other," she stammers. "It just kind of seemed, at the apartment, like maybe…"

"Like maybe what?"

"Like…" Rowan is stumbling over words she isn't saying, and Leti cuts her off.

"If you don't think Shawn is hot, you're blind. Or gay." He points a French toast bite at me. "Are you surfing the rainbow?"

I cock an eyebrow at him.

"Then you think Shawn is hot. Stop denying it."

Rowan waits patiently for my response, but I just roll my eyes. "Okay, sure, yeah, I think he's super-duper hot."

Leti grins at my sarcasm, but Rowan just looks confused, or disturbed, or…curious. I'm praying she lets it go—and then she does.

But Leti doesn't.

"What do you like best about him, hmm? Those sexy green eyes? That wind-swept black hair? The way he touches his guitar like he wants it to scream his name?"

When I blush, Leti's grin is triumphant.

"So all of the above then."

I roll my eyes as hard as I possibly can, kind of hoping I give myself an aneurism or something else to get me out of this conversation. "Sounds like you have a crush of your own."

"Oh, I *so* do."

"I just think he's really talented," I lie. "And yeah, maybe I had a little crush in high school, but that was six years ago. If I wanted Shawn now, I'd just have him."

Damn, that came off cocky. Confident and cocky and awesome. Leti turns to Rowan and smiles wide.

"Have I told you I love her?"

I manage a grin I don't quite feel, wondering if it would really be that easy—if I could make Shawn like me, if I'd even *want* Shawn to like me.

And then I kid myself into believing that I wouldn't.

That I don't.

It's another lie I tell myself, one I force myself to believe.

Chapter Five

THE FIRST FAMILY dinner after meeting Leti, my brothers give me four tons of shit for not showing up at the last one. My mom does her best to save me, but attempting to derail my brothers is like trying to stop a stampede of obnoxious shithead elephants.

"Forgetting about us already, huh?" Mason chides.

Of course, every single elephant is sitting on his lazy ass while my mom and I set the dining table, with Mason reclined in his high-backed wooden chair, his arms crossed over a shirt that's too small for the muscles bulging in his chest. With his dark eyes, buzzed hair, and bad attitude, most people know not to mess with him, but if he thinks I won't crack him over the head with one of the spoons I'm setting on the table, he's dumber than I thought.

"Were you busy writing music?" my mom asks as she sets a basket of dinner rolls in front of Mason, but Bryce opens his big mouth before I can open mine.

"She was probably busy with her new boyfriend."

"You have a new boyfriend?" Ryan asks, but it's Bryce's turn for silverware, and his stupid remark was magic—it turned the metal spoon I'm holding into a weapon. A satisfying "POP!" sounds against the back of his skull, and his hand flies up to his head with a holler.

"OW!"

Mason makes a move to grab the spoon from my hand, but I rap him hard on the knuckles, leaving both boys nursing their wounds and Kale chuckling openly at the other side of the table.

"No, I don't have a freaking boyfriend," I finally answer Ryan, placing a spoon peacefully on the napkin by his plate while my mom returns to the dining room with a big pitcher of water.

"That's too bad," she comments as she begins filling glasses.

I hold back a disgruntled groan. Every dinner, it's the same thing from her. *Kit, have you met anyone? Kit, why not? Kit, Mrs. So-and-So has a son I'd really like you to meet.*

"How can you expect me to get a boyfriend when I have him?" I point to Mason, who grins ruefully. "And him." I point to Bryce, who doesn't even notice because he's too busy grabbing a dinner roll before we're all even seated.

Our mom gracefully circles the table, grabs a spoon, and cracks him on the back of the head.

"OW! MOM!"

Everyone except Bryce breaks out laughing, and Mom shoots me a wink from behind his chair before making her way back out to the kitchen.

"You had boyfriends in college," Kale comments from the seat beside mine—because he's a damn cold traitor who probably tried to absorb me in the womb and is still bitter I survived.

Now everyone's eyes are on me, but there's not a spoon in the entire world big enough to fix this. My brain stutters through a million responses that aren't good enough, and I somehow end up sitting in my chair.

"And high school," Kale adds, and I kick him so hard with the heel of my combat boot, he squeaks like a little girl.

"Who?" Mason and Bryce demand to know simultaneously.

"No one." I glare at Kale while he cradles his shin in his palm. "Kale is full of crap."

"Am not," he mutters under his breath—because he *clearly* wants to get kicked again.

My boyfriends in high school were just friends I experimented with. In college, they were just...fun distractions. They weren't puppy loves or true loves or any kind of loves. They were just...there, and then they weren't.

I'm saved from having to lie my face off some more when our dad enters the room, patting his big belly loudly enough to break sound barriers. "Needed to make some room!" he proudly announces, sitting at the head of the table and laughing like he's the funniest guy he knows. He's been stationed in the bathroom for God knows how long, exercising his Sunday pregame in preparation for Mom's big meal—a ham big enough to feed a literal football team.

"So, Kit," she begins while the boys practically dive face-first into it, "have you made any friends other than the band?"

"The lead singer's girlfriend is really cool," I answer as I scoop some mashed potatoes onto my plate. "She goes to the school out there. And she has this friend, Leti. He's awesome."

"And cute?" my mom not-so-subtly suggests.

I nod while scooping some corn into my mashed potatoes—a habit I learned from my dad. My mom does this almost every dinner, so I'm ready for her. "And funny. And smart." Her face begins to brighten. "And gay."

She dims and sighs, her hopes for girl talk squandered again. I've never been the type to have tea parties or swoon over boy bands or wear frilly dresses. Instead, I come home with piercings and blue hair and boots. Two words, and her maternal battle is lost again—*he's gay*.

"That's such a shame," my mom laments, and I cringe for Kale's sake. Her words are like an invisible whip that lash right in his direction with no one even knowing it—no one but me, and it takes every ounce of restraint I have to not turn to my twin and throw a protective arm around him.

If my mom knew her youngest son was gay too, she wouldn't be so insensitive. Or at least I don't *think* she would…but I have no way of knowing, and neither does Kale. All he knows now is that she just heard I had a gay friend, and her response was *that's such a shame*.

"I just don't get it," Mason interjects. "Why would any guy sleep with other guys when there are millions of gorgeous women just begging for it?"

"Guys are less drama," Ryan jokes with a smirk on his face.

"Are you kidding?" Bryce says. "Gay dudes are the most dramatic of all. Always with the hand motions and shit." He flicks both hands flamboyantly in the air, his voice a lispy stereotype when he says, "Everything is *sooo* fabulous."

Anger bubbles somewhere down deep in my belly, erupting in my voice when I snap, "You're an ass."

Normally, my mom would lecture me about the cursing, but at the anger in my voice, she settles for a cautious, reproachful look.

Bryce starts laughing and grabs his third dinner roll. "Don't get your panties in a bunch, Kit. I'm just playing."

Just playing? Just *playing*? I haven't spared a glance at Kale yet, but I can already see the look on his face. I can feel the hurt.

"It's not fucking funny."

"Kit," my mom warns this time, but I make no apology. Bryce is lucky my fork is still lying on my napkin instead of lodged in the meat of his shoulder.

Dismissively, he says, "Okay, sorry, *jeez*." But it does nothing to cool my temper, and I finish my dinner faster than everyone else, tapping Kale's knee under the table before excusing myself.

I'm waiting for him in my old room upstairs when my phone dings and Shawn's face flashes onto my screen.

Can I come over?

And if I thought I couldn't hate my brothers more right now, I was wrong. I'd give anything in the world right now to be at my apartment, with Shawn just a twenty-minute drive away, but here I am, stuck with a bunch of bigoted jerks who unfortunately share my last name.

The first time I called Shawn was three days ago, when I had a riff playing over and over on my fingers. My excitement about the sound outweighed how nervous I felt about dialing his number, and it wasn't until the phone was ringing in my ear that I nearly passed out from the blood that rushed to my head. I *knew* he wouldn't answer. I *knew* he wouldn't call me back. I knew—

He picked up on the first ring, showed up at my door less than half an hour later, and stayed until I was almost too tired to keep my eyes open.

I never would've asked him to leave, but sometime after midnight, he ended up on one side of my door while I stood on the other. The good-bye was awkward as hell. No goodnight kiss. No promises to call. No promises to text.

But I did text—the very next day, and the next. And never once did he leave me hanging.

Now, he's texting *me*, and asking if he can come over?

God, that shouldn't make me as giddy as it does, but I find myself smiling down at my phone anyway.

I'm at my parents'. :(
Why the sad face?
I kind of hate everyone right now.
Why?

It surprises me how badly I want to tell him all about what happened downstairs, but that would require telling him about Kale, and I've never told *anyone* about Kale.

My thumbs twitch over my phone until I finally type, *Why do you want to come over?*

Because I want you to tell me what happened at your parents'.

I smile down at my phone, because that is *so* not why he texted me in the first place, but the fact that he wants to know why I'm sad makes me feel all tickly inside. I roll my eyes at myself, and when my door begins to open, I wipe the grin from my face and shove my phone under my pillow.

Kale's shoulders are slumped, the fight drained from his expression when he closes the door behind him and leans back against it. And just like that, the butterflies in my chest are gone, replaced with a quiet aching that I always feel when I know my twin is hurting.

"I am so, so sorry about what happened down there," I say, and Kale closes his eyes and rests his head against the wooden frame.

"It's not your fault."

"I shouldn't have brought it up."

My twin sighs and opens his eyes, sliding to the floor with his bony elbows propped on his big knees. "You shouldn't have to keep secrets just because I do."

This is normally where I'd try to convince him to just come out—to be who he is, who he has *always* been—but after what happened downstairs...

"They're just being stupid," I say, like that makes things any better.

The look Kale gives me says that it doesn't. I read his expression like a book—one that says in bold italic letters,

I don't believe you. Stop kidding yourself. They meant every word.

"They're always stupid," he counters, and I desperately want to argue with him. I want to insist that what happened downstairs isn't how our brothers—or our *mom*—really feel, but Bryce's lispy impersonation is still fresh in my mind, and maybe Kale is right. Maybe I give them too much credit.

"Do you know what Leti would have done?" I ask instead of disagreeing. Every morning since we met at Starbucks last week, when he predicted we'd be third-best friends, we've met up there, and now I guess it's become our thing.

Kale looks up from the floor to catch my answer, and I use my hands to demonstrate. "He would've responded *extra* flamboyantly just to make everyone uncomfortable."

When I finish flicking my wrists around like Bryce did downstairs, Kale cracks a smile and lets out a little chuckle. I join him on the floor a moment later, my back resting against the door and my shoulder attaching itself to his.

"They wouldn't act like that if they knew," I say.

"You don't know that."

"If they did, I'd beat the shit out of them. You know I would."

"I know," Kale agrees, resting the side of his head against mine.

We sit like that forever, neither of us admitting that we miss the hell out of each other. Even after three years of sleeping under different roofs, I miss being able to sneak over to my twin's room at night to share blackmail on our older brothers or watch scary movies that leave us both too terrified to sleep.

Sometimes, Kale works on my nerves. But most of the time, he makes me feel…whole. Like a piece of my heart that sometimes leaves my chest.

"I want you to meet Leti," I say with my head still resting against his.

Kale doesn't budge. "You're not setting me up."

"Of course not."

It's a lie, and because he's Kale, he knows it, and because I'm me, I know he knows it.

When he elbows me, I elbow him back, and we keep going like that until I'm sure I have a bruise on my arm and he's rubbing his and telling me he gives up. "Mean," he scolds.

I move to sit on the edge of my bed, resisting the urge to rub my tingling bicep. "You started it."

"It's not my fault you're annoying."

"It's not my fault I met the guy of your dreams."

Kale shushes me and shifts away from the door to peek out of it. He closes it softly and scoots across the hardwood floor toward my bed. "Just because you met one gay guy, *one*, does not make him perfect for me. Being gay does not make him my soul mate or something."

"He's also funny and sweet and smart." Kale rolls his eyes, and I grin like a Cheshire cat. "And ridiculously hot. He's tall, with a great body and this sexy golden-bronze hair. He can rock a pair of sunglasses like nobody's business."

"Then maybe *you* should date him. God knows you're boyish enough."

"You're going to regret saying that when you're begging me to set you up."

"In your dreams."

When I smirk at Kale, he scoffs at me. "If you want to talk about boys so much, why don't we talk about Shawn? Are you back in love with him yet?"

When I lose my smile, his falls away too.

"Oh God...you're in love with him again."

I groan, collapse sideways onto my bed, and bury my face under a pillow—coming face-to-face with my phone and desperately wanting to check to see if I have any more texts from Shawn. I'm *not* in love with him again, am I? Even when all I want to do is rush Kale out of my room right now so I can stare at his face on my screen some more? So I can giggle in my Jeep, break traffic laws all the way home, and—ugh, *God*.

"Seriously, Kit?"

"He's stupid," I whine into my pillowcase.

"Why is he stupid?" Kale asks, and I inhale a slow breath through the cotton.

"Because he makes *me* stupid," my muffled voice complains. He makes my heart do cartwheels. He makes me *giggle* at my freaking *phone*.

Another pillow smacks me hard over the pillow covering the back of my head. "Stop being annoying and tell me what the hell you're saying."

I pull the pillows away and glare at Kale through the thick web of hair falling over my eyes. "Why do you want to know anyway? You hate Shawn."

"Which you should too."

"That was six years ago, Kale."

"Has he said he's sorry?"

"How can he be sorry for something he doesn't remember?" While Kale grimaces at me, I struggle to sit up and brush the hair out of my face.

"He should say sorry for not remembering."

"Now who's stupid?" I whack him with a pillow, catching only the forearm he lifts to block me.

"Still you. Why not meet some of the other hot guys in town?" He snatches the pillow away and continues rubbing Shawn in my face. "You live by a huge college, for God's sake. You've got to be swimming in them."

"They're all Polos," I complain, and it takes Kale a little longer than usual—two seconds, almost three—but eventually the static on our twin frequency clears and he shoots me a flat look.

"Maybe you're just not looking hard enough."

Or maybe all I can see is Shawn.

Even in college, no guy ever made me feel like Shawn made me feel, even if it was just for one hour on one night at one party six years ago. No one else can compete with him—I just never fully realized it until I was sitting on that couch with him after band practice, watching him play that vintage Fender and remembering what it felt like to have my heart do that thing in my chest.

That dancing, twirling, fluttering fucking thing. That thing straight out of books and Lifetime movies.

"There's no one like him, Kale."

I don't even know what it is about him. It's the intense way he stared down at his guitar when he was playing, the soft way he looked at me when I made him smile. It's like there's an even more beautiful person beneath his beautiful shell, and all I want to do is *be* with that person. I want to be the only girl he smiles at like that.

Kale sighs, his chest deflating and the worry lines around his mouth deepening. "You should hate him."

"Forever?"

"At least until you remind him what he did."

I never can.

"He needs to know, Kit."

He never does.

"And you deserve to hear an apology."

I never will, and that night, when I'm in my own bed under heavy covers, I don't ask for one. Instead, I text Shawn, tell him I'm home, and answer my phone when it rings two seconds later.

Actually, I answer it when it rings ten seconds later, because it takes me that long to stop smiling around the lip I'm biting and feeling like I'll start giggling as soon as I hear his voice.

"Hello?"

"You're home now?"

Three words, and that giggly smile is back on my face. I pull the phone away until I can get a grip on myself, and then I answer, "Yeah, I'm in bed."

"Oh…"

Shit…did that translate to, *I don't want you to come over*? Because that is definitely *not* what I meant. What I meant was, *Yes! I'm home! Come over! Stay a while! We can do…stuff!*

God. It's like I've never talked to a freaking boy before.

"So what happened at your parents'?" Shawn asks, interrupting my spastic inner monologue.

I make a noise and answer, "You don't want to hear about it. Trust me."

"If I didn't want to hear about it, I wouldn't ask."

Soft heat radiates beneath my cheeks, soaking into the fingertips I press against them. "What if I just don't want to talk about it?"

"Then can I play you something?"

I slide my fingertips away when that soft heat turns to fire. "On your guitar?"

"No, on my harmonica."

I'm *way* too nervous to form a smart-ass reply to his tease. "Over the phone?"

"Yeah. I want to come over tomorrow, too, if that's cool with you, but I've been waiting all day for you to listen to this song I've been working on."

That smile I gave to the darkness earlier comes back full force, and I swallow another stupid giggle. "Sure. Play away."

And then, he does. He plays his guitar just for me, and I close my eyes and let myself dream.

I dream that the song is mine, that the night is mine, that Shawn is mine.

"So what do you think?" he asks when he's finished. "Do you like it?"

And with that dreamy smile still on my face and his song still in my heart, I answer him.

"No," I say. "I love it."

Chapter Six

OVER THE NEXT couple of weeks, my mornings are usually filled with Starbucks and Leti, and my afternoons are usually filled with practices or jam sessions, playing music or writing music. Most of the songs I learned that day in Shawn's apartment end up getting changed anyway—the old guitarist's parts getting replaced with new ones I write myself. The guys love the fresh flavor I add to their sound, and I love that they love it. We grow together flawlessly, and it's all easy. Mike always has my back, Adam always makes me laugh, Joel always entertains my corny jokes, and Shawn...

Shawn is the only part that's not easy.

Time alone with him is tough. I try to keep it professional; he has no idea that I have to try so hard, and I always feel like I'm going through withdrawal of him as soon as he leaves my place. Texting him and hearing my phone ding a response becomes an addiction, one that tugs at the strings of my heart, pulling it closer and closer to a place I swore I'd never go again.

Sometimes we meet up at his place. Sometimes the whole band practices at Mike's. But it's the times when it's just Shawn and me sitting on the roof outside my bedroom window that I look forward to the most.

"Do you hear that?" he asks as he plucks the E string of my guitar. The sound carries on the breeze blowing my hair into my mouth, and Shawn smiles as I try to brush it away.

It's been a few weeks since our first band practice, but the late May weather still hasn't realized it's almost summer, and even though the cold is demanding I crawl back through my window to put on socks and boots, I don't listen. Instead, I curl my toes against the roof and tell Shawn, "Still flat."

The icy shingles pressed against the bottoms of my feet help keep me grounded, reminding me that I'm not in a dream, reminding me that I called Shawn and he called me back—six years late, but he called. And now he's sitting next to me outside my bedroom window, looking perfectly comfortable with my guitar on his lap.

He tightens the string and plucks it again. "What about now?"

"Perfect," I say with an easy smile. I crisscross my legs and tug my frozen feet into my lap, wrapping my hands around my icicle toes to warm them. "Who taught you to play?"

"Adam and I taught ourselves," Shawn answers, a nostalgic smile curling the corners of his mouth as he places my guitar back in its case. He flips the locks and settles back against the roof, his strong arms holding himself up and his long legs stretched out in front of him.

It would be so easy to crawl on top of him—to straddle those beaten-up jeans of his and taste the breeze on his lips.

I force my eyes back up to his. "How long have you been friends?"

"First grade," he says with a little chuckle I can't help smiling at.

"What?"

"I dared him to try to walk on top of the monkey bars, and he got all the way to the last one before a teacher caught him and gave us both detention for the whole week."

"So you're the bad influence," I tease, and the pride in Shawn's grin confirms it.

"He dared me to try it as soon as our detention was up and we were allowed to go outside for recess."

"Did you do it?"

He laughs and shakes his head. "Nope. I told him I didn't want to get more detention, and when he tried to convince me I wouldn't get caught, I dared him to do it again himself."

Almost twenty years, and those two haven't changed at all. "Did he get caught?"

Shawn nods proudly. "We got two more weeks of detention, plus they called our moms."

When I laugh, he laughs too. "I'm surprised your moms let you be friends," I say.

"We were already brothers by then. It would have been too late."

I don't know why that makes me want to kiss him, but it does—just like every other damn thing he ever says. And just like every other night I've found myself alone with him, I bite the inside of my lip and try not to think about it. "So why guitar?"

"Adam's mom bought him one for Christmas, and I played around with it until he decided he wanted to learn too." Shawn's smile brightens as he travels back in time. "I think he only wanted to learn for the girls, but after a while, he started writing lyrics and singing them. And I guess the rest is history."

"What about you?" I ask, and he tilts his head to the side. "Adam wanted to learn for the girls, but what about you?"

He rakes a hand through his hair and says, "It's going to sound stupid."

"Tell me."

"It just felt right," he explains after a moment. "It came naturally...I never wanted to sleep or eat."

"Or go to school or bathe," I add, because I know exactly what he's talking about.

"Or do anything but play that guitar," he agrees. "I just wanted to keep getting better. I wanted to be the best."

"You still do."

He considers that for a moment, and a smile sneaks onto his face—one of his rare ones, the kind that makes his eyes shine a whole shade brighter, the kind that makes me wonder how my feet can be so cold when the rest of me is burning hot.

"So do you," he says, and when I say nothing back—because my tongue is tied and my heart is in knots—he asks, "Are you nervous about performing at Mayhem this Saturday?"

Our first show. Hell yes I'm nervous, but I'm too excited to feel anything but anxious. The new songs we've been working on are amazing—ridiculously freaking amazing. Working with Shawn has been like...like working with a legend. Like creating the very piece of art I've been a fan of all my life.

"Are you kidding?" I ask. "I was born for this."

With my pale knees poking through my shredded jeans and my wild black-and-blue hair jutting out of a clip, there's no question that I look the part. My eyelashes are painted as black as my toenails, and my nose ring is glittering like a snowflake in the cold.

Shawn grins and asks, "What about going on tour?"

We leave in two months, and that daily countdown has kept me up at night ever since he told the guys and me about the tour last week—but not because I'm nervous about performing in big cities for four weeks, which I kind of am, but because I'm nervous about where I'm going to sleep once I'm on the bus. I lie under my warm covers at night wondering if Shawn will be in a bunk above me, below me, across from me...I wonder if he's a night owl or an early riser. I wonder what he wears to bed—if he wears anything at all. I wonder if he'll bring girls on the bus after shows, and then I imagine myself being the one who shares his covers. We haven't even left yet, but I'm already fighting the imminent urge to crawl into his bunk, straddle his hips, and—

"Nah," I say with a shake of my head to clear my thoughts. Shawn eyes me curiously, and I ask, "Are you?"

"A little," he confesses, and my eyebrow lifts.

"Really? You still get nervous?"

"Not really about performing...more just about everything else. If the crowd is going to be good, if the equipment is going to work, if we're going to be on time—"

"So basically everything you can't control," I say, and he smiles at my assessment.

"Pretty much."

"It must be hell working with a bunch of rock stars."

"You have no idea. But record execs would be worse."

"Really?"

"You'll see. The music industry is one giant cannibal, especially big labels. Like Mosh Records—they've been after us for years. But they want you to look a part and play a part and be this *part*, and the whole time, they're just eating you alive."

"Awesome," I say, and Shawn shrugs.

"That's why we're not with them."

"Even though we could be..."

"Even though we could be."

I wonder how many offers Shawn has gotten, and which labels they've been from, but instead of asking about any of that, I coil my hands around my ice-cold toes again, and say, "What do you think I should wear to

Mayhem on Saturday?" Even though I know I don't have to look a part or play a part or *be* a part like Shawn just said…I kind of want to, at least for our first show, and these shredded hand-me-down jeans I'm wearing just aren't going to cut it.

"Something warm," he teases, and I lift my eyes to find him smiling at the way I'm holding my feet.

I sneer at him, he grins at me, and I say, "Maybe I can get Dee to make me something."

Dee is making a name for herself by designing shirts for the band's website, but maybe she could do a cute dress or something…something Leti would approve of.

"You've talked to her?"

"A few days ago at Starbucks." Whatever happened between her and Joel…it left the girl empty. She wasn't the spirited, catty chick who swung open the door at Mayhem the day of my audition and basically told me to get lost. She's as broken as Joel, only with better fashion sense.

Shawn sighs and pulls a knee up, balancing an elbow on it and scratching his hand through his hair. "How was she?"

"Hanging in there, just like Joel," I say, obeying what I'm guessing is some kind of inner girl code by telling the truth without really telling it. The comparison alone says enough, because Joel is the same sort of shell. He goes through the motions—shows up at practices, hits his marks, forces a laugh when everyone else laughs—but even someone like me, who hadn't really known him before, can tell his light his out. The one that lit for her.

Shawn sighs and looks out over the big yard behind the old woman's house, and I'm content to watch him think. It's like watching the northern lights, a breathtaking phenomenon that not many people get to see. Guys like my brothers can simply space out, think about nothing, but not Shawn or even Adam. It's a songwriter thing, a constant introspection, and it's why the band's songs resonate with so many people. It's why they've always resonated with *me*. And now, watching Shawn climb inside himself, I wonder if I'm witnessing the lyrics of our next hit being drafted, if this is what that looks like.

"I used to wish they'd stay apart," he says. "Now, I wish they'd just get back together."

"Why?"

"I think they need each other." Shawn glances over at me, like he just realized he's talking to another person instead of himself, and then he lets out a breath and stares back over the yard again. "I don't think they needed each other before, but…I don't know. It's like none of us ever realized he was half a person until she came around. Not even him."

"Maybe that's true of everyone," I say, barely noticing the numbness in my toes anymore, because I'm too lost in this moment. It would take me ten seconds to get my socks and boots, but those are ten seconds with Shawn I'm not willing to lose.

He's quiet for a long time. A long time. And then he looks over at me, his green eyes making my heart beat faster, just like they always do. "Do you believe that?"

I shrug a shoulder. "I don't know. Maybe."

"Are you half a person?"

In the depths of his eyes, I feel like I might find my answer...

"Are you?" I ask, stopping myself from searching.

"How would I know?"

"I guess you wouldn't."

The silence doesn't have answers, and neither do the ribbons that rise out of the horizon. Blues, pinks, purples. Shawn and I sit out there, content to watch them dance.

"So you've never been in love before?" I ask the air between us. I don't know why I need to know, but sitting up here on my roof, with the sun setting just for us, I do.

"No." His answer comes quickly. He doesn't even glance at me.

"Not even once?"

When he finally looks over at me, I almost regret asking. "Have you?"

I look away, not giving myself time to think about it. "No."

"No boyfriends? You had to have had boyfriends..."

"Of course I've had boyfriends," I scoff. Still sitting guru-style, I try to tuck my feet in the creases of my knees to warm them—and fail miserably. "I just never loved any of them," I say as I try to tuck a foot into the opposite leg of my jeans. "Do you want me to tell you about each one? Because I can tell y—"

"No," Shawn interrupts, scooting over and tugging at the crisscross of my legs until I'm nearly toppling backward. My feet get pulled into his lap, and I grip his shoulders for balance as he wraps warm fingers around my toes. We're suddenly inches apart, and when he turns his face to look at me, there's nowhere for me to run, nowhere for me to hide. "Trust me," he says, "I really don't want to know."

Chapter Seven

THE NIGHT OF the roof, with my feet in Shawn's lap, we talked about everything and nothing. Or, more accurately, he talked...and I just kind of squeaked back a reply once in a while.

Long after it got dark, long after he left, I snuggled tight under a mountain of heavy blankets and smiled into the cold breeze that blew in through my open window. The night air smelled like him, or maybe he smelled like the night air, but either way, I let it in. I closed my eyes, and with the kiss of the wind on my cheeks...my nose...my lips...I could almost imagine he never left.

Even now, I can still feel the way he held my legs in his lap, and that memory has been both inviting and haunting over the days leading up to tonight, our first performance at Mayhem. He and I haven't been alone since the roof. Instead, we've seen each other only during group practices, and that has made the day of the sunset feel like a dream, a fluke. Shawn goes back to being Shawn, and I go back to being Kit—a punk rocker who doesn't do embarrassing things like blush and giggle and act like a total *girl*. I'm a guitarist, one of the guys, and I regret asking Dee to make me a dress for tonight's performance.

In the only private room of the band's double-decker tour bus, I finish putting it on—a flattering black minia-ture *thing*, adorned with blue safety pins that barely hold the slinky garment together. Dee made it from one of the dresses she already had in her closet, and even though she warned me it had been short even on her, my eyes go wide when I realize how *super* short it is on me. I take a deep breath and ignore how much pale skin is show-ing, using a compact mirror to cake on my lengthening mascara. I apply an extra layer of super-strength deodor-ant and brush my hair until it flows like water over the bristles.

"Are you nervous?" Shawn asks from the other side of the closed door.

Nervous about the crowd? No. Nervous about open-ing that door? I stare down at my legs again.

"Yeah, a little."

"You rocked soundcheck this morning," he assures me. "Just bring that same confidence tonight and you'll be fine."

I sit on the edge of the black satin bed and tighten the strings of my combat boots. If Dee knew I was wearing *this* dress with *these* boots…well, it might reignite some of that fire missing from her eyes. "You can go in without me. I'll be done in a minute."

The silence that stretches and stretches tells me he took me up on my offer and I'm finally, really alone. I finish tying my second ass-kicking boot, let it fall back to the ground, and take another rib-straining deep, deep breath. Nervous invisible butterflies swarm in my stomach until I heave them out in a heavy sigh.

Tonight is the night. Every choice I've made—picking up the guitar, dedicating the past few years of my life to it, auditioning for the band, not quitting after I threw a guitar pick at Shawn's chest and had my chance to get away—it all comes down to this.

When I slide open the door, Shawn pushes away from the hallway wall, his wide eyes traveling down, down, down. They linger on my bare thighs, which probably blush as pink as my cheeks, my neck, my ears.

"I thought you went inside," I stammer.

His gaze is in no rush as it lifts back to mine. "Wow."

"Wow?"

"I…"

When he doesn't finish his sentence, I say, "You?"

His eyes finally lock on mine, and he swallows and runs a hand through his hair. But then those eyes are dropping again, and when they catch my lips, I bite the bottom one between my teeth. It's a nervous gesture that makes his eyes dart to the wall behind my head. "You ready to head inside?"

"Not until you say what you were going to say."

I surprise even myself, and God…I don't know why I want to hear it. I don't know why I *need* to hear it. But the girl inside me, the one who never got a call from him, the one who giggled with him on the roof…she needs to know. She needs to know what he was going to say after "wow."

"You look…" Shawn's eyes start to wander again, but he stops them short of diving into the cleavage peeking out from behind bright blue safety pins that Dee strategically fastened in the dress. He drags that fiery green gaze back up, his fingertips wearing at an already-worn spot on his jeans while my heart pounds pulse-by-slow-pulse in the hollow of my chest. "Dee made this for you?"

My inner rock goddess wants to take his fidgeting hands and fit them against my curves. Wants to suck his fingertip between my lips to make him think about other things he'd like to put in its place.

My inner girly-girl is a pussy.

"Yeah," I say. "Do I look okay?"

Do I look okay? In lieu of mimicking oral sex on his finger, I opt for *Do I look o-freaking-kay?*

An amused smile touches his lips, and he answers with a slight shake of his head. "Yeah, Kit, you look fine."

It isn't until he starts walking down the bus hallway and I fall in step just behind him that I finally find my nerve again. "Is that what you were going to say?"

"Huh?"

"Back there, when I opened the door"—I'm on his heels as we descend the stairs of the double-decker—"is that what you were going to say? That I look fine?"

Outside, my combat boots hit the pavement, and we walk toward Mayhem side by side. "Does it matter?"

When I stop walking, Shawn takes a few more steps ahead of me before he stops walking too.

"What are you doing?"

I level a stubborn gaze on him. "Waiting."

He steps closer so we can see each other in the dim orange glow of the parking lot, and it's ridiculous what a perfect model he'd make for Goodwill—because it's like every single T-shirt he wears beat itself up just to be with him. "I have no idea what I was going to say."

"Yes, you do."

"No, I don't," he argues. "It was like my brain stopped working for a minute, so I honestly have no fucking idea."

Silence, and then *giggling*. From *me*. I can't stop myself from doing it, and even though I feel dumb as hell, it does nothing to wipe the ear-to-ear smile from my face.

A smile teases at Shawn's lips too, which only makes me feel even dumber. "Happy?" he asks.

I walk ahead of him to hide my goofy grin. "Maybe."

He opens the door for me, his hand finds my lower back to usher me inside, and that smile on my face blooms to epic proportions. I'm escorted backstage to catcalls and whistles from the staff, and I flash them my middle finger even though my heart isn't in it. Even when Shawn's hand drops away as we approach the guys, my mood is indestructible.

Because I broke Shawn Scarlett's brain. Shawn Scarlett thinks I'm hot.

Mike whistles louder than anyone, earning me the sudden attention of the entire band. Rowan and Leti are backstage too, and when all eyes turn to me, I brace myself for their ambush.

"Oh my," Leti says, circling around me like I'm some kind of safety-pinned maypole. "Oooh my."

"You look *gorgeous*," Rowan praises, rubbing her fingers over a safety pin on my shoulder and admiring Dee's work.

"That *ass*," Leti admires from behind me, and I whirl around and smack him on the shoulder while he laughs.

"Did Dee make this?"

I turn back around to find Joel studying me, the rest of the guys gathered around. His eyes are for the dress and not at all for what's underneath, and when I confirm that she did, his answer is blankness. No full smile, no half smile, no frown, no nothing. He nods and walks away, and everyone stares after him with no right words to say, because no right words exist. Shawn and I exchange glances, and when he replies to my worried expression with a slight shake of his head, we both let Joel go.

"You're going to have a fan club," Adam tells me with his arm draped heavily around Rowan. He's grinning like he's about to award me some kind of secret honor, and I grin right back.

"Good. I've always wanted a fan club."

"Not this kind of fan club," Shawn warns, like I have no idea what it's like to have fans, like I've never had guys in the pit shout my name. First, he thinks I've never had a boyfriend, and now, he thinks I've never had someone try to hook up with me after a show? I scoff at him.

"What, the kind that jerks off to my picture at night? I think I can handle it."

Mike bursts out laughing and maneuvers his way to my side. He wraps his arm around my shoulder and diffuses me with a warm smile. "You ready to bring the house down?"

"Always." I beam up at him, and he turns back toward the rest of the guys.

"Sounds to me like she's ready."

"This girl was born ready," Leti praises, and I wink at him before prepping for the show. I strap my guitar around my neck. I insert my in-ear monitors. I shift from leg to leg as I stand between Adam and Shawn at the darkened side of the stage.

"I'm going to play up the fan club thing," Adam says with a devilish smile. "Don't hate me for it later."

I think I hear Shawn sigh to my left, but when I look over at him, he's busy adjusting the strap of his guitar.

The lights of the house cut to black, and it takes my eyes a moment to adjust, but then the guys are walking onstage and so am I. The crowd goes fucking crazy. The screams are loud enough to make the soles of my boots shiver and the blood in my veins hum. In the dark, a roadie helps me get plugged in, and I take a deep breath. I adjust my in-ear monitors. I wait for my mark.

Shawn's Telecaster starts the band's most popular song, and I try to not go completely fangirl about sharing the stage with him, with Adam Everest, with Joel Gibbon, with Mike Madden. My face breaks into a huge smile, and then Joel's bass joins in, then my Fender, then Mike's drums. Adam's voice carries into my ear, but I know the crowd is hearing it blare from the massive speakers at the sides of the stage. Their arms are in the air, bouncing up and down, up and down, in a turbulent sea of bodies. I know that feeling—that feeling of having your pupils get big, your skin blaze hot, your blood turn electric. But onstage, that feeling is multiplied by a hundred, a thousand. I'm high on the crowd, the music, the dream.

By the time the first song ends, the entire crowd is screaming its collective head off. It's been over two months since The Last Ones to Know performed here, and it's obvious their fans missed them.

Still, Adam baits them.

"MAYHEM!" he shouts, tugging his mic from its stand and walking to the very edge of the stage. "God, I've missed you!"

The girls in the pit start screaming that they've missed him too, that they love him, and Adam turns to Shawn and smiles. He tugs his shaggy brown hair away from his face and glances across the stage at me with sparkling gray-green eyes before turning back to the crowd.

"We've got some new songs for you tonight! But first, do you see this smoking-hot chick we've brought with us?"

A deep voice in the pit shouts, "HELL YEAH!"

Adam chuckles into his mic. "That's our new guitarist, Kit. We went to school with her, and she's talented as hell." He walks the length of the stage, engaging the entire crowd. "How many guys here want to join Kit's fan club tonight?"

The deafening cheers that spring from the pit this time are different from when Adam's silhouette first walked onstage—now, male voices dominate the noise. Most of the guys are probably here with girlfriends, but none of them seem to care as they answer Adam's call.

I've played for crowds before, but none this size, and never with a lead singer like Adam. He knows just what to say to get the fans worked up, and I follow his lead by blowing a kiss down at the pit. The girls in the front row cheer me on, screaming at me like I'm some kind of hero.

Adam grins at my showmanship, fueling me with his approval. "Sounds like you have a few takers. Ready to give them a show?"

I play a riff on my guitar that leaves the crowd screaming, and even Adam doesn't interrupt the applause. With the walls threatening to come down, I glance at the other guys to find them beaming at me—Joel behind me, Mike in the back, and Shawn at the other side of the stage, illuminated in blue light. Then, before I know it, Adam introduces the next song, and the next.

I lose myself in the music—in the heat of the lights, in the sound of Adam's voice, in the beat of Mike's drums. I focus on my instrument, letting my fingers do what they were trained to do and giving in to the high. My mind is present on the stage and above the stage and in the crowd, and beads of sweat are pooling at the base of my neck and trickling down my spine. By the time the first "last song" ends, my skin is blazing hot and my brain is completely fried. When I walk out of view of the crowd, it doesn't even feel like walking. It feels like floating, like flying. It feels like dreaming.

"You were fucking AWESOME," Adam praises backstage before our encore. The fans are already shouting for one more song, one more song, one more song, and I want to give them a thousand more. I want to play until my fingers fall off, and then I want to glue them back on and keep playing.

"You guys!" I shout, bracing my hands on Mike's shoulders because I desperately need to latch on to something. "That was AMAZING!"

When Leti taps me on the shoulder, I spin around and throw my arms around his neck.

"How great was that?"

He laughs and asks me if I need to be "spun around or something."

"YES!" I shout, barely getting the word out before he whips me around in a circle. My feet leave the ground, and I squeal and feel like kissing him or finding religion or, hell, stripping naked and going back onstage that way.

We played some of the new stuff, and the crowd ate it up. Not that I doubted that they would, but to hear them applaud the songs *I* helped write…songs played by The Last Ones to Know…it was indescribable.

"Here," Shawn says, handing me a water, and to keep myself from jumping into his arms instead of Leti's, I take it and gulp it down.

"I told you there was nothing to be nervous about," he says, flashing me that heartbreaker smile that makes my skipping heart remember exactly why it was so nervous. His dark band T-shirt is damp with sweat, his messy black hair soaked at the tips and curling at the base of his neck. His skin is flushed and probably as scorching hot as mine, and I wonder if I pressed up against him, if we'd both burst into flames.

"One more song!" The crowd's chant gets louder, pulsing under the soles of my feet. "One more song!" My scalp prickles, sending electric waves down my spine. "One more song!" My guitar pick calls to me even though the pads of my fingers are numb. "One more song! One more song! One more song!"

"You ready?" Adam asks me, and I nod as I finish my water. I wipe my arm across my mouth and toss the bottle in a bin, and then my guitar is strapped heavily around my neck and I'm walking back onstage in a line. Joel, Mike, me, Shawn, Adam.

The Last Ones to Know.

Chapter Eight

THE GUYS AND I play one final crowd favorite before we exit the stage, followed by a deafening roar of screams and applause. I almost feel bad for the post-concert hangover we're leaving those kids with, knowing that each one of them is going to be going through withdrawal for days.

But for now, there's only mayhem as we march right into the thick of the crowd. Shawn tells me to keep close, but in the chaos, I get thrown into a cyclone of fans and pictures and autographs—more fans and pictures and autographs than I've ever dealt with in my life. Sometimes, the pictures are of me and the band. Sometimes, they're of me and a few girls. Sometimes, they're of just me and a guy. And most of the time, those guys offer to buy me a drink or take me home.

"After merch," Shawn manages to shout to me over the noise while Mike and I are taking a picture with a fan, "we'll go to the bus." Our group has been broken up by the crowd, with Shawn and Adam being swallowed by the teeth of it.

I shake my head and shout back at him. "No way! I was promised like thirty freaking drinks at the bar!"

Some random guy hollers his approval, and I laugh. The best way to get fans to love you is to love them back, and I already do. Come to see them, and they'll come to see you.

"Joel!" Adam shouts with Rowan pinned to his side. "Kit says we're going to the bar afterward!"

Joel looks up from a girl who's uselessly trying to give him her number, giving a thumbs-up. It takes two and a half more seconds, but he weaves away from her like some kind of seasoned ninja, and then he's at my side, his blond Mohawk adding another few inches to his already solid six-foot-two.

"You doing okay?"

I beam up at him. "I'm doing awesome."

"She's a pro," Mike says from my other side, and I beam up at him too.

Joel's arm wraps tight around my shoulder to escort me through the crowd, and Mike helps part the sea to get me to the merchandise booth.

It's near the bar and absolutely swarmed, with girls buying Dee-designed T-shirts and asking where and when they can buy my dress. There are chicks with blonde hair and pink hair and brown hair and blue hair, but when I finally see Shawn again, the girl hanging off of him is one with auburn hair that made it through the show in much better shape than mine. I'm covered in at least five layers of dried-on sweat, with my runny mascara probably making me look like I belong in Twisted Sister instead of The Last Ones to Know, and she's standing over there looking like she just had her lip gloss applied by Kim Kardashian's makeup artist.

While the band and I mingle with fans at the merchandise booth, she waits. When the house music starts and we make our way to the bar, she follows. When we sit, she sits.

"Can I buy you that drink now?" one of the guys from before asks me, and I stop scowling at the girl's stupid catwalk-ready face long enough to answer him.

I should be celebrating right now. I should be happy and excited and *not* daydreaming about swinging some chick around by her hair. I turn a manufactured smile on the guy and tell him I'll have a rum and Coke, and he buys it for me while telling me how awesome I was, how hot I look, how talented I am.

I soak it all in, sipping on the drink he buys me and a drink another guy buys me and a drink another guy buys me, and there might be another guy or two but I honestly lose count. I mingle with girl fans and guy fans and try to give some of my attention to everyone who wants it, which isn't nearly half as many people as those who are competing to talk to Adam and Shawn.

An hour after the show has ended, the house music is pounding against my eardrums, the alcohol is thinning my blood, and Shawn makes eye contact with me from down the bar. Most of the fans have left or gone back on the floor, but the auburn-haired girl from before is still hanging off of him. She's treating him like her own personal jungle gym, talking his damn face off, and I'm suddenly on my feet.

"Dance with me," I order, grabbing his hands and leaving no room for argument. The other guys watch me drag Shawn onto the dance floor, and Rowan and Leti stand side by side grinning like cartoon characters, like their mouths are going to stretch off the sides of their faces at any given moment.

I imagine the girl with the stupid hair is glaring poisoned daggers at the back of my head, but I'm too busy towing Shawn into the crowd to enjoy it. The drinks I've had are making the shiny dancers blur, the laser-filled room tilt, and my lips feel numb, but my feet don't fail me. When Shawn's hand squeezes mine, it's enough to keep me sober...Kind of.

In the middle of the floor, I spin around and wrap my arms around his neck. He's tall, but so am I, so I don't have to crane my neck very far to catch his bright forest eyes. They're locked on me, but the rest of him doesn't make a move. He's a statue, and I'm desperate. I step into him, pressing my every soft curve against his every hard plane, holding his eyes with every centimeter I close between us. He looks like he has no idea what I'm doing—and that makes two of us. My fingers play in the back of his hair, and when he still makes no move to put his arms around me, I make a soft plea against the shell of his ear. "Please."

Shawn's head is the only thing that turns, his hands hanging at his sides and his body stuck in place. He angles his chin toward my ear, his stubble brushing my cheek when he says, "Please what?"

Please touch me. Please hold me. Please want me. "Pretend I'm someone else."

He pulls away to stare down at me, but I keep my arms around him, begging him with my eyes to *please* just let me pretend. Tonight, I don't want to be the girl he left behind in high school. I don't want to be his buddy from the band. These past few weeks with him have been torture, and right now, I just want to be a hot girl in a hot dress. I want to be the girl he was with at the bar. I want to be one of thousands.

When he shakes his head, my heart sinks. The word "No" leaves his mouth, and I turn to walk away from him. But then his hand catches my waist and pulls me backward. My back molds to his chest, my ass fits against his jeans, and his fingers slide up my arms, lifting them until my hands are curling behind his neck. With my body flush against his and me not daring to let go, his capable fingers slide back down my sides until he's clutching my hips again.

I turn my head to stare up at him, and he doesn't shy from my gaze. Instead, he pulls me even tighter—as tight as we can possibly be—and his hips rock mine from side to side. I turn away and close my eyes, tunneling my fingers into his soft, messy hair and grinding against him on the floor. There's no mistaking that my dress is thin, that his jeans are stiff, and that whatever I'm doing, I'm doing it right.

Where Shawn's hands move, a trail of fire follows. He ignites my sides, my arms, my thighs. A safety pin in the side of my dress gets unfastened, and then that hand is boldly sneaking inside my dress, caressing my blazing-hot stomach before flattening against it to hold me even tighter against him as his hips rock with mine on the floor. I long for him to move that hand up, or down, or, fuck, I don't even know. I just want to feel him. I want to feel him like I felt him six years ago.

Kale told me I should hate him, should make him get on his knees. But how can I hate him when he makes me feel like this? When his fingers set my world on fire. When his eyes make my heart flip in my chest. When his voice calls to something in me that no one else knows is there.

When I slide his hand out from my dress and spin around, Shawn's eyes are almost as dark as mine. I wrap my arms around his neck and forget everything. I forget the past six years, I forget all the drinks I've had tonight, I forget the warning Kale gave me.

"I forgive you," I blurt.

And I kiss him.

I don't even give him time to respond before I rise onto my tiptoes and do what I've been wanting to do for days, for weeks, for years. And God, his mouth is so warm, so soft. I savor it and breathe him in, letting his spicy-clean scent fill my lungs and thicken the fog in my head. His lips taste like a young whiskey, my heart drums against my ribs, one song stops and another begins—and everything I forgot comes back in a fucking rush.

I open my eyes and jerk away, covering my mouth with my hand because *oh my God, I just kissed him.* Shawn looks stunned, like I just ambushed him—*because I just ambushed him.* "Oh my God," I gasp, dropping my hand from my mouth in a panic. I seriously just kissed him. I just kissed Shawn. "I'm so sor—"

One second, I'm panicking. The next, his lips are crushing mine. His fingers dive into my hair, leaving no room for me to get away if I'd even want to, and he kisses me like he's stealing something. Like he's on fire and needs me to put him out. But as his lips brush and tease and feed on the raw heat of mine, that fire blazes even hotter. His tongue teases the open seam of my mouth, doing things that have me melting into him and desperately gripping at the sleeves of his shirt. He's close, but I need him so much closer. I pull and tug and relish the feeling of his fingers in my hair as he writes a song in the rhythm of my breathing. His kiss is an inferno, consuming all of the air in the room and lighting every nerve in my body on white-hot fire.

"Fuck," he pants against my mouth, the hardness in his jeans throbbing under my hand, which got there all on its own.

When I pull it away—pushing it under his shirt instead because I need more of him, now, right now—Shawn plucks it from his body and links his fingers with mine. He starts pulling me from the dance floor, but stops three steps later to put those delicious lips on mine again. "I'm taking you to the bus," he growls against my mouth with one hand squeezing my ass through the silky fabric of my barely there dress. He tugs me tight against him so I understand exactly why he's taking me there, and I bite my bottom lip to keep myself from moaning. His stubble brushes against my temple as he moves his lips to my ear. "Right now."

"Okay," I purr against his throat, and then my hand is in his again and a hundred bodies are blurring by us. We break through a steel exit door into the frigid night air, and then we're across the parking lot and Shawn is practically carrying me onto the bus.

I don't make it easy for him to get me up the stairs to the first level. As soon as the door is closed behind us, I'm in his arms and his lips are mine. I'm insatiable, but so is he. I don't try to make it nice for him, he doesn't try to make it nice for me, and I'm so fucking hot for him I feel like I'll explode if he doesn't tear this dress off me soon. "What are you waiting for?"

The backs of my legs collide with the edge of one of the long leather benches on the lower level, and when Shawn lays me down on top of it, I bunch my fist in his shirt and pull him down with me. He settles between my legs and I arch up to meet him, loving the way he groans and pushes back against me, the way he grips my hip so desperately that it's sure to leave marks for days. He rocks against me as he controls the kiss, making me light-headed as he claims every last centimeter of my lips. I turn my head to the side and pant for fresh air, and when he drops his hungry mouth to the curve of my neck, my eyes roll back behind closed eyelids.

I feel like I'm not even inside my body anymore. I feel like I could pass out. I feel... *fuck*... I'm going to throw up.

All of the free drinks I had at the bar hit my stomach at once, threatening to come back up before I even have a chance to get out from under Shawn. I frantically push at him until he gives me enough space to roll out from underneath him, and I shake my head when he asks me what's wrong. When I slap a hand over my mouth, realization dawns on his face.

"That way," he says, pointing toward what I'm praying is the bathroom. I turn on my heel and race my way there, nearly tripping over the lip between rooms before yanking open the bathroom door. I drop to my knees in front of the toilet and grip its edges to keep from falling face-first into the bowl. The entire room spins as I puke my freaking guts out. My hair gets pulled away from my face and a rough hand rubs my back. Shawn's voice attempts to comfort me, but it doesn't stop the tears from springing to my eyes as I heave over the toilet.

I'm puking in front of Shawn. After almost puking in his mouth. Nothing could make this night any worse.

No, that's wrong—the only thing that could make it any worse is *me fucking crying*.

I lock down my emotions and finish throwing up all of my cocktails, resting my forearm on the seat of the toilet and dropping my forehead to my elbow—because I'm too wasted to stand, I'm too stubborn to lie down, and I'm too embarrassed to let Shawn hold me.

"Can you stand up?"

I try to say "no" but end up puking some more instead. My head is spinning faster and faster with every second that passes, and eventually I start dry-heaving into a toilet bowl that won't stay still. My arms are noodles, tossing me from side to side while my entire stomach climbs its way into my throat.

"I'm going to carry you upstairs, okay?"

Someone who sounds kind of like me mumbles something unintelligible back. Then there's Shawn's scent against my cheek and his voice in my ear. I become vaguely aware that I'm floating. And then, it's just dark.

In the morning, I can't remember how I got into my bunk, and Shawn isn't around for me to ask, not that I would if I could. I'm tucked under sheets that smell like him, wishing I was dead. Drinking too much is one thing. Drinking too much, throwing myself at Shawn, mauling him on the bus, and then puking my guts out in front of him?

I close my eyes and pretend it was all a bad dream, but the black hole that's blossomed in my head screams otherwise. It sucks painfully at my brain, my eyeballs, my eardrums—like it needs to devour the entire contents of my skull before it can escape and suck the rest of the world into its hole as well.

My feet are heavy as I throw them over the edge of the bunk and plant them on the icy floor. I stare down at my star-print socks, imagining Shawn carrying me up here, taking my boots off, tucking me in…and shaking his head at what a complete mess I was—the so-called rock star who thought she could hang with rock stars.

I rub a hand over my face and fit my feet into my boots one at a time. Then I attempt to finger-comb my hair, give up, and swipe my fingers under my eyes instead to clean up my mascara. Each step down the stairs to the lower level of the bus feels like an ice pick to my frontal lobe, and I'm praying there's some coffee I can make in the kitchenette—because if not, I'm going to lie on the floor and just die.

The smell of dark-roasted beans hits me as soon as I step off the last stair, but my brain is too hungover to process what that means. I follow the smell like a worn-down bloodhound, dragging my sorry ass toward it until I emerge in the kitchen and meet forest green eyes.

Because, apparently, humiliating myself last night wasn't enough. Now I need to rise from the dead with my brain throbbing out of my ears, my hair looking like something straight out of a B-rated horror film, and my wrinkled dress still ten sizes too small.

"How are you feeling?" Shawn asks, like it's not written all over my face. I plop down in a chair at the corner table and immediately curse myself for it when lightning bolts shoot into the backs of my eyes. I hiss a curse word and bury my face in the darkness of my elbow.

I have two options. I can be an adult, apologize for going all alien-sucker on his face, promise it won't happen again. Or...

"What happened last night?" I groan into my arm when I hear him sit across from me and slide a cup of coffee in my direction.

When Shawn doesn't answer, I lift my head enough to peek up at him, and he asks, "How much did you have to drink last night?"

His five o'clock shadow has turned a day old, making him look even sexier and more disheveled than he normally does. His navy blue band T-shirt is hanging loose across his collarbone, stretched by my frantic fingers the night before.

"I don't know. Five? Six?" I sit up and prop my forehead on my fist for a moment just to get myself used to being in an upright position. "Too many."

Shawn studies me while he sips his coffee. His eyes are bloodshot like I'm sure mine are, a sign I wasn't the only one who overdid it last night.

"How much do you remember?"

Everything. I remember the way his fingers skated across my stomach on the dance floor, the way his hips moved with mine. And I remember the weight of those hips on the bus, the way they rocked between my thighs.

It's the moment of truth, and I lie my ass off. "I don't know," I mutter. "Did…" I give him my most confused look. "Shit. Did I kiss you? In Mayhem?"

Shawn stares at me while rubbing calloused fingertips over his eyebrow. "A little."

If that was just *a little* kissing, this dress is just *a little* short. "Oh God. Then what? I was so wasted, I can't remember shit."

"You got pretty sick," he says as I blow nervous ripples into my coffee. Then he skips all of the in-between and jumps right to the end. "I brought you back here and put you to bed."

So I'm not the only one who's full of shit. Interesting. I continue blowing on my coffee while my swollen brain tries to make sense of what's happening. Shawn is lying, and it's either to save me the embarrassment of remembering what I did, or more likely, because he regrets it just as much as I do.

My coffee burns my tongue when I take a sip, but the sting is nothing compared to the sudden burn in my heart.

"Did anyone see me kiss you?" I ask, and Shawn shakes his head.

"If they did, they would have said something. Peach texted me, but I told her you were trashed and I was dropping you off at your place."

"Won't they think it's weird you didn't come home last night?"

"Not if I tell them I called that annoying chick who was digging her claws into me after the show."

I nod and take another scalding sip of my coffee, wanting desperately to ask him why he's lying, why he kissed me back. I was drunk, but I wasn't too drunk to know what I was doing, and I don't think he was either.

But I guess it doesn't matter, because whatever spark flared between us, it's clearly been put out.

Or maybe it was never there. Maybe I imagined it. Maybe I was just what I wanted to be—just a hot girl in a hot dress.

Maybe I meant nothing more to him than that girl with the auburn hair, nothing more to him than I did the last time he made me feel like this.

I hate myself for letting him. For letting him make me feel like this *again*.

Chapter Nine

I WAS LATE to the first band practice we had after Shawn and I made out on the bus. I was late, but he said nothing. I missed my marks, but he said nothing.

So I started missing them more. I started plucking the wrong strings. I started telling the guys that *Shawn* was the one who was off.

Still, he said nothing.

Whatever lies he told the guys about what happened after I dragged him on the dance floor at Mayhem, they believed him. And whatever lies he told himself, he believed those too.

The entire practice, I searched for any sort of acknowledgment in his eyes—I looked to see if he'd look at me the way he did when he was kissing me, when his hands were on my skin and his heart felt like it was beating in my own chest—but he barely even looked at me at all.

It was like nothing happened—*less* than nothing. It was like he'd forgotten the way he danced with me on the floor, the way he buried his hands in my hair. It was like *I* was nothing.

It was just like before.

Before writing songs in my apartment. Before sunsets on my roof. Before tugging my feet into his lap.

And I didn't dare tell a soul about what happened between us—not until this weekend at Dee's, when it was weighing so heavily on my mind that I accidentally blurted that I slept with Shawn in high school. I was at Dee's apartment with Rowan and Leti to help Dee pack up her stuff since she was planning on moving back home, and then we were going to celebrate her birthday before she left, and…yeah, it just came out.

The girls surprisingly kept their questions to a minimum, but that night after they were both fast asleep in a blanket fort in the living room, Leti locked himself in the bathroom with me—while my pants were down around my freaking ankles—and grilled me like an overcooked sausage. He held me hostage until I confessed every last detail about Shawn, with only one that I managed to keep to myself: I didn't tell him that the night I slept with Shawn in high school was the night I lost my virginity.

I could barely sleep that night, and the next morning, after a trip to IHOP for coffee, Shawn showed up with Adam and Mike to help move Dee's boxes out of her apartment. He ignored me while we loaded the van, and he continued to ignore me that night while we all drank ourselves stupid in her empty living room. I sat right next to him, and it was like I wasn't even there.

It hurt until it didn't. Because eventually, all I felt was pissed the fuck off.

"I CAN'T BELIEVE you called him *scrawny*," Leti says from the far side of my tiny apartment. I'm busy tossing things into a suitcase, and he's busy studying my wall full of pictures—of my family, of big shows I've been to, of the band.

At Dee's birthday party last night, I sat next to Shawn, had a little bit too much to drink, and…yeah, I called him scrawny. And I poked his bicep to prove my point, even though it did the opposite. I pulled my finger away, hating him for being so fucking perfect I could hardly stand it.

Leti shoots me a grin over his shoulder. "So cold, Tourni-Kit."

"He *is* scrawny," I insist. And smart. And funny. And hot.

"And hot," he counters, and an image of Shawn pops into my mind: the way he looked when he was loading Dee's things into a moving van. The way his lean muscles flexed under his T-shirt. The way the heather-gray cotton clung to his skin. The way sweat beaded at his temples.

I hated it so much, I couldn't stop staring.

"You think everyone's hot," I scoff.

"Only rock stars," Leti fibs.

"And my brothers."

I glance at him out of the corner of my eye, and the smile he shoots me is all trouble.

Tonight, I'm dragging him along to my family's Sunday dinner, then driving him to his parents' place and spending the night before coming back to town. Because maybe a few cities' worth of distance will help me forget about Shawn. Even if only for five freaking minutes.

Leti returns his attention to my picture-wall and whistles. "Your brothers are even hotter than you are."

I throw a dirty shirt at him and continue rifling through my things.

"Tall, dark, and handsome. Mmm, mmm, mmm. Are any of them gay?"

The pair of socks I'm holding freezes in midair for a moment before finishing its journey into my suitcase, and Leti misses nothing.

"Silence," he observes too quickly. "Iiinteresting, Kitana."

"Huh?" I say to recover, pretending I hadn't heard him.

"So which one?" One corner of his mouth lifts into an intrigued little smirk.

"What are you talking about?"

Leti turns back toward the picture-wall, his sunshine-yellow Felix the Cat T-shirt hanging loose between broad shoulders. "My guess would be this one that looks like he just broke out of prison," he says, and I don't need to join him at the wall to know he's talking about Mason. "He looks like he's overcompensating for something."

I snort out a laugh, and Leti continues guessing.

"Or maybe it's this one. Who's this?" When I finally walk to stand beside him, he's pointing right at Kale.

"That's Kale," I answer, and then I casually continue going down the line of brothers standing in the picture, arms around each other and smiles on their faces. "And that's Bryce. That's Mason. And that's Ryan."

"So which one, Kitastrophe? Or am I going to have to guess?"

I chuckle and retreat to my bed. "Still don't know what you think you know, but please, try to guess."

He continues guessing until my bag is packed, and during the hour-long ride, I warn him all about my family. I'd already told him how offensively they behaved at the dinner when I told them I'd made a gay friend, but I think that only made him want to come home with me even more. And when we step inside my house, he proves it. My brothers are expecting us, and when they flock to the front door from different corners of the house to greet me, Leti's one-man performance begins.

"You must be Mason," he says before wrapping my most intimidating brother in a fearless hug. My jaw drops to the foyer floor, Mason's brows turn in with something between shock and confusion, and Leti tightens his squeeze. "Kit's told me so much about you."

I glance at Kale over Mason's shoulder, and his black eyes are just as wide as mine. He looks at me, I look at him, and our mouths mirror each other as the corners tip up…up…up. We're kids on Christmas morning, watching Leti as he ends the hug with a firm kiss on Mason's cheek. He leaves my hulk of a brother stunned, like he's not sure if he wants to punch Leti in the face or apologize for not hugging him back, and I have to resist the urge to jump up and down while applauding the show. Leti is getting even—for me, for himself, for the entire gay community—and I am so, *so* on board.

I hold back an ecstatic giggle when it dawns on Bryce that he missed his opportunity to escape. But then it's too late, because Leti's arms are around him. "And you must be Bryce."

Another kiss, another set of traumatized dark eyes, and then Ryan is in Leti's arms next, but at least *he* has the decency to lift his arm and hug Leti back. I smile with approval.

"Nice to meet you, man. Kit's told us a ton about you too."

Leti pulls away and grins. "Ryan, right?"

Ryan nods and claps Leti on the shoulder, and then Leti is turning to Kale.

"And Kale," Leti says, smiling at my twin before stepping in to give him a hug. He wraps his arms around my brother, and I find myself wanting to squeal again, but for entirely new reasons. They look so good together—both tall, both fit, both cute as hell. Leti's arms wrap around my brother easily, and Kale hesitates for only a moment before hugging him back. "It's good to finally meet you."

Leti kisses Kale on the cheek, and Kale blushes almost as brightly as Mason had. I swallow another giggle, and Leti asks, "Now where's Mom?"

He follows the scent of lasagna to the dining room, and my brothers helplessly trail after him. While everyone is distracted, I bump Kale with my hip.

"Told you he was cute," I whisper, and Kale turns his "shut up" glare on me before pinching my arm and following Leti's testosterone-filled conga line.

In the kitchen, my third-best friend kisses my mom. He kisses my dad. And at the table, he raises the bar.

"This lasagna is delicious, Dina," he tells my mom. "Are you sure you're not Italian?"

My mom chuckles and waves him off. I'm pretty sure it took Leti only two seconds and half a compliment to become her first-favorite person.

"Seriously," he continues as he carves off another bite. He's sitting next to me, at my mom's end of the table, my three oldest brothers on the other side. "I had an ex who was Italian, but he didn't make it even half this good." Leti's eyes swing to Mason, and a mischievous smile touches his lips. "He actually looked kind of like Mason. All big football-player muscles and bad-boy tattoos." He leans in close to my mom and whispers loudly enough for the rest of the table to hear, "But he was kind of a nympho."

My mother's nose turns red, and I choke back my laughter.

"Was he the one with the weird fetish?" I ask even though I have no freaking clue who Leti is talking about and I have no idea if this person did or did not have a fetish. All I know is that Leti is making my family ridiculously uncomfortable, and I'm *totally* down for being his partner in crime.

He nods with his mouth full of lasagna. "Yeah." An exaggerated chill shivers over his body as he continues chewing. "I'll never look at Slinkies the same way again."

This time, I actually do laugh, but only because I can't help it. My entire family looks thoroughly disturbed—all except for Kale, who's heard enough about Leti to guess what's going on. He grins from down the table, enjoying the show and maybe the view.

"I had to break up with him after 'the incident,' " Leti continues, holding everyone's rapt attention. Even my dad can't pull his eyes away.

"Oh God, the incident," I echo.

"What incident?" Bryce makes the mistake of asking, and Leti shakes his head like he can't bear to remember it.

"Let's just say it involved a hot tub, some pop rocks, and a pineapple."

Kale's laughter booms from my left side, and I'm quick to join him, followed by Ryan and even my mom and dad.

Bryce just sits there with his eyebrows turned in and his mouth hanging open, a piece of lasagna dangerously close to dropping off the fork he's holding in the air.

"Dude." Leti laughs. "We're just messing with you."

"Wait…" The lasagna plops onto his plate, but Bryce just stares around the table like we're the ones who are missing something. "So then what was 'the incident'?"

Even Mason can't help but laugh at our brother's expense, and by the time dinner is over, my entire side feels like it's splitting in half and I'm pretty sure everyone is in love with Leti—Kale most of all.

"So, Leti," Mason says after my dad has retired to the den and my mom is busy washing dishes. He leans back in his chair with his hands behind his buzzed head like he owns the place, his muscles threatening to split the shirt he's wearing. "The guys in Kit's band...they good guys?"

Ryan on Mason's right, and Bryce on Mason's left, both hang on the response Leti isn't giving because I'm too busy interrupting him and digging my heel into his shin. In my rush to prepare him for my brothers in the car, I forgot to tell him the most important freaking thing: that they have no idea I'm in the same band we went to high school with. "Give it a rest, Mase. I already told you that Bill and Ty and the guys are great."

Leti's eyebrow lifts at me, and he responds without looking away or putting it down. "Yeah...Bill and Ty and the guys...stellar dudes."

"Any of them hooking up with our sister?" Bryce asks, and even in my discomfort, I bark out a laugh and get cocky.

"Yeah, Bryce, because Leti would tell you even if they were."

"So they *are*," he accuses, and I roll my eyes.

Kale leans over the table to look past me to Leti. His chin is propped on his hand and his black hair is tumbling over his forehead. "Our brother is a little slow."

He barely dodges a half-eaten biscotti when Bryce chucks it at his head. It explodes on the floor behind Kale's chair, and Kale simply smirks and says, "Mom is going to kick your ass."

"Language!" she shouts from the kitchen, and all of us laugh while Ryan gets up to pick up the pieces.

My oldest brother finishes finger-sweeping them up, drops them onto my napkin, and kisses the top of my head. With his hand on my shoulder, he says, "Stop giving them such a hard time. You know they're only asking because they love you."

Mason shoots me a triumphant grin and goes back to being a pain in my ass. "Any guys we need to worry about?" he asks Leti.

The answer is a face that springs into my mind. One with heart-crushing green eyes. Calloused fingertips. Black hair a shade lighter than mine. And a voice that's still the last thing I hear at night, because it plays over and over again in my mind.

"I don't think you ever need to worry about Kit at all," Leti answers.

He's lying. He might not know it, and my brothers might not know it, but I know it, and I love him for doing it.

We sit at the dinner table long past dark, until I convince my brothers to let us go and I convince Leti that we really need to hit the road. Kale walks us out to my Jeep and gives me a long hug good-bye.

"Don't miss any more Sunday dinners. They aren't the same without you."

I smile into his shoulder. "What about when I go on tour?"

There are only six weeks left until we leave, in mid-July. Shawn has been busy making arrangements and working on publicity for the album we're recording next week and releasing two weeks before our first tour date. And I've still been busy wondering where I'll sleep. Before, I wondered if he'd bring girls on the bus after shows. Now, I wonder how I'll react when he does.

Will I cry? For four straight weeks?

"Take me with you," Kale answers before letting me go, and I wish I could. Mike, Adam, and Joel are great, but it'd be nice to have my twin with me. I miss him more than I'd ever let his punk ass know, and I know he can see it by the way he pulls me in to give me a kiss on the cheek before moving on to Leti.

My favorite brother stands across from our dinner guest, with his hands tucked in his back pockets and sincerity in his dark eyes. The boys are eye to eye under the glow of the security lamp hanging beside the basketball hoop in our driveway, Kale in a fitted checkered button-down and Leti in hot pink hoodie the same bright shade as his hot pink Chucks. "Thanks."

"For what?" Leti asks.

Kale gives him a smile that means everything. "For being yourself tonight."

If I didn't know Leti better, I'd swear his cheeks turn almost as pink as his outfit. A smile touches his lips and he never takes his eyes off my brother. "Before we came here tonight, I told your sister her brothers were hot and asked if any of them swung my way. Do you know what she said?"

Kale just waits, and I swallow hard.

"She said she had no idea what I was talking about. Do *you* know what I was talking about?"

Again, Kale says nothing. But because I'm his twin, I can tell the words are right on the tip of his tongue. I can see it in the way his fingers fidget in his pockets.

Leti waits a moment longer, and then he smiles again. "Well, if you *do* ever figure out what I'm talking about, give me a call." He pulls my brother in for a hug, unlike the one he gave him when he got here. This one isn't for show. And it isn't romantic either. He's giving my brother his support, and when Kale frees his hands from his pockets and hugs Leti back, hope blooms in my chest and I walk around the hood of my Jeep to crawl into the driver's seat.

"Love you, Kale," I call after Leti slides in next to me.

"Love you back," Kale says. His eyes flit to Leti before I put the Jeep in reverse, and then they drop to the driveway just before he turns to walk away.

"How'd you know?" I ask as soon as Leti and I are on the road. We're both wrapped in our hoodies, drenched in the chilled night air that blows past us faster than the light of fireflies dancing by the side of the road.

"Maybe I was just hoping," he says, and when he turns to me, his right hand soaring in the wind, he looks the most boyish I've ever seen him look.

"Are you crushing on my brother?" I ask, and he laughs and looks back out of the side of the Jeep.

"Have you *seen* your brothers? I'm crushing on all of them. Even your dad is hot."

My nose scrunches at the thought of Leti and my...no, not even going to go there. "I don't think you're my dad's type."

"I'm everyone's type," he counters, and I can't help smiling.

"Why'd you lie to your brothers about the band you're in?"

And just like that, my smile vanishes. The road gets my undivided attention as we break through the suburbs and head toward the highway to Leti's parents' house.

"Because they wouldn't like it."

"That's a shitty excuse for Kale and an even shittier one for you. What's the real reason?"

I think about it for a long time—for so long that my answer cuts across a silence that's become as impenetrable as the dark.

"Because Shawn was a secret…" I admit, my voice quieting with the second half of my confession. "One I wanted to keep."

"What about now?" Leti replies, and a million images flash into my head—the sunset, the stars in Shawn's eyes, how his voice sounded when it carried on the breeze. Every single one of them ends with the way he won't look at me now—not even to chastise me for being late or sucking at my job.

"Now?" I ask. "Now I know better."

Chapter Ten

NONE OF US—*none of us*—could have predicted the way our album would blow up the first week of its release. Big bands like Cutting the Line and The Lost Keys are extremely vocal about loving our work, and all it takes is a few shares from a few big names. Social media explodes, shows sell out, and we add even more dates to our already booked tour.

Which means more time on the road. More time with Shawn.

"What's with the purple?" he asks as I lug my guitar case and overstuffed backpack toward the bus, one slung over my left shoulder and the other slung over my right. My shades are down, my hair is a freshly dyed mix of midnight purple and black, and my asskickers are laced tight.

"What's with your face?"

I walk past the irked look he gives me and stare up at our new bus. It's gray and silver, a single-level behemoth that's still tall enough to put most tour buses to shame. The guys apparently know someone who owns a whole fleet of RVs, and for this month-long US tour, we needed something that could actually make it under overpasses without getting split in half. Taking back roads on the tight schedule we've booked just wasn't going to cut it, so the guys scored us two sleeper buses—one for the band, and one for our crew.

"What's your problem?" Shawn asks from beside me, and I let out a heavy sigh. The past eight weeks since we nearly hooked up on the bus have been miserable. It's not that I enjoy being a bitch to him...it's just that I can't help it—not after being ignored by him for almost an entire month and having my anger fester the entire time. Now he's talking to me, but now I couldn't care less what he has to say.

If I was a mature, rational, reasonable adult, I'd realize he made a mistake that night just like I did and that I shouldn't hold a grudge. I'd forgive—or at least pretend to forget—and act like a professional. I'd move on.

But as it is, I grew up with not one, not two, not three, but *four* older brothers. I grew up teasing and pranking and learning how to be a giant pain in the ass. "Moving on" isn't part of my repertoire, but "getting even" is.

"Are we seriously going to continue talking about your face?" I ask, and when I glance over at him, the look he's giving me isn't nearly as satisfying as I thought it'd be. I'm not sure which is worse—having him forget me, or having him hate me.

It hurts to know that he's probably already forgotten the way he kissed me, when I can't stop thinking about it.

It makes me want to hate him, which just makes me that much more frustrated that I can't.

With his eyes on me, I sigh. "I didn't get any sleep last night," I offer in the most apologetic tone he's going to get.

It's not a lie. I tossed and turned in anticipation of today. For the next month, I'll spend every single day with him. Every. Single. Day. We'll travel together, perform together, sleep practically on top of each other.

I thought about not showing up this morning.

"Better get used to it," Shawn says, and I can't even look over at him as he talks to me. I'm sure the morning sunlight is hitting his hair just right. He probably has a layer of scruffy stubble because he can never just do me a favor and give himself a clean shave. And he's probably wearing a T-shirt that feels just as soft as it looks.

A few roadies pile off the smaller bus to finish loading equipment into a trailer attached to the back. One takes my guitar from me.

"I think you've got the last bunk," Shawn adds, and then he walks to the door of the bigger bus, stepping one foot up and turning around when I don't follow. "Are you coming or what?"

And of course, he's right. In all of my stalling this morning, I'm the last to show up, which means I get last dibs on bunks, which means I'm on the bottom…right across from Shawn. I stare down at the black comforter like it wants to chew me into pulp, swallow me down, and throw me back up.

Joel startles me out of my misery by hooking an arm roughly around my neck and staring down at the bed with me. He turns a bright smile in my direction—one I hadn't seen before he and Dee made up. It was the night of her birthday party at the end of May—he drew her a picture, she kicked his door down, the rest of us waited to see whose body we'd have to bury, and then we found out they made up. I'll never understand those two, but at least they're both smiling again.

"I hope you brought earplugs," he says, and—*oh, God, no.* Everyone had warned me about his snoring—Dee, Rowan, Adam…*everyone.* And still, I forgot my damn earplugs.

"Shit," I hiss. "Please tell me you have extra."

"Why would I have any?" he says with far too much amusement. "I sleep just fine."

My face falls, and his blue eyes glimmer as he laughs.

"Drink enough whiskey before bed and you won't hear a thing, I swear."

"Really?" I counter. "*That's* your solution?"

"Or you could ask Shawn," he offers with a shrug. "He's usually the guy to go to. But you've been kind of a bitch to him lately, so—" I shoot him a glare, and his arm slips away from my shoulder as he takes a quick step back. "Don't get me wrong, I think it's funny as hell."

"Anyone ever tell you you're annoying when you're happy?"

"Dee," he answers with a big grin. "All the time."

I grunt at him, toss my bag into a storage area near the bunks, and make my way through the rest of the bus. The first section, behind the driver's quarters, is filled with leather benches for sitting. Then there's the bathroom and lots of personal storage. Then five bunks—a stack of three on one side, a stack of two plus extra storage on the other. Then a kitchenette complete with seating, a minifridge, a microwave, an oven, plenty of storage and counter space, and a massive TV that Mike is already hooking gaming systems up to while Rowan unloads groceries. It's like she bought out the local supermarket and thinks it's all going to fit in our cupboards. I consider pointing out that all of the guys are way too lazy to cook and there's no way in hell I'm cooking for them, but I can tell she's keeping herself busy to keep from missing Adam before he's even gone. He's sitting on a bench watching her, fiddling with the wristbands on his wrists and looking like he wants to pull her into his lap and keep her there for the entire tour. Both Rowan and Dee are taking summer classes— Rowan at the local college and Dee at the local fashion school—or I don't doubt they'd be coming along.

"Where's Dee?" I ask.

"She has class." Rowan throws the last box of pancake mix into a cupboard before turning around. She leans back against the counter, her bottom lip red like she's been gnawing on it all morning.

"We said good-bye last night," Joel says from behind me, and when I look over my shoulder at him, he's smirking at the memory. "She made sure I'd miss her."

I scrunch my nose at his oversharing, and Mike chimes in with his hands full of wires, "I give it three days before you start whining like a baby."

"I give it two," I challenge, and Mike chuckles while he programs the TV remote.

"You're on."

"I give it one," Joel confesses, and Adam laughs before finally reaching out and tugging Rowan into his lap. He nuzzles his nose into her hair, and her eyes close as she hugs his arms around her.

It takes another twenty minutes to get Adam to let her go, but when he finally does, Shawn practically sits on top of him to keep him on the bus. The roadies pile onto theirs; our bus driver, Driver, starts our titanic engine; and then we're on the road and there's no turning back.

The first venue is only a few hours north, in Baltimore, and we do an early afternoon soundcheck before breaking for dinner at a local hibachi place and then coming back to mingle with fans standing in line. We take pictures, sign autographs, and get to know all the kids who showed up over an hour before the doors are set to open. Then we head inside and hang out up on the shadowed private balcony to watch everyone file inside.

The first girls to enter practically sprint up to the barrier in front of the stage, securing their places front and center in hopes that they'll catch Adam's eye. They all dream that he'll sing part of a song to them, which he probably will; or that he'll reach out and touch their hands, which he might; or that he'll invite them backstage, which he definitely won't, not with Rowan waiting for him back home.

"Tonight's going to be crazy," Joel notes with his entire body stretched over the balcony rail as he watches the rows in front of the stage thicken from two, to three, to four, to five deep. "Was this one sold out?"

"Not as of this morning," Shawn says, but as the rows continue multiplying, it becomes pretty obvious that more than a few tickets have sold between this morning and now.

"What are we doing after the show?" I ask, my stomach churning with nerves I wish I could control. Venturing into the pit after a show at Mayhem is one thing—most of the fans have seen the guys perform a hundred times and are used to having access to them—but performing out of town is different, and I have a feeling this crowd would eat us alive.

"We'll hang out backstage until shit dies down," Shawn says, calming my upset stomach. "Then we'll head to the bus."

My attention drifts to the pretty girls in the front row again, and I wonder if any of them will be coming back with us. Ever since my drunken night with Shawn, there's been nothing to stand in the way of groupies and him after shows. I've made a habit of ending the night early just so I don't have to see him go home with them.

"There will probably be some fans hanging out near the bus," Mike adds, answering my unspoken question: Shawn won't have to take them back to the bus, because they'll already be there waiting, like hot and fresh delivery. "But it won't be anything too crazy."

AND HE'S RIGHT—it isn't anything too crazy. After the show—a loud, manic, incredible first show of our tour—my tired muscles carry me across the parking lot and I realize that what *is* crazy is how groupies can dress in public without getting arrested. My eyes rove over tits hanging out of tops, asses hanging out of skirts, bellies on full display. A few of the girls have their boyfriends' arms draped around their shoulders, but I'm guessing that isn't going to stop them from slipping the guys their numbers, not if I'm judging by the desperate way they shouted at the band from the crowd tonight, or the panties that kept flying onstage.

I root a hair tie from my pocket and pull the thick of my long purple-and-black hair up into a knot on top of my head, casting a glance at Shawn while I fight with the flyaways. I wonder which hair color he'll opt for tonight. Bottled red? Boxed brunette? Bleached blonde?

My eyes swing back to the group clustered in front of the bus, and I try to concentrate on only the fans—the ones with their tits and asses covered, the kids wearing gear they've purchased from the merchandise booth during other tours, the ones who look like a hot mess because they moshed their asses off inside and didn't immediately run to the restroom afterward to straighten their hair extensions and reapply a metric ton of makeup.

Everyone applauds and whistles as soon as they spot us, with the groupies already pushing out their chests and playing with their hair. Adam uncomfortably hugs one who throws herself at him, and then he has to physically peel her hands from around his neck when she won't let go. Joel sticks to one-armed hugs and his slip-away maneuver, intentionally throwing all of his attention at the fans who aren't half-naked. Mike, the trooper that he is, intentionally intercepts the most desperate of the groupies when they won't let go of Adam or Joel. And Shawn gives a lot of attention to the groupies too, but he looks *much* happier to be doing it.

I smile for pictures and sign things—and try not to glare at the blonde who's busy taking a selfie with her lips on Shawn's stubbled cheek.

"Do you three want to see the inside of the bus?" Driver asks the three bodies in the three smallest skirts after all of the fans have gotten pictures and autographs. He's playing the role of recruiter, which I don't doubt he's done a thousand times before. It's probably in his job description: find hot chicks for Shawn to bang, invite them on bus, drag them off afterward.

Shawn's eyes dart to me at the same time mine dart to him. "Oh, uh, not tonight," he stammers, shaking his head at Driver. "I told you, not this tour."

Not this tour?

Not *this* tour.

It hits me then, *why* he's saying no. It's not because he doesn't want them to come on board. It's because he thinks *I* don't want them to. He thinks he's doing me a favor. Like he'd be hurting my damn feelings. Like I *have* feelings.

I deliberately roll my eyes at him and smile at Groupie One, Groupie Two, and Groupie Three. "Shawn's just a party-pooper. Come on, I'll show you where he sleeps."

ON THE BUS, I walk the slut parade back to the bunks, pointing out Shawn's bed and ignoring the irritated look he gives me as I play the role of tour guide.

"Where does Adam sleep?" the bleachiest bleached blonde asks, casting a flirtatious smile over her shoulder at Adam, who isn't paying her even the least bit of attention. He's sitting on a bench next to Mike, his black-painted fingernails typing texts back and forth with Rowan.

"Adam sleeps with his girlfriend, Rowan," I answer in a no-nonsense tone that shuts the girl right up. They always want the lead singer first, *always*—because they think he's the fastest way to get their name in a song or their face in a gossip column.

"Oh."

"Yeah."

Undeterred, she turns that flirtatious smile on Shawn, just like I knew she would. "But you don't have a girlfriend, right?"

Shawn tears his gaze from her to shoot me a cold stare that I return with an oversweet smile. I continue leading the girls to the kitchen, where he leans against the wall with his arms crossed over his chest. Joel locks himself in the bathroom, probably to call Dee, while I pour the groupies drinks.

I offer Shawn a drink too, but he's a statue. With the way he's looking at me, I'm guessing the only thing he wants is to tape my big mouth shut or kick me off this bus. But I keep egging the girls on, like I have something to prove. Because I feel like I do.

I don't like Shawn. I don't need Shawn. I don't want Shawn.

"Yeah, Shawn, drink with us," Groupie Number Three says, positioning herself in front of him and lifting her lipstick-stained glass to his face. Her red hair is a silken waterfall tumbling over her shoulders, and I have to look away.

I'm driving a knife farther into my own heart—because I need him to know it.

I don't like him. I don't need him. I don't want him.

I don't love him.

I need myself to know it too—to believe it—but when the girl giggles, I can't help it…I listen, I watch, and I hurt.

I watch as Shawn's hand covers hers, as he lowers the glass she's holding, and as he leans in to whisper something in her ear. She giggles again, and he grins before turning those green eyes on me. "Sure, Kit, pour me one."

He turns on a charm I've always wished he'd direct at me, using that voice and those smiles that I've always wished I could claim for myself. He hijacks the tequila bottle from my hands and pours the girls drink after drink after drink while I stand by pretending not to care—even though I can't help noticing that Groupie One's breasts are bigger than mine, that Groupie Two's lips are fuller than mine, that Groupie Three's legs are longer than mine.

I stay until I can't take it anymore—until their hair-flipping makes me want to claw my eyes out and their giggling makes me want to gouge my eardrums out. Shawn is too busy being fawned over to even notice me go, so I sulk my way down the long aisle of the bus, closing curtains behind me until I'm plopping down on a bench next to Mike. Joel is still holed up in the bathroom; Shawn is back in the kitchen with Big Boobs, Perfect Lips, and Long Legs; and Adam…

"Where's Adam?" I ask. Mike hands me a half-finished beer I desperately need, and I gladly accept it. "Thanks."

"He said something about seeing if he could get on the roof, and then he was gone," Mike says.

"What about Driver?"

"Probably went to the other bus to take bets on Adam falling and cracking his head open," Mike says dismissively. I chuckle until he says, "Any reason for your sudden love of groupies?"

"Who doesn't love groupies?"

It doesn't escape me that I'm asking the only guy in the world who doesn't love groupies. Mike isn't in the band for the girls or the fame. He's in it because he loves the drums—and because the guys are his family, and he's theirs.

"Tonight?" he says by way of answer, his eyes big, brown, and sincere. "Shawn."

I grunt and take another sip of his beer, staring longingly toward the first closed curtain separating me from the kitchen, because I could really use a stronger drink but would rather swallow broken glass than go back there. "Shawn was enjoying himself in the kitchen, trust me."

"Shawn didn't want them on here in the first place."

"Shawn thought he was doing me a favor."

"So?"

"I don't need his favors. I'm just one of the guys."

"Hmm," Mike hums.

"What?"

"Nothing."

"What?"

I'm seriously going to punch him if he says "nothing" again, but he doesn't get the chance because Joel emerges from the bathroom looking ragged, like he's been scratching his fingers through his Mohawk until the spikes are jutting in every possible direction.

"What's wrong?" I ask, wondering what the hell happened during his phone call to make him look as lost as he does.

"I miss Dee."

Mike and I both start laughing. "You win," I tell Joel, and his sandy blond eyebrows tug together. "You didn't even last a day."

He groans and collapses next to me, and I hand him what's left of Mike's beer. He sighs and finishes it off. "Where is everyone?"

A giggling from the back of the bus answers the question about Shawn, so the only name I bother saying out loud is Adam's. "Adam is outside trying to crack his head open."

"On the roof," Mike agrees at the same time we all hear heavy footsteps above us. Three pairs of eyes turn to the ceiling as we listen to Adam's footfall walk the length of the bus and then stop. There's cheering from outside, and Joel stands up to leave.

"Let us know if he's dead," I call as he walks toward the door to the bus. His fading laughter is cut off by the door that closes behind him.

With it just being Mike and me again, I'm afraid he's going to pick our conversation back up. It's late, I'm tired, my high from the concert has worn off, and Shawn is doing God knows what with three ridiculously willing girls just two curtains away. The last thing I need to be doing is talking about it.

What I *need* is for Mike to go back there and get me another beer.

Instead, the closest curtain opens, and my head jerks in that direction. Groupie One and Groupie Two emerge, unsteady in their heels as they make their way down the aisle.

"Are you two leaving?" I ask with unrestrained surprise in my voice.

Groupie One presses her bare knees up against Mike's leg. "Unless you want us to stay," she suggests with her eyelashes batting down at him.

He holds up the empty beer bottle that somehow got passed back to him. "Can you toss this in the trash on your way out?"

She rolls her eyes but doesn't stop smiling, and when she and her friend begin leaving the bus without taking the beer bottle, I call after her, "What about your friend?" Three gold diggers came on this bus, but only two are leaving. It's been a long night, but simple math says they're forgetting someone.

Groupie One tosses her blonde hair over her shoulder and stops only long enough to giggle and answer, "We're going to the other bus. Shawn said he was a one-girl kind of guy."

I STAY PARKED on the benches long after the first two girls leave and the last one's giggling behind the curtain dies down. Long after Mike ventures through it with his eyes covered to get to the TV in the back. Long after my eyelids start to droop and my head starts to roll forward.

I stand up, take a deep breath, and move to the heavy curtain separating me from the bunks, imagining what I'm going to see on the other side. Clothes on or off? Shawn on the top or bottom? Ugh, I should just sleep on the fucking bench.

Instead, I grit my teeth and yank the curtain back—to find Shawn lying fully clothed on top of his bedcovers, his long legs crossed at the ankles and a book on his lap. His reading glasses are low on his nose, his pillows are piled behind his head, and he definitely does *not* look like someone who just spent the past hour playing rock god with queen of the groupies.

My confused gaze travels from him to the bunk across from him—*my* bunk—which now holds said queen, also fully clothed. She's passed out under *my* covers, drooling on *my* pillow, and when my gaze slowly swings back to Shawn, he's smirking at me over the top of his book.

"What the hell is she doing in my bed?" I snap.

"You're the one who invited her on here. What was I supposed to do, let her sleep in mine?"

I hear Mike laugh from back in the kitchen, but I ignore it and bark at Shawn. "You sleep with her and then put her nasty ass in my bed?"

The girl under my covers stirs and mumbles something in her sleep. Then she goes back to smearing lipstick all over her drool-coated cheeks.

"Who the hell said anything about sleeping with her?" Shawn asks, closing his book and uncrossing his ankles to sit up.

"Then what the hell have you been doing for the past hour?"

"Cleaning up the mess you made."

"What about her?" I snap, pointing to the body attached to the widening puddle of drool on my pillow.

Shawn has the nerve to smirk at me. "Figured I'd leave some of the mess for you."

He leans back, recrosses his ankles, reopens his book...and I stomp over to him and slam it closed. "No fucking way. Get her out of my bed."

"Do it yourself."

"SHAWN."

"Yes?" he says sweetly, and my fingers itch to strangle him. Instead, I growl so loudly, Mike laughs from the kitchen again.

I turn to the girl and yank my covers off of her. She's curled up with her glittery silver heels still on, and I poke her shoulder with the tip of my finger and then wipe it on my jeans. "Hey."

She groans in her sleep and turns her pink-stained mouth all the way into my pillow.

"Dude," I say, "get up." I poke her again, harder this time.

She starts snoring, and Shawn chokes back a laugh from where he's lying comfortably behind me.

"She drank like half the bottle," he says. "She's not waking up anytime soon."

I turn around and glower at him. "Then get up."

"Why?"

"Because I'm taking your bed."

He casually flips the page of the book he's reading. "Don't think so."

Adam and Joel appear in the doorway, Adam rubbing his elbow like he nearly cracked that instead of his head open when he climbed down from the roof of the bus. "What are you two fighting about?" he asks.

"Her." I point an accusing finger at the skanky lump in my bed, and Joel raises his eyebrow.

"Why is she in your bed?"

"Because Shawn's an asshole!"

Shawn chuckles, doing nothing to erase the confused expressions from Adam's and Joel's faces.

"Where are you going to sleep?" Joel asks me, and I turn on Shawn again.

"Get up."

"Nope."

"Shawn, I'm not playing."

"Then you shouldn't have started this game in the first place."

I'm not sure what possesses me, but I grab his book and he grabs it back, and then I grab his hands and pull. Mike catches me around the waist before I can yank Shawn's arms off, manhandling me into the middle bunk on the other side. "Take mine, for God's sake."

He yanks the blankets off of the passed-out chick on my bed and drags them toward the benches at the front. "Now everyone shut up. I'm going to bed." I move to hop out of the bed and stop him, but he yells at me without stopping or turning around. "Go the hell to sleep, Kit!"

I freeze with one leg hanging off the mattress and watch him close the curtain behind him, flinching backward when Joel nearly knees me in the face to climb into the bunk above me. Adam crawls into a top bunk too, and I glare at the smirk still planted on Shawn's stupid face as I settle back into my cubby.

"You realize this means war."

"Your face means war," Shawn counters, stealing my insult from this morning.

"Oooh," Joel and Adam mock in unison.

"Them's fightin' words," Adam adds in a deep southern twang.

Shawn holds his middle finger out high enough for them to see, and both of the idiots up top start laughing.

"What part about SHUT UP did you fuckers not understand?" Mike shouts from the front of the bus, making the other three giggle so immaturely that I almost laugh too.

Almost. Instead, too bone-tired and too irritated to climb back out of bed, I crawl under the covers and slip out of my jeans, stuffing them into the corner of my bunk and rolling away from Shawn. If he wants war, I'll give him war. Tomorrow morning, I'm going to replace the sugar for his coffee with salt, or burn every pair of boxers he owns, or…

I fall asleep thinking of a thousand forms of payback, and later, I wake up to the demons of hell trying to escape from Joel's mouth. Or at least that's what it sounds like. It sounds like his soul is being dragged into the ninth circle of hell and his body is barely clinging to life. From Mike's middle bunk, I roll over and glance down at Shawn. He's still awake, still reading, and in the dark, I doubt he can tell I'm awake. I keep it that way as I reach for my jeans and root a pair of stolen earplugs from the pocket.

In complete silence, I fall asleep quickly, but I haven't slept nearly long enough when someone nudges me into the wall. It's still dark outside, and uncompromising fingers are pushing and prodding and *begging* to be broken.

I'm scowling before I even turn around, my eyes dry from not taking off my eye makeup before bed.

"Where are my earplugs?" Shawn growls in a voice that barely makes it to my eardrums.

I pull one of his earplugs out of my ear just to get him riled, keeping the confused and irritated expression on my face even though it's taking everything I have to not smile or start laughing. I stole his earplugs from his bag this afternoon, long before groupies or tequila or snoring, and now I'm only glad he did something to deserve it. "What the hell are you talking about?"

"Where did you get those?" He pulls my fingers closer to his face and then glares at me.

"What is your problem?"

"Did you steal my earplugs?"

"Why would I steal your earplugs when I have my own?" I yank my fingers from his grasp and stick his earplug back in my ear, shaking my head pityingly. "Are you getting paranoid already? Because I haven't even *started* messing with you, Shawn. If you're losing your mind already, that's really not a good sign."

I roll away from him before he can glare at me some more, hiding my troublemaker smile in Mike's pillow and making a mental note to switch my dirty sheets with Shawn's clean ones as soon as I get a chance.

Chapter Eleven

WAKING ON A moving bus isn't the same as waking in a moving car. You're in a bed, complete with pillows and warm blankets—and you're moving. When you roll over and look into the aisle, you can't figure out exactly where you are. When you attempt to crawl out of bed without being careful, you smack your head on the bunk above you.

"Motherfucker," I hiss, rubbing my forehead while dangling both legs over the edge. I slide off Mike's mattress, underestimate how far my sleepy legs have to drop, and narrowly avoid plowing teeth-first into the bunks on the other side of the aisle.

"Go awaaay," Adam whines from the top bunk, blindly swinging his arm out and nearly smacking me in the head. His face is buried under a pillow, and his covers are hanging mostly off his bunk. I bat his hand away with one arm and rub my sleep-filled eyes with the other.

Joel's face peeks through the curtain separating the bunks from the kitchen, and he smiles before dipping back inside. "She's up!"

I cast a quick glance at the bunk below the one I slept in, relieved when there's no sign of the drool machine who got her nasty all over it the night before. I scrunch my nose and grab my bag from storage, removing and reapplying my makeup in the bathroom before growing some balls and joining the guys in the kitchen.

I plop down in a bench next to Mike, across from Joel, and avoid eye contact with Shawn as he pours me a coffee I didn't ask for.

"I'm hoping you guys dumped that chick's body somewhere along the interstate," I mutter while staring at the steaming cup in front of me.

Mike shakes his head. "We only did that once. Shawn said it's bad for publicity."

I grunt and take a reluctant sip of my coffee, which tastes so good that I almost want to thank Shawn for making it. He's leaning against the counter, not saying a word, and I'm busy pretending he doesn't exist.

I pretend he doesn't exist the whole way to Philly. I pretend he doesn't exist at soundcheck. I pretend he doesn't exist while I'm washing my hair before the show, in a shower that he just climbed out of. He always smells so fucking good, I'm tempted to replace all of his sexy man-scented body wash with my vanilla-jasmine exfoliating wash—and then I do.

After drying my hair and reapplying my makeup, I emerge from the bathroom to find that I'm alone. And seeing my opportunity, I make quick work of switching my nasty bedsheets with Shawn's. I even make sure the lines are crisp when I make the bed back up, just like Driver had done while the rest of us were at soundcheck. The guy is spacey as hell, but he can make a bed like no one's business. He fixed everyone's up but Adam's, who apparently prefers that his covers be just as messy as the rest of him.

I'm sitting at the booth in the kitchen, munching on the peanut butter cookies that Joel tried to hide for himself in the back of the cabinet, when the guys pile back onto the bus and commandeer my snack.

"Where are we going for dinner?" I ask as I get up to follow them back through the bus. My stomach growls, and Shawn stops in his tracks to turn around and face me.

"They're going to a burger joint. But you," he says as he starts stripping the sheets off his bed, "are coming with me to the Laundromat." When my face twists with confusion, he glances over his shoulder and tosses a pillowcase at me. "Did you really think I wouldn't notice? Every inch is covered with glitter."

"And drool," I add with a chuckle that he mocks.

"Ha, ha, ha. Yeah, and a million other things I don't want to sleep in."

He finishes stripping the bed, grabs a bag from the closet, and ushers me off the bus. And outside, I begrudgingly fall in step behind him, dangling the pillowcase from my fingertips like it's covered in something I could catch—which I don't doubt it is. "Shouldn't you be used to it by now?"

The frays of my cutoff shorts tickle my thighs along with a strong summer breeze. After all the trouble that wearing that safety-pinned dress Dee made me for our first performance at Mayhem caused, I've decided it's easier—and safer—to just be myself, mismatched wardrobe and all. My oversized My Chemical Romance tank is tucked into the front of my shorts, my hair is twisted up into a clip, and my boots are eating the sidewalk one crack at a time.

"Used to what?" Shawn asks. His shirt is just as time-worn and dark as mine, but he lets it hang loose over the aged threads of his worn vintage jeans. His long arms are full of black bedsheets, his green eyes full of question as he waits for my answer.

"Sleeping in groupie-whore filth," I reply bluntly while discarding the pillowcase on top of the pile he's carrying. He doesn't even try to fight me, the teasing mood between us shifting somewhere in a fleeting second I feel like I missed.

Shawn's eyes are back on the littered Philly sidewalk when he says, "Would it make you hate me more or less if I told you I didn't sleep with them?" I have no answer to give him, but he doesn't wait for it anyway. "I'm not going to lie, Kit…Yeah, I've fucked groupies before. A lot. Too many to count. But it's not like we cuddle after." He looks over at me again, his gaze unreadable in a way that makes me wish I still had something to carry. "So are you going to hate me more or less, Kit? Because I don't know what to say to you to get you to stop looking at me the way you do."

I don't know how I look at him now, but I know it's not how I looked at him a few weeks ago.

And I guess he knows it too.

"I didn't invite those groupies on the bus," he adds.

"Why didn't you?"

Shawn stops walking to question me with a piercing gaze.

"Why didn't you want them to come on?" I repeat.

"Because I didn't want you to look at me like you're looking at me now."

"How am I looking at you?"

Shawn's thick eyelashes fan down over his eyes, and then he opens them back up to look at me, everything about him calling to that thing in my chest that used to beat for him, that thing that still beats fast even now. "Like there was never a time when it was just you and me hanging out up on your roof," he says. "Like I never made you laugh or smile or…" He sighs, and those fissures in my heart start to pull again. The regret in his eyes breaks them open. "Just because we kissed in Mayhem doesn't mean things have to be like this."

It mattered to me more than he knew, more than he can *ever* know, and that's exactly why that kiss meant things *did* have to be like this. I couldn't keep falling and letting myself do it.

I can't.

My defense mechanisms go on high alert, the alarms in my head drowning out the sound of that pounding behind my ribs. "You're getting awfully sentimental, Shawn."

We're walking shoulder to shoulder in the heart of the city. There are cars passing and sirens in the distance and people shouting back and forth—but I hear none of those things, not one, when Shawn says, "Maybe I miss being on the roof with you."

My eyes flit in his direction—hoping to catch a smirk or a glint in his eye or something else that would tell me he's just teasing. But when he won't even turn his head to look at me, I know he's telling the truth.

"That was corny," I reply.

"I meant it."

In a signature Kale move, I twist my bottom lip between my teeth. What exactly does he want from me? He misses being on the roof with me? What does that even *mean*?

When Shawn opens the door to a place called Laundrorama, I refuse to go in. "How am I supposed to look at you, Shawn?"

This time, when our eyes lock, he doesn't look away. "Like you did before," he says. "Like we're friends."

I don't tell him that never—*never*—have I looked at him like we're just friends. Instead, I silently walk through the door he's holding open for me, and with my back to him, I quietly say, "Okay."

"Okay?"

"I'll try to get my eyes to…I don't know, what are they supposed to do?" I turn around with my eyes intentionally as crazy and wide as I can get them, and when Shawn laughs, I ignore the way that sound calls to my heart again, and I force a smile back at him.

I pick up a pillowcase that drops to the floor as he sets the sheets at the side of a machine and opens the lid. He unties the bag he brought with him and pulls out two mysterious, unlabeled plastic containers—one with white powder, one with blue.

"Detergent and fabric softener?" I ask while I gaze around the Laundromat. Washers are lined in the middle, with dryers stacked along the walls. The place is mostly empty, save for a woman smoking right next to a No Smoking sign and a leering old man in a robe and pair of jeans.

I shrink closer to Shawn, my shoulder pressed against his when he says, "Mmhm." He measures the powders out in marked cups and empties them into the machine.

"What kind?"

"Some shit I can't pronounce. Something Italian."

"Is that how you get your clothes so soft?" I ask, and he turns a tender smile on me that makes my cheeks redder than the No Smoking sign being ignored at the corner of the room.

"Yeah. It also makes them smell really good."

Uh, yeah, I've freaking noticed. But that does nothing to stop me from wanting to turn into him and bury my nose in the neck of his tee.

"Want to smell?" he says, shifting toward me like he's offering to let me do just that. His collarbone looks good enough to eat, just begging to be nibbled on under the thin black fabric of his T-shirt.

I pick up the powder and sniff that instead, coughing when some gets huffed up my nose. "Smells like dead brain cells."

Shawn barks out a laugh and takes the container from me, closing both up before pushing the sheets in the washer and closing the lid. He roots some change from his pocket and feeds the machine, and then we take two seats in front of the big bay window of the Laundro-freakin'-rama.

The bells on the door jingle as we both watch a very pregnant woman wearing too-tight boxer shorts and a two-sizes-too-small top enter the Laundromat. She has two little kids screaming and chasing each other around her flip-flop-clad feet, and I can already tell the next hour or so is going to be a blast. Shawn twitches like he wants to offer to help her with the laundry basket she's balancing on her hip, but with the way her suddenly heated gaze homes in on him like he could be her next baby daddy, he settles back in his plastic chair. The kids start running through the aisles making enough noise to drown out the dryers, and Shawn stretches his arm behind my seat.

"Kill me now," I say, and his head turns in my direction, a smile on his lips.

"So what did you do when you left the kitchen last night?"

I'm distracted by the glances the woman keeps stealing at Shawn while she fills one of the washers, so I barely hold back a snicker when one of her kids face-plants on a dryer and starts screaming his head off so loudly that she can't continue ignoring him.

"You're evil," Shawn says with a grin when I'm too busy laughing to answer his question.

"You do realize she wants you to mount her on a washing machine, right?"

He chuckles and says, "So are you going to answer me or not?"

"About what?"

"What'd you do after you abandoned me in groupie hell last night?"

I lift an eyebrow when he acts like he didn't enjoy himself. "You mean before or after you slept with the glitter-chick?"

"I told you I didn't sleep—"

"Fucked her, I mean."

After I correct myself a little too loudly, I glance at the baby mama, who should definitely be offended on behalf of her small children, but she's too busy ogling Shawn to give a damn about what I just said. I'm thankful when she ushers her little monsters toward the door. She casts Shawn one last sultry look before she goes, but his gaze is locked on me and nothing else.

"I didn't sleep with her or fuck her," he says when my eyes reconnect with his.

I narrow my gaze on him. "You didn't?"

He shakes his head. "I told her I did so she wouldn't be pissed when I practically threw her off the bus this morning, but no, I didn't."

"Why?"

"I don't fuck everything that walks, Kit."

Of all the lines that could make a girl feel special, I wouldn't have expected *that* to be one of them. But my heart flutters anyway. "She was pretty," I protest, for God only knows what reason.

"So?"

"So." I struggle to find some way, any way, to claw my way out of this hole of a conversation I've dug myself into. "I hung out with Mike at the front of the bus," I say, finally answering his question about where I went after I fled from the kitchen.

"Was Adam the one making all that noise on the roof of the bus?"

I chuckle at the memory. "Yeah, I think Joel joined him up there."

Shawn's grin puts the world's smallest, most adorable dimple in his cheek. "I would've guessed you'd be up there too."

"I was too tired to be scaling buses."

"Just wait until we're a few weeks in. You won't even be able to tell the difference between dreaming and being awake."

I rest the back of my head against the top of my plastic chair, tired just thinking about it. "Sorry about stealing your earplugs."

Shawn slouches low in his seat to stay level with me, turning his head with that heart-melting smile still on his face. "They were yours anyway."

"What are you talking about?"

"I'm used to Joel's snoring. I brought them because I figured you might need them."

I shrink to two inches tall, my voice teeny-tiny when I say, "And then I stole them…" When he chuckles softly, I close my eyes and curse. "Shit."

"Apology accepted."

With my eyes still closed, I can't help laughing. "I'm also sorry for dumping your body wash down the drain and replacing it with mine." I peek an eye open, and he lifts an eyebrow.

"But you didn't..." Realization dawns on his face, and his eyes go flat. "You did."

"I did."

"Why?"

Because you smell too fucking good. Because I can smell you from here. Because it makes me want to crawl on your lap and see if you taste as good as I bet you do. I shrug. "The good news is you'll smell like vanilla and jasmine."

"Every guy's dream."

"See?" I say with a big smile. I sit up straight and criss-cross my legs on the chair before spinning to face him. "I'm being a great friend already."

Shawn grabs the bottoms of my calves and flips them up until I'm tumbling backward and squealing while trying to catch myself. When I finally regain my balance and sit back up to whack him in the arm, all he does is grin. I cross my arms over my chest and sit back in my chair with my boots firmly on the floor, trying not to smile.

I missed this. Just hanging out with him. Talking to him because it's the easiest thing in the world to do, despite the way my heart races and the way my cheeks flush. I missed his laugh and his smile and his eyes.

I missed *him*.

"I missed this," Shawn says, and that hidden smile finally breaks free across my face.

"Me too."

We talk, we joke, we toss the sheets into the dryer and watch the baby mama come and go again. We're sitting on a bench at a sub shop across the street, trying Philly's famed Philly cheesesteaks, when Shawn asks me what Mike and I talked about while we were alone at the front of the bus.

There's no way I'm telling him we talked about *him*, so I sidestep, sidestep, sidestep. And as soon as I get the chance, I change the subject by asking Shawn something I've been wondering about since last night. "Has Mike ever hooked up with a groupie?"

Shawn shakes his head as he chews. How he makes even *chewing* look cute, I have no idea, but he's so adorable with his clean bites and good manners, I want to eat him up, even though it would probably make me sick. "He's hooked up with a fan or two, but never a groupie. Not girls like we had on the bus last night."

"Why?"

He takes another bite as he thinks about it. "Do you remember the girlfriend he had in high school?"

"Wasn't her name Danica or something?" I ask. I remember her having flawless honey-brown hair, and bright white teeth inside an expensive designer smile. She was on the cheerleading squad, and knowing Mike like I know him now, I have no idea what he ever saw in her.

"He dated her for like three years," Shawn confirms. "He put her on a pedestal, but she dumped him right before we moved out here."

"Because of the long distance?" I bunch up my trash and discard it in the basket my cheesesteak was in.

Shawn shakes his head once. "Because she was a gold digger who tried to force him to quit the band. She said he wouldn't amount to anything."

"What a bitch," I scoff, and Shawn nods emphatically before taking the last bite of his sub. He gathers up our trash, and I follow him to the trashcans.

"Yeah. She broke his heart."

"Do you think he wants a girlfriend now?"

"Maybe. But he's...careful, you know? He deserves someone special."

"Someone who deserves him," I agree, and as we cross the street, Shawn flashes me an approving smile that ripens the pale apples of my cheeks.

When he opens the door of the Laundromat, I enter with the inside of my lip pinned between my teeth. I'm nibbling at the skin when I finally ask what I'm wondering. "What about you?"

I glance at him out of the corner of my eye as I open the dryer and start gathering the clean sheets into my arms. He used more fabric softener in the dryer, and the sheets are all as soft as the clothes he wears. I resist the urge to bury my face in them and breathe deep.

"What about me?" he asks.

"Ever want a girlfriend?" I walk ahead of him so he can't see how red my cheeks are glowing. I don't know why I'm even asking. I don't care. Can't care. Shouldn't care.

"She'd have to be one hell of a girl," he says as he catches up with me. The bells jingle as we leave the Laundromat behind, and I know I should close my mouth. I should stop asking questions. I should let the conversation drop.

"Like what kind?"

My question hangs suspended in the air between us, the inside of my bottom lip getting nibbled sore as what seems like an eternity passes in just a few hard thumps of my heart. My palms start to sweat and I think of a million jokes I could tell to make him forget the stupid, impulsive, stupid, stupid question I just blurted. But then he answers me.

"I don't know..." he says, his magnetic gaze pulling at me even though I resist the urge to meet it. "Maybe a girl like you."

I DON'T SAY anything on block one, minute five, or step 152. My thoughts are traveling faster and further than my feet are moving, and each step of the way, Shawn is right beside me.

Maybe a girl like you.

A girl like me? Not *me*, but a girl *like* me... Why a girl *like* me? What the hell does that MEAN? Why is he always so goddamn confusing?

My mouth has opened and closed at least five times when my phone rings, tearing me from the eternal echo of Shawn's words.

My twin's face flashes onto the screen that I free from my back pocket, under letters that spell "Butthead." He's wearing a cowboy hat that I plopped on his head while we were Christmas shopping last year, and he has an unamused expression on his face that makes me grin every time he calls.

Well, almost every time. This time, I simply cast an uncomfortable glance at Shawn before handing off the sheets and telling him I really have to answer the call. My phone has been on silent all day, but I have it set so that if anyone calls twice within three minutes in case of an emergency, the call comes through.

"What's wrong?"

"Aside from the fact that I've texted you like a million times since yesterday and you clearly aren't dead?" Kale asks.

I feel bad for worrying him, but not bad enough to say sorry. "Should I apologize for not being dead?"

Shawn turns his head with his eyebrow lifted, and Kale answers gruffly. "For starters."

"I'm sorry the bus didn't crash and burn," I offer, nearly snickering when I picture the way his brows probably just slammed down with frustration.

"Good," he says. "You should be. Now tell me all the reasons you couldn't pick up a phone."

I finger-comb the loose strands of hair away from my face to prevent myself from glancing over at the reason Kale is asking for—a reason with messy hair, gorgeous eyes, and a smile that makes a girl forget to check in with her family. "The show was awesome, but the crowd was crazy, so we had to hang out inside for a while. And then we went out to the bus, and there was a crowd there too." I add the last part with a lightning-quick tongue—"And some of them came on the bus and—"

"Wait, what?" Kale interjects. "They didn't—they brought girls on the bus? Did Shawn—"

"Have you called Leti yet?" I interrupt, discreetly turning the volume on my phone as low as possible so Shawn won't be able to hear anything Kale is saying.

"Nuh-uh," my meddling twin counters, refusing to let me change the subject. "No way. What happened?"

"I can't really talk right now, Kale." I glance at Shawn again, wishing there'd be anything else on this busy street to steal his attention: a near car accident, a hot chick, a crazy homeless person throwing hamsters at people, *anything*.

"Why?" A moment of silence. "Is he with you right now? Can you not talk because he's with you?"

"Something like that," I answer.

"Fine, then just say yes or no."

I hold the phone with one hand and rub a spot between my eyes with the other. "Can we not?"

"Did he bring groupies on the bus?"

"No."

"But groupies did come on the bus?"

"Yeah."

"And he fucked one of them?"

I growl into the phone, and Shawn gives me a look again. I ignore him and answer Kale. "No. Can I go now?"

"But you're mad at him?"

Is everything okay? Shawn mouths, and I wave him off to answer my brother. "Not anymore. And Kale?"

"Yeah?"

"I love you. I'll call you tonight."

I hang up before he can argue, letting out a deep sigh as Shawn and I round a corner to the lot the buses are in.

"What was that about?" he asks as my phone rings again.

I silence it all the way and shrug. "Wrong number."

Chapter Twelve

THAT NIGHT, AFTER sweating out another five pounds under the blazing-hot lights of a packed-to-the-rafters venue, Leti's call is the one that comes through my silenced phone.

"We're here."

"Huh?" I towel off my forehead and tip my head upside down, drying off my neck as the blood floods my skull. The crowd is still screaming, high off our set, and Leti is making zero freaking sense.

"You looked amazing. Are those leather pants?" I furrow my black eyebrows at my shiny black leggings. "And your boobs looked fantastic," Leti adds. "I almost went straight for a minute, but your brother was standing right beside me, so…I was torn, Kitty-Bitty."

I flip my head back up and look around the green-room the band and I are in. The guys are chatting with the sound crew as bottles get passed around and drinks get poured. "You're *here*?"

"Yep. Standing in front of some 'roided-up security guy who's giving me a dirty look right now." His voice gets a little quieter, like he pulled the phone away from his mouth, when he says, "What's your problem, man?"

"And Kale's with you?"

His volume goes up again. "Currently looking very worried that I'm going to get my ass kicked by said 'roided-up security," Leti answers. "Are you going to come to my rescue, or are you going to let me get pummeled? I mean, your brother here would make a super-cute nurse, but—"

"I'm coming," I interrupt. I hang up before Leti can put any more scarring visuals in my head, and then I tell the guys I have to go find my brother.

Shawn's black kicks are in step with my even blacker combat boots as I walk through the halls of backstage, ranting about my brother being the evil twin and me having no idea why he and Leti showed up here tonight. I didn't ask Shawn to come with me to find them...but I didn't try to stop him, either.

When I finally do spot them, they're standing with a security guard who's impossible to miss. " 'Roided up" was an understatement, but I march right up to him. "It's okay. They're with me."

The security guard huffs and gives Leti a final dirty look before turning and walking away, a big body on big legs.

Leti grins like a loon as he watches him leave. "I think he wanted me."

My twin is standing next to Leti in a fitted red tee, his black hair looking perfectly washed and styled, I'm guessing for Leti's benefit. "What are you doing here?" I ask in a not-exactly-happy-to-see-him voice.

"Waiting for you to call me back," he replies coolly, his gaze hardening when it drifts to Shawn. It's a look I've seen before—from every single one of my brothers at some point or another. It growls, *Stay away from my sister.* And Kale's holds a touch of, *I know you brought groupies on the bus, you asshole.*

"Oh, don't even act like you're mad anymore," Leti teases Kale. He smiles at me and continues. "He *loved* the show. He just kept going on like, 'That's my sister! That's my sister!' "

Kale nudges Leti with his elbow, Leti smiles fondly at him, and I'd feel giddy as hell about them being so close with each other if it wasn't for the thick tension between Kale and Shawn. Kale's black gaze is razor-sharp, but Shawn doesn't shy away from its edge. The two of them are in a stare-down, both standing tall and still. I look up at Kale, at Shawn, at Kale.

"This is Shawn," I say.

Kale tucks his hands in his back pockets instead of reaching out to shake Shawn's hand. "I know who he is."

Leti's eyebrows fly up almost as high as mine, and I stammer, "Uh…"

"It's nice to meet you," Shawn says, extending his hand with a smile on his face that isn't at all like the smiles he gives me. It's the smile he gives fans who overstep boundaries—nice, believable, but counterfeit.

Kale lets his eyes fall down to Shawn's hand, looking like he'd rather latch on to it with his teeth instead of touching it with his skin. I'm wondering if I'm going to have to pry his hands from his back pockets and puppeteer him into playing nice with Shawn myself, but then he reluctantly peels five fingers out of his dark denim and reaches forward. "Kale."

During the walk back to the greenroom, Leti graciously fills the awkward silence, and Shawn and I learn a few things. One, Kale called Leti to get him to call me, but Leti insisted they just come up here. Two, Leti set a condition for the impromptu road trip, and that condition was that they go to a hot new club before they leave. Three, the guys and I *have* to come along.

"THIS IS A gay bar!" Adam squeals between his giggles as we all step up to the flashing rainbow entrance of Out, the "hot new bar" Leti somehow got Kale to agree to go to—along with the rest of us. Mike, Shawn, and Joel are all standing shoulder to shoulder on the sidewalk, staring at the psychedelic door like they might get lost forever inside. It's like nothing I've ever seen—all plasma-like technology and Technicolor swirls that flash and dance while tossing their glow into the dark. Adam, always up for anything and everything, spins around, his eyes bright with excitement. "It's a freaking gay bar!"

"Why are you so excited?" I ask, unable to stop myself from chuckling at him. Heavy bass is pulsing inside the club, making the summer-warmed hair on the back of my neck stand up. The lights, the music, the long line of people stretched around the block—they make midnight seem like a magic hour, a time for dancing and laughing, not for warm beds and sweet dreams.

"I've never been to one!" Adam answers.

"Are we even allowed to go in there?" Mike finishes scanning the long line and turns a skeptical eye on Leti.

"Of course you're allowed," Leti answers from beside me. He shoots Mike a grin and adds, "My people don't discriminate."

Joel, with his Mohawk dyed a kaleidoscope of rainbow colors in the reflection of Out's flashing door, gives us an uneasy glance over his shoulder. "Won't they think we're gay?"

Leti chuckles and shakes his head, the bright lights illuminating his already-bright smile. "Trust me, they'll be able to tell you're straight in three-point-four seconds."

"Doesn't mean you're not going to get hit on though," I tease, and Leti winks at me before walking ahead of everyone toward the door. He bypasses the impossibly long line, full of mostly guys and a few pockets of girls, to flash his trademark grin at the bouncer, and after a minute of smooth talking, he waves us all over and we cut the line to get inside.

"They didn't even check our IDs," I note as we enter a pitch-black corridor that's lit only by the rainfall of spots still peppering my vision.

"You're rock stars," I hear Leti's voice explain as we make our way forward, toward a thin line of light on the floor. My arms spread as I attempt to feel my surroundings, but then a heavy arm curls around my shoulders, and a familiar scent envelops me in the dark. I cling to Shawn's T-shirt and let him guide me toward the light, the music at the end of the dark tunnel growing louder and louder with every cautious step.

The click of a door, and then I'm blinded by blues, reds, yellows, greens. Lasers and glow sticks flood the room, and there is nothing I can see but dancers—dancers on the floor, dancers in cages suspended from the ceiling, women dancing with women, women dancing with men, and everywhere, men dancing with men. Everyone is dressed in something spectacular—or barely dressed at all—and in my faux-leather leggings and Dee-designed tank top, I almost fit in.

"How are we supposed to get anywhere?" I shout over the music, and Leti's grin turns devilish a second before he grabs my brother's hand and yanks him into the crowd. They disappear into the glittering sea of bodies, and I'm left standing with four straight guys who are busy looking at me like I have all the answers they don't.

Shawn's arm dropped from my shoulder sometime before the door opened, which is why I'm free for Mike to pull to his side when he says, "I call Kit!"

We get sucked into the crowd, leaving Adam, Shawn, and Joel standing there staring at each other with lost expressions on their faces.

Mike and I don't dance so much as maneuver. We weave with each other in and out of free spaces until I finally spot an open set of stairs leading down to a long, glitter-topped silver bar at the other side of the room. "There!" I say, pointing at the bar and getting my hand snatched out of the air. A guy with wide pupils spins me around faster than the disco balls suspended from the ceiling, making me so dizzy that I'm not sure which is still spinning—me, the room, or the floor beneath my feet. When I'm thoroughly light-headed, he hands me back off to Mike, who steadies my still-spinning body, helps me to the bar, and deposits me in a vacant standing-room-only spot in front of the bartender.

"That was scary," he says while chuckling behind me, and I turn around and laugh along with him.

"I wonder how Leti and Kale are doing."

Mike flags the bartender over my shoulder, and I order raspberritas for the both of us before he can object. He's sipping on the sugar rim and making a face at me, when I see a group of hot girls pass behind him to find a free spot at the bar.

"I bet you could find a nice girlfriend here," I shout over the music, and Mike's warm brown eyes follow mine to the group clustered a few spots away. They're all wearing tight dresses, lots of makeup, and pounds of sparkling glitter. They look the way most girls look when they're trying to be pretty for themselves instead of for someone else—shiny and colorful and happy.

"Don't girls come here so that they don't get asked out?" Mike counters.

"Exactly! Which is why their defenses are down!" When he laughs like I'm joking, I pout. "Seriously Mike, you should ask one out."

"Why?"

"You deserve someone."

"So do you," he counters. "But you don't see me pushing you at anyone."

"That's because everyone here is gay!" I protest, but Mike's response comes quick.

"Not everyone."

My eyes narrow with suspicion, and I swing a finger back and forth between us. "You don't mean…"

"God, no," he rushes to say, his hands out like he's going to physically stop me from dropping to one knee and proposing to him or something. "You and me?" He starts laughing again—hard.

I prop a fist on my hip in mock offense. "Are you saying I'm not your type?" When he can't stop laughing, I hold back a smile. "What's your type then?"

"Someone…not-mean," he says, and when I burst out laughing too, it only encourages him. "Someone not-loud, someone not-crazy."

"I get it," I interrupt. "Someone nice and calm and sane."

Mike grins and nods his chin toward the girls I pointed out earlier. "A.K.A., definitely not those girls."

When I turn my head to find them cackling like drunken hyenas and falling over each other, Mike and I laugh even harder. Those girls would be a sure thing, a trio of one-night stands he'd never have to call again, but I should've known Mike better than to think he'd go for glitter and glam and easy. Whoever captures his heart is going to be class and brains and worth waiting for.

By the time Shawn, Adam, and Joel finally track us down, Mike has finished a beer and a half, and I'm double-fisting raspberritas—mine, and what's left of his.

"Are those raspberry margaritas?" Adam immediately asks, stealing one from my hand and taking a big swallow before I can answer.

"You fit right in here," Mike teases him, and Adam flicks him off with a black-painted fingernail while still taking a long drink from my glass.

"What happened to your shirt?" I ask, my eyes traveling past Adam's newly acquired glow necklace, past the Magic 8 Ball tattoo inked on his left pectoral, and down to a unicorn stenciled on his stomach. Mike wasn't exactly wrong about him fitting in.

"Some dude offered to trade him a glow necklace for it," Shawn explains, and Adam chuckles into the raspberrita at Shawn's disapproving tone. He coughs and wipes his mouth with the back of his hand, and I stiffen when Shawn squeezes into the space half beside, half behind me to order a drink of his own. His front is pressed tight against my back, and his fingers find my side as he places his order.

"Where are Leti and your brother?" Joel asks me, oblivious to the way Shawn's hand on my side is making it impossible for me to talk.

"Still haven't come back yet," Mike answers for me, still shaking his head at Adam's bare chest. Adam wraps an arm around his shoulder and flashes him a white smile.

"Is he gay?" Joel asks me point-blank, tearing my attention from Adam and Mike. "Your brother?" His voice holds no disapproval, no judgment, but I avoid the question anyway.

"Is Adam?" I reach out and poke Adam's unicorn, and he barks out a laugh, snapping Mike's head forward when his arms jerk down to protect himself.

The boys get into a scuffle that forces me even tighter against Shawn, and it's impossible to miss the way his body reacts to mine. We both feel him between us, but neither of us moves an inch, and neither of us says a word. Instead, I nibble at the inside of my lip when his fingers close even tighter around my waist.

Shawn and I stand like that, listening to the guys act like idiots under the downpour of techno bass—and ignoring one big, pressing, unspoken thing between us— until Leti and my brother emerge from the crowd, looking like they just danced twenty pounds off. My brother's cheeks are red—from exertion or from crushing on Leti too hard, it's impossible to tell. I try to shift away from Shawn before they can reach our group, but he catches the curve of my waist and refuses to let me budge. And all I can do is stand there, my heart doing flips and tumbles and cartwheels in my chest.

Does he know what he's doing? He has to know what he's doing. Why is he doing it? And why does he feel so. fucking. good? I purposely shift against him, and his fingers draw me even closer.

"Dude." Leti laughs as he practically skips up to our group. Kale is right beside him, but they don't so much as brush elbows. Leti may have gotten my brother out of the house, but he's still firmly in the closet. "You know what those mean, right?" He points at Adam's glow necklace, and when Adam simply lifts it up and raises an eyebrow, Leti starts laughing again. "They mean you're DTF."

"DTF?" Mike says.

"Have you never watched *Jersey Shore*?" Leti asks like it's a crime.

"It means you're down to fuck," Kale answers, and Adam looks around to find that no fewer than ten guys are eyeing him up.

My bandmates get into a hilarious conversation about why Adam won't take it off—with him insisting that he's used to the attention and that glow necklaces are "cool as hell," and Joel teasing that he's been away from Rowan too long—while Shawn and I stay quiet on the fringes of the group, his front glued to my back and his hand stuck to my hip. I pretend that the way he's touching me is normal, that this is what friends do, that I'm not tuned in to every breath he takes or every line of his fingerprints indenting themselves in my skin.

When I feel eyes on me, my gaze drifts to Leti to find him grinning my way. My brother, standing beside him, is busy glaring at Shawn's hand.

"Come dance with us," Leti coaxes, tugging my reluctant body away from Shawn's.

Shawn's hand slowly slides from my waist, and Kale finally meets my eyes.

"No way," my twin says. "I'm not dancing with my sister."

But Leti is on a mission, and he starts walking backward with my hands ensnared in his. "Suit yourself."

He lures me up the stairs and onto the floor, and we drift deep, deep into the crowd. In the middle of it, Leti rests his big hands on my shoulders, his golden-honey eyes flashing with glee as multicolored lasers cut across our skin. He presses his mouth into my purple-and-black hair and shouts over the throbbing music, "He is *so* into you!"

When he pulls away, I simply shake my head. Shawn's body might be into me, but the rest of him? That would be into a girl *like* me, if he was into anyone at all. I'm not even on his radar. *I'm* just one of the guys, which is a good thing. A really good thing. Definitely good.

I pull Leti down and rise to my tiptoes. "He said he could date a girl like me. *Like* me."

"That's a good thing!" he shouts back.

I shake my head against his cheek. "I'm not even an option."

Leti is frowning when I pull away. He lowers his arms to wrap them around my waist, pulling me close and pressing his lips into my hair again. "You didn't see the way he kept looking at you while you guys performed onstage tonight."

I rest my forehead against Leti's shoulder, because I know no amount of trying to convince him is going to make him believe that Shawn and I were over before we even began. I feel him sigh against me, and then the room is spinning, laser lights blurring as he twirls me in circles and makes me squeal and laugh. We dance until one song ends and another begins, until I finally feel far enough away from Shawn to think of something—anything—else.

"You and Kale…" I question with Leti's arms around me, and he grins down at me, the honeycomb in his eyes sparkling.

"He's a really good kisser."

My jaw drops in a gasp, and Leti's cheeks burn red as he chuckles and I enter freak-out territory. "YOU KISSED HIM? HERE? JUST NOW?"

When Leti shakes his head, that grin still plastered all over his face, I furrow my brows in confusion until he explains.

"He kissed me!"

My eyes open saucer-wide, and he laughs again before spinning me some more. I have a million more questions I want to ask—questions I *need* to ask before I explode—but the music between us blares loud and Leti spins me and twirls me and dances me like a marionette until I'm light-headed and loving it. My arms become weightless, my legs become lighter than air, and I float behind Leti all the way back to the sunken bar. I grin at my brother as I glide down the stairs, delighting in the way he blushes when he tunes in to our twin frequency and realizes I *know* what he did. I *know* he kissed Leti.

"Where'd everyone go?" Leti asks our group, sidling up to Kale while still keeping an ambiguous distance.

"Out for a smoke break," Shawn answers as he takes in my sweat-tipped hair, my damp top, my pink skin. I'm sure I look like a hot mess, but there's no point in trying to fix it. "Adam kept getting hit on."

"Did he take the necklace off?" I ask, and Shawn makes me laugh when he shakes his head.

He hands me a full raspberrita he must have ordered while I was away, and I can't help the shy smile that dimples my cheek as I lift it to my lips.

"Shawn," Leti asks, "want to dance?"

Shawn coughs out a laugh that does nothing to dim Leti's smile.

"Oh, come on. You haven't danced at all!" Leti complains. "If you're not going to dance with me, you should at least dance with Kit."

I find myself shaking my head as everyone watches—because I remember all too well what happened the last time I danced with Shawn. I made a damn fool of myself and then nearly barfed in his mouth.

"I'm actually getting tired," I say, turning my not-at-all-tired gaze on Shawn. "Think the guys would be cool with heading back to the bus yet?"

"Nooo," Leti whines. "You can't leave."

I flash him a secret smile. "Kale can stay with you! We'll catch a cab back."

Even though Leti pouts about me leaving early and putting the kibosh on his evil plan to hook me up with Shawn, he lets us go. Kale hugs me tight before I do, warning in my ear, "I don't like him, Kit. I came up here because I was worried about you."

"I'm fine," I say back, kissing his cheek. He frowns at me as I back away. "And you have better things to do than worry about me!" I wink at him and yell at Leti to make sure my brother gets home safe, and then I turn around and walk out to the sidewalk with Shawn to join our three missing rock stars. We hail a cab driver, tip him in advance for letting the five of us break the law by cramming into his taxi, and pile inside.

On the way to the club, Kale had driven and we'd all squished in tight, with me on Leti's lap. This time, Adam calls shotgun; Shawn, Joel, and Mike claim the backseat; and I end up on Shawn's lap with my legs tangled with his. The night is dark, with the city lights flashing in and out of the car, and this time, when Shawn's fingers find my hip, there's no music pounding in my ears, no lasers filling the room. It's just us in the dark, my skintight leggings heavy on his lap and his fingers slipping under my loose tank top to caress my goose-bumped skin.

In the dim glow of the cab, while the other guys are talking, I gaze down at him. My arm is curled behind his neck, and those impossibly green eyes are all mine, staring up at me from under black lashes that look soft enough to kiss. The streetlights flash across his face over and over and over again, highlighting the emerald specks in his eyes, the perfect shape of his nose, the shadow on his jaw. Each span of darkness makes me want to kiss him, and each flash of light reminds me that I can't.

When the cab drops us back off at the bus, I stumble out of the backseat first, not waiting for the rest of the guys before I climb on board our gray-and-silver sleeper. I immediately grab my bag from a cabinet and head for the shower, taking it cold. The water rains over my face, washing away makeup and dancing and the heat on my skin. The cold makes Shawn feel like a dream, even though the ghost of his fingertips clings like an invisible print on my sides—one I can feel, one that's impossible to wash away.

I take a deep breath and run my hands over my face, standing under the ice water until both my body and my memories are numb, until the entire night seems like yesterday. When I step out of the bathroom in fresh pajamas, with a fresh-washed face, it's a new day, one I can face. One that doesn't make my heart hurt.

The guys, including Driver, are all gathered in the kitchen, drinking and gaming and watching TV, and I say a quick goodnight to all of them, careful to avoid meeting Shawn's eyes before I close the curtain and slip into my bunk.

My pillow, my blankets…My entire bed smells like him. After I switched his sheets with mine this morning, I didn't think to take both sets to the Laundromat with us, and now I'll be sleeping in his scent. It wraps itself around me when I pull the covers up to my chin and close my eyes. I can almost imagine I'm waiting for him in his bed, that he'll crawl in next to me at any moment and hold me even tighter than he did inside the club.

My thoughts drift to what would happen after the holding…

And after the kissing…

I toss and turn, turn and toss. I'm alone, lying on my back while staring at the wooden beams above me, thinking of that night six years ago and how it feels like a lifetime ago, when a sliver of light cuts onto the aisle floor. When Shawn lets the curtain fall shut behind him, that sliver disappears again, leaving nothing but the dim glow of city light sneaking in through gaps in the curtains and blinds. I keep my eyes glued to the bunk above me as he slips out of his jeans, crawls under his covers, and settles in his bed. But when I feel his eyes on me, I roll onto my side to face him.

Across the aisle, he watches me, his scruffy cheek sunken into his pillow and his green eyes the brightest things in the room. He doesn't look away when I stare back at him, and I couldn't look away if I tried.

"Stop," I say, so quietly that I barely reach him across the aisle.

"Stop what?" The softness in his voice tickles over my skin, lighter and warmer than the scented sheet caressing my shoulder. He's in my head, wrapped around me, staring at me from so, so close.

Stop making me forget. Stop making me remember. Stop making me fall for you.

What I want to do is slip out from under the covers, close the space between us, drop to my knees, and press my lips to his. I want to kiss him until his fingers find my sides like they did in the club, like they did in the car, and then I want to put my hands on him the same way. I want to touch him until he's as lost as I am, until we're both just *gone*.

What I actually do is close my fingers around my second pillow and toss it across the aisle. Shawn laughs and catches it, tucking it under his head with no intention of giving it back. I can't help smiling at him before rolling toward the wall, burying my nose in his pillow, and closing my eyes tight.

I wish Shawn had called me six years ago. I wish he didn't regret kissing me on the bus.

I wish he didn't want a girl like me.

I wish he wanted *me*.

Chapter Thirteen

A GIRL LIKE YOU.

Those four words plague me for the next seven days. When Shawn's smiles give me butterflies, I think he must have been trying to tell me something. When he makes fun of me like I'm one of the guys, I change my mind.

The thing is, he's *not* shy. I remember the way he was in high school, the way he took me upstairs like there was no question I'd follow him anywhere. If he wanted me now, he'd tell me. He'd take me into a dark room again. He wouldn't say "a girl like you."

And anyway, he's full of shit. Shawn doesn't want a girlfriend, or he'd have one. It's not like he's hurting for options to choose from. Each night we perform, he can have any girl in the crowd. Girls hotter than me, more girly than me, more his type than me. They wait for him at the bus, in their short skirts and plunging tops. And even though I'm thankful he never invites them on board—that he spends his nights reading or teasing me with smiles across the aisle—it's impossible to forget that if I wasn't here, that if I wasn't a girl on his bus, he'd be sampling different groupies every night. And maybe one of them would become his girlfriend, maybe not, but either way, he'd be more himself than when he's with me. And I'd still be just that girl—that girl he left behind. That girl he forgot.

"This last one's a new one," Adam says into the microphone during our ninth day on tour. It's our sixth performance, and the sixth time he's said those exact words. Most shows start the same—with him flirting with the front row before building up my sex appeal to the guys in the crowd. Then he belts lyrics into the mic, with Shawn singing over him and under him and after him and before him. Joel rocks the bass, Mike pounds the drums, and I lose myself somewhere between the spotlights suspended from the rafters and the strings of my guitar.

But this night has been a little different, with a blonde twenty-something standing just offstage, watching us with her arms folded and a confident smile on her face. She showed up sometime around the third song, on Shawn's side of the stage, and when we took a break just before the encore, she hugged the guys like they were old friends, and giggled condescendingly when I had to ask her name.

Victoria Hess.

Apparently, she's some hot record exec's daughter. And she thinks *everyone* must know this.

My guitar pick strums the final song to its end, and amidst the thunderous applause, my humming legs carry me back to her annoying smile. I busy myself with chugging down the contents of a water bottle next to Mike, and Adam ignores Victoria, clapping everyone on the back and congratulating them on another successful show.

My head is pointed toward Adam, but my eyes are focused on Victoria as she sidles up next to Shawn. She's wearing an all-white skirt-and-top combo that might look professional if it wasn't for all the skin she's showing. The top is beyond tight, with a plunging neckline that's about four buttons too low, and the skirt is high-waisted and mini, flaunting an ass that's barely there. The outfit is complete with a super-skinny pleather belt that's hardly necessary, considering the clothes are practically painted to her preteen-sized curves. She's the exact kind of way-too-perfectly skinny that high school girls develop complexes over.

"So," she says, pushing a strand of pale blonde hair away from her face and hooking her arm in Shawn's, "who wants to pour me a drink?"

I glare daggers at the back of her silky blonde head the whole way down the backstage hallway to the greenroom. Victoria is front and center, squeezed between Shawn and Adam, and I'm in the back between Joel and Mike, trying to avoid getting smacked in the face every time she flicks her stupid hair over her stupid shoulder.

"I guess you know why I'm here," she says, her white heels clicking loudly off the laminate floor. "Jonathan still really, *really* wants you to sign with him."

She turns a snooty upturned nose over her shoulder when I interrupt with, "Who's Jonathan?"

"Jonathan," she repeats, like I'm an idiot for having to ask. "President of Mosh Records?"

"You mean your dad?"

Mike snickers when she turns away without answering me.

"So anyway," she continues as if I'd said nothing at all, giving her attention back to Shawn and missing the look I share with Mike and Joel. They both stop walking with amused looks on their faces, hanging back as Victoria drags Shawn and Adam into the greenroom. She's going on and on and on about how selling out would do wonders for our band, and the three of us wait until she's gone.

"She hates being reminded that the only reason she has her job is because of who her dad is," Mike explains, and Joel nods in agreement.

I remember Shawn mentioning Mosh Records—something about them being cannibals...

I don't doubt Victoria would just *love* a taste of him.

"Is she in love with Shawn or something?" I ask, and Joel continues his vigorous nodding.

"She's an opportunist," Mike reasons. "So yeah, right now, she's in love with Shawn."

Joel stops nodding long enough to argue, "She had a thing for him way before we started getting big."

I look to Mike for confirmation, but he simply shrugs, doing nothing to calm my nerves as we finish the short walk to the greenroom.

This past week and a half with Shawn, I've learned that he's an early riser, that he never takes his coffee the same way two days in a row, that he usually wears chunky-framed glasses when he reads. I've seen the way his chest rises and falls when he sleeps, the way his hair looks when it's wet from a shower, the way he twirls a guitar pick against his lip when he's trying to brainstorm lyrics for a song.

Onstage, Adam is the frontman, but behind the scenes, it's Shawn's show. He books our performances, plans fun things to do on our days off, picks up our coffee orders every time we park within walking distance of a Starbucks. He's organized, meticulous, and impossibly charismatic. Backstage, he's always saying the right things to the right faces and shaking the right hands, and everyone in the industry loves him. They love him because in spite of it all—the spotlights, the fans, the attention—the music is still number one for him, always will be, and even the sellouts have to admire that. They see a genuine artist in him, and I see it too—along with a guy who smiles at me before my head hits the pillow, a guy who gives me butterflies along with my morning coffee.

I don't know what I expect to see when I turn the corner into the greenroom, but it definitely isn't Victoria curled on his lap with her twiggy arms coiled around his neck. The room is buzzing with people anxious to congratulate us on a great show, and the blonde-haired cannibal in white makes sure she's right in the middle of it.

"Joel!" she shouts as soon as we step inside, ensuring that she's the star of the show. Her voice is so annoying and whiny, I'm not sure how anyone could miss it. "I heard you got a girlfriend!"

Joel collapses next to Adam on the couch opposite Shawn, propping his feet on a coffee table and linking his fingers behind his head.

"So did Adam," he says, and Victoria grins.

It's like I'm not even here. It's like I'm invisible, and if I wasn't sure Shawn's eyes were on me, I'd believe it. I feel them—those bottomless greens—staring at me even though I won't meet his gaze. How can I, with her arms around him? It's like he's watching me to...to what? To see if I mind that he has a hot chick on his lap?

If he wants my approval, he's not going to get it. But he's not going to get my disapproval either, because I have no right to give it.

He's not mine. He never was.

"I heard that too," Victoria says as Mike's shoulder parts from mine. He heads for a table full of food and drinks in the corner, and I gravitate toward Joel's arm of the couch, watching as Victoria turns her smile down at Shawn, who looks like he always does after a show— worn out but wide awake, like he pushed past exhaustion and decided he never needs to sleep again. His irises are darker, his hair is damp and curling at the tips, and his entire body looks like it would sizzle at the touch. I've spent nights wondering how his chest would feel against mine, right after a show, when we're both still fueled with adrenaline and stage light. Now, Victoria is the one trailing her fingers over his collarbone.

He turns his chin up and meets her gaze.

"Not you though, right?" Victoria continues, her hazel eyes sparkling down at Shawn as she brazenly asks if he has a girlfriend. "You're still up for grabs."

Aaand that's my cue. Not waiting to hear his answer, I push off the couch and meet Mike at the food table. I grab a cookie, take a bite, and pour myself a much-needed shot of vodka, swallowing it down and scrunching my face at the aftertaste—a welcome distraction.

"When we get big enough," Mike says as I try to reverse-lick the cookie-hairspray taste out of my mouth, "I'm demanding there be pizza at every show." His big fingers lift a petite mini-sandwich to his mouth, and he makes a face at it before popping it in his mouth.

"I'd ask for a froyo machine," I counter. And right now? I'd drown myself in it.

"What flavor?"

"All of them."

Mike chuckles as we both turn back toward the room and lean against the table. I stand at his side—trying to avoid glancing at Shawn, and failing. My heart aches with jealously at the way Victoria can flirt with him like I never could. At the way she can touch him like I never can.

"I heard Van Halen likes M&Ms," I continue, "but with all the brown ones removed."

Mike swallows down another mini-sandwich. "Seriously?"

"Yep." I peel my eyes from Shawn, pinning them on Mike and commanding them to stay there. "And Mariah Carey likes furry animals backstage." When he lifts a thick brown eyebrow, I explain, "Like kittens and puppies and stuff."

"You're kidding…"

"Nope. I did a paper on backstage request lists in college. And that's not even the weirdest thing. Marilyn Manson requests a bald hooker with no teeth."

Mike's disturbed expression gives way to a short laugh, and then he shouts across the room, "Joel! Did you know that someday, you'll be able to put a bald toothless hooker on your backstage request list instead of having to track one down yourself?"

And of all the questions Joel could ask after he spins around on the couch, the one he chooses is, "What the hell is a backstage request list?"

"It's a list you give the tour organizers," some random person in the room answers, "of all the shit to have ready for you backstage."

Joel's elbows slip from the back of the couch as he whirls on Shawn. "Why don't we have one of those?"

"You could," Victoria croons, her long fingernails dancing up the side of Shawn's neck. "Most of our bands—"

"Not happening." Shawn unceremoniously shifts her off his lap before making his way over to me and Mike. As acting manager of our band, it's his job to handle music execs like Victoria's dad. The guys support his decisions, and so do I—especially if they involve pissing off Victoria in the process.

"You could be so big!" she protests.

"Will be," Shawn corrects. His shoulder brushes mine as he collects the vodka bottle and a stack of disposable shot glasses, but he doesn't even glance at me before walking back over to Victoria.

"Don't you want the fame? The money? The girls?"

He sinks back into the couch and sets the vodka and shot glasses on the table, immediately unscrewing the cap. "Not if it means selling my soul."

"Vicki thinks souls are overrated," Adam taunts, earning a smirk from Shawn, who's busy pouring the world's messiest round of shots. "Isn't that right, Vicki?"

Victoria sticks her tongue out at him while Shawn swallows two shots in short order, but she loses her good mood when he holds the third up for me. "Kit?"

My name on his lips is like a foreign thing, something that happened before Victoria and not after. I take the shot in a sort of daze, feeling her eyes on me as my fingers close around the clear plastic. When Shawn settles back into the leather couch cushion, she crosses one of her legs over his, and I get her message loud and clear. I sit on the arm of the opposite couch, declining the second shot he offers me because the last thing I need to do tonight is get drunk and emotional. He shrugs and downs his third.

"Look, I get it," Victoria says, her pink tongue flicking over the vodka on her lips. "You're not ready to sign with anyone. Whatever. You have my number when you are. I didn't come all this way just to talk business."

"What'd you come for then?" Joel asks, taking the bait she dangles.

"To see all of you, of course." She turns her meat-eating eyes on Shawn and gives him a photo-ready smile. "I missed you."

Her hand falls from his chest when he leans forward to pour another round of shots, but it finds its way home as soon as he sits back. And all I can do is watch. Even when other people join in the conversation, my eyes keep drifting back to Victoria's fingers on Shawn's chest, her bare calf on his thigh, her lips against his ear.

She's the type of girl he needs, even if he doesn't sign with her. A hot, rich, take-control girl. One who's unforgettable. One with a name like Victoria Hess.

I'm staring at him—at *them*—when his gaze locks with mine, and Victoria tracks its movement, hers narrowing my way. They can tell I've been staring at them like some jealous love-struck creeper, and with two sets of eyes on me, all I can do is stand up. Brush myself off. Announce that I'm going to the bathroom.

"Are you okay?" Mike asks, cutting off the conversation he's having with some of the stage crew.

"Not feeling so well."

"Want me to come with you?"

"No," I stammer as I make my sloppy escape. "No, I'll be back later."

I make my way through a maze of hallways, all the way to an exit door that gives way to a burst of star-sprinkled air. I have no intention of ever going back inside—not with my heart having manicured fingernails scratched all down its neck—so my combat boots punish the asphalt all the way across the deserted lot to the bus. We've been in that greenroom for so long that the crowd that normally waits for us has gone home, and I'm fumbling with the keypad next to the door when calloused fingertips curl around my arm.

Shawn spins me around, and my chin lifts to meet the intense way he's staring down at me. "Why did you leave?"

The seriousness in his voice leaves no room for jokes, lies, or anything else I could possibly say. The vodka he drank is practically swimming in his electric-green gaze as he waits for my answer, but I have no answer to give. He brushes soft, black strands of hair away from my face until he's palming the side of my neck. Then, with his fingers threaded in the thick of my hair, he steps forward and cages me against the bus.

"Why'd you look so pissed when you walked in the greenroom earlier? Why couldn't you look at me? Why'd you leave?"

There's nowhere left to run, but I can't answer him...I can't. "Why did you follow me?"

"For the same reason you left." His face lowers closer to mine, and my lips quiver with the touch of his breath. "I want to kiss you."

My heart kicks against my ribs, my palms flattening against the metal behind me. He's asking me to make the same mistakes all over again. He's asking me to revisit a party, relive a night on the dance floor, re-create a memory on the bus. And I know I shouldn't want to...but I do. God, I want to.

I want him.

"No."

"Please." Shawn's whisper pleads with me, his lips pulling closer and brushing mine on the word. I turn my face away, but his uncompromising fingers turn my chin back until there's no more escaping. "Please," he says again, just before his hungry eyes drop to my mouth. His lips follow, nipping at the closed seam of a kiss that's threatening to consume me. All of me wants to bloom for him, wants to open wide and let him in. "Let me. Just once."

His voice is like a kiss in itself—smooth and warm against my mouth, melting my resolve. I wouldn't have the strength to tell him no again, but he doesn't give me the chance to. Instead, he draws me closer, and he kisses me with such insistency that the soft petals of my lips are helpless against the heat of him. He kisses me with his eyes open. And, eyes open, I melt.

Kissing Shawn sober is like jumping off a cliff. Like realizing you can fly. Like welcoming the consuming rush of air. Like falling.

It's like embracing the very ground that's going to shatter you to pieces.

A moan escapes from a locked-away place inside me when his hips press me into the bus and his fingers clasp with mine, lifting my hands higher and higher until my breasts are pressing against his chest and every chemical in my brain is rushing like white-water rapids. My hands are trapped against chilled metal, his to control, and my knees are barely holding me up.

"Shawn," I pant when I finally summon the strength to turn my head away from the kiss that's making it impossible for me to breathe or move or think.

His name on my breath sounds like a protest, it sounds like a plea for more.

"I'm not finished," he promises in my ear, his nose brushing my hair away so he can nip at the exposed lobe. When I squirm, he lowers those lips to my neck and closes them over a spot that floods a pool of heat in my belly. All I can do is tighten my knees, let him kiss me, and try not to moan his name. His tongue does things that send tingles racing from my head to my toes, and those lips trail lower, lower, peppering kisses against my skin until he's exploiting the curve of my neck and I'm burning from the inside out.

What we're doing is wrong—the forbidden resurrection of a secret that's been kept too many times. And it feels good, *so* fucking good—but I can smell the vodka on his lips.

When I break away from him, it's not pretty. It's not clean. It's messy, with my hands jerking out from under his and my body stumbling away from the cage of his arms. He looks at me with half-lidded eyes, and I'm sure I'm mirroring that look right back at him. I can feel it in the way my nipples are perking, the way my skin is blazing, the way I still can't quite breathe evenly.

"No," I say, and Shawn steps forward before reconsidering and staying put.

"Why?"

"You're drunk."

This is the night after our first performance all over again. I want him, but I can't take another morning-after. I can't take him regretting what he did, him choosing to forget it. I can't be forgotten again.

I walk away from him because it's the only choice I have. If I stay...

I can't stay. Not with him looking at me like that. Not with every fiber of my body wanting to wrap itself around the softness of him, the hardness of him.

"Kit," he calls after me as I retreat toward the door to the venue. Every step I'm taking hurts, like I'm resisting the pull of something I belong to. The farther I get, the harder it is.

I don't turn around.

"No, Shawn. I'm not doing this again." What I'm not saying is that I can't...I *can't*. Every time we do this, I lose another piece of myself, and another.

I hear his footsteps following me.

"Kit," his voice pleads before I swing the metal door wide open.

"No. Talk to me when you're sober."

I don't look back. Shawn's presence behind me tingles at the back of my neck, but the whole walk to the green-room, I pretend he doesn't exist.

I'm not a toy. I'm not something he can just play with each time he gets bored and then forget about until he feels like it again.

"Guys," I say from the doorway, flinching when a heavy hand lands on my shoulder. I turn my head to glare at Shawn, sighing when I realize he's simply lean-ing on me to steady himself, staring down at his feet like they're about to jump out from under him. "Shawn is drunk as hell," I finish. "Can someone help me get him to the bus?"

A roadie walks over, clapping him on the shoulder so hard that Shawn is nearly knocked off his feet. The roadie laughs and dips his head under Shawn's arm, holding him up while Adam attempts to crawl over the back of the couch, trips in the process, and proves he's just as wasted as Shawn. Shawn starts giggling, and Adam lies on the floor laughing his ass off while I roll my eyes.

Joel is the one with enough sense to stand and walk around the couch instead of scaling over it. He stares down at Adam with glassed-over blue eyes of his own. "Dude, you are so trashed."

When Adam holds up a hand for help, Joel is about to reach down and take it, but Mike jumps in instead to prevent both of them from ending up on their asses. "Alright, let's go."

"Are we taking the party back to the bus?" Victoria suggests in that annoying daddy's-girl voice of hers, and my mouth is quick to open before anyone else's can.

"Sorry, invitation only." I shoot her an oversweet smile and wait for Mike to haul Adam off the ground.

Victoria is in my personal bubble before I know it, turning her big hazel eyes on Shawn, who still has his hand on my shoulder. "Can I come, Shawn?"

We're both staring up at him, waiting for his response, when he starts chuckling again and challenges, "Were you invited?"

I'm still too pissed off at him to appreciate the support, but I do grin at the way Victoria's face twists from the rejection. I turn my back on her without another word, my heavy boots leading my hot mess of boys back to the bus. They're loud, they're obnoxious, and on the bus, I can hear them even through the walls of my running shower.

Shawn's kisses linger on my skin. His lips still tingle on my neck. His fingers are everywhere, and I brace my hands against the linoleum wall and let the water rush over the back of my head as I try to block them out.

Kale warned me that joining the band was a bad idea, and I knew it would be hard…I just didn't know it would be like this. I didn't know I'd kiss him in Mayhem. I didn't know he'd kiss me back.

I lift my face into the water.

This time, *he* kissed *me*. And just like that girl who would have followed him anywhere six years ago, I let him. I kissed him back. I knew I shouldn't, but still, I couldn't *not* kiss him back. He's like an addiction that's always coursing through my veins, waiting to flare at the slightest spark.

It's his lips. Those eyes. His scent. That touch.

It's the way he looks at me in the dark. The way he kisses me when my eyes are closed—the way he kisses me when my eyes are open.

I don't bother drying my hair. I tie it up in a knot on top of my head and emerge from the bathroom in an oversized band T-shirt that swallows up the silky pair of pajama shorts underneath. The guys are still trying to raise the dead in the kitchen, so I huff out a breath and make my way back there.

"Seriously?" I say, my eyes scanning over the shot glasses and liquor bottles decorating the table they're at.

"I'm not drinking," Shawn offers, but I ignore him and start rummaging through the cupboards.

"What are you doing?" Joel asks from where he's sitting on top of the table, a bottle of gin between his legs.

"Making you something to eat."

"Oh!" Adam pushes Shawn's head out of the way so he can see me better. "I want…cheesecake! Can you make cheesecake?"

"Yeah, Adam, let me pull a cheesecake out of my ass for you."

As I root through a cabinet, there's so much laughter from behind me, I can't even tell who all it's coming from. I wish I was one of them, drunk off my ass and laughing about shit that's not even funny. Instead, I'm a model of sobriety to prevent myself from soaking Shawn's sleeve with my tears and asking him why he can't just want me when he's sober.

I pull every bready thing I can find out of the cabinet—crackers, cookies, pretzels—and trade them for the bottles on the table, stashing them away before threatening to murder anyone who dares wake me up. When I finally crawl under sheets that still carry the faint scent of Shawn's cologne, I'm exhausted—from the long day, from the concert, from having to deal with Victoria Hess…

From having to say no to Shawn Scarlett.

SHAWN'S GREEN EYES are the last thing I think of before I fall asleep, and the first thing I see when I wake. The dark is just beginning to give way to light, a hazy glow begging entry through the closed blinds of the bus, while Shawn's soft fingers brush my elbow. He's crouched next to my bed—his shirt, clean; his eyes, clear; and his breath, minty fresh when he orders, "Come with me."

Without waiting for me to argue, he disappears behind the heavy gray curtain leading to the kitchen, and I lie in bed until I'm sure I'm not dreaming. Joel is snoring, traffic outside is moving, and my heart is waking up without me, forcing my feet to free themselves from my covers and swing over the side of my bunk. The chill beneath the pads of my toes confirms that I'm awake as I slip silently between the bunks, careful not to wake anyone as I prepare myself for Shawn's apology. He'll say he's sorry for kissing me, explain that he was drunk, and I'll accept all the promises he'll make that it will never happen again. It'll be awkward, and we'll agree to keep things professional, and that will be that. Simple and impossible.

When I push back the curtain and slip inside the kitchen, he turns to face me, the glassy sheen from the night before gone from his eyes. "You said to talk to you when I was sober."

My heart sinks when he confirms that he remembers— the way he touched me, the way I let him. He was drunk enough to come on to me, but not drunk enough to forget it.

I kissed him back. I wasn't the one who was drunk, but I kissed him back.

Shawn steps closer, my breath catching in my lungs when both of his hands tunnel into my hair—still damp from my shower last night. Without my boots, I'm tilting my chin high to stare up at him.

"I'm sober," he says.

"What?"

"You said to talk to you when I'm sober," he explains. And then, he kisses me.

My eyes are already closed by the time his lips press against mine, and that furious addiction in my veins boils until I'm kissing him back, until I'm breathing him in. I fist my hands in the slack of his T-shirt, and he spins us around and begins walking me backward.

He's sober. The way he looked at me, the way he's touching me—strong, deliberate, steady.

The kitchen counter gets in my way, and then Shawn's hands are gripping my ass and lifting me onto it. The stubble on his jaw prickles my palms, my cheek, my neck, my chin—until every part of me, seen and unseen, is marked as his.

I want him, but not just for a moment. I want him, but not just this once.

I break my lips away and hold his shoulders at a distance when he tries to reclaim them. The smoldering look in his eyes is shaking my resolve when I warn, "You can't regret this, Shawn."

Whether he's sober or not, I can't lose another piece of myself. I can't just throw it away.

He pulls me to the edge of the counter so that my thighs are snug around his hips and the firm press of him is hard between my legs. His eyes are full of promises when he says, "I won't."

His lips crush mine again, and the squeeze of my knees draws him even closer. Shawn's hands slide down to my ass, and when he rocks me against him, my moan mingles with his, a low, quiet, breathy sound that makes my insides coil tight.

I'm ready to give him whatever he wants when his lips suddenly part from mine, brushing across my skin until they're pressing hard against my temple. His words are at my ear and his shoulders are trembling under my hands when he says, "You can't regret this either."

"I won't."

"Mean it." His voice is uneven, his hands unsteady—like it's taking everything he has to keep them from taking me.

"I promise," I say, and he pulls away to see the truth in my eyes a moment before he kisses me.

He kisses me like he plays the guitar—a mix of passion and technique that makes me feel like a sundae he's determined to savor, like my tongue is the ripened cherry on top. And I kiss him back until I'm melting under his lips, his tongue, his touch. My skin ignites when his lips drop lower, and lower. They explore my neck and the exposed parts of my chest, finding my hot spots and exploiting them until I'm biting my lip between my teeth to keep from waking the entire bus. My tiny whimpers only encourage him as he pushes a hand under my shirt and palms the swell of my breast, greedy and massaging and...fuck, I'm throbbing between my legs, and the way he's moving against me isn't helping—not with my pajama shorts as silky as they are, and my panties getting as wet as they are.

With his hips between my thighs and his hand under my shirt, my fingers detach themselves from the shoulders of his T-shirt in a rush, diving to the button of his jeans instead. I'm fumbling with the denim, desperate to feel him inside me, when Joel groans from his bunk behind the curtain, "Shaaawn, make me a coffee."

Shawn and I freeze—me with my hands ready to tear apart his jeans, and him with one hand on my breast and the other under my ass. He slowly straightens back up, my fingers not moving from his button and his eyes not straying from my mouth. We wait and wait and nothing.

In the silence, he nips softly at my lips, and in the silence, I kiss him back.

"Do you think he went back to sleep?" I ask in a whisper.

"No." Shawn's searing lips catch mine again in a soft yet dominant caress, but then something heavy drops to the ground, and in a second, his hands are out of my shirt, mine are off his jeans, and he's taking a hasty step back.

Joel bursts through the curtain a second later, a hungover mess as he walks right past Shawn to get to the coffeemaker. He loads a filter into the machine, oblivious to the way my heart is pounding out of control, the way my lips are a bright kiss-swollen red, and the way Shawn is staring at me like he's seriously contemplating finishing what he started regardless of who is or isn't watching.

"Why the hell didn't anyone make coffee?" Joel complains, and I bite my bottom lip between my teeth.

Shawn takes a little step toward me, and I subtly shake my head. He hesitates, then nods toward the curtain, silently asking me to leave the bus with him. For once, he's asking, and for once, I can think.

A satisfied smile touches my lips, and I shake my head again.

I've always made things too easy for him. Too quick. Too forgettable.

"Don't make me any," I tell Joel as I hop down from the counter, determined to make myself memorable. "I think I'm going to try to get some more sleep."

I smile at Shawn as I walk past, my fingers brushing his in a move that makes my heart pound even harder than it did while I was on the counter. His fingers curl with mine before letting them go, and that morning, I fall asleep not minding the scent stuck in the fibers of my pillowcase. I turn my face into it and smile, because those green eyes were sober this time and they were honest and they still wanted me. I smile because he said he wouldn't regret it. I smile because I believe him.

Chapter Fourteen

THERE ARE A few things most people don't know about being on tour. One is how things change.

The first week, the big shiny bus smells like excitement and fresh leather, but by the fourth week, it smells like exhaustion and boys' gym shorts. The kitchen loses its shine, the road loses its magic, and the towns all start to look the same. Each night is the best night of your life, and each morning is déjà vu.

The first week, saying good-bye to friends and family is easy. Hugs, kisses, waves from windows. But by the fourth week, saying good-bye—even over the phone—feels like cutting an invisible tether that's tying you to home. Sometimes, it feels like you'll never see home again...because how can you when home is so, so, so far away?

Adam gets restless, taking late-night walks and filling notebook after notebook with lyrics for our next songs—anything to distract himself from how much he misses

Rowan. Joel develops an unhealthy attachment to his phone, sleeping with it right next to his pillow and constantly whining about how much he misses Dee's ass, her legs, her mouth—anything to disguise how much he really just wants to wrap her in his arms and never let her go again.

Mike complains about missing his house, his entertainment center, his studio.

But Shawn and I...Shawn and I don't complain. Because how can we when each new morning, each new city, brings quiet kisses behind the kitchen curtain?

Sure, I miss Kale. I miss Leti. I miss the rest of my brothers and my mom and dad. I miss Rowan and Dee, and even my old-lady landlord. I miss my own bed and having more than just a few pairs of clothes to wear. I miss primetime TV and watching Sunday night football on my parents' couch. But I don't miss not being kissed by Shawn or not being touched by him. I don't miss wondering what being wanted by him would feel like.

For me, the tour becomes a different life, one of toe-curling kisses and secret smiles. Shawn and I keep whatever is going on between us a secret from everyone else, because I don't think either of us knows what it actually is...

It's waking up early to giggle against his lips in the kitchen. It's sneaking away from crowds to moan against his lips in the dark.

This morning, I opened my eyes to find him smiling at me from across the aisle, and I hid the goofy grin that consumed my face deep in my pillow. When I peeked over at him again, he winked at me, and it took everything I had to not wake the rest of the boys up with a stupid girly giggle. Shawn pointed toward the kitchen, and I shook my head. He pointed again, and I gave him another troublemaker smile and shake of my head. He gave me a devilish smile and picked up his phone.

Shower?

As I read his text, I bit my lip between my teeth, forgetting that he could see me. When I looked his way, I was pretty sure he was going to pick me up and carry me there whether I wanted him to or not.

More sleep. :P

Then I'm crawling in bed with you.

You wouldn't.

My head whipped in his direction when I heard him start to slip out of his covers, but I slid into the aisle before he could beat me to it. And in the kitchen, he swept me into his arms and punished me for my teasing—with scorching kisses that left me breathless and soft touches that drove me insane. He treated my body like a toy he was learning, and I was happy to let him play. He took his time teaching me my lesson—too long, because the bus started, the boys woke up, and Shawn and I nearly got caught with our hands buried under each other's clothes. For what seemed like the hundredth time.

I've spent the afternoon frustrated, but it was worth it. The fact that we're a secret makes this thing between us even more fun, makes us even more desperate, and every moment I have with him feels like something I'm stealing for myself.

"Kit?" Kale's voice asks in my ear, and I shake my head of thoughts of my morning with Shawn to answer him.

I'm sitting on a curb outside of a Bojangles fast-food joint while the guys finish their breakfasts inside, a phone to my ear and my skin melting off.

"I'm sticky."

"Huh?"

"Georgia," I grumble, wiping the sweat off my arms and peeling myself from the curb to find the shade of an overhang. "It's sticky. Seriously, my skin is like goo right now."

"Ew."

"I look like a melting wax figure. I swear to God, the insides of my ears are sweating."

"You're nasty," Kale says.

"I know." I cradle the phone against my shoulder and flap my arms like a chicken to get some airflow. "Don't you dare bury me in Georgia. Scrape me off the sidewalk and ship me to Antarctica or something."

My brother chuckles, and I lift the back of my oversized band tank to press my back against the shadowed brick of a nearby building, ignoring the judgmental looks I get from passing pedestrians. "So I take it you're ready to come home this weekend?" he asks.

My thoughts immediately jump back to Shawn and the way he kissed me in the kitchen this morning. The one morning Adam decided to wake up early, it had to be today. Every damn time Shawn and I start getting too hot, something always happens to hose us down, and I'm not sure if I should be thankful for it or flatten all six tires of the bus.

"No," I admit, and then I sigh and start pouring my heart out. "Shawn and I—"

"Uuuggghhh," Kale groans. "I knew it! I *knew* it."

I close my eyes behind the dark shades I'm wearing. "I don't know what's going to happen when we get home."

It's not like I haven't thought about it a million or two million times. I don't want us to stay a secret forever, but *I'm* the one who made us one in the first place, by hiding what we were up to in the kitchen from Joel, and Shawn has been content to keep it that way. How will I look if I change my mind now? Needy. Desperate. Pathetic. Shawn hasn't said what he wants from me, and I'm too scared of disappointment to ask. I'm too scared of having my heart broken. Again.

"Did he actually ask you out, or is he just using you as a fuck buddy?" Kale asks.

"We haven't fucked."

"Answer the question."

"I don't know."

"How do you not know?"

"I think we're together," I say, mostly to appease my brother, because honestly, I'm not sure *what* I think.

"You *think*?"

I wipe a layer of sweat off my brow. "I think I'm falling for him again."

"Bullshit," Kale says, like I'm his petulant kid sister, which I am. "You love him, and we both know it. You never stopped."

My twin says out loud what my heart already knows, and there's no use denying it anymore. "I thought I was over him."

"Yeah," Kale says as I wipe my clammy hand on my shorts, "because you're stupid."

I slink down against the brick wall until I'm sitting with my knees against my chest. I don't bother arguing with him, and he doesn't bother rubbing it in. We both know I'm teetering on the edge of another heartbreak, and we both know I'm going to risk it anyway. Because Shawn has *always* been worth the risk to me, and these past few weeks have only given me a million more reasons why.

It's because he puts honey in Adam's whiskey before shows to help his voice, and because he tapes a bottle of aspirin above Joel's bunk when he's doomed to wake with a hangover. It's because he makes me smile when he smiles, and makes me laugh when he laughs.

Getting to know him—*really* know him—has only made my feelings for him deeper. What I felt for him when I was fifteen is nothing compared to what I feel for him now—now that I know he feels something for me too, even if I don't know exactly what that something is.

Kale and I let my confession hang between us, not needing to say anything else because we both know what each other would say. He'd say I need to stop messing with Shawn before I get hurt again. I'd say it's too late for that. He'd tell me he doesn't like him. I'd say I know. He'd ask what I plan to do when he *does* hurt me again. I'd sigh and have no answer to give him.

"Leti wants me to come out to Mom and Dad," he says, and I'm thankful for the favor he's doing me by changing the subject.

"Of course he does."

Leti and Kale really hit it off the night we all went to Out. Even though I texted them to tell them they could sleep on the bus that night before heading home, they never showed up. They partied all night, have talked almost every day since, and have even gone out a few times. I've rubbed it in Kale's face that I told him they'd be perfect together, and he hasn't denied any of it.

When he goes as quiet as I had, I ask, "What are you going to do?"

"I don't know."

"Well, you know what I think." I push to my feet as the guys file out of Bojangles, with Adam already lighting a cigarette and Joel already complaining about the heat. Shawn has his cell to his ear, and the look he gives me when he sees the way my ripped white tank is clinging to my skin makes my sunburned cheeks blaze even hotter.

"I know," Kale replies. He pauses and then adds, "Kit, no matter what happens with Shawn, you know I'll always be there for you, right?"

I never doubted it, not even for a second. "I know. I love you, Kale."

"Love you too, sis. Call me if you need me."

I join the rest of the guys to walk back to the bus, asking Mike who Shawn is talking to.

"Van."

One word, and I'm nearly tripping over my combat boots. The guys give me weird looks, and I blame an imaginary crack in the sidewalk.

Van Erickson, a name so big that the surname is optional. He's the lead singer of Cutting the Line, one of the most popular bands around right now. I scored tickets to one of their shows last year, and even though my friend and I showed up three hours early, we still ended up being far, far back in line, and then right in the middle of the pit. I got clobbered, but it was one of the best shows of my life. Every single person there that night knew every single word to every single song, and we all screamed them at the tops of our lungs, hands in the air and chaos in our veins.

I shamelessly eavesdrop on Shawn while Adam, Joel, and Mike joke and carry on—like having Van Erickson on the other line is no big deal—but I barely catch the tail end of the conversation before Shawn hangs up and goes into business mode.

"Change of plans," he says. "We're heading back to Nashville."

"When?" Adam asks between puffs of his cigarette.

"Now."

Shawn's ear is back to the phone in no time, and I manage to get only short answers from him while he simultaneously talks to Driver.

Apparently, Cutting the Line's opening band came down with a nasty bug that's putting them out of commission, and Van wanted to give us first dibs on filling in. Shawn said yes, and in a few hours, I'm going to be opening for Cutting. The freaking. Line.

WHEN WE GET back to the buses, the engines are already running. Driver pulls out of the parking spot practically as soon as the last man's foot leaves the ground, and then we're on the highway toward Nashville.

Joel chuckles as I pour myself a Red Bull and sip it while staring absently at the kitchen wall. "You nervous or something?"

My eyes drift to him, and I realize I'm as white as the T-shirt he's wearing. "Aren't you?"

He shakes his head and sits on the tabletop. "I've played with them before."

"You've *played* with *Cutting the Line*?"

"Their bass player drank way too much at Manifest," he explains.

I would've sold every last inch of my hair to go to that festival last spring, but tickets sold out before I could get my hands on any. "What was it like?"

"Loud." His devilish grin gives me chills that stay with me the whole way to Nashville, and when we pull up to the venue, my eyes go wide in a window of the bus. The line for the show tonight stretches for blocks and blocks, kids with dyed hair and piercings and T-shirts even more faded than mine. I swallow thickly and peel my eyes from the window when Shawn sits next to me on my bunk.

"There's only one thing you have to remember," he coaches. He's dressed for the show, in exactly what he wore this morning—faded, ripped jeans and a vintage Nirvana shirt.

"What's that?"

"You're the best damn rhythm guitarist these kids have ever seen." He smiles softly at the look of doubt I give him and tucks my hair behind my ear before standing up to walk to the front of the bus.

"Shawn," I call after him, standing up and facing him in the aisle. "How do I look?"

I'm wearing a cute black bra that's peeking out through one of Dee's creations—a cut-up purple top that hugs where it should hug and drapes where it should drape. It matches the highlights in my hair and sports a Photoshopped image of Marilyn Monroe on the front. She's complete with heavy makeup and tattoos, both hands in the "rock on" symbol, looking just as badass as I hope I do. My legs are snug in shredded black skinny jeans, and my combat boots are laced up tight.

Shawn's green eyes scan over me before he steps in close. We're alone between the privacy curtains, and when he kisses me, it makes me forget. I don't care about Van, or performing, or who might walk in on us. I only care about how warm his mouth is, how good he tastes—like dark-roasted coffee and sugar.

He pulls away first, my heart pounding hard when he purrs low in my ear, "You look like trouble."

BY THE TIME I exit the bus, a second road crew is already outside helping ours rush things inside. Adam immediately lights a cigarette since he's banned from smoking on the bus—even though half the time he does it anyway—and Mike stretches his arms toward the sky, growling a tired groan. When Shawn finishes shouting at the new road crew to be careful with our stuff, the rest of us follow him inside.

Seeing Van Erickson onstage—looking like a rock god in black jeans, a fitted black T-shirt, and a studded belt that's hanging loose at the end—makes me feel two inches tall. He hops off the stage and immediately starts walking toward us, even his confident stride screaming "rock star." His hair is black, shaggy, and dyed red at the tips, and he has tattoos crawling up both arms. His grin is completely confident as he approaches the guys of my band. His eyes scan over Shawn, Adam, Joel, Mike, and then they rake over me from head to toe. He smirks and then claps hands with Adam and Shawn, pulling each into a guy-hug.

"Owe you one," he tells Shawn.

"You're up to like five now," Shawn corrects, and Van laughs as he pulls away and hugs the rest of the guys too. When he gets to me, instead of a hug, he takes both of my hands and stretches them away from my sides so he can get a good look at me.

"Damn. You're the new guitarist?"

If any other guy was inspecting me like he is—like I'm a juicy piece of Grade A meat—I'd yank my hands away and probably knee him where it counts. But because he's Van Erickson, because he's one of my idols, I just stand there with my tongue tied in my sandpaper mouth. "Kit," I finally rasp in a single quick syllable.

Van smirks and lets my hands fall back to my sides. His arm wraps around my shoulder, and he turns to face the guys.

Shawn is watching me closely, and I suddenly realize that I'm standing there with Van's arm around me, like I'm his property, like I'm a fucking *groupie*. My cheeks redden, and Van's implication is barely veiled when he glances at me one last time before saying to the guys, "You're sticking around after the show tonight, right?"

He's asking if *I'm* sticking around after the show—me, the girl with her bra mostly showing; me, the girl who just let him inspect her like a cut of prime rib; me, the sure thing.

In a moment of absolute insanity, I lift my hand to my mouth…

I suck on the tip of my finger…

I shove it right in Van Erickson's ear.

In an instant, his arm is flying from my shoulder and he's jumping out of reach, hollering at the top of his lungs, "What the fuck!"

A heartbeat of silence, and then every single one of my bandmates is laughing his ass off—loud, probably loud enough for the kids to hear outside—while I just stand there with an oh-my-fucking-God look on my face.

Did I seriously just give VAN ERICKSON a wet willy?

Oh my God. Yes. I just gave Van Erickson a wet-freaking-willy.

"Why'd you do that!" he shouts at me.

With my eyes still wide, I simply say, "It seemed like the thing to do…"

"It seemed, it seemed—" Van is stuttering his ass off, which only makes the guys laugh even harder. Mike grips his side as his laughter echoes off the walls of the venue. Shawn and Adam are cracking up so hard they're crying. Van stops stuttering to gape at me and say, "You're fucking crazy!"

Mike howls, and I just nod. "A little…But I play good guitar."

"You—" Van cuts himself off as his brows pinch together. He studies me for a long, long moment, before his expression softens and he shakes his head. "You play good guitar," he repeats, like it's the craziest thing he's ever heard, and then he laughs a little. When his face cracks into a smile, I manage a cautious one back. "Okay, Kit. You play good guitar? Let's hear you play guitar."

DOING A SOUNDCHECK with Van Erickson and his band watching is even more nerve-racking than playing a full set for a sold-out venue, but I'm the only one who seems to think so. It isn't until Adam starts belting out lyrics to Donna Lewis's "I Love You Always Forever" that I have no choice but to loosen up. I can't help laughing along with everyone else, and when Joel accidentally snorts, I have to let my guitar hang loose from my neck because I'm laughing too hard to support it.

With a crowd this big, here to see a band as popular as Cutting the Line, the opening act can go one way or another. The audience can like our sound and we can gain new fans, or they can get impatient and float in the pit like dead fish in the sea.

The first song, we get mostly dead fish. A few kids know us and sing along, but most are just biding time until Van takes the stage. Then comes some banter, during which Adam introduces our band, gives our names, tells where we're from. He explains what happened to the scheduled opening act, and then he and Shawn joke back and forth about rushing four hours to get here to give the kids a show. They tell the entire crowd about my wet willy incident, teasing me about it until the crowd is cheering loudly and my cheeks are burning red.

By our third song, we've completely won them over. Everyone is jumping in place, hands in the air, screaming their heads off at the end of each song—and even though most of them don't know the lyrics to our stuff at first, by the third time Adam sings the chorus, new fans are singing along with him.

Song after song, we convert them, and at the end of our set, Adam makes them go crazy. "ARE YOU READY FOR CUTTING THE LINE?"

The crowd cheers for the headlining band and for the kick-ass performance we put on, and I practically bounce off the stage, high off the show and for a chance to see Cutting the Line—from *right* backstage. A year ago, I would've killed for this, and now, this is my life.

Van's band is heavier than ours, with his backup singer growling hardcore lyrics into the microphone and Van's voice assaulting all sides of the room. The girls in the front row are showing even more skin than Adam's groupies do, considering they all have breast implants that are about five sizes too big. I wonder if that will be us someday, staring down at G-cup tits and playing to a room this big.

When Shawn's hand discreetly sneaks into my back pocket and gives my ass a squeeze, I don't risk acknowledging him. The guys and I are all standing in a line just offstage, and he's using the leverage of my pocket to coax me closer to his side. I pin my bottom lip between my teeth as he teases me, and then, when I can't take any more tempting or I'm seriously going to mount him where he stands, I slip my hand in the back of his T-shirt and rake my fingernails down his lower back.

Shawn's hand stops moving, and then we're both just standing there tortured. We were supposed to have today off, and I'd planned on sneaking away with him to a Laundromat or something, but instead, I'm stuck with his hand in my pocket and not a damn thing I can do about it.

When he gives me a look, I give him one back, and I realize what he's seeing—me, with my big black eyes, staring up at him with a pouty bottom lip bitten between my teeth. He frees his hand from my pocket like he's considering using it to haul me somewhere private, but then he rakes it over his scalp and strangles his hair between his fingers.

The corner of my mouth kicks up into a satisfied little smirk at how frazzled he is, and he immediately pulls his phone from his pocket, typing something out before mine buzzes in my jeans.

If you don't want to be dragged back to the bus, you have to stop.

You started it.

Let's finish it.

I peek up at the promising expression on his face, my blood flashing white-hot before I turn my attention back to my phone. The desire to go with him is so, so strong. For the past few weeks, all I've wanted is half a damn hour of privacy so I could see if fitting together with him would feel as good as I remember.

But what happens after? What happens when that half hour is up? What happens when we get home?

"We're going to Van's hotel party after this, right?" Adam asks, giving me a much-needed excuse to tuck away my phone before I type something stupid—like, "Can we talk about our feelings first?"

"Yeah," Shawn answers Adam. "I think we have to."

Chapter Fifteen

ONCE, WHEN MY parents took our seven-person family to Florida for summer vacation when I was ten, we all packed ourselves into one giant hotel suite. It had two bedrooms, a small kitchen, and a modest living space. My parents got the first bedroom; I shared the second with Kale, Bryce, and Ryan; and Mason took the couch. We were all in awe of how big it was.

Van's penthouse hotel suite, which is filled with the most decadent furnishings I've ever seen, could easily fit ten of that Florida suite within its two-story walls.

Crystal chandeliers sparkle from the ceiling, glinting off of black marble columns that stretch all the way to a black marble floor. A bar lines most of the left wall, and beyond that, tropical fish swim in a built-in aquarium that stretches halfway around the room. The water casts waves of light onto the diamond-dust bar top and across the floor, which steps down into a sunken seating area in the middle of the suite. Sparkling side tables, priceless antiques, plush leather couches—Van's suite was built for a king, and the far wall proves it. Made entirely of glass, it boasts the glimmering Nashville skyline, a kingdom to be admired.

His Royal Highness's private quarters are to the left of the suite, and in another room off to my right, I catch a glimpse of a lap pool as someone splashes into it. A hairspray-scented group of girls races by me, already giggling and tearing off their clothes, and in front of me, Van spins around. He faces me and the rest of my bandmates, spreading his arms wide with a proud smile on his face. *"Mi casa."*

Someone turns on the music, and the entire suite comes to life. Van's entourage doesn't stop racing past me—girls, girls, guys with girls, more girls. I get jostled by one and step forward, angling my body to get a better look inside the pool room.

"If I put my arm around you again," Van questions from beside me, "will I be safe from getting another wet willy?"

I straighten and shake my head. "Nope."

He chuckles and throws his arm around me anyway, leading me to the bar and telling the guy who's busy stacking liquor bottles on top of it to pour me something. Everyone else is helping themselves, pouring top-shelf tequilas like they're nothing but unfiltered water. All of the guys but Shawn have dispersed throughout the room, and when he presses up against my other side, the air charges with a static that fizzles thickly in my throat.

"So on a scale of one to ten," Van says, "what are my chances with you tonight?"

I turn toward him so that his arm drops from my shoulder, smirking at the overconfident grin he gives me. My back is pressed against Shawn's front when I hook a thumb over my shoulder. "You realize Shawn has a better chance with me tonight than you do, right?"

Van glances at Shawn and laughs, but he has no idea how serious I'm being. He toasts my jab and tells me to have fun, and when he disappears, Shawn's fingertips slip into the waistband of the tight jeans I'm wearing.

"On a scale of one to ten," he echoes in my ear, "what are my chances with you tonight?"

With goose bumps skipping down the back of my neck, I turn around to meet his eyes, but instead, I catch myself staring at those impossibly soft lips. I know what they feel like against my neck, my shoulders, my chest. And I can think of a dozen other places I'd like to feel them.

When he leans in, I don't stop him. I know that anyone could see us—Adam, Joel, Mike, any of the roadies we brought with us tonight—but I don't have it in me to care. I'm lost in him, lost in some place I never fully escaped from and now never want to. His lips are a caress against mine, a promise that deepens until I'm drowning in it, and it isn't until someone pops a bottle of champagne that the spell is broken. Shawn and I both jerk out of the trance we're in, my heart hammering against my ribs as my eyes swing up to meet his shocked expression.

"Oh my God," I blurt, and we both start chuckling. I look around to see if anyone saw us, but the only people looking our way—*Shawn's* way—are a few scantily dressed groupies who undoubtedly caught our performance tonight and are patiently waiting their turn for his attention.

I'm glaring at them when Shawn's lips press against my neck, making my toes curl. My fingers press into my palms, and I nibble my lip between my teeth.

"I'd rather be back on the bus right now," he says, and I couldn't agree more, but that doesn't stop me from wondering why the hell two of those chicks are still staring at me—*me*, not Shawn. When they grin at each other and start walking my way, I can't help feeling like a meal about to be made.

"I'm Nikki," the taller one says when she's finished stalking across the black marble floor. She's only an inch or so taller than me, with hair as long as mine, a nose ring even sparklier than mine, and curves a hell of a lot curvier than mine. She's one of the prettiest girls here, but not a single guy is hitting on her, and I'm guessing that's for a damn good reason—she has *Van's groupie* written all over her.

"And I'm Molly," her shorter counterpart says. The girl is five foot even at best, and petite all over, with an eyebrow piercing and the most doe-like eyes I've ever seen. Both girls have fake lashes, fake nails, neon pink hair, and an air about them that says they're well-taken care of.

"I'm…" Confused, curious, lost. "Okay?"

Molly giggles. "Nice to meet you, Okay! We loved you at the show tonight. You're like this hot dangerous sex kitten that can play the guitar even better than Asshat over there." She nods across the room, to where Cutting the Line's rhythm guitarist is drinking Cîroc straight out of the bottle, and then grins up at Shawn. "Isn't that right, Shawn?"

It clicks in my head then, what those predatory smiles meant. They saw me kiss Shawn. They know Van. Van knows Adam, Joel, Mike.

Shit, shit, shit.

"Stop being a pain, Molly," Nikki scolds. "Shawn, we're borrowing Kit for a minute. Go take a cold dip in the pool or something."

I follow them because I have no choice. They have unspoken blackmail, and I have everything to lose. Shawn and I aren't ready for the world to know about us because, frankly, I'm not even sure there *is* an us. He likes me…I think. Or maybe he just likes kissing me. Maybe we're friends with benefits.

God, are we friends with benefits? Am I a fuck buddy like Kale said?

The girls lead me through open glass doors out onto a balcony that has what I have no doubt is the best view in the city. The skyline twinkles before me, a collection of sparkling skyscrapers that don't hold a candle to the magic-filled suite behind me. But out here, I'm swathed in shadow.

"So, you and Shawn—" Nikki starts, but the vulnerable girl I was with Shawn is still somewhere at his side, and I cut her off.

"What are we out here for?"

She looks through the glass wall separating the balcony from the suite. Everyone is laughing and carrying on in a frenzy of excitement, but her voice is apathetic when she says, "We were bored."

"Are you and Shawn a thing?" Molly asks excitedly, but when she sees the worried look that must spread across my face, she scrambles to add, "Oh, don't worry, we won't tell!"

"It *is* a secret, right?" Nikki asks, and I give her a half confession.

"How'd you know?"

My question makes Molly scoff, and my head spins back in her direction. I'm going to need physical therapy for whiplash if these girls don't stop answering for each other.

"We knew Joel and Dee were together before *they* even did."

"You know Joel and Dee?"

"I got the first Dee original T-shirt creation there ever was!" Molly squeals, and Nikki smiles at her. "I love yours though. That shirt is so hot."

I stare down at my cut-up purple shirt, feeling so weird being out here with two *very* girly girls. I think I'm supposed to act like a girl too, but, uh…how? "Thanks…"

Nikki turns around and leans back against the glass. In heels, booty shorts, and a curve-flattering belly-top, I'm sure she's getting way more attention than the one-of-a-kind art pieces sprinkled throughout the suite. A breeze blows her hair back. "So why the big secret?"

"It's complicated," I answer truthfully. At first, we kept the secret for fun, but now, it's for a million reasons—none of which seem quite good enough any-more. It's because I have no idea what Shawn wants, and I don't want to embarrass myself by asking. What if he says he wants us to stay a secret forever? What if he says he *doesn't*? When he finds out I want more from him than he's probably willing to give, will the kisses stop coming? Will it be another six years before he calls me again?

A reckless part of me almost *wanted* Adam or Joel or Mike to catch us when we were kissing. Then, it would've been out in the open, and it would've been out of my hands. Instead, it's still a secret—and it's still mine to keep.

"Oh, sweetie," Nikki says, patting me on the shoulder. "It always is."

I'M THANKFUL WHEN Adam appears a few minutes later, outside for a smoke break that interrupts the girls' inter-rogation about me and Shawn. I practically drag him into the conversation, and Nikki and Molly behave themselves well enough for me to actually start to like them. They don't seem as desperate for attention as the other girls here, but maybe that's just because they don't need to be.

We talk about touring and buses. We talk about Rowan and Dee. And when Adam's cigarette is noth-ing but a dimming red cherry in the dark, he smashes it under his shoe and we all head back inside. The four of us pass by the sunken sitting area, where Van's drummer and bass guitarist are hanging out with a cluster of other people. There's smoke and bottles and paraphernalia on the table that I know better than to inspect too closely or ask questions about, and I let the pool room distract me as a wall of bubbles wraps itself around the laces of my boots. A hot tub in the corner is overflowing with half-naked chicks and vanilla-scented suds, and Nikki ignores the girls calling to her as she beelines straight for Van. He's sitting on the opposite side of the pool, in a makeshift sitting area of leather couches and chairs that look like they've been moved from some other room. The other guys from my band are all with him—aside from Joel, who's cannonballing into the pool. His splash arcs toward the ceiling, and my eyes travel up to the LED lights sprinkled in the deep blue concrete sky. The pool room is just as magical as the rest of the suite, even when the spray of chlorine-scented water wets the bottoms of my shredded black jeans.

"KIT!" Joel yells from the water, his voice bouncing through the cave-like room. "Get in!"

"Nuh-uh," I say from the edge, shaking my head for extra emphasis.

He argues, argues, and stops. And then his eyes flit behind me and my training kicks in—all eighteen years of it that I got from living with Kale, Bryce, Mason, and Ryan. In one swift movement, I sidestep and spin, latching on to Adam's reaching arms and using them to launch him into the pool.

I'm caught off guard when Molly grabs on to me, but end up laughing when she simply starts bouncing up and down, laughing hysterically as Adam's head pops back out of the water. He's laughing so hard he can barely breathe, and when Joel jumps onto his back and dunks him under, I'm pretty sure he might die.

I turn to Molly and shrug. "Serves him right."

"I fucking love you!"

I jump out of the way of the splashes that come my way from Adam and Joel as I circle the pool, flicking them off when they boo me. Karma attempts revenge by making me slip and nearly eat floor, but Molly catches me at the last moment, and we both laugh as we cautiously finish maneuvering around the pool. When I get to the couches, I take the first seat I see, which also happens to be right next to Shawn. I'm propped on top of the plush leather arm of his couch when his fingers brush the suds away from my shins, traveling much higher on my leg than they need to. He gazes up at me, and the red in my cheeks boils to the surface.

"What are the boards for?" Molly asks about the mini dry-erase boards on each of the guys' laps.

Shawn hands me his, and I give him a confused look as Van says, "You'll see." He gives Molly a playful smile, and then he pulls a megaphone from next to his leather chair. Where in the hell these guys got dry-erase boards and a freaking megaphone, I'm sure I'll never know. "Okay! Contestant one!"

A member of the bikini brigade in the hot tub climbs out and positions herself at the arced entrance of the room. In a sparkling pink two-piece that's covering her crotch, her nipples, and little else, she faces the pool and waits as Van chants, "On your mark! Get set! No!" Van chuckles as the chick jumps forward a step, tries to stop herself, and slips around like a newborn donkey on ice before he shouts, "Go! Go! Go!"

She's barely regained her footing when she takes off running, her bouncing boobs threatening to knock her head right off her shoulders. She nearly slips again, catches her footing again, and makes a poor attempt at cannonballing into the pool. The guys are all unmerciful, holding up ones and twos as her wet blonde head emerges. When I realize everyone is staring at me expectantly, waiting for my score, I uncap my marker with my teeth.

"NO. JUST NO." is what my sign says when I finally lift it above my head. The guys all laugh, the girl giggles like she's cute, and I roll my eyes as she makes a show of climbing up the ladder of the pool, her bikini bottoms pinched between tan ass cheeks that are pushed out for Van's benefit.

"NEXT!" he shouts, simultaneously curling his finger at a different girl in the pool. No questions asked, she hauls herself out of the water and rushes to his side. "Grab me something to drink, will you?"

She turns toward the bar like it's her privilege to serve, and even though it's a total bitch move, I seize the opportunity before she gets too far. "Me too!" I shout, and when she turns back around, Van gives me an appreciative smile before smacking her on her ass.

"Her too."

Nikki, sitting on Van's lap as he pays attention to every girl but her, hooks her fingernail under his chin and stares down at him until she's the only girl in the room. When she kisses him, I look anywhere else, accidentally meeting Shawn's eyes while my cheeks are flushing as red as the next contestant's bikini. It's decorated with tons of polished hardware, and when it's clear Van's thoroughly preoccupied, his lead guitarist picks up the megaphone and shouts, "GO!"

Van tears his lips from Nikki to watch the second contestant frolic the length of the floor, stop at the edge, and pinch her nose. She jumps in toes-first—in a *cannonball* competition—and I'm left sitting there with my face scrunched up and my head shaking in disgust.

"What the fuck was that?" I ask, but when her top floats back up without her—yanked off by her pathetic splash—most of the guys start cheering. They hold up eights and nines as the girl covers herself with one arm and tries to catch her drifting top with the other. Adam—fully clothed, dripping wet, and sitting on the side of the pool—covers his eyes while Joel lifts it with two fingers and launches it in the girl's direction before she can get too close to him.

Another few pathetic jumps. Another few pathetic scores.

"I think we need some kind of incentive," Molly suggests as she squeezes onto the arm of the couch with me. I inch over to make room, but she continues nudging me until I have to grab on to Shawn to keep from tumbling into his lap. I catch myself just in time—

And squeal when he tugs me the rest of the way.

"The winner should get to spend the night with Mike," Nikki suggests with a mischievous undertone to her voice, and Mike's protests are lost under the volume of Van's megaphone. I might have been able to help back him up if I wasn't so busy trying to act normal, like being on Shawn's lap in front of *everyone* isn't making my heart want to explode.

"Highest score gets a night with Mike!" Van shouts, laughing when Mike makes a play for the megaphone.

I laugh too, quieting when I realize how much it makes me wiggle on Shawn's lap. Adam and Joel don't even seem to notice us, but when I glance up at Molly, I can tell she knocked me off the arm of the couch on purpose. She winks at me, and Shawn's middle fingers thread through my belt loops, his thumbs caressing the sensitive skin under my top.

"NEXT!" Van shouts again, and I take the drink his groupie finally brings me, sucking it down to calm my nerves. I'm on Shawn's lap, struggling to breathe evenly as he touches me like he doesn't even care who sees us.

The next few girls to compete are all just as pathetic as the first—some in bikinis, some in skimpy underwear. One falls. One suddenly realizes she can't swim—*after* she jumps in the water. And the rest barely manage a splash because they probably don't even break a hundred pounds.

"NEXT!" Van shouts once again, and a girl in a blue bikini, with implants bigger than my head, climbs out of the hot tub. She makes a show of rubbing the suds from her body in the brightest spot of the room.

"Oooh, she's pretty," Molly says. "What about her, Mike? I think she's winning."

"She'll probably float," he argues, and I chuckle against Shawn. He pulls me tighter against the ridges of his body, giving me one big reason to bite my tongue—and my bottom lip. It's all I can do to not beg him to take me somewhere private so we can finish what we've started.

"You ready, sweetheart?" Van asks the G-cup groupie, and she nods her tiny head.

"GO!"

I expect her to rush, and hopefully fall, but instead, she's unhurried and confident. She walks to the edge of the pool, curls her fingers under her bikini top, and lifts it up over her designer breasts. At least ten jaws fall to the floor, including mine, and then earsplitting cheers and hollers fill the room. Dry-erase boards start flying up, all with giant tens on them, and while everyone is distracted, Shawn's fingers slide up and trace the underwire of my bra. When I gaze down at him, his molten green eyes are only for me, and my heart skips into my throat.

"We have a winner!" Van shouts, and Shawn's thumbs swipe delicately over my pert nipples, once, twice—

Oh God. I'm so hot, I'm squirming. Every inch of me is arching into his hands as he teases my primed, eager nipples. My eyes close, and his thumbs continue torturing me until they slide back down to my waist. Both of us are breathing heavy, and every muscle in my body is coiling, squeezing, demanding I get the hell out of this room and drag Shawn along with me.

I finish off my drink in one big swallow.

"Van," I say in a voice I'm hoping doesn't sound as breathless as I feel. He turns his head toward me. "I think we need more drinks."

He gazes down at his full glass, grins, and calls a random girl over, ordering her to bring us something. The remainder of his tequila is gone in two or three big gulps, and then he sets his glass on the floor and we all watch attentively as Mike's winner circles the pool to stand in front of him.

"Uh, I'm Bob," Mike lies as he stares up at her. "You're looking for Mike. I think he's at the bar. Skinny guy, lots of curly orange hair." He finishes describing our bus driver and points to the other room. "Have fun."

The girl looks doubtful, but she follows his finger anyway, and I'm smiling like a lunatic when Nikki pouts, her face twisting with disappointment.

"Boo. Why'd you do that?"

When he doesn't answer, Molly teases, "Maybe he's not into chicks."

It's a bitch thing to say, and I get nasty right back—throwing out the equivalent of a bitch slap to Molly's face. "Maybe he's just not into groupie whores."

"Hey," she rushes to say, "I mean, that's cool if he isn't…"

My teeth are grinding, but Mike doesn't sound angry at all when he says, "Look…when I meet my wife, I don't want to have to explain to her why I slept with a hundred chicks before I met her, okay?"

Every single person within earshot shuts up and stares at him, with every single girl melting for his words. Even Molly and Nikki are looking at him like they wish they were that girl he's waiting for: because Mike could be Van—he could have taken that implant connoisseur somewhere private and had her do anything he asked—but he's staying loyal…loyal to a girl he hasn't even met yet. And that's so much more than Molly or Nikki can ever hope for.

"More for me," Van chides, jostling Nikki when he reaches over to clap Mike on the back. He shuffles her off his lap and stands up, stretching his arms out before heading for the hot tub.

Neither Nikki nor Molly bothers following him.

The rest of the night is filled with drinks and laughing, with pushing people in the pool and ordering forty dozen Krispy Kreme donuts from concierge. The music doesn't stop, and neither does the party. Sometime around three in the morning, when Shawn's discreet touches have grown too much for me to bear, I meet his eyes across the sunken sitting area in the middle of the suite and chew my lip between my teeth. When I stand up, his eyes follow me. When I turn away and cross the room, I know they're still watching. When I slip outside the suite into the hotel hallway, I know no one notices—no one except him.

I'm leaning against generic eggshell wallpaper when the door opens, and when he steps through it, I grin. But only for a second, because that's how long it takes him to cross the space between us, thrust his fingers into my hair, and pin me against the wall. His lips cover mine in a kiss that's been building all night, and breathing becomes something I no longer need to do—because his fingertips are sliding down my neck, over my shoulders and arms, and around my wrists. He stretches my arms above my head, and I'm so *his* right now, I let him. He parts my thighs with his knee, pressing up against thin jeans until I'm squirming on top of him, making sounds against his mouth that are desperate and pleading. I'm on fire, and Shawn kisses at the flames, making them burn hotter and hotter until I'm devouring his lips just to keep them off my molten skin. If only I could free my hands, I'd be able to put us out, but each time I tug against Shawn's grip, he pulls them even higher.

Light and music from Van's suite suddenly spills into the hall, but Shawn doesn't stop kissing until I do, and even then, he doesn't release his hold on my wrists. He watches me as I watch over his shoulder—a new cluster of girls enters the suite, and when my dark eyes turn back to Shawn's, he's staring at me like nothing else in the world matters. When I try to lower my hands, he refuses to let them budge, and I surrender control faster than I ever thought I would. His eyes darken, my knees go weak, and I just wait. And wait. When he brings his lips to mine again, it's powerful, dominant, and it makes me squirm between his body and the wall.

"I want you," he breathes against my neck, sending a sweet rush of heat between my legs. His breath is warm against my skin, his tongue smooth as he dips it into the hollow of my collarbone. With my hands restrained, there's nothing I can do except let him have me. And God, I want him to have me.

"Let's go somewhere."

He lifts his head from my skin to meet my eyes, and the smoldering look in them makes my heart trip and stumble. When I move to lower my hands this time, he lets me, and when I step away from him and start walking backward, he calls after me.

"Where?"

"Anywhere."

I give him a devilish smile that he can read like one of his books, and when I start to sprint down the hallway, he's right on my heels.

I have no intention of getting away—I never have, never did—but the fact that he's chasing after me...it makes the running worth it.

Chapter Sixteen

ON THE ROOF of the hotel, under a thick blanket of summer stars, Shawn and I are completely, *completely* alone. During our sprint through halls and stairwells, I nearly crashed into housekeeping, who we ultimately convinced to let us on the roof. I pretended to be a groupie, Shawn pretended to be a member of the "huge rock band" the entire staff had heard about, and by the time we got on the roof, we were both giggling like mischief-making kids. Shawn tried to kiss me, I laughed and jumped away, and he chased me to the edge of the roof. But the view is what caught us, and now, as we stare out over a city that seems to shine just for us, he takes my hand in his.

"It's beautiful," I say, mesmerized by the skyline. Touring hasn't left much time for sightseeing, but I know none of it would have been like this—just Shawn and me, alone, standing at the edge of the world.

When his soft chuckling sounds from beside me, I turn my head and say, "What?"

"Is this the part where I'm supposed to stare at you instead of the view and say something corny like, 'Yeah, it is'?" I laugh and look back out at the lights, but from the corner of my eye, I can see him still staring at me. His voice becomes exaggeratedly serious when he says, "Because it is. Beautiful, I mean." I laugh harder and nudge him with my shoulder, and he wraps his arm around me.

"You're a dork."

"Only around you."

I smile out at the sky, content under his arm because there's not a single place I'd rather be. The breeze carries the crisp scent of his cologne, and it wraps itself around me like a cool summer blanket as the silence between us stretches and stretches, out into the dark, winding through sleeping city streets.

When it reaches too far, I ruin everything by opening my mouth. "I thought we'd have our clothes off by now."

I blush fiercely as soon as I say it, curling my toes tightly in my boots to punish my foot for putting itself into my mouth, but Shawn's voice is honest, soft, when he says, "So did I."

I relax under his arm, thinking—and hoping—that this isn't something friends with benefits would do. They wouldn't race to an abandoned roof just to laugh and hold each other. They wouldn't stand here like we are, creating a memory like this.

When I turn toward Shawn this time, curling my fingers around his shoulders and bringing my lips to his, the kiss is soft, controlled. It's not a fire. It's a message. It's a million things I can't say, and I when I lower from my tiptoes, I can't help smiling up at him, warming from the inside out when he mirrors that smile right back at me.

Clothes and all, it's perfect, and we eventually settle with our backs against the brick wall of the hotel, our shoulders touching and my arms wrapped loosely around my knees. The view really is gorgeous up here, but a poor substitute for Shawn's green eyes. I can't stop myself from stealing glances at them, and each time he catches me and smiles, I have to look away to keep myself from giggling like the girly girl I'm not.

"I'm going to ask you to do something," he says after a while, "and it's going to be weird. But don't laugh, okay?"

He makes it sound so ominous, I prepare myself for the worst. A guy I dated in college asked me to refer to him as "Daddy" once while we were making out, and I laughed so hard as I walked out of his life, I'm pretty sure I never gave him an answer.

My voice is nervous when I answer Shawn. "O…kay…"

He spreads his knees and pats the ground between them. "Can you sit here? And…let me hold you?"

Butterflies swarm out from my heart, through my veins, and into my stomach. They're fluttering wildly, their wings forcing goose bumps to the surface of my skin, as he waits for my answer. The nervousness in me wants to stall by asking him why, by ruining the moment, but instead, I swallow thickly and push that reaction down deep. I crawl between his knees, settle with my back against his chest, and swoon when he wraps his strong arms around me.

"Are you comfortable?"

I can't help it this time—I giggle quietly—and when he asks me what I'm laughing about, I say, "You act like you've never been with a girl before."

"Never like this. Not with a girl like you."

If only he knew—that he was with me once, years ago, far more intimately than this. On a night like this, at a party like the one we just left, before he let me walk away. Before he forgot my name, my face, our story.

I try to push the memory away, but it's hard when his arms are finally wrapped around me and only one of us remembers the first time our eyes met, the first time our lips touched.

My very first time ever.

"I used to have a crush on you in high school, you know," I confess. I know he doesn't remember, but I can't stop myself from hurting, or hoping. My heart reaches for his in the dark, trying to make him remember.

"Did you?"

I let out a little sigh when my heart comes back empty, and he rubs his thumbs over my arms. "Yeah," I say.

Shawn starts playing with my fingertips, his hard-earned calluses rubbing against mine. "You shouldn't have."

"Why not?"

"I wasn't a good guy in high school." When I lift my chin to gaze up at him, he brushes my hair away from my forehead and tucks it behind my ear. His T-shirt is soft against my cheek, his voice even softer when he says,

"A guy like me wouldn't have been good for you in high school."

I want to argue with him, but I don't know that I can. And anyway, what would be the point? I turn back around, settle against his chest, and let him tighten his arms around me. "What makes you good for me now?"

"Probably nothing. But I want you anyway."

Part of me sighs in contentment while the other part wants to ask for how long. For the rest of this tour? For until he gets bored? For tonight? For forever?

"You don't really know me," I say, but Shawn's response is quick.

"I know you talk in your sleep."

I push off his chest and shift to look at him. "I do not."

"Yes, you do," he says with a playful smirk. "Last night, you kept saying, 'Oh, Shawn, oh, you're so hot, I want you so bad—'"

My jaw drops in a gasp. "You're so full of shit!" When he starts laughing, I smack at him until he wraps me in his arms and tugs me back against his chest. I laugh along with him, delighting in the way his body shakes against my back, until I'm smiling out over the roof again.

"Tell me something I don't know," he asks of me after a while, and I can hear him smiling too—it's shining through his voice.

"I like ketchup in my macaroni sometimes."

His thumbs stop tracing over my arms when I say the first thing that pops into my head, and the night is silent when he says, "Damn. That changes everything. I think you should go back inside."

I laugh, and his thumbs start up again, keeping me still in his arms.

The smile is still in his voice when he says, "Tell me something else."

"It's your turn," I argue.

"What do you want to know?"

"Have you ever been to a party like that?"

"Like that?" With my head nestled in the crook of his shoulder, he says, "Nah. I've been to some crazy parties, but none like that."

"If you'd sign with Victoria's dad, you could have them every night."

"Why would I want to?"

I spin around and face him, bending my knees over his thighs. "Isn't that the dream?"

He rests his hands on the worn knees of my jeans, twining his fingers into the threads. "You mean having someone else tell us what to do?" When I wait for him to elaborate, he says, "It's not worth it. I never want someone telling me what to write or what not to write or how fast we have to put stuff out there. Cutting the Line is good, but compare them now to how they sounded five years ago."

I know exactly what he means. "Their first album was amazing."

"And Van knows it." His fingers continue navigating every slit and fray in my jeans—every single one, like he needs to touch every inch of my exposed skin, even though I doubt he realizes that's what he's doing. "He loves the life, but he hates what he has to do to have it.

Vicki's dad has him under his thumb. That would kill it for me and Adam, and I know Mike and Joel wouldn't like it either." His fingers glide into a slit behind my calf, and I pretend not to notice, not to love the way he's touching me as much as I do. "What about you?"

"I like things the way they are."

His smile warms the chill of the wind on my cheeks. "They're going to change, either way. It'll just be slower this way."

"I like slow."

"I'm starting to like slow too." His eyes drift to my lips, and the breeze itself seems to still. "Like now...I really want to kiss you."

"Why don't you?" My voice is shallow, hollowed by breath he steals.

"Because I like this." His fingers crawl back up my legs until they're twining into the ragged threads stretched over my knee again. "Tell me something else."

"Like what?"

"Where do you see yourself in five years?"

My attention lifts from his fingers to his eyes. "Jeez, you couldn't have gone with something easy?" He grins, and the adorable line that sets in his cheek makes me want to answer anything he asks. "I don't know, hopefully still playing music."

"That's it?"

"That's the only thing I can say for sure."

There are things I know I *want*—like Shawn, every single bit of him—but I don't know where we'll be tomorrow, much less five years from now. And when I try to guess, it just hurts. Because five years is almost six years, and six years is such a long time.

He nods with understanding, and I ask, "What about you?"

"Definitely still playing music. Hopefully with you." He smirks, and I smile. "By then, maybe we'll be on a label."

"I thought you didn't want to be on a label?"

"Not right now," he explains. "I want to be big enough that when we draft the papers, they have to kiss our asses instead of the other way around." I chuckle and shift closer to him, listening as he continues. "And I don't know. Adam and Peach will probably be married or something by then, so I'll probably be homeless."

I laugh and joke, "I'd let you live with me."

"So there then," he says with one of his unguarded, bright smiles. "We have a plan."

I look away, at a piece of gravel next to my boot, and I can feel my own smile dimming as I pinch it between my fingers. "Part of me never wants this tour to end."

"Why?"

I lift my gaze back to his, my eyes making a confession even as my mouth asks the question my heart has been too afraid to. "What happens when we get home? To you and me?"

Do we pretend the kisses we shared over coffee on the tour bus never happened? Do we keep fooling around in secret? What happens when he meets someone better than me, prettier than me?

"What do you want to happen?" he asks.

"Don't do that," I plead.

"Do what?"

"Make me embarrass myself."

He studies me for a long moment, and then he says, "I told you I wanted you. You think that wasn't embarrassing?"

"What does that even mean?"

"What do you mean, 'what does that even mean?' It means I want to be with you." A subtle blush creeps onto his cheeks, but I still can't believe Shawn is saying what I think he is.

"Be with me how?"

He laughs and shakes his head. "Christ, Kit, do you not see how into you I am? I'm saying I don't want us seeing other people, okay? I want you for myself. I want to see where we might be five years from now."

The smile that consumes my face turns night to day, pushes the dark into tomorrow. "Ask me."

"Ask you what?"

"Ask me," I press again, and he chuckles as he picks apart a thread in my jeans.

"You're the worst, you know that?" When I just keep smiling at him, he can't help smiling back. "I swear, if you say no—"

"Ask me."

He takes his time, inhales a deep breath...and then, he asks me. "Will you go out with me?"

"Can you be more specific?"

When he starts to argue, I laugh and kiss him, silencing him with my answer. I kiss him until his arms are circling around my waist, until I'm his and we both know it. "Okay," I say when I part my lips from his. "But if I'm yours, you're mine."

My thumb traces the curve of his jaw, memorizing the brush of his stubble, the way his eyes look in this moment, the way his voice sounds when he says, "I've been yours for a while."

When I kiss him again, it's the seal to a promise. It's telling him that I want this. That I want him.

It's telling him where I want to be in five years. In six.

Chapter Seventeen

I WAKE UP with an ache in my back, the sun in my eyes, and I smile. I turn my face into Shawn's hard chest, breathing into his fabric-softened T-shirt and loving the way his arms tighten around me like he's never going to let me go.

We talked all night, until we curled up under the stars and fell asleep where we lay. He told me about meeting Mike and Joel, about starting the band with them, about discovering Mayhem for the first time. I learned about his mom, his dad, an older stepsister he has. We told each other our favorite colors, our favorite places, our favorite songs. We shared childhood stories, and all the crazy things we want to do before we get old. We laughed and smiled and held each other, and this morning, nothing's changed.

What happened between us last night was real. It still is.

"Dude," says a voice, and I jerk myself awake. Mike is standing over us, kicking the sole of Shawn's shoe, and I remember in a daze that the click of the steel hotel door is what woke me in the first place. I shield my eyes from the sun and attempt to sit up, shrinking under Mike's gaze. I feel like I've been caught red-handed—because in Shawn's arms, I have been. But he's my boyfriend. He fell asleep holding me. There's no need to hide it anymore.

Nervous butterflies flutter wildly in my belly, and I manage a pathetic, "Hey."

My entire body gets jostled when Shawn sits up in a rush, a curse word already flying from his lips. "Shit. What time is it?"

Mike's eyes slowly swing to the disheveled boy next to me. Shawn's hair is poking out everywhere, mussed by the sleep and the way my fingers twirled in it as we both drifted off last night. "Half past nine."

"You're kidding." Shawn is already pushing to his feet, and I'm left sitting on my sore ass, rubbing my sore back, looking like a sore mess.

"*Everyone* is looking for you," Mike tells him, and I don't doubt it. We were supposed to leave for the next city before the sun broke the horizon this morning, but now it's high in the sky, casting light over a secret Shawn and I have been keeping for weeks. Mike's gaze swings down until I'm shrinking again. "And for you."

Under the sun and our drummer's scrutiny, last night suddenly seems a little less real, a little further away. It's not just Shawn and me anymore. It's not just us in the dark.

When calloused fingers drop in front of my face, both Shawn and Mike watch me, waiting to see if I take

Shawn's hand. My palm is clammy when I do, but I hold on tight and let him help me up.

The contact is broken as soon as I'm on my feet—by me, by Shawn, by habit. I brush myself off while trying to think of what I can possibly say to Mike.

But Shawn beats me to it.

"Hey," he says as he combs his fingers through his hair, "don't say anything to the guys about this, okay?"

I can feel Mike shift his attention to me, but I'm too busy staring at Shawn with my stomach dropping to my knees to care. When I finally turn my head, Mike reads the hurt in my eyes and then looks back at Shawn. He shakes his head and sighs. "Whatever you say, man. See you back at the bus."

With that, the steel door of the hotel clicks shut behind him, leaving Shawn and me just standing there. Alone. Again. And last night suddenly seems impossible—if Shawn told me it was all a dream right now, I'd believe him.

He finally turns toward me, but I quickly drop my chin. The gravel crunching under my boots is real. The way my fingernails are stabbing into my palms is real. The metallic taste of my lip between my teeth—that's real too.

"Hey," Shawn says, his finger lifting my chin. Enchanted green eyes search mine.

"What do we do now?" I ask with his fingers gliding over my cheek, threading into my hair.

"What do you mean 'what do we do now?'"

I step away from his touch, and his hand falls from my face. "Last night," I stammer. "It's cool if you...I mean,

I'm sure Mike won't say anything…and, I understand, you know…"

Jesus, I'm tripping over words and feelings, crashing with no one to catch me. But then Shawn steps forward, his hand capturing mine. "Whoa. You're not changing your mind, are you?"

My brows knit at him. "You just told Mike not to tell anyone…"

A smile tugs at the corners of his mouth, which only makes me want to yank my hand away, but he squeezes it tighter. "We're trapped in a tin can with those guys," he says, like that should be explanation enough. "We'd never hear the end of it, trust me. And there are only two days left of the tour." When I continue frowning, he threads both hands into my hair and presses his forehead against mine. "I'm still yours."

My hands close over his, and I don't know what comes over me—maybe the spell in those green eyes. "Prove it."

His lips are against mine in an instant, warm and intoxicating as they part mine and prove that last night happened, that what I felt between us was real. His fingers curl in my hair, and my hands slide to his wrists. I hold on as he kisses me—until my knees are weak, until my thoughts are miles away. My back collides with the brick building we'd fallen asleep against, and my fingers are tugging him close when I bite down on his lip, his body trembling against mine as a deep moan sounds from his lips.

Last night, this had been building. For *weeks*, this has been building. We postponed it, but now there's only me, him, and nothing else to stop us.

When I release his lip from my teeth, he stares at me with a green fire flaming in his eyes. He kisses me until I turn my head, giving him access to erogenous zones that he knows intimately by now. His tongue flicks over a sensitive spot below my ear until my fingers are clawing desperately into his shirt. I'm squirming against him, my breaths coming out in twos and threes, when I finally find the sense to remind him, "We're late."

Mike said *everyone* was looking for us this morning, and Shawn and I are acting like *no one* matters.

"Adam's always late," he counters, his lips trailing lower, lower. He hooks a finger into the collar of my shirt and tugs it down to taste even more of me, heat pooling low in my belly—lower, lower.

"Shawn," I protest, but it sounds like a prayer even to my own ears, and when he drops to his knees in front of me, my fingers bury in his hair.

"Five minutes," he says, already pushing my shirt up to play his lips along my stomach.

Lower, lower.

He makes short work of my button, and then my jeans are being tugged down. Quick fingers tug at my boot-laces, and then I'm stepping out of those, out of jeans. My panties get tugged down too, but Shawn doesn't even wait for me to step out of them before his lips press forward.

Heat—molten-hot heat—closes over where I'm already wet for him, and my head falls back in a moan that makes my knees quake. His strong hands hold my hips in place, pinning them against the wall and holding me up as the aged brick bites against my ass. My eyes are rolled back between closed eyelids, my fingers gripping Shawn's hair as he devours me with the firm tip of his tongue and then presses forward even farther. Wetness rushes between my legs just as his hand slides up my stomach, over the swell of my bra, teasing at an impatient nipple that strains against the black lace. My entire body is alive, nerve endings dancing as Shawn tunes them like a neglected instrument, and when I open my eyes and gaze down at him, his green eyes are staring up at me under thick black lashes. He lifts a hand between my legs, finds the wet trail his tongue has paved, and buries two fingers deep, deep inside of me.

And God, the moan that pushes out of me as my knees begin to quiver, it only makes me hotter, makes his eyes darker, makes me so, so close.

"Shawn." My voice is raw, needy, desperate. My hands are out of his hair, gripping the sides of the building because I feel like I'm about to pass out. I've been with other guys, but never—never—have I felt like this. I'm about to come apart. A white spark is climbing inside me, threatening to explode into a shower of fireworks.

"Come for me, baby," Shawn says, his low, husky voice bringing another rush of warmth between my legs as his fingers make the world fall away. "We're not leaving here until you do."

And God, I believe him. The way he moves his talented fingers inside me, he'd be here all day, all night, forever if he—

"Oh my God," I say as my seams burst apart, every single thread at once. My knees nearly buckle, and Shawn's strong hands latch on to my waist, pinning me against the wall. He devours me with his tongue until I'm melting all around it, and then he catches every last bit of me, greedy as he continues licking for more and more and more and—"Oh my fucking *God*," I moan as a second wave of pleasure rushes over me, taking control of my body until I'm not even sure I'm inside it anymore. "Shawn…oh…oh, *God*…"

My moans become intelligible as the most intense orgasm I've ever had overtakes me, and Shawn stands in a rush, claiming my lips in a way that makes me want to reach down low.

I want to find his button and tear it from his jeans. I want to feel him inside me—deep, where I'm still pulsing for him. But he kisses me ravenously, stealing words from my mouth and thoughts from my mind. I'm his—utterly his, following him blindly as the kiss deepens, slows, calms. When his lips part from mine, I'm still breathless, my eyes half-lidded as I stare back at him.

In a daze, I want to tell him I love him. I want to say the words, sleepily with my eyes half-open. I want to repeat them and repeat them until he kisses me again.

Instead, I rest my forehead against his, and he smiles.

"Thank you," he says, and an exhausted laugh escapes me as my eyes drift closed.

"Yeah, Shawn. You're welcome."

He kisses me softly, so softly, and then he brushes my hair from my eyes and presses his hand against my cheek. "Open your eyes."

"Why?" I ask, already parting my lashes to the captivated way he's looking at me.

"The way they look right now…" His thumb strokes my skin. "I've wondered what they'd look like right now."

My cheeks burn pink, but he's too busy studying my eyes to notice. A soft smile blooms across his face, stoking the hibernating nest of butterflies in my stomach until they're flapping nervously against my heart. I'm not used to this—to wanting to tell him I love him so badly, to having him make me feel like I could.

"We're late," I remind him once more as I reach down to lift my panties back up. My knees are still trembling as I step into my jeans and my untied boots.

"I had five minutes," Shawn teases as I reach down to tie my laces. "I'm pretty sure I still have two left."

I angle my chin to glare up at him, but I'm smiling, and so is he.

WITH MY HAND in Shawn's, I float my way to the bus, my entire body buzzing with Shawn's personally gifted brand of satisfied exhaustion. Every time my thoughts drift back to the roof of that hotel, tingles trickle across my skin and I have to resist the urge to tug him into an alley, an empty parking lot, a bathroom stall in the nearest fast-food joint. I keep stealing glances at him, he keeps catching them, and I curse every giggle that frees itself from my lips, because I'm helpless to stop them.

"Can I tell Rowan and Dee?" I ask, needing to tell someone, *anyone*, that Shawn and I are together. *Really* together. Shawn shakes his head, and I pout.

"They'll tell Adam and Joel," he reasons, "and they'll make these last two days on tour hell."

"What about Leti?"

"He'll tell Peach and Dee, and they'll tell Adam and Joel."

"Okay, well, what about Kale?"

"Your brother?" Shawn slows to a stop just before we reach the parking lot that the bus is in. His smile is gone, and when I nod, he says, "Let's…let's just wait, okay?"

"Why?"

A beat of silence passes, then another and another, before he says, "He's friends with Leti, right?"

"Yeah…" *Friends*…sure.

"So he'll tell Leti, and Leti will tell Peach and Dee, and—"

I sigh, and Shawn squeezes my hand.

"Later," he promises. "Just not yet, alright?"

He kisses me before I can answer, a soft touch of his lips that magically puts a smile back on my face. "Okay."

Just before we enter the parking lot, he drops my hand, and I force myself to ignore the way that makes my chest pang. I follow him to the bus, and when he holds the door open for me, I climb up onto it.

The guys immediately jump on us, and each thing they accuse us of is a truth or damn close to it. We snuck off together. We've been having secret hookups for weeks. We're in "looove." We banged each other's brains out on the roof before Mike found us.

Shawn rolls his eyes, and Joel laughs. "We got locked up there, asswipe."

"Uh-huh, sure," Joel teases.

"Kit was drunk and determined to get up there. What was I supposed to do, let her fall over the edge?"

Shawn lies easily, and if I didn't already know the truth, I wouldn't even doubt him. The deception melts on his tongue like sugar, and I'm sure I would've eaten it right up.

When Joel looks to me, I rub my temple like I have a hangover. "Don't ask me. I don't remember shit."

I'm no stranger to lying myself, especially when it's convenient, but this one…this one tastes sour.

"I almost fell off a roof once," Adam offers as the bus merges onto the highway, carrying us to a new day, a new city, a new show. "Actually"—his brows furrow—"I think I *did* fall off a roof once. Shawn, do you remember that after-party in Cold Springs?"

Shawn chuckles as he gathers his things for a shower. "Yeah, man, you definitely fell off the roof."

Adam nods to himself and rubs a phantom lump on the back of his head. "Yeah…I thought so."

When Shawn slips into the bathroom, Joel's attention snaps to me. "So you guys seriously just got locked up on the roof?"

I stick to Shawn's story, and Joel pouts, but he lets it go—and so do the rest of the guys, even the roadies. After another round of harassment at soundcheck, the entire morning gets discarded and forgotten. And I don't text Rowan. I don't text Dee. I don't text Kale. I don't text Leti.

At soundcheck, Shawn resumes our covert flirting, and even though all of his touches are secret and fleeting, they still make my heart rush just as fast as it had this morning when he was…when we were…

My cheeks flush fire-red at the memory as we perform that night for a sold-out crowd, and when I glance across the stage at him and his eyes are already on me, I giggle. I giggle in the middle of a damn song, with muscle memory being the only thing that keeps my guitar pick hitting the right strings. Even though it's still a secret, he's my boyfriend. My freaking *boyfriend.* The smile on my face is a living thing, sneaking there at inopportune moments and threatening to tell all my secrets to every single face in the crowd.

I hate that we didn't tell the guys about us, but I get it...I guess. Yeah, they'd be annoying. Really freaking annoying. We wouldn't hear the end of it until the tour was over and we were home. But the girly part of me would've welcomed that. She would've stoked the fire with an unrivaled level of PDA that would've embarrassed the hell out of everyone—herself most of all. Because Shawn was finally, *finally* her boyfriend, and she didn't want to hide that—ever, at all, from anyone.

But he was right about there being only a day and a half left of the tour, and I get that too...I guess. I'm sure he doesn't want the guys giving him a hard time. Or maybe he doesn't want them giving *me* a hard time. Or maybe he just wants to be able to steal another quiet morning in the kitchen with me without everyone hooting and hollering at us from the bunks...and after what happened on the roof? Yeah, I can live with that.

I smile at him across the heads of fans in the parking lot. The show tonight was incredible, and when we finally walked out to the bus, it was surrounded. I've taken so many pictures, spots dance behind my eyes as I leave Shawn, Adam, and Joel behind and step up onto the bus.

Mike is already on board, and I follow him to the kitchen in the back. Shawn mentioned that he'd talk to him about this morning, but after being caught like a rebellious teenager about to do the walk of shame, I feel the need to say something too—even though I have no freaking idea what that something is.

"You had a lot of fans tonight," I tease in spite of how nervous I'm feeling. I plop down on a leather bench, careful not to steal Mike's usual gaming spot, and wait to see if he brings up this morning. He grabs two beers from the fridge and closes it with the toe of his shoe.

"That one woman was like fifty years old," he exaggerates of a cougar dressed in, yes, cougar print, who was waiting outside the bus. There are some women who just have a thing for drummers, and this one made no secret of it—which, I'm guessing, is why Mike is currently glancing toward the front of the bus like she's about to storm onto it SWAT-style at any given moment.

I laugh and tease him some more. "Not all of your fan club was that old."

He gives me a look and collapses onto the seat next to me, handing me one of his beers before starting his Xbox.

"How are you going to meet your future wife if you won't give any of them a chance?"

"Trust me, any girl I'd want to be with is not one waiting outside of a tour bus."

"I've waited outside of my fair share of buses," I counter. For autographs, pictures, hugs. Nothing more, and I certainly wasn't dressed in cougar print.

"Exactly," Mike says, and when I drop my jaw and smack him hard across his shoulder, he laughs.

I smile and relax back against the seat, waiting until he's playing a game to say, "Thanks for not saying anything to the guys about me and Shawn this morning."

"You should've just told me," he says with his eyes on the screen and his fingers frantically pushing buttons. "I knew there was something going on with you two."

"That obvious, huh?" I try to ignore the fire-breathing dragon beneath the brightening skin of my cheeks.

Mike glances at me and chuckles. "Yeah. But don't worry. You're a much better liar than Shawn is."

I grin at the smart-ass compliment, and then I ask, "How so?"

"Dude," Mike says, "he gave it away from the moment you auditioned. I just never really got why he looked at you like that."

My nose crinkles. "Huh?"

"At first, I honestly thought he just didn't like you." Mike laughs. "I had no idea you guys hooked up in high school."

A ringing in my ears. A loud, loud ringing. "Wait… what?"

All sorts of warnings are flash-firing in my brain, causing my heart to protest painfully against my ribs. He had no idea we hooked up in high school? In *high school*?

Mike glances at me again before turning back to the TV with a chuckle. "Relax. Shawn told me everything. Your secret's safe with me."

"He… told you we hooked up in high school?"

That's impossible. He doesn't *remember* we hooked up in high school…

Mike curses and jerks to the side along with the character on the screen. Then he regains his composure and says, "At Adam's graduation party, right?"

"Yeah..."

"Kind of epic, if you think about it. It's like you guys were always meant to be together or something."

"Yeah," I mutter again, with dread pooling coldly in the pit of my stomach.

Shawn remembers?

Shawn remembers.

When Mike glances at me again, I disguise my emotions with a fake smile, and he smiles back at me before returning to his game. "I think you guys will be good together."

I walk away from him in a daze, icy shivers dancing over my arms and up the back of my neck as I replay his words over and over again in my head.

I had no idea you guys hooked up in high school.

Shawn told me everything.

You guys hooked up in high school.

In high school.

At Adam's graduation party.

Shawn has remembered this *entire* time. He's known since my audition, since the first time he locked eyes with me after six years of *nothing*. He knew when he gave me a hard time at our first practice and I ended up throwing a guitar pick at his head. He knew when I kissed him in Mayhem, when he kissed me back and I ended up making an idiot of myself on the bus. He knew when we sat up on the roof of the hotel and I admitted I had a crush on him in high school. He knew with every kiss he stole, every smile he took, every time he made me look like a stupid fucking girl harboring the crush of a fifteen-year-old freshman.

Betrayal plants in my belly and spreads like a weed, choking out the butterflies and making one thing perfectly clear: he doesn't want to tell the guys about us because he *never* wants them to know. He didn't want them to know back then, and *nothing* has changed. He only told Mike because Mike caught us and he had some serious explaining to do. But he doesn't want me to tell Rowan, or Dee, or Kale, or Leti, because after all these years, I am *still* just his dirty little secret.

When he climbs onto the bus and smiles at me, it takes everything I have to not cross the distance between us and clock him in the face. He's not my boyfriend anymore, not the guy who made me giggle tonight onstage. He's the guy who fucked me in a dark room and never called. He's the guy who has lied to me for *months*. He's the guy who broke my heart—twice.

Once, shame on me. Twice, you are *so* fucking done for.

After Adam and Joel pass by me to get to the back, I catch Shawn's arm and haul him to the front, closing divider curtains the entire way. Driver is still on the other bus, and I have only minutes before he appears to drive us to the next city.

"You looked hot onstage tonight," I say, my voice carrying a manic sort of recklessness that I'm hoping he can't hear. I boldly reach up and curl my fingers in his hair, a wild energy buzzing in my veins and threatening to make my fingers shake.

It would be easy to confront him, and it would be easy for him to lie. I'd look absolutely crazy—like just another one of the scorned groupies I'm sure he's collected over the years. Shawn could deny everything—every kiss, every touch, every word…every goddamn fucking thing I was stupid enough to think meant anything. And honestly, I'm not sure who the rest of the guys would believe. The forgettable little girl from high school? Or their best friend since forever?

Yeah.

So instead of screaming and crying and kneeing Shawn where it counts, I twirl my fingers around and around in his hair, flashing him a wicked smile that's full of bad intentions. And when the green flames in his eyes ignite, I can tell he's misinterpreting every single one.

My fingers are still twirling when his lips drop to mine. He kisses me just like he had last night, and the sting of it makes me pull away, but slowly.

"Can you imagine how many times we would have hooked up by now if you had known about the crush I had on you in high school?" I whisper, watching his reaction closely and trying not to get my hopes up.

I'm giving him an opportunity to come clean. All these months, all he would've needed to do is tell me the truth and say two words. "I'm sorry" would've been all I needed to hear to forgive him, and I'm giving him one last chance to say it.

His smoldering gaze meets mine from centimeters away, and I watch the way it dims and sobers. Now that I know what to look for, I spot it—the recognition.

He kisses me again, and I spot that for what it is too—a distraction. The hope in my chest dims, and I pull away again. "I thought about it, you know." He watches me, and I watch him right back, trying to see him for the guy he was with me last night, and not the one who has lied to my face for four and a half straight months. "About what it would be like to be with you...I bet we would have been amazing."

I'm desperate for him to just admit it—to tell me I'm not forgettable, to tell me I was worth remembering, to make me believe I still am.

"We're amazing now," Shawn says, and this time, when his fingers tangle in my hair, there's no pulling away. The way he kisses me makes me want to pretend. I feel myself start to fall—start to forget, to forgive—and the only way I can save myself is to bite down. *Hard.*

"Fuck!" He jumps away from me, his hand flying to his mouth. He stares at me like I've been possessed, and maybe I have been, because all I can do is stare blankly back at him. It's like I'm seeing him for the first time, through someone else's eyes.

"What the hell was that for?" He wipes his thumb across his bottom lip and glances at the streak of red blood that clings to the lines of his thumbprint.

"I guess I got carried away."

His dark eyebrows are pinched tightly in my direction when the nearest curtain swings open and Joel saves me from having to explain myself any further. "What the hell are you yelling about?"

Shawn's torn jeans get stained red when his thumb wipes across them. "Nothing. I bit my lip."

Another lie. And it rolls off his tongue so easily, my blood boils.

"Oookay…" Joel stares back and forth between us—at Shawn, glaring at the apparition I've become, and at me, with the taste of his blood still on my tongue. "What are you guys doing up here?"

"Obviously having another secret rendezvous," I answer flippantly, and Joel has no idea how honest I'm being when he brushes me off.

"Ha, ha. Seriously though, what are you doing?"

"Wondering where Driver is," Shawn answers for me, but I'm already walking away from his forked tongue, back through the bus. In the bathroom, my back slides down the closed door until my ass hits the floor and the world stops falling out from under me.

Pathetic.

Disposable.

Shawn threw me away after having me six years ago, and now? Our last show is tomorrow night. Just one more day on tour…and then what? Were we ever going to tell everyone? He said that we would, but he never said when, and even if he had, it wouldn't have mattered.

Because Shawn said a *lot* of things. And all of the things he *didn't* say mattered just as much.

I used to have a crush on you in high school, you know. Did you? he asked.

It was one of a thousand lies left unspoken. One of a thousand, and I fell for every single one.

Chapter Eighteen

WAKING UP THE morning after the veil is yanked from my eyes is déjà vu, but not the kind of déjà vu that reminds me of waking up in a new city yesterday, or the day before that, or the day before that. It's a déjà vu that carries me back to the summer after my freshman year of high school, to another morning-after. Then, I cried into a pillow. Now, I'd sooner gouge my eyes out.

I roll away from the metal wall of the bus and stare through the pale rays of sunlight separating me from Shawn. He's facing me, like he'd been watching me sleep, and his face looks peaceful. Beautiful. Deceiving. His black hair is a tangled mess against his pillow, his jaw dusted with shadow and his dark lashes fanned against his cheeks. It was almost impossible to sleep last night, with him right across the aisle as the bus ferried us to a new city. Part of me wanted to crawl across the impossible space separating us and kiss him until I forgot about all the things he said and all the things he didn't.

But an even bigger part of me wanted to punch him in the face and then smother him with his pillow.

I fell asleep angry, I woke up angry, and after tugging on a fresh pair of clothes, I leave the bus angry. Driver parked us in a new lot hours ago, and with the sun peeking through the windows, I know Shawn will be awake soon. He'll expect me to meet him in the kitchen before everyone else is awake, just like I have every other morning for far too long, and maybe he'll want to finish what we started on the roof of Van's hotel, or maybe he'll want to ask me why I went all zombie on his face last night, but either way, I hope he feels as lost as I do when he realizes I'm long gone.

Block after block, crosswalk after crosswalk, my combat boots gain the distance I'm so desperately in need of. The city is buzzing with people heading to their day jobs, dressed in suits and formal wear that stand in stark contrast to my shredded jeans, my band tee, my black-and-purple hair. I don't even know where I'm going—I only care that it's *away*. Because I can't think around him. I end up kissing him or biting his fucking lip off, or both.

When my phone buzzes and Shawn's face flashes onto my screen, I don't slow down. I don't turn around. Instead, I toss a few choice curses at his face before making it disappear. My contacts get pulled up. My thumb hovers over SEND. I make the call.

"Hey," Kale answers, the sound of his voice lifting an invisible weight off my chest.

I take a deep breath and say the three words he's probably been dying to hear. "You were right." My voice is firm—loud enough to make the confession real even to my own ears.

"Of course I was right," Kale agrees. "What are we talking about?"

"Shawn's an asshole."

"O...kaaay..."

"He remembers."

With the phone pressed tight against my ear, I wait for Kale to cuss Shawn out or rub it in or say *anything*, but my twin is silent for so long, I end up pulling the phone away from my head just to make sure I didn't lose the call.

"Hello?" I prompt with it back under my hair.

"Sorry...He *remembers*?"

"Everything."

"Like...He remembers you from high school?"

My heart twists in my chest, the writhing of a million jagged pieces that will never be put back together. "*Everything*, Kale."

"He told you that?"

A single laugh escapes me, cutting into the morning air of a city much too far from home. "No, Mike told me." I slip inside a random coffeehouse, the jingling bells on the door taunting me as my choice attire earns stares from the patrons. I dare them to give me a look, or say something, or breathe the wrong way. "But two nights ago, before I found out," I say as I approach a wary barista, "he asked me to be his girlfriend." I make a noise at the end, something between a scoff and a choked-out laugh. "I'll take a large coffee. Black."

"And what happened after that?" Kale asks as I hand the barista my money.

I laugh again, the wry sound a cruel reminder of just how much he hurt me. "Trust me, you don't want to know."

Long seconds pass, and I try to block out the memory of all the sweet things he said to me that night, and all the dirty things he *did* to me the morning after. "You said yes?"

"I did a lot more than say yes."

I woke in his arms and let him pin me to a wall. I let him kiss me, touch me... I let him drop to his knees. I let him—

My skin heats from the memory of what we did on that roof, and my fist clenches with the urge to punch myself in the face for the way my body betrays me. Even after everything, part of me—an untrusted, carnal part of me—still floods hot for him, and probably always will. He's still gorgeous. Nothing can change that. And he's still talented and smart and funny. And my heart...

My heart can't be trusted either.

"You slept with him?" Kale asks, worry seeping through the phone from hundreds of miles away.

"No. Almost... but no."

His sigh is heavy, and the weight of it bears down on me as I move to the edge of the counter to wait for my coffee.

"Kit..." Kale says after a while. "Are you okay?"

"No." My anger resurfaces with the admission. "No, I'm not fucking okay, Kale. He's been lying to me this *whole* time."

"Start at the beginning," Kale orders, and I collect my coffee and find a table. I sip at the rim of my recycled-paper cup, welcoming the way the scalding liquid burns away any last traces of Shawn's lips. And then I tell Kale everything, even though I swore to myself I never would. I tell him about the kiss in Mayhem before the tour, about the way Shawn pretended nothing happened. I tell him about the kiss the night I met Victoria, and the way Shawn pinned me against the bus. I tell him about sober kisses and drunk kisses and secrets—all of them, every single one.

"I feel like a fucking idiot," I finish. "I feel like I don't even know him. I guess I never did."

"What are you going to do?"

I press my knuckles into my eye. "I don't know."

"How do you not know?" Kale snaps. "Come home, Kit. Fuck him. He's not worth it." My twin's voice is stern, and there's no mistaking that he's related to Bryce, or Mason, or Ryan—or me. He's repeating the exact words he said to me that summer after our freshman year.

He's not worth it. He's not worth it. He's not worth it.

"Do you even know what the worst part is?" I ask, not waiting for an answer. "He told me not to tell anyone about us. He said I wasn't even allowed to tell *you*. I guess he just wanted me to be some dirty little fling again."

I can feel my brother's anger radiating through the phone during the silence that spans between us. I don't even hear him breathe, and in the quiet, I stare out the coffee shop window, watching the nine-to-five parade pass me by. Pantsuit, pantsuit, pantsuit, pantsuit. My eyes swing to the mismatched bracelets on my wrist and the chipped black polish on my nails, and I know with absolute certainty that I could never do what the people outside are doing—wake up at the same time every day, do the same job every day, come home at the same time, eat at the same time, go to bed at the same time. This band is my shot, my *one* big shot. And I want that, even if I don't want Shawn. Even if Shawn doesn't really want *me*. Even if he never did.

When Kale finally speaks again, his voice is a coiled snake. "Kit, listen to me. You need to come home. Right the hell now. Do you hear me?"

"We have a show tonight."

"So? Shawn is a fuc—"

"I'm not going to let the rest of the guys down just because Shawn's an asshole."

"Are you really sure they didn't know about that night too?" Kale snaps, and my heart sinks even further into my bottomless hole of a stomach.

"Mike didn't," I answer as I continue staring hopelessly out the coffee shop window. The sun is too bright, the glass is too clean, and I'm too many worlds away from home. I *do* just want to go home, but I can't. Not yet. "I don't think Adam or Joel do either," I finish.

"Just like you thought Shawn didn't…"

My knuckles gravitate to my eye again. "I don't know, Kale. This whole fucking thing is so fucking fucked."

A woman at a nearby table clears her throat in an obvious objection to my language, but I'd sooner bite her head off than worry about one more thing.

"Kit," Kale pleads, "just come home. This isn't worth it."

It's what he's been saying from the start—and from the start, he's probably been right. But here I am, with one show left to do, one day left to bear. "I'll be home tomorrow."

"No way—"

"Tomorrow, Kale. I'm finishing this."

It takes me forever to get Kale off the line, and after I finally manage it, I just sit there, staring at my phone and remembering Shawn's unopened text. I haven't wanted to *want* to read it—but here I am, *wanting*, staring. I watch the black screen until I light it up and make one final call.

"Did you just get off the phone with your brother?" Leti asks by way of greeting. He and I have kept in touch these past few weeks, but I haven't told him a thing about Shawn. He's asked, I've avoided, he's persisted, and I've changed the subject by getting him to dish about Kale.

"Yeah, why?" I rest my elbows on the table and slouch forward, burying a set of fingers under my hair. My forehead hovers over the laminate surface until I give up the good fight and let my head thump down against it.

"He's blowing up my phone."

"Tell him to get bent," I mutter to the floor.

"Oh, I just might, Kiterina. Do you know what he said to me the other day?"

"What?"

"That it was *easier* for me to come out than it would be for him. Just because I won prom queen does *not* mean it was easier!"

I wish I could laugh, but without the energy to even fake it, silence is all I can give.

"Okay," Leti says after I've been quiet too long. His tone has changed, becoming the tone of the guy who knew we were going to be friends before I even knew who he was, and who has always been there for me when I've needed him. "Tell me everything."

I unstick my forehead from the table and sit up, resting it heavily on the heel of my palm instead. "What did Kale tell you?"

"Nothing. I've been talking to you and ignoring his closeted ass."

The impatience in Leti's voice might sound like a joke to anyone else, but I know he's getting irritated, and I know Kale knows it too. Ever since Out, he and my look-alike have been kind of an item, but Kale wants to keep Leti a secret, and that's not the way to keep Leti at all.

"So are you going to start talking," Leti continues, "or should I start going into detail about the prom king and all the scandalous things we did in the limo after the—"

I interrupt Leti to tell him everything—everything I told Kale, from the beginning to the end. When he asks for details, I give them. When I realize I've forgotten something, I go back. I tell him every secret, every lie, every mistake.

"What did Kale say?" he asks when I'm finished.

"He told me to come home."

"Which means you decided you're staying."

"Do you think I should?" The question leaves me in a moment of weakness. I shouldn't need him to tell me what to do, but I just need someone—someone who hasn't inherited my stubbornness or infamous last name—to tell me something, anything, that will make this better.

"I think you're a bona fide rock goddess," Leti says. "I think you should do whatever the hell you want to do."

"What would you do?"

"Hmm," he hums, and I get a pang of homesickness as I picture his face and the vintage cartoon tee he's probably wearing. My Little Pony? Rainbow Brite? He pauses for a moment, and then he suggests, "Is Mike still single?"

I roll my eyes. "Thanks for the talk, Leti."

He snickers into the phone. "Look, Kit-stand, I'm not going to give you advice—"

"Apparently."

"Because you don't really want it. You only want me to tell you what you want to hear."

"And what's that?" I counter, not even trying to hide how frustrated I am. He's as bad as Kale. Worse.

"Shawn is an asshole and you should castrate him while he sleeps."

"Is that what I *need* to hear?" I counter, and a faint sigh drifts through the phone.

"Beats me. You're asking someone who's dating a guy who's still in the freaking closet."

WITH NO HELP from Kale, and even less help from Leti, I finish my coffee, order another, and wait for the clock to tick down. I arrive back at the bus just before morning soundcheck, toting a carrier full of specialty coffees and giving them to the guys with the fakest smile I've ever delivered. They immediately ask where I've been, and I put on the performance of my life. I pretend to not be broken. To not be an absolute wreck inside. My brain wants to hate Shawn. But my heart...my heart is useless.

Where was I? A walk to find a coffee shop. Why? Because I wanted to bring back a surprise. No more questions asked, and even though Shawn's eyes are curious, he says nothing that would make him seem any more or less concerned than anyone else—because we're a secret he's determined to keep. Or maybe because he just doesn't care.

I still have no idea what I'm going to do tomorrow, but for today, I have a plan, and that plan is to just get through it. I get through soundcheck, I get through lunch. I act normal. I play games with Mike, I make a casual phone call to my mom. I do whatever I need to do to avoid getting caught alone with Shawn.

That evening, I think about changing into something that will make his blood pump in all the right places and give him blue balls for the rest of his life. I could grab something from our boxes of Dee's merchandise, guaranteed to flaunt my ample chest, my tight stomach, my long legs...

But then I just say *fuck it* and grab the first clean things I find, not caring in the slightest that I turn out looking much more grunge than gorgeous. My jeans are tight and worn to pieces. My tank top is loose and falling apart at the collar. Complete with an oversized flannel, I look like I'm ready for a night on the couch instead of a show on the stage. I look like I'm ready for a tub of ice cream and a marathon of *Ice Road Truckers*, and if I had just listened to Kale when I had the chance, that's exactly what I'd be doing.

Instead, I drag my ass outside and sandwich myself between Mike and Joel to avoid walking next to Shawn. We haven't shared more than a few words since last night, and the short stroll to the venue is no different. But inside, swallowed by the darkness of the balcony, he places himself beside me.

I can feel his gaze burrowing into the side of my face, searching for something that's now missing between us, but I ignore it. And when he discreetly links his fingers with mine, one by one by one, I ignore that too. I silently stare over the railing, contemplating my next move. If I break this off between us—whatever *this* is—it will make things too easy for him. He'll get over me as easily as he had before, and I'll be the only one hurting.

He is the one who needs to hurt.

So instead of pulling away, I clasp my fingers with his, holding on tight and refusing to let go. I'm contemplating a million different ways to get even, each one threatening to destroy me just as much him, as I watch the crowd pour through the freshly opened doors. Red hair, brown hair, blue hair. Each one of those kids is already buzzing, ready for the best night of their lives, while I stand in the shadows with my hand trapped in Shawn's. Blonde hair, purple hair, pink hair. And then...

Black hair, black hair, black hair, black hair.

My hand wrenches from Shawn's when I suddenly gasp and grip the railing of the balcony, my eyes wide as I watch four extremely tall, extremely familiar, extremely far-from-home guys venture farther and farther inside. "Oh my God."

My knuckles flash white as I lean farther over the rail to get a better look. And, as if Kale can sense me, his chin turns up and our dark eyes lock. He elbows Mason, and Mason looks up too. Bryce, Ryan. "Shit!" I back away from the railing, running my fingers through the thick mess of my hair as I try to figure out what to do. My brothers are here. All FOUR of my fucking brothers.

Doing a kamikaze jump over the railing is sounding better and better and better.

"What?" Shawn asks, but I'm already making my way toward the stairwell. I look over my shoulder to see every single one of my bandmates following me. I hold up a hand. "Stay here."

Of course, they don't stay there. When I get down to my brothers, who are already busy scaring the shit out of the security guard they're dwarfing, four pairs of hard obsidian eyes skim over my face before stabbing a direct line of sight straight past me. They lock on the four pairs of eyes at my back—a rare gray-green, a boyish blue, a steady deep brown…and an enchanted, poisonous green.

Mason takes them in, his gaze sharpening before it challenges mine. "Outside. Now."

To me, his growled order is just my pigheaded older brother being his pigheaded bossy self. But to anyone else—

"Whoa," Shawn says, stepping past me defensively. "What's your problem?"

"Was I talking to you?"

The warning in Mason's voice triggers the sirens in my head, and instinctively, I grip Shawn's arm to keep him from moving even another half centimeter forward. I may want him to pay for what he's done to me, but that doesn't necessarily mean I want him to die tonight.

Unfortunately, Mason's black eyes narrow on my hand around Shawn's arm, and I'm pretty sure I just signed Shawn's death wish. I step forward in a hurry and do what I do best, throwing my attitude forward in an arrogant wave.

"Stop being an asshole, Mason. Say 'please' and maybe I'll think about it."

"Kit—" Ryan cautions, and I snap at him.

"Why are you guys even here?" I know it's because Kale opened his big fucking mouth, but I have no idea how much he told them. Enough to get them to come here, yeah. But judging by the fact that Shawn is still on his feet instead of lying in a bloody pulp on the floor, I'm also guessing that Kale didn't tell them about what happened six years ago, or about all of the confessions I made over the phone this morning.

"Kale told us you had a show not too far away," Mason spits, and even though he confirms Kale didn't say anything about me and Shawn, my twin is a dead man walking. I don't even bother looking at him, because when I *do* look at him, I'm pretty sure his eyes are going to be bugging out of his head from how hard I'll be strangling him.

"Nice of you to tell us you were on tour," Bryce complains, reminding me that I had told my family I wouldn't be able to make it to Sunday dinners because I'd started giving weekend guitar lessons, just like our mom always wanted. It was easier than telling them about the tour, about the band, about the hundred fibs I'd piled on top of each other.

"Nice of her to tell us she's in a band with the clowns from her high school," Mason snarls. Even without my brothers to back him, he'd still be this damn cocky. Big muscles, black tattoos, buzzed head. I cross my arms and stare him down.

"And you wonder why I didn't tell you."

"You didn't tell them?" Joel asks, but it's Adam's voice that makes things go from bad to *really* fucking bad.

"These are the crazy brothers you told us about?"

"Who the fuck are you calling crazy?" Mason growls.

"Uh, probably the big crazy dude with the big crazy eyes?"

I throw myself in Mason's path even before he takes his first step forward, knowing full well that he could knock Adam into next year and probably *will* if Adam doesn't learn to keep his mouth shut. The club is getting packed, and it's like every single light in the damn place is shining its bright heat on us—on the four giants at my back, the four giants at my front, and me in the middle, trying to control all eight of them like some insane miniature giant-tamer. "Look, guys," I say in my biggest voice, "we're about to go on. I'll talk to you after the—"

"No fucking way." Mason grabs my arm when I start to turn away from him, and then, the worst happens.

Shawn pushes his shoulder to knock his arm off me. And he doesn't back down.

In a blind panic, I push Shawn hard, so hard that he stumbles backward and nearly loses his balance. I'm so fucking pissed off, I don't know who I'm angrier at— Shawn for breaking my heart, or Mason for being *Mason*. I slam my open palms into Shawn's chest again, glaring at the way he looks at me—like I'm the one betraying him instead of the other way around.

I spin around when I can't stand to look at him anymore, getting all up in my violent older brother's face. "What the fuck are you so mad about?" I bark. "That I lied? I'm sorry! That I'm in a band with a bunch of players from high school? Not your fucking call!" He starts to interrupt, but I raise my voice even louder, like I'm screaming to the back of the fucking pit. "That I'm touring with them? I'm a grown fucking woman, and if you don't calm down right the fuck now, I'm getting you thrown the fuck out of here!" F-bombs are detonating left and right, each one doing nothing to calm the explosive rage inside me. Today was *so* not the day for Mason to push my last button. It had a big red sign on it that said Do Not Push, and like an idiot, Kale dragged him straight to it.

"Do you hear me?" I continue, knowing damn well that everyone within a five-mile radius heard my every last word just fine. "You have two options. Wish me a good show and I'll talk to you after, or keep pissing me off and go the fuck home."

My tone is deadly serious, and by the way Mason considers my words, he knows it. If he pushes his luck again,

I'll call security, and it'll take ten guys to throw him out, but they'll do it.

Dark eyes stay pinned on me until they lift to Shawn over my shoulder, and I watch as they transform into deadly black diamonds, promising untold pain if Shawn ever touches him again.

"You have two seconds," I warn.

Mason looks down at me, takes way longer than two seconds, and grunts. And when I see my opportunity, I lift onto my tiptoes and throw my arms around his neck like a snare, locking him in a strong-armed hug that I'm hoping cracks the shell he has up. I love my brother. I love my brother to death. And I won't hesitate to love him to death *right now* if he continues acting like a silverback gorilla on crack.

Luckily, his rock-hard shoulders soften under my embrace, losing the rest of their tension when I say, "I'm glad you're here. I missed you."

His tree-trunk arms lift to hug me back. "You're still in trouble."

"No, I'm not." I kiss him on the cheek and turn toward our other brothers. "If you can behave"—I lock eyes with every single one of them—"then you can watch from backstage. Can you behave?" When none of them answer, I sigh and say, "Fine, come with me."

WITH MY BROTHERS standing just offstage, I put on the performance of my life—just like every other night we've been on tour. I should be nervous. I should feel insecure. But instead, all I can think about is why they're here.

They're here to take me home.

And I'm going to let them.

Tonight is the last show. As soon as it's over, the band's plan is to drive the three hours to get back home. Adam and Joel have missed Rowan and Dee so much, I doubt they'll even spend much time with fans before climbing onto the bus. Instead, they'll probably pack the trailer in record time and get home well before sunrise.

I don't care when I get home. All I care about is that I don't have to hold Shawn's hand again tonight. I'll figure out what to do about him tomorrow, or the next day, or never. I really don't even care anymore. I just want to be *home*, in my own bed, in my own world. I want to be out of Shawn's.

I feel his green eyes on me as I play, and I gaze through the orange glow illuminating the stage to stare back at him. He's shouting lyrics into his backup mic, his fingers viciously strumming the strings of his guitar, looking like the rock god I could never help falling for. Every girl in this place is wishing they could go home with him tonight, and I'm the one who could. I could ditch my brothers, pull him somewhere private after the show. I could let him take me and pretend it means nothing to me. I could be his secret.

I could let him break my heart.

Again.

I watch him watching me, missing him already. I miss the dream of him. I miss the lie of us.

I look away because stupid tears are stinging, and the only way I fight them back is by pouring myself into the music. I close my eyes, I bounce with the beat. I jump, I spin, I shred my fucking guitar like it's never been shredded before. When I have a freestyle opportunity, I play my fucking heart out for him.

Because I'm *not* that same pathetic girl who thought her name wasn't worth telling. I'm Kit Fucking Larson. I'm a goddamn fucking rock star.

When I open my eyes again, the faces in the crowd are wild, and so am I. The pit is the sea in my storm, pitching crowd surfers over its waves. They reach for us with desperate fingers before getting snatched by security and tossed away. Adam is singing his heart out, Mike is pulverizing the drums, and the crowd is a thrashing, living beast dancing to our chaos. I play for them. For this.

I lose myself in the music, the motion, the lights. My heart pounds, my blood rushes, my skin blazes. In a damp shirt, with numb fingers, I hit a break in the song and pin my guitar pick between my lips, yanking off my flannel and chucking it into the crowd. The churning ocean catches it, and I watch it sink beneath the swell. Then I drop the pick back to my fingers and hit my next note— flawlessly, like the mid-song striptease was fucking *easy*.

It's the kind of show that should last forever. I'm the kind of lost that should never be found. But all too soon, our first "last song" ends and the guys and I walk offstage. My brothers are still there, Shawn is still breathing, and even though Adam is normally the one to rave about how great everyone was, tonight Bryce beats him to it.

"Holy shit!" he says while I wait for the backlash. I'm expecting my brothers to bitch about my career choices, clothing choices, life choices. But instead, he shouts, "You were fucking awesome!"

He claps me hard on the shoulder, and my thoroughly worked body nearly topples. But Mason catches me before I stumble, wrapping a big arm tight around my shoulder to hold me steady. "You're a damn rock star, sis."

I tilt my chin to stare up at his big smile…and then, I fucking *cry*. I hiccup, and then I *cry*.

I don't even know *why* I'm breaking down. Maybe because I'm happy my brothers love me. Maybe because I'm devastated Shawn doesn't. Maybe because I'm homesick. Maybe because I never want these past few weeks to end. Maybe because I'm not dreaming anymore. Maybe because I *can't*.

Kale's arms are the next to wrap around me, and I soon find myself smothered in a four-brother hug—in Mason's big arms, under Ryan's careful gaze, in front of Bryce's twice-broken nose, with Kale squeezing my shoulder until I pull myself together. They shield me from the world until the hiccups stop coming, and I kiss each one of them on the cheek before I let them go.

"Are you okay?" Ryan whispers in my ear on the last hug.

I sniffle and wipe my nose on the shoulder of his button-down shirt. "Yeah, I think I'm just a little homesick. Are you guys driving home tonight?"

He pulls away to study me. "Yeah, why?"

"Do you have room for me?"

I force a reassuring smile at his worried expression, and eventually, he nods. "Of course we have room for you. Come on…Let's get you home."

Chapter Nineteen

ARE WE OKAY?

In the light streaming through my childhood bedroom window, I read Shawn's text for the millionth time.

We're fine, I typed back last night on the car ride home with my brothers. Ryan's SUV was a mobile interrogation unit, and I wasn't sure which made me feel worse—dealing with their questions, or drifting farther away from Shawn, mile by mile, minute by minute. I felt like I should have confronted him, should have called him out about everything and heard what he had to say for himself. But I wanted him to come to *me*. I wanted him to come clean while he had the chance, to tell me he cared about me enough to shout it to the whole world. But he never did.

We don't feel fine.

You're coming to meet my parents tomorrow.

My thumbs punished the letters on my touchpad as I typed. I was angry with my brothers for inviting the band to a Saturday family dinner, angry with the band for agreeing to come, and most of all, angry with Shawn. For everything. When my brothers invited the guys to dinner before we left for home, I tried to object, but without being able to give the real reason, it was pointless. It was four against one. Even Kale wasn't on my side, and Shawn said nothing. He just stared at me like I had broken his heart and not the other way around.

I guess losing a toy can be pretty devastating.

You've been avoiding me since this morning.

"What are you doing?" Kale asks, and I look to my doorway to see my twin leaning against the jamb. I hadn't responded to Shawn's text last night, and I woke up this morning to one more.

I'm sorry.

I lay in bed with my heart pounding so hard, it threatened to throw my covers off me. He was apologizing. Too late, but he was doing it.

For what? I typed back. My fingers were shaking, the mangled pieces of my jigsaw heart quivering as they promised to either put themselves together or impale themselves into the walls of my chest.

For everything.

When I put down my phone, Kale must be able to see the hurt that swallowed me whole this morning. It must be written all over my face, because he sits on my bed and frowns at me. "What did he say?"

I hand my phone over, and my twin's brow furrows at the text conversation he pulls up. "For *everything*? What the hell does that mean?"

When his black eyes flick up to mine for an answer, all I can do is shake my head and stare at him through a blurry veil of tears, a wall that I refuse to let crumble. Kale's hard expression immediately softens, and my voice breaks when I say, "I don't know."

He's sorry for *everything*. For sleeping with me six years ago? For leading me on? For never calling? For lying about forgetting me. For kissing me on the tour. For making me think we could ever *be* something.

"Jesus, Kit," Kale says as he pulls me into a hug. He shifts on the bed until I'm wrapped tightly in his arms, and I turn my face into his shoulder to dry my eyes, but I don't break down. If I break down now—if I break down *again*—I'm afraid I'll never be able to put myself back together. "Tell me how to fix this."

"You can't."

"What can I do then?"

"Nothing."

He squeezes me tighter, rubbing my arm like he's trying to physically wipe the pain off of me. If only it was that easy. "Who do I call to cancel this dinner tonight?"

"No one."

"What do you mean, 'no one'?"

When I sit up straight, his hand slowly slips away from my shoulder. I take a deep breath until I can see clearly again. "I don't want to cancel. I'm not quitting the band, and you know Mase and Ry and Bryce are still going to want to meet everyone."

I've thought about it—a lot—and I want to stay in the band. I won't be Shawn's toy, not anymore, but that isn't going to stop me from being the rhythm guitarist for The Last Ones to Know. I've worked too hard, have given too much. I'm not walking away. Not now.

"Not if they knew—" Kale starts.

"But they *don't* know…They're never going to."

"So you're just going to—"

"Let Shawn come."

Kale studies me for a long time, his lip twisting and disappearing between his teeth before reappearing an entire shade brighter. "Kit…"

I just sit there staring flatly at him, resolute despite my own apprehension. It's probably a terrible idea to let the band come tonight, but Kale and I both know I'm right—my brothers will insist on meeting them sometime, and if I cancel dinner tonight, it will only trigger the alarms in their heads. It'll only make things worse.

Kale sighs when he realizes I've already made up my mind. "What are you going to say to him?"

I shake my head. "Nothing. It's done."

"Bullshit," he says. "You guys are never done."

"We weren't ever *not* done."

"You're stupid."

With my legs crisscrossed and my hands curled around my shins, I furrow my brows at him. "*You're* stupid."

"At least I'm not delusional," he argues with his legs crisscrossed and his hands on his shins, my mirror image.

"Oh yeah?" I'm about to throw Leti in his face, about to call Kale delusional for thinking he'll be able to keep him while still hiding who he is from the rest of the world, but I bite my tongue.

Hurt flashes across his face anyway, and I realize it's too late. He's done that annoying twin-telepathy thing again, and I've already said too much.

"Well, whatever," I say to end the conversation, hating my quick tongue and even quicker temper. I let myself collapse back against my pillows to avoid having to acknowledge the damage I've caused in the person I care about most.

"I know Leti and I are done too," Kale says. "You don't have to tell me."

"I didn't tell you," I counter without conviction.

"You might as well have."

When I say nothing, Kale sighs and stretches out on my bed. My feet are by his head and his are by mine. "You could fix it, you know."

He doesn't argue, and he doesn't agree. Instead, he considers what I said for a moment, and then he presses his gross-ass sock against my cheek. I knock it away, and he counterattacks by rubbing both sets of funky toes all over my face. I yell and scramble to push him away, he laughs and accidentally kicks me in the eye, and all hell breaks loose. Kale and I attack each other with toes and heels and ankles—until he gets a bloody nose and I get a throbbing knot on the back of my head from falling off the bed. We're both laughing hysterically as we nurse our wounds when Bryce walks in, rubbing the sleep from his eyes and scowling at us.

"What the fuck is wrong with you two?"

With his head tilted back and his fingers pinching the bridge of his nose, Kale mutters, "What the fuck is wrong with *you*?"

And then, I laugh so hard, I can't breathe. I laugh until I snort, which only makes me laugh harder. I laugh until this morning almost seems to not matter, and this evening almost seems far enough away.

Almost.

"Are those two up?" my mom yells from the bottom of the stairs.

"They're bleeding all over Kit's comforter!" Bryce shouts back, and I sneer at him when he rats us out.

"WOULD EVERYONE SHUT THE HELL UP," Mason hollers from behind his closed bedroom door. A split second passes before he quickly amends, "NOT YOU, MOM," but my mom is already trumping up the stairs, and I'm already laughing myself breathless again.

There are the familiar sounds of her feet pattering down the hall, Mason's door squeaking open, and my brother grunting while my mom smacks the crap out of him. The whole thing is punctuated by Kale's socked feet thudding past Mason's room to get to the bathroom, because he's laughing too hard to keep the blood from spurting from his nose. Bryce continues rubbing the sleep from his eyes like all of this is normal—because it is, and the tears that wet the corners of my eyes are only partly from laughing so hard.

It feels good to be home...safe—bloody noses and all.

"Kit," my mom says after she nudges Bryce out of my doorway. She crosses the distance to my bed and wraps me in her arms. "You're in so much trouble, young lady." She rubs her hand up and down my spine before pulling away and capturing my chin in her hand. She turns my face from side to side to side. "What have you been eating? Have you lost weight? You look like you've lost weight..."

"Kale kicked me in the face," I snitch, and she huffs at me.

"Come downstairs so I can feed you something." She pats Bryce on the shoulder before she leaves my room, and from the hallway, she scolds Kale. "Don't kick your sister in the face."

"She broke my nose!" Kale shouts after her as her footsteps clack against the stairs.

"You probably deserved it!"

"KALE, YELL ONE MORE TIME AND YOUR NOSE IS GOING TO GET BUSTED FOR REAL," Mason bellows from his room, and this time, Kale and I both shut up. But when Bryce winks at me and disappears, I know nothing good is about to happen.

Bryce becomes a drummer as feverish as Mike as he pounds bloody murder against Mason's freshly closed door, and he gets a nasty case of karma when he slips on the hardwood while trying to escape down the stairs. Mason is on him two seconds later, and by the time Kale and I descend the stairs to get to the breakfast my mom is setting on the table, Bryce is nothing but a groaning, battered heap on the floor. We gingerly step over him and take the seats we've had since we were old enough not to use high chairs.

The morning is filled with my mom's own personal brand of interrogation, which I'm guessing is where my brothers learned it. Why'd I lie about the band I was in? Because I knew my brothers would overreact. Why didn't I tell anyone about the tour? Because I knew my brothers would overreact. Why didn't I tell *her* about the tour?...Because I'm a bad daughter, I'm sorry.

Did I meet anyone special while I was away? Are any of the boys in the band cute? Do I like any of them?

No. No. Not in a million years.

I lie by the skin of my teeth, and if she can tell, she doesn't say anything. My brothers provide commentary after every question and answer, and eventually, my dad puts his daily paper down and tells everyone to let me eat in peace.

"Did you at least have fun, Kitten?" he asks, and I force a smile at him that eventually becomes genuine.

The tour was unforgettable. I'll never forget the bad parts, but I'll never forget the good parts either. I'll never forget the shows, the fans, the friends I made. I'll never forget how insane opening for Cutting the Line was, or how ridiculous rating groupies afterward with the guys felt. I'll never forget getting my ass handed to me by Mike at *Call of Duty*, or nights spent taking shots with the rest of the guys every time he made a headshot. Part of me missed my brothers back at home, but the other part of me already misses the ones I gained on tour.

"Yeah, Dad, I did."

"Well, good then. Now eat your eggs. You're getting scrawny."

I finish breakfast thinking of Mike, of Joel, of Adam. And even though I try not to, I think of Shawn. My mom's coffee doesn't taste like his, and I find myself wondering what he's doing as I sip it. I check my phone once, twice, a million times, and throughout the day, Kale mirrors my every move. He never hears from Leti, I never hear from Shawn, and as the hour hand on the clock ticks up—one, two, three, four—I type a million texts I never send.

Don't come tonight.

Are you still coming tonight?

What does sorry for *everything* mean?

Why didn't you want anyone to know about us?

What the fuck does *everything* mean?

I hate you.

Please don't come tonight.

I loved you.

I never wanted this.

At five 'til six, I type two words and finally press SEND.

Don't come.

But at 6:02, the doorbell rings and my heart plummets through the floorboards beneath my feet. Ryan answers the door, and I let the sound of voices draw me to the foyer.

Shawn's eyes find mine across the room, giving no indication if he read my text yet or not. His shirt isn't faded. His jeans aren't torn. He looks…nice. God, really nice. He looks like someone I could bring home to meet my mom and dad.

I wish someone had slammed the door in his face.

"Is this them?" my mom asks from behind me, and I silently squeeze myself against the wall to let her pass. The rest of the band is making their way into my house, all looking equally as presentable—all except for Joel's blond Mohawk, and Adam's black nails, torn jeans, stacks of bracelets, and…well…yeah, everything about Adam, who would probably show up at his own grandmother's funeral wearing the same stuff.

Shawn introduces himself first and holds out his hand, but my mom ignores it and pulls him in for a hug instead. He hugs her back, his gaze locking with mine over her shoulder. I don't know if he wants to talk to me because of the texts I didn't send, or because of the text I did send, but either way, I look down at my socks to keep from falling for the spell in his eyes again.

"And you must be Adam," my mom says as she begins moving through the band one by one. Shawn shakes hands with my dad, who dragged himself from the den, and I slip closer to my brothers. Kale presses his shoulder against mine, reminding me I'm not alone.

My dad asks the guys which instrument each of them plays, and when Mike says he plays the drums, my dad starts talking about how my Uncle Pete played the drums in high school. All of the guys entertain his reminiscing as they follow him to the den, and somehow, I end up at the back of the man-parade with Shawn on one side and Kale on the other. I'm ignoring everything that isn't front and center, but when Shawn clasps his hand with mine and tugs me to a stop, I have no choice but to stay in the hall with him or risk causing a scene. Kale stops too.

"Can we talk?" Shawn asks.

"Can we not?"

"What's this about?" He shows me his phone, confirming that he got my text, and when I meet his eyes again, I can tell it isn't something he's going to let me ignore. With a sigh, I nod at Kale, giving him the okay to leave us for a minute. He doesn't look happy, but when I nod again, he reluctantly slips into the den.

"Why'd you come here tonight when I asked you not to?" I snap at Shawn as soon as we're alone.

"I was less than ten minutes away from your house," he snaps back.

"So?" God, I sound like a child. And by the way his brows knit, he knows it.

"So...what the hell, Kit?"

Kale pops his head around the corner, since he's obviously been eavesdropping and doesn't like the way Shawn's talking to me. "Are you guys coming?"

"In a minute," I say, and when he gives me a look and disappears again, I resume barking at Shawn. "Can we just get through this? Then you can go back to being sorry. For *everything*." I practically spit the last word, and then I escape to the den before he can stop me. I ungracefully plop down on the arm of Mason's chair, gnawing on the inside of my lip to keep my lightning-quick tongue from striking out again.

It takes approximately two and three-quarters seconds for me to regret the past one and one-quarter minutes. I release my lip, glance at Shawn when he enters the room, and then bite down on it again. That didn't go at all like I had planned. I didn't keep my cool. I wasn't aloof or even halfway professional. God, it was like the scorned fifteen-year-old girl inside of me clawed her way to the surface and threw her little fit.

But who was I to deny her?

Can we *talk*? No, we cannot fucking talk. There's nothing to talk about. All we'd be able to talk about is all the things we *weren't*, and what the hell is the point in talking about something that never mattered and never will?

I should have known better. I shouldn't have expected a call from him six years ago, I shouldn't have expected anything but more bullshit from him from the moment I joined the band, and I shouldn't have expected this to end in anything but disaster.

I'm sorry too. Sorry for *everything*.

"She used to have this little Mattel four-wheeler," my dad says. "Used to raise hell on that thing."

"Ass naked," Ryan adds, bringing me back to the present.

My dad chuckles. "Just her in her little diaper."

I look down at Mason. "Is this really happening?"

He grins at me before turning toward the guys. "Who wants to see pictures?"

I punch him in the arm, and he pushes me off the chair.

"Dad," Bryce says as I force my ass onto the cushion with Mason, "you should've seen her last night. She was amazing."

When my mom calls us out for dinner, the conversation continues as we migrate to the dining room, drawn by my mom's dinner-bell voice and the smell of a fifteen-pound turkey. Wooden chairs scrape against the hardwood floor as everyone seats themselves at the table that my mother set for eleven—with Shawn hijacking the spot right next to me. I ignore him and look *anywhere* else.

My mom is the last to sit down at the immaculately set table, her smile bright as she grins at the mess of overgrown boys stuffed into her dining room. "I just want to thank you kids for coming tonight. And for being so good to Kit. Even though I really think all of you need to eat better while traveling—"

"Mom," I interject, and a few snickers sound throughout the room. Joel and Adam grin at my mom like she's the best thing since fried cheese.

My mom takes my cue and gets back to her point. She raises her water glass. "To good friends and good food."

Everyone raises a glass in a toast, and before mine is even back on the table, all four of my brothers stand at once to grab the best parts of the turkey. I chuckle as I catch Adam, Joel, and Mike sharing looks from my dad's end of the table, but they catch on quick. Within seconds, we're all on our feet except my dad, who waits for my mom to make him a plate, since she's always liked waiting on him and he's never minded it.

I circle the table to get some space from Shawn, but my plate fills up quickly, leaving me no choice but to sit back down at his side.

"Oh my Goddd," Joel groans as he chews on his first bite of my mom's turkey. "This is the best turkey I've ever had."

She beams, and I catch Mason grinning approvingly. But then he catches me catching him, and he ditches the smile. "So, Adam, I kind of remember you from high school," he says, and the fact that he's talking at all means he's up to no good.

"Oh yeah?" Adam asks. He's seated between Joel and Ryan, reaching across the table to grab a dinner roll.

"Actually, I don't think I remember you. I just heard a lot about you."

Adam smirks like he knows what's coming. "People like to talk."

Undeterred, Mason continues prodding. "Yeah, they said *a lot* of things."

My mom takes the bait, her brow furrowed as she washes down a bite of stuffing. "What kind of things?"

"Adam hooked up with practically every chick in school," Bryce offers with unbridled admiration. I'd reach across the table and punch him in the head if I thought I could even make a dent in his caveman-thick skull.

"Oh…" my mom says. She glances at me, and I sigh. "Adam has a girlfriend now. So does Joel."

"Does Van Erickson have a girlfriend?" Mason goads.

"Who's Van Erickson?" my mom asks, but Joel is already chuckling and giving Mason an answer.

"He has tons of them."

My mom starts asking who he is again, but Mason interrupts her. "Was one of them my sister?"

This time, Mike is the one to set his fork on his plate and stare at my brother like he's an idiot. "Do you really think your sister would be Van Erickson's *groupie*?"

"Thank you!" I say with my hands thrown dramatically in the air.

Ryan grins and finally answers my mom. "Van Erickson is some big rock star. Kit's band opened for them a few days ago."

"One of the biggest rock stars there is," Kale adds to throw glitter on my parade. When I look at him, wondering how the hell the guys know about us opening for Van in the first place, Kale shrugs and swings his finger at all four of them. "They looked you up online. There *is* this thing called the Internet, you know."

"She gave him a wet willy," Shawn volunteers from beside me, and the entire table explodes with laughter.

I'm staring at Shawn, wondering why he's acting like he's proud of me or something, when Bryce shouts, "She did not!"

Shawn gives a half smile and nods. "Five seconds after meeting him."

Even Mason laughs so hard he has to set his drumstick down. My dad joins in from the end of the table.

"Kit," my mom manages through giggles, "did you really?"

I shrug. "He deserved it."

Shawn grins at me, but the gaze I return to him is hard. This doesn't make us friends. This doesn't make us even. And it sure as hell doesn't make us okay.

I thought I could pretend not to hate him, but I can't. Not with him smiling at me like it's *okay* to smile at me. The light fades from his eyes, his lips, his face, and we're just staring at each other with a million unspoken things in the air.

Don't come, I texted him. And now all I'm thinking is, *Get up, go home, don't call me. Ever.*

"That's so badass." Bryce praises my wet willy incident and then turns to my mom. "Mom, you should've seen her onstage last night. She was such a fu—" He coughs to stop himself from getting whacked in the head for cursing. "Freaking rock star. She took her shirt off and threw it out into the crowd and—"

"She took *her shirt off*?" my mother practically shrieks, stealing my attention from Shawn. But then his hand finds mine under the table, and when he tries to hold it, I jerk it out of his grasp.

My fists start to shake. My arms, my legs. What the fuck does he think he's *doing*?

I don't look at him. I can't. I'm two seconds from standing up and running from the table in an angry fit of tears. Either that, or stabbing a fork in his eye.

He tried to hold my hand. Why *the fuck* did he try to hold my hand?

"Her flannel," Kale corrects Bryce, but Mason cuts in before my mom can be relieved.

"She was practically getting naked."

I break my thoughts from Shawn to glare at Mason from across the table. He challenges me with his stare, and I'm silently promising to murder him, when a pea hits me right in the cheek. Ryan laughs down at his plate, and I make a mental note to get revenge for the pea after dinner, because if I do anything about it now, every single person at this table will end up covered in mashed potatoes—and Shawn will probably end up with a chair smashed over his head.

"No more taking clothes off," my dad proclaims with his eyes on the stuffing he's soaking in gravy, and everyone at the table snickers. Everyone but me and Shawn.

"So, Mike," my mom says when the madness has died down, "what about you? Have a girlfriend?"

He shakes his head as he finishes chewing his food. "Not for a while."

My mom shoots me a quick smile, and I roll my eyes.

"Oh," she says. "Why not? A handsome guy like you, I figured you'd be beating them away with one of your drumsticks."

"Nah," Mike says with a bashful smile and his cheeks turning pink, "I leave that to Adam and Shawn."

My mom turns her mischievous grin on the boy who broke my heart. "No girlfriend for you either?"

When Shawn's gaze slowly lifts to lock with mine, I curse the day he was born. I curse the day *I* was born. There's not a damn person at this table who doesn't see the way he's looking at me—except maybe my dad, since he's eyeball-deep in stuffing—and Shawn's answer makes things even worse. "I'm not sure."

"Oh?" my mom asks, and Shawn holds my lethal gaze for a moment longer before finally turning away.

"I don't know."

He doesn't *know*? He lies to me for months, keeps me a dirty secret, apologizes for *everything*, shows up at my house after I ask him not to come, tries to hold my hand when I'd obviously rather shove his in a meat grinder, and he doesn't *know*?

"What's not to know, sweetie?"

I surprise myself by slamming my fork down so hard on my plate, even my dad gives me his undivided attention. Ten sets of eyes are on me when I snap at everyone, "I can actually think of a lot of things you don't know." With all those eyes on me, with Shawn at my side playing the victim, I can't stop. I see the cliff I'm about to career off of, and my foot punches the gas. This has been a long time coming. Six fucking years, and then some. Everything I've ever wanted to say to Shawn comes exploding to the surface, and I say it in front of *everyone*.

With my dark eyes bouncing between my brothers, I bark, "Like, did you know that Shawn fucked me at Adam's party the day you guys graduated?"

The way I stare around at all four of their white-stricken faces without batting an eye stands testament to how much of my mind has officially left the building. Even the guys from the band have lost their color, but more and more secrets keep pouring from my mouth.

"That was the reason I was so depressed that summer. He asked for my number like he was going to call me, but then he never did. He fucked me in Adam's bedroom and then he *never even called me*."

Everyone just sits there, stunned into frozen silence, and I laugh when I remember the most important detail. My head whips in Shawn's direction, my fierce gaze stabbing him between the eyes.

"Wait, I haven't even gotten to the best part yet! Did you know that was the night I lost my virginity?"

His face falls, and I go for the kill.

"Yeah, Shawn, that was my FIRST fucking time. I wanted it to be you. I wanted you to be the one, because you were the only boy I EVER fucking loved. And still, you're the only one…the only one I've ever…"

Tears scorch my eyes, and my voice cracks. When I glare at him from inches away, a few spill into the void between us. I blink hard and shake my head to regain my composure—however unstable it was in the first place. Turning my hard stare on my brothers and everyone else gaping at me at the table, I continue raving.

"I was *fifteen years old*, and then he just picked up and moved and never thought of me again. And I thought he didn't remember who I was when I auditioned, but it turns out, he's known this entire fucking time. And then he asked me to go out with him, and you know what? I said yes." I start laughing again, or sobbing—the sounds blend together in the hysteria I'm in. "But then, he said I wasn't even allowed to tell anyone. Because he never wanted anyone to know. All I've ever been is a dirty, pathetic, disposable fucking secret to him." My anger bubbles to the surface once more, and when I turn my head and latch on to Shawn's wide green eyes again, I scream at the top of my lungs. "Isn't that fucking right, Shawn?"

I'm pretty sure words start coming from his mouth, but it's lost under the sound of my chair crashing to the floor. I stand up so violently from the table that it flies backward and topples, and I'm pretty sure I broke it, but I don't fucking care. I'm storming away from him, from everyone.

"Kit!" Shawn's voice calls, and I hear a chorus of chairs scraping against hardwood, the thunder of footsteps following me.

I don't stop until I'm at the front door. When I turn around, Shawn is right there. I swing open the door and stand on the threshold.

"Where are you going?" he pants, and if I didn't know better, I'd think the look in his eyes is panic. Regret. A million things that I want to believe are there, but that I know damn well are not.

"NOWHERE."

With the force of a woman's scorn, I snare my fingers in the front of his shirt and yank him toward the door. Then I spin around and push him so hard, he stumbles backward onto my porch. I barely catch the pleading look he gives me before I slam the door as hard as I can in his face. The foundation shakes, my hands shake, the world crumbles, and when I turn around, *everyone* is staring at me. *Everyone* knows.

My mom, my dad, my brothers, the band. All of them are staring shell-shocked at me as I put all of my effort into simply staying on my feet. My heart is jackhammering against my ribs, threatening to tear me apart from the inside out. My skin shrinks along with the rest of me, and I can tell my eyes are wild. I'm trapped in open space with nowhere else to run.

In an attempt to stay on my feet, I find my twin's face in the crowd, but his eyes are just as panicked as mine. I'm falling, sinking, and he's feeling every bit of my desperation, making it his own.

I want to run. I want to hide. But there's nowhere, nowhere, nowhere. I'm shaking in my own skin, about to lose what's left of my dignity as I break down in hysterical, inconsolable, mortifying tears right here on my foyer floor—but before I can, before I can make the worst night of my life so, so much worse, Kale shouts at the top of his lungs, his voice echoing off the walls—

"I'M GAY!"

Chapter Twenty

MY MOM PASSED the fuck out.

One minute, she was gaping at me, at Kale, at me, at Kale, and then her eyes just kind of rolled back in her head and she dropped like a sack of bricks.

Mike half caught her since everyone else was too busy doing the same thing my mom had been doing—big eyes darting from me, to Kale, to me, to Kale.

Fast-forward to Ryan rushing to call an ambulance, a swirl of red and blue lights flashing through our windows, a team of medics sprinting into our foyer…and, yeah, tonight was a disaster of epic fucking proportions.

"She's going to be okay?" Kale asks the medic standing on our doorstep, guilt weighing down his words.

"She'll be fine," the EMT assures him. "Just keep her hydrated and make sure she takes it easy."

I don't watch the ambulance pull away—because Shawn is still out there somewhere. When my mom finally regained consciousness and we were waiting for the ambulance, Adam gave me a quick hug, told me Shawn is an asshole, and went out to stand by his best friend's side. But Mike and Joel are still in my house, with Mike running his hands anxiously through his hair and Joel gnawing on a thumbnail, neither of them knowing what to say or what to do.

Tiny step by tiny step, Joel backs toward the front door. "I'm…just gonna…" When he's almost there, he stops to rub the back of his neck. "Do you need me for anything?"

I shake my head. "Go."

"I'll see you next practice?"

"Yeah," I say, not sure if I'm lying to him or not.

Joel slips outside, and Mike sighs before wrapping me in a strong hug. He keeps me pinned tightly against him when he says, "Look, Kit, Shawn only told me what happened between you guys after I found you on the roof, and when he told me…it's not like he was proud of it. He knows he messed up." Mike pulls away to study me, concern coloring his deep brown eyes. "If I had known you didn't know—"

"Don't say it." I know he wouldn't have told me, and then I never would have known.

Mike frowns. "I'm just saying…" Another sigh escapes him. "If you really do love him—"

"Mike."

"You should give him another chance. That's all I'm saying." When I just stare at him, he adds, "I really do think you're good for each other, and I really do think he cares about you." When I open the door a little wider for him to leave, he takes the hint. But just as I'm about to close it, his hand wraps around the edge and his head pokes back inside. "Don't leave the band over this."

"I'll call you."

The frown he gives me says he isn't satisfied with my answer, but he releases the door and leaves anyway, and then it's just me and Kale standing helplessly in my foyer. I lean back against the door and close my eyes. "You didn't have to do that."

Of all the ways Kale imagined coming out, I'm sure that yelling "I'm gay!" at the top of his lungs in a room full of strangers wasn't one of them.

"I know."

"What are we going to do now?"

"Dad said we're supposed to meet everyone in the den."

I open my eyes, dead serious when I say, "Want to run away instead?"

"Only if we can be snake charmers."

"I hate snakes."

"Looks like we're staying then."

When I frown at Kale, he gives me a weak smile and pulls me into a tight hug—the kind that prevents you from breathing or thinking or feeling. I give him the same kind.

"I'm with you," he says, and I tuck my face into the crook of his shoulder.

"I'm with you too."

"Then we'll get through this."

"I know."

"Are you ready?"

"No. Are you?"

Kale shakes his head against my cheek. "Not even close."

Shoulder to shoulder, we cross the distance to the den and step down into it. My mom is lying on the couch, her head on my dad's lap as he presses a damp washcloth against her cheeks. She sits up as soon as she sees us, batting my dad's hands away when he tries to force her back down.

My brothers are camped on chairs and arms of chairs and the brick base of our fireplace. No one says a word. Everyone just stares and swallows and blinks and stares.

Kale sucks his lip between his teeth. I twirl the diamond in my nose.

"Why didn't you tell us?" Bryce begins, and both Kale and I stare back at him. I don't know who he's talking to, since he's looking at both of us, and neither Kale nor I are in a rush to answer him. "It doesn't matter," he continues. "So you like dudes, so what."

When I gaze over at Kale, his eyes are already glistening. God, I want to hug him. I want to wrap him protectively in my arms. But Bryce beats me to it. He crosses the distance in no time, yanking my brother into a hug that brings tears to my eyes too. My hand lifts to my mouth, and I step away to give them space.

"You're my brother," Bryce says, and those three words say everything. When he pulls away, he smiles at Kale. And then he pushes his shoulder and crosses the room to sit back down.

Kale stares at everyone else—at our mom, our dad, at Mason, at Ryan. My mom slides her feet from the couch and pats the cushion next to her. "Come sit down."

My brother does as he's told, and my mom takes his hands in hers. "Before I say anything, tell me this isn't just something you did to help Kit out."

Kale silently shakes his head.

"And the reason you've been checking your phone for days…"

"Leti," Kale answers, and I hold my breath as I wait to see what everyone does.

A soft smile curls my mom's lips. "But before Leti, you were still…"

"Still gay," Kale confirms, and my mom's eyes drift to mine.

"And you knew?"

I swallow thickly. "Since sixth grade."

She lets that sink in, but it's Mason who barks out a response, his black eyes pinned on my twin. "Since *sixth grade*? You've been keeping this from us for…for…How many fucking years is that?"

"Ten," Ryan answers, disappointment quieting his voice. "Ten years. Kale…why? Why would you…" He chokes up and rubs his eyes, and Kale wipes the heel of his palm under his own thick lashes. "I don't understand," Ryan finishes.

My dad reaches over and pats Ryan's knee, and Kale stares down at his feet. "I'm sorry."

"What the hell are you apologizing for?" Mason snaps, and Kale just shakes his head at his socks.

In a quiet, broken voice, he says, "I don't know."

"It better be for waiting so long to tell us, and not for anything else," Mason warns, and a tiny gasp leaves my mouth. He is furious—furious with Kale for not telling us and for hiding who he is. For nothing else.

Kale looks up again, his eyes trained on our brother until the tears start to slip down his cheeks. When I lift my fingers to my own, I realize they're just as wet.

Mason curses and stands up, yanking Kale off the couch and breaking his back in a hug. "I fucking love you, Kale. Stop being a baby."

Kale laughs through quiet tears, and my dad is the next to stand. He pulls Kale in for another bone-crushing hug, and one by one, my family accepts him. They forget about me until a sob bubbles out of my chest and all eyes turn my way.

"Oh, for Christ's sake, Kit," Mason says. "Get over here."

It's corny. It's the corniest family hug in the history of family hugs everywhere. But it heals some broken part inside Kale, or at least I hope it does. Ten years of fearing this moment, and the only thing anyone is upset about is the fact that he spent ten years fearing this moment.

"So...Leti, huh?" my dad asks, and Kale blushes as red as Bryce's sneakers.

"I knew there was something going on with you two," Bryce chimes in, but Mason laughs and elbows him in the arm.

"Did not."

"Did too!"

I'm smiling when my mom's hand lands on my shoulder. "Don't think we've forgotten about you," she warns.

My heart sinks, and the quietness between us spreads throughout the room. Kale's moment is up, and now it's mine. And mine isn't going to be nearly as Hallmark, because I'm pretty sure my family's introduction to it involved me shouting the word *fuck*—a *lot*.

"Can we talk about it tomorrow?" I ask, taking a step backward, toward the doorway of the room.

"Sit down," my dad orders, and I do as I'm told. "Now, the rest of you, out."

My brothers begin to protest, but when his gaze is just as hard and stony as theirs, they groan and follow his orders. Even Kale has to leave, closing the door behind him and leaving only my mom and my dad sitting on the couch cushion next to me.

I swallow thickly.

"I'm not going to yell at you about what happened at dinner," my dad says, and my brain takes a minute to process and then reprocess his words.

"You're not?"

He shakes his head. My mom is holding his hands on her lap, in silent support of everything he's saying. "Nope. I'm going to keep you in here for five minutes so your brothers think we handled it, and then I'm going to let you go."

My mom stares at him over her shoulder, a soft smile touching her face. Then she turns back toward me and says, "Do you want to talk to us about anything though? Or just me...I can kick your dad out."

I can't help laughing a little despite the vise-grip squeezing my heart. "I don't think so."

"You sure, honey?"

I take a deep breath and nod. "I'm sure."

"Okay. Well, then I'm just going to tell you this one thing, and then you can go." I wait, and she pats my knee. "That Shawn boy is a fucking tool if he doesn't see how special you are."

I gape at my mom and the curse word she just blatantly said, and she nods to emphasize her point, absolutely serious.

"A motherfucking *tool*."

And oh God, I can't help it—I start laughing. Hard. And both she and my dad smile at the sound.

"Any boy who wants to keep you a secret isn't one worth getting angry over," she adds. "Kick his ass to the curb. But I will tell you this…" She squeezes my knee before letting go. "I saw the way he looked at you tonight, and when you stormed away from the table, he didn't seem to want to keep you a secret then. He was out of his chair even before your brothers, and do you know what he did? He chased after you. He didn't hesitate."

I chew on the inside of my cheek, the lightness gone from my broken heart. It's heavy again—jagged, confused, bleeding.

"I don't know exactly what happened between you two in high school," she continues.

"Don't want to know," my dad tosses in.

"But…I just saw him, okay? I just…I saw how fast he ran."

I don't know what to say to that, so I say nothing. And when my dad checks his watch and says I can go, I go.

MY BEDROOM DOOR is locked that night when someone knocks on it for the thirty-millionth time. First, it was Mason. Then Bryce. Then Mason. Then Ryan. Then Mason. Then Mason again. Now...

"What's the password?" I yell to the closed door, and Kale yells back, "Bangarang!"

I can't help cracking a weak smile as I drag myself off my bed to let him in. I have no idea why he yelled "bangarang," but I kind of love him for it. The password thing is a game we've played since we were little—there never is a password and never has been, but for years, we had my brothers convinced that I made up a new one every day, and that Kale was the only one who ever knew what it was.

When I swing open the door, he slips inside before any of my brothers can careen down the hallway to barge their way in. I'll talk to them eventually. Just...not tonight. Tonight, I don't need their personal brand of psychosis. I have enough of my own.

"Hey," Kale says as I engage the thirty-dollar lock I bought with the money I got for my eleventh birthday. When you have four brothers and are starting to wear training bras, you have priorities.

"Hey." I plop down next to him when he makes himself at home on my bed.

"So tonight was pretty epic."

I force a fragile smile. For him, tonight will always be the night his heart became whole. For me...tonight will be the night I threw mine outside. "Have you told Leti yet?" I ask.

"Not yet. I wanted to talk to you first."

"About what?" I ask a dumb question, and he gives me a dumb answer.

"Oh, I don't know. Did you hear the Patriots beat the Packers last week?"

He meets my flat stare with a flat stare of his own, and I sigh.

"What did Mom and Dad say?" he asks, and a little chuckle escapes me.

"Mom called Shawn a tool."

"She did not."

I nod with a breakable smile on my face. "She totally did."

"I don't believe you."

"Her exact words were, 'motherfucking tool.'"

Kale gapes at me a moment before barking out a loud laugh that simmers into belly chuckles. "Oh my God, that's perfect," he says, and I force a half smile that makes him lose half of his. "What else did she say?"

"You know Mom," I say as I rub my finger across a worn part of my blue comforter. "Always trying to get me a boyfriend."

Kale places his hand over the worn spot to reclaim my attention. "What did she say?"

"She said Shawn didn't seem like he wanted to keep me a secret tonight…She said…" Kale waits patiently when I trail off, and I let out a bone-weary sigh before I continue. "She said she saw how fast he ran to catch me."

Kale's dark eyes hold mine for a long moment before dropping to that worn-down spot on my bedspread. His fingers follow, fidgeting with the same threads he pushed mine from seconds earlier. "Everyone saw it. I did too."

We sit like that for a while, both lost in some imaginary place, when Kale says, "Kit, I need to tell you something."

I look up at him first; he looks up at me second.

"I know why Shawn never called you." My nose wrinkles with confusion, and he gnaws on his lip before rattling off the last part. "I told him not to."

I hear him, but I can't understand a word coming out of his mouth. He *told him not to?* He *told him not to call me?*

Kale starts pacing my room. "I couldn't believe he took you upstairs and just…that he used you liked that. He was a senior, for God's sake, and some kind of rock star, and you…you're my sister, and you'd always had such a crush on him, and he just…" When Kale glances at me, guilt eclipses the blacks of his eyes. I see a flash of it just before he drops his gaze back to the floor. "I only let a day pass before I found out where he lived. I went over there, and…"

Kale trails off on an exhausted breath, and I scoot farther toward the edge of my bed. "And *what*?"

My twin's eyes are full of more regret than I've ever seen in them when he says, "I told him to stay away from you. I told him if he ever tried talking to you after what he did…that Mason Larson was our older brother, and he'd break every one of Shawn's fingers. I told Shawn he'd never play the guitar again."

I stare at him. And stare. And stare. Something in the pit of my stomach is simmering to a boil, and I can feel it in the way my blood starts to sizzle under my skin.

"I thought I was helping. I thought—"

"You thought you were *helping*?" I hiss, and Kale cracks.

"I didn't think he cared about you...But, Kit, I saw how he was with you tonight, and—"

"Get out," I order, my voice a cold chill that punches through the room.

"Kit—" Kale pleads.

"Get out!"

My anger knocks him back a step. "Please. Just let me—"

"GET OUT!" I launch off my bed and fly straight at him. "GET OUT, GET OUT, GET OUT!" I'm all up in his face, forcing him toward the far side of my room and reaching behind him to unlock my door. It hits him in the side as I swing it open, and I shove at him until he's in the hall, screaming at him to get out, over and over and over again, until the door is slamming between us. I throw the lock and glare where I'm sure Kale's face is probably still staring at the other side, knowing the rest of the house is probably already on their way upstairs to demand that I open up and explain. But then I'm at my window, throwing it open and climbing over the sill.

I don't think. I just jump. And on the ground, my socked feet race desperately across the lawn—into the dark, past houses, past trees, past borders I've never crossed.

I run until I can't run anymore. Until I can't breathe or think or feel. I run until I'm lost.

And then, I fall apart.

Chapter Twenty-One

I WAKE WITH a gnat trying to crawl up my nose, a rock burrowing into my spleen, and Leti...flicking an ant off of the log he's sitting on, looking entirely out of place in the middle of wherever-the-hell I fell asleep last night.

"This is really not in my job description as third-best friend," he informs me, his golden eyes utterly serious when they swing to mine. "In case you couldn't tell"—he gestures at his vintage Thundercats T-shirt, his faded jeans, his hot pink Chuck Taylors—"I'm not exactly cut out for this 'being one with nature' stuff."

I groan and rub my crooked back as I sit up. My face is stiff with sun-dried tears, and my mess of black-and-purple hair is a literal *nest*, complete with dried leaves and what I don't doubt is an army's worth of creepy crawlies. I turn my head upside down and do my best to finger-comb the heebie-jeebies from my scalp. "What are you doing here?" I ask with my nose still pointed at the ground. My voice is hoarse from crying all night, and I hear Leti sigh.

"Coming to your rescue?" he suggests. "I'm pulling a Robin Hood or something."

My eyebrow is raised even before I turn my head upright. "Robin Hood?"

"Well, I'd love to be your Prince Charming"—an amused smirk sneaks onto his face—"but I believe that ship sailed over the rainbow, Sleeping Hot Mess."

"Sleeping Hot Mess?"

Leti chuckles as I wipe a smudge of dirt from my cheek. "You're certainly no Sleeping Beauty."

I glare at him, and he shrugs.

"Just telling it like it is, Kitterbug. And apparently, I'm the only one who does."

"What are you talking about?" I grumble. I'm sore, I'm exhausted, and my head is throbbing with each shift in the breeze. I have no idea why Leti is here—or *how* Leti is here—but trying to figure that out would require thinking, and thinking is the last thing I want to do right now. Last night feels like it was five minutes ago, and even though I try to forget the details, they ambush me one by one.

The way I screamed at Shawn at the table. The way I pushed him out the door. The way everyone just stared at me.

The way my mom said, *I saw how fast he ran.*

The way Kale said, *I told him to stay away from you.*

Leti stretches his long legs out, crossing them at the ankles. "I'm talking about all the lies you and everyone else in the world has been telling. I've spent all night hearing about the absolute chaos that went down here last night."

"From who?"

He flutters a hand in the air. "From *everyone*. Rowan, Dee, Adam, Joel. Mostly from your brother."

"Did he tell you about the other secrets that came out last night?" I ask, and Leti's grin answers me even before the contentment in his voice does.

"He did."

"So you guys are good?"

He nods with that bright smile on his face, and I almost feel happy for them. But my voice sounds of resentment when I mutter, "Glad Kale got his happy ending."

Especially after he ruined mine.

"Which brings me to why I'm here," Leti says, his smile slipping away, and I finally bother asking—

"Why *are* you here? How'd you even find me?"

"Kale found you." He dismisses me with another swat at a gnat in the air. "But he thought it would be better if he wasn't here when you woke up."

I snort, because all that proves is that my twin has half a brain in his head. "So you're here to get me to go back home? Hate to break it to you, Leti, but I would've had to go back anyway. I don't have my Jeep."

"If surgeons dissected your head," he counters as he picks at the log he's sitting on with a well-manicured fingernail, "do you think they'd discover your skull is missing-link thick? Or full-on cavewoman thick?"

When I glare at him, he smiles.

"I'm here to talk sense into you."

"And what kind of sense is that?" I'm practically growling as I struggle to get comfortable against the trunk of a thick-barked tree. That rock I slept on seriously might have poked a hole in something vital, because all of my muscles feel battered and bruised—maybe from the rock, or maybe from the way my body racked with heartbreaking sobs as I cried myself to sleep on top of it.

Leti runs his hand through the sunlit hair on top of his head. "Where should we even start? Kale or Shawn?" When my expression hardens on his last word, he nods to himself and says, "Kale it is. You're mad at him for telling Shawn to stay away from you in high school, right?"

I stare back at him, refusing to answer such an idiotic question.

"You realize you were fifteen, right? And Shawn was eighteen? An eighteen-year-old hot musician who'd slept with more girls than most guys twice his age? And you were a virgin? And he was moving away anyway? And you had an unhealthy obsession with him?"

I cut in when he gets to the only part I can argue with. "I was *not* obsessed."

"Love, obsession…" Leti flicks his fingers in the air. "When you're fifteen, it's all the same thing. What do you think would have happened if Kale hadn't told Shawn not to call you? Do you really think he would have called?"

"I'll never know," I answer angrily.

"Okay, let me ask you this then. Do you really think Shawn—*Shawn*—would have stayed away from you just because your macho-man brothers wanted him to? If he really wanted to be with you, like your little-girl heart wanted to believe, do you think he would have let them stand in his way? For *six years*?"

A sharp stinging surges against the back of my eyes, and I blame it on the even-worse stinging in my chest. It feels like my heart is a twisted, gnarled mess, like it's been thrown into a food processer and then run over with a Mac truck. "I get it, Leti. Shawn never wanted me. Is that your point?"

"My point is that Kale was just trying to protect you. He's an idiot, but he's an idiot who loves you."

"Lucky me."

Leti sighs and watches me wipe the heel of my palm over my eye. "You *are* lucky. Extremely lucky. Which brings us to Shawn."

"If you say I'm lucky to have Shawn," I warn, "you're getting a rock chucked at your head."

"Baby steps, she-devil," Leti replies, like I didn't just threaten to murder him where no one would find his body. "I'm not going to tell you Shawn cares about you or anything." He fakes a cough that sounds an awful lot like, "He does," and then he wipes a self-satisfied grin from his face and continues. "But I am going to point out that you are a giant—and I'm talking giant, massive, enormous, colossal—"

"Get to the fucking point," I order.

"Hypocrite." Leti matches my hard stare with one of his own, not backing down from the darkness in my eyes or fearing the way I weigh that promised rock in my palm. "All you've done since the moment you walked back into Shawn's life is *lie*."

"I'm not the liar," I argue, letting the rock fall back to the ground.

"Yes, you are."

"But he—"

"Did exactly the same thing as you." In my silence, Leti emphasizes, "*Exactly* the same thing. You pretended not to know him. He pretended not to know you. How are you going to be mad at him for something *you* did?"

"*I* did it to protect myself," I insist, but the argument sounds weak even to my own ears.

"And you just assume he did it for a different reason? Like just to hurt you or something? This is Shawn we're talking about. Since when have you known him to go around trying to hurt people?"

Shawn puts honey in Adam's whiskey before shows. He goes on coffee runs for the roadies. He brings earplugs for girls who steal them.

I feel my anger waning with the absolute sense Leti is making, so I narrow my eyes even farther and continue protesting. "He wanted to keep me a secret."

"Did he tell you he wanted to keep you a secret?"

"YES!" I bark at him. "He told me not to tell anyone about us!"

"Forever?"

I want to scream at Leti again, but instead, I think back and remember what Shawn had said. He said that he didn't want Adam and Joel to know because they'd make the rest of the tour hell. He looked down into my eyes and said, "Later. Just not yet."

My molars ache when I stop grinding them together. "I think he wanted to wait until after the tour…"

"And did you give him the chance to tell people after you guys got home?"

God, last night…Last night, my mom had asked him if he had a girlfriend, and he said he didn't know. He looked right at me. In front of everyone. Like it was my decision. And after my outburst, he chased me. He chased me like I was the only thing he cared about.

When a fresh round of tears springs to my eyes, Leti stands up, wipes off his jeans, and holds a hand down for me. "Are you ready to go back now?"

"What do I do?" I stare up into his golden eyes, set into a soft face illuminated by the sun's golden rays. He smiles warmly at me when I give him my hand.

"You chase him."

Chapter Twenty-Two

ON THE HIGHWAY, my foot weighs heavy on the gas pedal of the beat-up Chrysler convertible that Mason and I fixed up my junior year of high school. I'm so distracted, I haven't even turned the music on. My thoughts are as blurred as the cars I pass, and all I can do is stare out the dusty windshield as I make my way toward the same city where Shawn lives, the same place where we tuned guitars together on my roof.

I'm not chasing him.

There are still too many questions left unanswered. And part of me is afraid to ask—to even wonder. I know why I lied, but I don't know why he did. *I* was the one he crushed six years ago. *I* was the one with everything to lose. But still, he lied just the same as I did, and I don't know what that means. I don't know what we are. I don't know what I ever meant to him, if I meant anything at all.

I only know what a mess I made last night.

My brothers could have killed him, and maybe that's what I wanted when I was screaming at him at the top of my lungs. I was furious—over a thousand lies he told, over a thousand lies I told, and over a thousand lies I believed even though no one ever told them. I thought he wanted to keep me a secret. I thought he was playing me for an idiot. I thought a lot of things, but after everything Leti said this morning…now I can't think at all.

All I can do is drive.

Because even if I *wanted* to chase him, no one knows where he is. Rowan was the one who drove Leti to my parents' house this morning, and before I left, she told me that no one has seen him since last night. He took off as soon as the guys got back to his apartment building, and now he's not answering his phone.

I thought about calling him to see if he'd answer for me, but something kept my fingers away from his number. Maybe it was embarrassment. Maybe it was pride. Maybe it was fear. Or maybe it was all of those—six years and three months of bottled-up emotions that made me feel more vulnerable than I ever had.

Had he really been chasing after me, just like my mom said? Did he mean what he said on the roof the night of Van's party? With my shades down and the wind in my hair, I want to believe it.

But it isn't until I see his car parked in my driveway that a little part of me starts to.

I coast into the driveway and park the silver Chrysler next to Shawn's black Mitsubishi Galant, hope flaring in my chest like a flame threatening to burn me alive. I clamp down on the fire, reminding myself that it's just an empty car. He could be here to chew me out for humiliating him. He could be here to kick me out of the band.

With my nerves bunched tight in my shoulders, I gather my things from the backseat of the car and carry them up to my apartment, half expecting to find him in my unlocked room. When I don't find him there, I dump my things in a corner and venture into the old lady's house, entertaining her warm welcome home and casually asking if a boy stopped by to see me today. But apparently, the only boy she saw today was the neighbor boy, Jimmy, who crashed his bike into her mailbox because he was trying to hold his Labrador's leash while he was riding, and thank God Jimmy was wearing a helmet, because he could've *died* on her lawn, and he broke her mailbox post, but his parents made him come over to apologize and fix it, and she wishes she knew if anyone did find that damn dog—

With my toes twitching in my boots, I back out of the room and eventually out of the house, with the old woman's voice still talking to herself somewhere in the living room. I slip back into the garage, back up the stairs, and back into my loft, with only one place left to check.

At my window, I stare out at Shawn sitting on my roof, his long legs stretched over the shingles as he gazes off into nowhere. He's in the same clothes he was in last night—a nice black button-down and an untattered pair of black jeans—and it's like the night stuck to him, preserving his dark form from the golden sunlight stretching across the rest of the roof.

He's untouchable, and even when I slide the window open, his concentration remains unbroken. I sit near him in the silence, having no idea what to say or feel or do. He could have gone anywhere last night—there have to be at least a dozen groupies within a one-mile radius of his apartment—but he's on my roof, outside of my room, where no one would find him but me.

My head turns in his direction, but it's like I'm not even here. He won't even look at me. His green eyes are pinned on some distant place, and I'm not sure I've truly found him at all.

Eventually, I stop searching, and together, we stare out at the same spot on the sunlit horizon—me with my arms around my knees, him with his hands flattened against the roof at his sides. When he speaks, even the sun shines behind a cloud that sweeps across the sky. "I've been thinking all night of what I could say to you." His voice is dry, unreadable, and it makes my stomach drop.

"Did you sleep here?" I ask.

When he finally gazes over at me, his thick black lashes hang low over tired eyes that tug at the splinters of my heart. His scruff is days old, his hair is an untamed mess, and in his all-black attire, he looks…beautiful. Heartbreakingly beautiful.

"I didn't really sleep," he says, and he stares back out at that invisible spot again. His chest rises on a heavy breath before deflating in a shallow one. "I don't know what to say, Kit. All night, I've tried to come up with some way to say I'm sorry, for every single mistake I've made with you, but I still don't have it."

The hopelessness in his voice manifests in my own chest—an empty aching that makes me want to wrap my arms around him and pray he holds me too. Even if it means nothing to him. Even if it doesn't change anything.

The sun peeks out from behind the clouds, and when he gazes over me, all I can do is stare back at him. "I lost you before I ever had you," he says, "and all I've been doing is sitting up here feeling sorry for myself." He shakes his head in silent admonishment of himself. "Do you realize how big of an asshole that makes me? That I'm so jealous of the guy I should have been for you, I can't even find the right way to apologize for the guy I was?"

He's saying all the things I needed to hear days, weeks, years ago, and I don't even realize I'm crying until a tear slides over my lashes and trickles down my cheek. It's hot and speaks of a million different things—of the sadness I feel that we're over, of the regret I feel that we never began, of the relief I feel that he's sorry, and above all, of the emptiness, of the distance that stretches between us until it's much too far to cross.

The clouds open up for us, and light raindrops begin to mix with the shallow streams of tears on my face. Shawn just stares at me from across the void, until his somber voice says, "I should go."

My head is shaking back and forth even before I find my voice. "No. Come inside."

I walk to my window ahead of Shawn, not waiting to see if he'll follow, and inside my room, I wait and I wait and I wait. When he finally climbs in after me, his hair and shoulders damp from the rain, I want to hold his face in my hands and kiss the raindrops from his cheeks. I want to tell him I'm sorry too. Instead, I lean against a wall, my arms crossed over my chest to keep them from reaching out. I have a million questions, and if I don't ask them now, I know I never will.

Shawn closes the window behind him, and then he sits back against the sill and waits for me to say something.

"Were we really together?" I ask in a moment of forced courage. I'm terrified of his answer, but I need to know it, even if it twists the knife in my chest. "After Van's party...the roof..." I wipe what I tell myself are raindrops from my cheeks. "What was I to you, Shawn?"

He considers his reply before saying, "Do you really think I wanted to keep you a secret?" When I say nothing, he sighs. "Kit, there isn't a man alive who would want to keep you a secret. You're..." He shakes his head to himself. "You're everything I never knew I wanted. I didn't realize what perfect was until I got to know you, and then I thought you were finally mine, and...I just didn't want the other guys making it impossible for us to get any privacy for those last two days. They would have been such assholes about it. I wanted you to myself."

Resisting the urge to go into his arms, to make myself his, I say, "Why did you act like you hated me when I first joined the band?"

"I didn't trust you," he explains. "I didn't realize you actually cared about the music. I thought you were only there to get even with me or something."

"What about when I kissed you in Mayhem? Before the tour?" He pretended like he didn't remember taking me to the bus, lying me down on a bench, or making out with me—right before I had to run to the bathroom to throw up.

"You were drunk," he says sadly. "I was so wrapped up in finally getting to touch you, I didn't even realize it…I felt like an asshole for taking it so far. And then…I thought you just wanted to forget."

Because I lied. That morning, I was the first one to pretend nothing happened. Shawn only followed my lead.

"And on the roof of Van's hotel? I told you about my crush on you in high school. I *wanted* you to remember."

"I know," he says, his expression hopeless before he drops it to the floor. "I know, but everything was going so perfectly, I didn't want to ruin it."

"I even tried to get you to remember on the bus after I found out. But you just kept lying…"

Shawn shakes his head at the floorboards beneath his feet. "I didn't want to lose you."

But he did lose me…And now, I'm just lost.

"And six years ago?" I finally ask. The words come out strong and confident, betraying the doubt, the hurt, the brokenness inside me. "What about then?"

Shawn sinks heavier against the sill on a defeated sigh. "This is the part where I don't know what to say." He hesitates before lifting his gaze back up to mine. "I wasn't a good guy six years ago. I'm sorry you thought I was, but I wasn't."

"Kale told me what he said to you," I say. "After that night, when we…" I trail off, unwilling to give life to the ghost of a memory, but understanding is clear in Shawn's eyes.

"Do you think that's why I didn't call?" he asks after a while, and I don't know if I truly want the answer to what I ask next.

"Is it?"

"Kit," he says, like the words coming out of his mouth are hurting him to say. "What happened wasn't your brother's fault. I could have called."

My voice threatens to crack when I ask, "Why didn't you?"

Shawn's eyes close for a moment, holding mine when they reopen. "I didn't know you six years ago. You were just a hot girl I met at a party."

Tears scald my face, and Shawn crosses the room to wipe them away. His thumb brushes lightly across my cheek when he says, "I'm sorry. I didn't know you were fifteen, and if I had known it was your first time..."

"You never would have done it," I answer for him, my voice holding years of knowing those words to be true. What happened between us was as much my fault as it was his.

"I wouldn't have," he agrees sincerely. "I fucked up with you, Kit, and I'm sorry."

"Did you ever even think of me?"

His palm is still cupping my face when he says, "At first...once in a while. But it's not like I've spent the past six years thinking about you. I didn't know what I lost when I let you go. You need to know that." Both calloused hands thread into my hair to gently hold my face in place. "I wasn't the guy you wished I was. I *did* forget about you up until you walked into that audition. I had no idea what I'd walked away from."

"What about now?" The words push free in a moment of desperation I wish I could take back. But with my face in his hands—with my *heart* in his hands—I have nothing left to lose.

"Now?" he asks, never breaking his eyes from mine. I'm drowning in them when he says, "Now I think I know the answer to what you asked me out on your roof." When I just stare at him, he says, "You asked me if I was half a person, and I asked you how I'd know." His thumb grazes my cheek, his eyes clinging to mine. "You. You're how I know."

I close my eyes and let his words consume me, remembering that day on the roof so many weeks ago. He said it was like no one ever realized Joel was half a person until Dee came around, and when I asked him if *he* was half a person, he asked me how he'd know. Neither of us had an answer. Now, he says he does.

And my heart tells me I do too.

With my face still cradled gently between his calloused hands, I open my eyes and lift onto my tiptoes, meeting him in a kiss that promises to put me back together—even as it breaks my heart. He's so close, but I feel like I *miss* him. Like I've *always* missed him. And I'm desperate to make this feeling go away—this distance, this emptiness.

His hands tunnel into my hair, and he draws me up as I draw him down, but we're still not close enough. I need more of him, and I find myself walking him backward, step by step to the edge of my bed. When the backs of his legs are against it, I crawl on top of him, my knees sinking into the mattress next to his hips and my lips forcing his head down to my pillow. We're both breathing heavy as I kiss him, as he kisses me back—little moans escaping my lips and big ones rumbling in his chest. His hands slide under the hem of my shirt, greedy for soft skin, and mine scratch over his scalp as I kiss him desperately, needing him more than I need to breathe.

He's hard beneath me when he begins to sit up, to take control, but when I push him back down against my mattress, that's when his self-restraint snaps. His fingers grip the hem of my shirt and yank it over my head in an unapologetic move that makes my skin burn hot. Even in just a bra, I'm burning up, so when he reaches behind me and unclasps it with an expert flick of his fingers, all I can do is thank him.

I thank him with my lips, my tongue, my hands—with the little sounds I make as he traces his tongue across my collarbone and dips scalding-hot kisses into the dip at the base of my throat. When he sits up this time, I let him, and the petal of my nipple is between his lips a second later. He curls his tongue around it—a wet, warm, breath-stealing sensation that has it blooming between his lips.

My back arches. My head falls back. My long hair cascades over his hand as he kisses and nibbles and pulls. And I don't know what comes over me, but when I tip my chin back down, my fingers grip tight around his hair and I break his lips from my skin. He looks up at me with blazing green eyes—the forest in them burning to the ground—and I devour his mouth a shallow breath later, my hips sinking low on top of the stiffness inside his jeans. I moan at the sudden heat between my legs, my blood pumping fast when Shawn's hands rock me even tighter against him.

"Shawn," I gasp, parting my lips from his on a moan, but he doesn't release his hold on the frayed back pockets of my jeans. He moves me against him in a heated rhythm that my hips are eager to match, and when I can't take the sparks that are flying between us anymore, I reach down and find the button of his jeans.

Shawn watches me as I unbutton him, as I unzip him, as I undo him by stripping out of the last of my clothes next to the bed—in full light, on full display, just for him. It's too late to feel self-conscious, because I've already put it all on the line. He shimmies out of the rest of his clothes as I fish for a condom stashed in a drawer I haven't gone to in forever, and when I hand it to him, he follows my silent request and slides it over himself—slowly, while I watch.

My bottom lip bears the sharp bite of my anticipation as his fingers glide over every hard inch, and I begin crawling on top of him before he's even finished. I walk my knees up the bed until I'm hovering over his hips, and he lies motionless on his back, staring up at me.

"Are you sure you want to do this?" he asks, but his eyes are betraying his self-control. They're on my lips, my breasts, my stomach, and lower. The feather-light touch of his fingers dances over my sides, then my thighs—giving me goose bumps, making my nipples harden, making it impossible for me to speak.

I don't answer him. Instead, I lower my lips to his, kissing him slowly as my fingers scratch down his chest, his stomach, the thin line of hair trailing south of his navel. I wrap my hand around him and tease him with my fingers, relishing in the way his grip tightens around my waist. When I can tell he wants to push me lower, to steal control, I lift him to meet me, and then I rock down on top of him, just enough for both of us to feel it.

My breath catches in my throat, and he squeezes my hips almost painfully. With his lip pinned between my teeth, I sink down lower, deeper, until I can't tell where he ends and I begin. The memory of how this felt with him in high school has faded, but God, I know it couldn't have felt like this. My heart feels ten times too big for my chest, and each beat makes it impossible for me to think. All I know is that it's Shawn between my legs, Shawn under my palms, Shawn holding me tight as I rock lower and lower still. There's so much of him for me to take, and I want him—all of him, every single bit.

He moans against my mouth, and I kiss the sound away until he's all the way inside me, my forehead dropping to the pillow next to his head. The length of him is making every nerve in my body flash-fire with electric heat, and all I can do is make tiny sounds of ecstasy against the soft shell of his ear as he begins moving in and out of me on his own, his strong hands holding my hips in place. With Shawn rocking in me, out of me, in me, out of me, I grip the bedsheets, the pillow next to his head, the roots of his hair.

The moans coming from my throat become quicker, more frantic, and his pace picks up to match. He's pushing me higher and higher, out of my fucking mind, and in the heart of the fire, I sit up straight and brace my hands on his shoulders. I steal the pace from him, my knees lifting me, rocking me, grinding me against him, until the world is spinning and I'm being flipped onto my back.

"I'm so close," I beg, and Shawn hikes my knees up to my chest, leaning back before pulling out and pushing back into me *agonizingly* slowly. His eyes are on mine as every single inch of him sinks deep between my legs, and my eyelids flutter closed as I burn alive beneath him.

The mattress beside me shifts as he lowers to his hands, and his breath is hot on my ear when he says, "Do you know what I remember about our first time?"

Every movement he makes inside me is so controlled, so deliberate, that all I can do is answer with a whimper.

"It didn't last nearly long enough," he says.

His lips capture the lobe of my ear in a warm caress that makes my toes curl, his heavy breaths stirring the hair at my temple and making my thighs tighten around him.

"Do you want me to touch you?" he asks, and the way I pulse around him is answer enough. He leans back, wets the pad of his thumb between his lips, and watches me squirm as he lowers it to the ready bud that has me crying out his name. "I want to see that look in your eyes again, Kit. Open your eyes."

It takes every ounce of strength I have to open my eyes and gaze up at him, but when I do, it takes only seconds.

"Oh my God," I gasp, my back arching off the bed, my fingers gripping the base of the headboard behind my pillow. Shawn's calloused thumb traces firm circles, and the image of him stays printed behind my eyelids even when they squeeze shut and my head throws back.

The way his arms are flexing as he reaches down to touch me. The firm muscles in his chest, his stomach. The scruff on his jaw, the brightness of his lips. Those green eyes, and the way they demanded I fall apart beneath him, *for* him.

The base of my wooden headboard is still biting into the palms of my hands when Shawn lowers back down to a missionary position. He kisses my neck, my jaw, my mouth. He's unhurried as he moves inside me, firmly enough to keep my orgasm going, going, going.

Eventually, my arms wrap around him, my nails digging into his back as I squeeze him close against my breasts. "I want you," I breathe against his damp temple. Because God, I haven't had enough yet. Not even close.

"You have me."

And when he pulls away and I see the look in his eyes, I believe him.

My hand curls behind the back of his neck and I kiss him—I kiss him like he's mine. I claim every inch of his lips, of his tongue, playing and sucking and nibbling until his pace becomes a little less sure, a little less controlled. Shawn tries to pull away again—I can tell he's getting close—but I suck at his tongue in long, seductive strokes that make him moan against my mouth.

And God, that sound. My heart kicks. My back arches. I fall apart again, my knees trembling against his body as mine loses control. I kiss him desperately, and the moans coming from deep inside his chest grow hungrier and wilder until he gives himself to me, his hips jerking within the tight squeeze of my thighs—until neither one of us has anything left to give.

And then, I hold him. I wrap my arms around him and hold him close, brushing my fingers through his damp hair, kissing the side of his face, biting my lip between my teeth when I pulse around him and his body responds. I hold him until he summons the strength to lift himself up and gaze down into my eyes.

He doesn't say anything, and neither do I. Instead, he lowers his lips to mine, and when he kisses me, softly with absolutely nothing separating us, I know with everything I am that he was right—

Neither of us is half a person. Not anymore.

Chapter Twenty-Three

IT'S WEIRD SEEING my twin with Leti…It's weird seeing my twin with *anyone*. Under the hazy blue lighting of Mayhem's main bar, I watch Leti whisper something in Kale's ear, and I watch Kale smile softly at the reflective black bar top, the back of his shoulder pressed tightly against the front of Leti's chest.

It's weird—like seeing a bunny giggle or a puppy with purple eyes—but I can't stop smiling.

Kale and I worked things out the day after Shawn and I spent countless hours making up for lost time. Everyone in the world tried to contact us that day, but we made the world wait.

The next day was chaos.

Shawn dragged me back to his apartment with him so we could tell Adam, Joel, Rowan, and Dee in person about us being together. Then he told Mike over the phone, with jeers and catcalls flying from the background. I finally understood why he wanted to wait until the tour was over to tell the rest of the band, but even with Adam and Joel behaving like the ten-year-olds they perpetually are, the smile was etched permanently on my face. Shawn told them about me like he was announcing an award he'd won, and the way he held me close, it made me feel like one.

I drove all the way home to talk to my family that same night—sans Shawn, in spite of his protests that we should go together. It was something I needed to do on my own. My talk with Kale was short—an apology from Kale, followed by a hug, an "I forgive you," and a bone-crunching punch to his arm from me. I gave him a bruise that lasted over a week, a black-and-blue reminder to worry about his own love life from now on.

Shawn was already waiting for me in my loft when I got home late that night, and I told him about the invitation my brothers not-so-kindly extended that he should-slash-better come to our next family dinner. And even though I tried-slash-threw-a-tantrum to dissuade him, Shawn wouldn't get the hell out of my Jeep that following Sunday, and I had no choice but to bring him along.

We arrived a few hours before dinner, with my brothers immediately suggesting a game of touch football that I knew damn well would involve a hell of a lot more than harmless touching. They had that dark look in their already-dark eyes—the one that told me they remembered every word I'd blurted at the dinner table, and that my explanations about Shawn being a good guy now had fallen on deaf ears.

"They're going to pulverize you," I warned with the hem of Shawn's shirt gripped between my fingers. We were standing on the sidelines of my front yard while my brothers waited impatiently on the grass for my boyfriend—like a pack of killer whales waiting for its prey to dive into the water.

"I know," Shawn agreed, unpeeling my fingers from his clothes one by one. A soft kiss on my cheek, and then he added, "Let them get it over with, okay?"

I gnawed on my lip, but let him dive into the infested waters. And I watched my brothers eat him alive. I cringed every five seconds while my dad watched approvingly from beside me, his broad arms crossed over his even broader chest.

Fifteen minutes in, when Shawn finally intercepted the ball and took off toward the end zone, I bounced onto the toes of my feet and screamed for him to GO, GO, GO. I was waving imaginary pompoms down the field, jumping on an invisible trampoline, when Mason charged at him and landed a vicious shoulder to the ribs. Shawn went airborne, his feet flying out from under him, before landing in a curled-up heap. I had just put one boot in front of the other, prepared to tackle my six-foot-three, two-hundred-forty-pound brother to the ground, when Shawn rolled onto his side and held up a hand for me to stay where I was. I froze, my hard eyes narrowed viciously at Mason while he hovered over Shawn and smiled.

"I think maybe we should call a doctor," he taunted while Shawn gripped his ribs and struggled to catch the wind that had been knocked out of him. "What do you say, Kit?" Mason's voice boomed from across the yard, and not one of our other brothers stepped in to help. "Should we wait six years to call?"

Everyone watched as Shawn coughed and writhed, and I was two seconds from showing Mason how deadly my combat boots could be—when his hand dropped in front of Shawn's face. I watched as Shawn took it, I watched as Mason lifted him to his feet, and I watched as every single Larson on the field that day landed an elbow or a knee or a well-placed shoulder. By the time I drove Shawn home that night, he was in no physical condition to be even sitting up straight. I cast a worried glance at him from the driver's seat of my Jeep, the light of passing cars chasing away the shadows on his face.

"I think they like me," he joked, and the only reason I could laugh is because I understood my brothers well enough to understand that they *did* like him. They beat the shit out of him, but they helped him back to his feet every time, and the fact that he was still breathing had to count for something. It was their way of making things right.

Shawn's body was still achy from that game when he came to the next family dinner, and the next. My brothers chided him about how tender his bruises still were—just like they would tease each other—and even though Kale was the slowest to come around, eventually he stopped narrowing his eyes at Shawn from down the table.

"You really do love him," he said to me quietly just before we left last Sunday.

Instead of denying it, I pulled away from our hug and smiled. Aside from my psychotic break during that

unforgettable family dinner, I hadn't said the words yet—
neither had Shawn—but I felt them. I felt them when he
smiled at me, when he held me, when he made me laugh.
And I felt them when he did none of those things. I felt
them all the time.

I expected Kale to shake his head or scowl or twist
his lip between his teeth, but instead, he gave me a small
smile—just a little one, but one that I remember perfectly
as I stand under Mayhem's blue glow with my elbow on
the bar, directing that same smile at him and Leti. I always
imagined what it would be like to see Kale with a boyfriend,
but I never imagined he would seem so…peaceful. Content.

Happy.

He turns around, Leti leans into him, and I blush when
my twin's hands find my third-best friend's waist, holding
it tight as he steals a kiss that makes my ears blush.

"You guys are disgusting."

Joel's voice snags my attention, and when I turn to
him, he's busy watching Shawn's fingers curl round and
around in my hair. Since we came out as a couple, Shawn
has made no secret that he and I are together—that I'm
his, that he's mine. His hands are always on me, always
grazing or holding or touching, and while I would never
have thought I'd like that so much…it's *Shawn*, and I'm
starving for the roughness of his fingertips when they're
not somewhere on me. I angle my chin to grin at him
standing behind me. "I think he's jealous."

Shawn smiles down at me, his green eyes content as he
continues playing with my hair. "Probably because Dee
makes him sleep on the couch all the time."

"I *like* sleeping on the couch," Joel protests, and Dee quirks a perfectly shaped eyebrow into her perfectly powdered forehead.

"You do?"

God, those two are still a mess. Fighting and making up, fighting and making up. I swear they do it just for the make-up sex, which Joel always brags about and—if Dee's constant antagonizing is any indication—she enjoys just as much.

Joel scrambles for a save. "I mean…I mean, no. No. I hate it. Seriously hate it."

I chuckle against Shawn's chest when Dee mutters something about making Joel sleep in the tub from now on, and Joel smirks at her before whispering something in her ear that I thank God I can't hear. Shawn's arms circle around my waist, tugging me tighter as I melt against him.

"I'm nervous about the show tonight."

I turn in his arms and wind my arms behind his neck, my nose scrunching up at him. "You're never nervous."

He gives me a soft smile and then kisses the tip of my nose, effectively unscrunching it. "I know."

"What are you nervous about?"

"You."

The scrunching starts again. "What are you talking about?"

Shawn smirks and checks his phone. "You ready to head backstage?"

On the way, I ask a million more questions he doesn't bother acknowledging. And none of the other guys bother answering me either, even though I can tell they know something is up. Shawn straps the guitar around my neck because I'm too busy harassing everyone, and I don't stop throwing questions at the backs of their heads until we're in full view of the crowd.

Shawn shoots me one last smile over his shoulder before taking his spot at the other end of Mayhem's stage.

The whole performance, I wait to find out what he was talking about. I wait for anything unusual, anything out of the ordinary. But nothing happens. We play our hit songs, the crowd screams them back to us, and the mania in the room builds and builds until I convince myself the guys must have just been messing with me.

Nothing happens.

Until it does.

"We want to do something a little different tonight," Adam announces into his mic toward the end of our set, and I stare across the stage at Shawn. He stares back at me, his tattered black jeans and his vintage black band tee absorbing the blue tint of the stage lights. "Shawn and I have been working on something new," Adam continues, his voice a muted sidenote to the cacophony of my thoughts. "Do you want to hear it?"

When the crowd's screams start bouncing off the walls, Adam grins at me. I finally pull my attention from Shawn to furrow my brow at our lead singer, who chuckles before turning back to the audience.

"It's something acoustic."

Roadies rush two stools onto the stage as Mike moves his sticks to one hand and Joel unstraps his guitar from around his neck.

"Shawn wrote this one, and it's pretty fucking amazing."

Adam takes the acoustic Gibson a roadie hands him, and Shawn trades out his guitar as well, for the priceless vintage Fender he played for me the first time I ever visited his apartment. He takes his seat on a stool next to Adam as Joel and Mike usher me off the stage.

"What's he doing?" I ask, unable to tear my eyes away.

The guys never answer me. Or maybe they do, but I just don't hear them. My eyes, my ears—every single part of me is tuned in to Shawn, watching him sit next to Adam with that Fender on his lap.

The last time I saw them like this was when I was in fifth grade, watching them at a middle school talent show. Then, I thought I was in love.

Now, I really am.

"This song doesn't have a title yet," Shawn says as he adjusts the mic in front of him, and I smile at the uncharacteristic nervousness in his voice. He clears his throat, locks the mic into place, and leans back. When he starts playing, forgoing any further introduction, his fingers strum chords that tug at the strings of my heart.

His beautiful voice fills the room, from wall to wall, touching every soul in the crowd. Every single fan is hanging on the tune of his guitar, the sound of his voice, the words of his song.

He sings of a girl who was the sun, and he sings of walking away from her. He sings of rooftops and sunsets, of secrets and dreams. He sings of heartache and six years.

He sings of love.

His green eyes find me from across the stage.

He sings of me.

Mike's arm wraps around my shoulder as tears start to drip down my cheeks, and when Shawn's song fades to an end, I can't help it—I cross the stage until I'm with him.

In front of his stool, I wipe the heels of my palms under my eyes, having no idea what to say.

"I love you," Shawn says first, his voice carrying through his mic and filling the entire room. He stands up and dries the rest of my tears with the gentle pads of his thumbs, and I know he's going to kiss me.

"I love you too," I say when his lips are halfway to mine, and he pauses before dropping them the rest of the way. Just a second, just long enough for me to lose myself in the promises in those green eyes, and then his lips claim mine.

The fans explode into applause, but Shawn kisses me like they're not even there. He kisses me like it's just us—in a kitchenette, on the roof of my apartment, on top of a penthouse suite. He kisses me in front of everyone, and in my heart, in his arms, on a stage for all to see, I *know*—

I know where we're going to be six years from now.

Epilogue

Shawn

"YOU'RE GOING TO make me late," I say, and Kit giggles against my mouth. I love that sound—because I'm the only one who can make her make it, and she hates that she can't stop me from doing it every chance I get.

"Go."

"Seriously," I say between kisses, too lost in the feel of her—of her long hair slipping between my fingers, her satin lips seducing mine, her sexy thighs cradling my hips. I force her farther onto the kitchenette counter as I press tighter between her legs. "We need to go in."

"Then stop kissing me," she orders, her voice a convictionless, breathless moan that makes me swell against the inviting heat of her.

I break my lips from hers to press them to her throat. "No."

Her fingertips scratch into my hair as she gives control without really giving it. She plays me just as well as a six-string guitar, knowing exactly how to touch me to get me to do whatever she wants. I'm sucking at the curve of her neck when I finally get her out of her jeans.

"Tonight's important," she reminds me as I tug them down over her thighs, her knees, her ankles. And in the back of my mind, I know that. Jonathan Hess is waiting inside Mayhem with paperwork, but Jonathan Hess can wait. If Kit and I go in now, neither of us will be able to concentrate. We're doing this for the show, the crowd, the band.

Or at least that's what I tell myself as I tug her panties down with her jeans. She kicks them off the tips of her black-painted toes, and I step back between her legs. "I love you," I say as I palm her ass in both hands, dragging her to the edge of the counter.

"I lov—" Her voice catches as I sink deep inside her, and she finishes with a low, sexy, "Shawn." Her moan is as deep as the path I pave inside her, her dull nails scratching over my scalp with every single inch. I peel them away and kiss the calloused pads of her fingers one by one, each lingering touch of my lips making her wetter until I'm seated all the way inside her, until I'm just as breathless as she is. My forehead glues itself to the shoulder of her T-shirt because she just feels so. fucking. good. She feels fucking amazing.

How we are now is nothing like how we were our first time. Now, when she says my name, I know she means so much more than Shawn Scarlett. When she looks into my eyes, she's seeing more than her own name in lights.

I should've seen it back then—the way she looks at me, the way she probably always has—but I was a blind man until she walked away...two, three, four times.

My fingers hook under the hem of the shirt separating me from her skin, and I impatiently tug it over her head. Then I'm reaching for her bra, she's grabbing at my shirt, and we're locked in a battle of wills as I try to strip her of her clothes at the same time she tries to strip me of mine. Both of us end up laughing, and I eventually let her win.

She continues giggling until I cup her breast in my palm and slide my thumb across her nipple. And at the quiet gasp that grabs her, at the look in her eyes—that dark, bottomless look that spells desire in the black of her gaze—I bend down and suckle a pink tip between my lips. Her back arches, her thighs squeeze, and I...I'm barely holding it together as her pretty little nipple pebbles beneath my tongue.

I take my time—because I *have* to with her if I'm going to last—teasing one blushing pebble and then the other before teasing *her* by asking, "How are we going to celebrate tonight?"

The soft moan that purrs from her mouth is more than I can handle. With her nipple still perked between the seam of my lips, my eyes travel up over the delicate curve of her neck, the line of her chin, the pink of her cheeks. Under thick lashes, she stares down at me, and I make a show of parting my lips and tracing my tongue over her in long, slow strokes that she watches for only a moment before her eyes flutter closed.

"Open them."

With her half-lidded gaze watching my every move, I make a feast of her. I nibble and flick and suckle until she's coiling tight around me, and then I bury my fingers in her hair and pull her to my mouth.

I lose track of time, of where we are, of everything but the way she kisses me senseless as I thrust into her over, and over, and over. She's so tight—her heat around my cock, her fingers on my back, her lips over mine. I'm so fucking lost, I don't even know how I keep moving inside her, except that I'm desperate—desperate to hear the sounds she makes when she comes for me, for the way her pupils swallow her irises and she looks at me like she wants to do it all over again.

"Fuck," I say, trying to slow my pace because I'm about to come undone.

"Don't stop," she begs, and when she asks me like that—like she *needs* me to keep feeding myself inside her—there's no way in hell I'll ever deny her.

I say a silent prayer that she's closer than I am, because God, I'm going to come soon if she doesn't—

A heavy moan rumbles in my chest when she clenches around me, her fingers digging into the coiled muscles of my back as I follow her over the edge not even a full second later. I empty into her as her insides hug me tight, squeezing and milking and unraveling me until I can't even think.

Kit is moaning into my ear, saying my name and stringing curse words together, but I can't stop—I push into her until I have absolutely nothing, *nothing* left to give. And even then, I want to give her more. I want to give her everything.

When I kiss her, she must be able to tell how badly I want to take her again, because her tired voice reminds me, "We are so fucking late."

IT TAKES ME a pathetic amount of time to pull myself together and collect our clothes from the floor, but then Kit and I get dressed and straighten her sexed-up hair as well as we possibly can. When we finally make our way inside Mayhem, hand in hand, Adam smirks his face off at me. I've spent most of my life lecturing him about being on time, but now, he's the one to say it—"You're late."

"Really late," Mike emphasizes.

"Good," I say. "John can wait."

"Yeah," Joel chides, "because I bet *that's* why you're late. And not because you and Kit were busy fu—"

Dee and Peach both elbow him in the ribs, and he grunts as he doubles over.

"You look great," Dee tells Kit, and Kit grunts a little too, which pulls a smile onto my face. She's friends with the girls, but she'll never really be *one* of the girls, and that's just one of the things I love about her. She's hot as hell, and she knows it, but she doesn't flaunt it—because she doesn't need to. Even when she's wearing one of my baggy T-shirts, an old pair of jeans, and an oversized flannel, she looks like a siren, smiles like a siren, laughs like a siren.

I drape my arm over her shoulders. "Is he waiting in the greenroom?"

When the guys confirm that Jonathan Hess is, in fact, waiting for me in the greenroom, I walk back there with

Kit still held captive under my arm. I shake hands with Jonathan. I try not to laugh at the sour look Victoria has on her face. I don't negotiate.

Ever since we performed with Cutting the Line at their show in Nashville last August, our popularity and sales have skyrocketed. Even Mayhem has had to close its doors to people standing in line, and now, Mosh Records is finally prepared to do the ass-kissing they've been wanting us to do for years. The lawyer I staffed checked out the paperwork this morning, and everything was in order. Jonathan's label is merely a name we're attaching to ourselves for mutual benefit—his people will help us, and we'll help his image. For a percentage of our sales, every resource of Mosh Records will be made available to us, and the label will have no say—none at all—over the music we produce or when we produce it. They'll help with marketing, producing, booking, networking—and all we need to do is keep doing what we're doing.

Every ounce of hard work I've put in over the past ten years gets poured into every letter I sign. I watch Adam sign, Joel sign, Mike sign, Kit sign. And then we all shake hands and leave. It isn't until we're backstage again that I pick Kit up and spin her around.

She laughs and squeezes my neck tight while everyone celebrates. "You did it," she says in my ear when I finally put her down, and when I pull away and see her smile, it's all the reward I need. Without her, I would've celebrated with the guys tonight—I would've gotten drunk and hooked up with a groupie after the show—but I would've gone to sleep alone.

Tonight, I'll be next to Kit. I'll be on her and inside her and it will be so, so much fucking better than it would have been if she wouldn't have stormed back into my life with her combat boots and her take-no-prisoners smile.

I kiss her one last time—two, three last times—and then we take the stage. Me, Kit, Adam, Joel, Mike. We're as high as the crowd, adrenaline-fueled by the time Adam finally pulls his mic from its stand and riles up the crowd.

"We just signed with Mosh Records!" he shouts, and cheers rise up from the crowd—along with a few boos. Adam laughs. "And they totally kissed our asses! I'm pretty sure I could say they suck a giant cock right now, and they wouldn't be able to do a damn thing about it!"

"But we're not going to do that," I chime in while the entire room screams, and Adam grins at me.

"What, do you think I'm an idiot? Of course we're not going to do that!"

I chuckle into my mic, and Adam spins back toward the crowd.

"Shawn has been working this out for us for years. And you guys helped make it happen. So I just want you to give yourselves and Shawn a huge fucking round of applause before we start this show!" The crowd screams, and Adam turns toward Mike. "I don't think that was loud enough, do you?"

Mike takes Adam's cue and shakes his head.

"When you think they're loud enough, go ahead and start."

Mike grins, and Joel, Kit, and I motion for the crowd to get louder. Louder. Louder. When every single person in the venue—including the bartenders, the security, our road-ies—are screaming at the tops of their lungs, Mike taps his sticks together and hits his first drum. The venue lights cut, the stage lights flare, and with the air glowing blue, I play my first chord. The music hums through my fingers and up my arms, swallowing my thoughts as I work my fingers to the bone. I shout backup into the mic, twining my voice with Adam's in a way that's as familiar to me as the weight of my guitar, and he plays to the crowd, the girls, the fans.

The groupies are ravenous tonight, screaming and reaching and threatening to bring down the barricade. We play song after song, watching everyone in the pit sing back to us with their hands in the air and their bod-ies bouncing to the beat. Two, three, four songs. I stare through the spotlights, skimming over the frantic first row, until—

Until my heart lodges into my throat and I nearly pluck the wrong damn string. If my Fender wasn't strapped to my neck, I probably would have dropped it.

"You see her, right?" Adam asks me as soon as the song is over. His mic is switched off, and I step away from mine and just nod my head.

Danica fucking Carlisle. Mike's fucking ex. Cheering from the front row. Desperate for Adam's attention, my attention, anyone's attention.

"What do you think she's here for?" Adam asks, and my fingers strangle the neck of my guitar.

To make Mike miserable. To mess with his head. To summon her hellhounds and ruin the show. "I have no fucking clue."

Six years ago, she tore Mike's heart right out of his chest, and now she's acting like his biggest fan, like she didn't completely *destroy* him when she tried to make him choose between us and her.

"Do we tell Mike?" Adam asks, and when I give him a look and shake my head, he nods in agreement. He gulps down his water and walks back to his spot front and center, ignoring Danica like she's invisible.

For everyone else, she's impossible to miss. When we start playing again, she jumps up and down, screaming her head off while the poor chick next to her barely avoids flying hair and elbows. While everyone else in the front row is reaching for Adam and losing their minds, *that* poor girl's arms are crossed over the railing she's hugging to avoid getting knocked backward into the pit. She's a tiny thing who keeps glaring at the bitch next to her, and when Danica yells something down to her and tries to lift her arm into the air, I realize they're here together.

Not surprising. Even Danica's own friends can't stand her. But Mike...I still don't think he's over her. Six years, and he's still never given another girl the chance he gave her. He probably still thinks she's the one who got away.

I try to put her out of my mind, finding Kit's gaze across the stage. She knows something's up, and I smile at her to ease the tension that's tightening the inside walls of my chest.

My smile gets bigger when I think about what she'd do if I told her that the girl who broke Mike's heart is here. She'd probably tear her guitar from her neck and do a kamikaze dive off the stage. Her entire family has a penchant for violence, and my girl is no exception.

"What's wrong?" she asks as soon as we're backstage before our encore, and I curse my face for giving me away.

"How do you do that?"

"Do what?" she asks, her hands curling into the soft fabric at my waist as she scrunches her nose at me.

"Know what I'm thinking," I answer.

She can read me like a book of music, and I'm not sure yet if I like it or not. But that's just Kit. Maybe it's the product of having grown up with four brothers. Or maybe it's something she learned from being a twin. Or maybe it's just because she knows me like no one else does, because she's close to me in a way that no one else has ever been.

Her dark eyes narrow up at me, her long lashes drifting together. "Stop trying to distract me."

Since we promised not to keep secrets from each other ever again, I take a deep breath and drop my lips to her ear. "Mike's ex is here."

And, being the pro that she is, she doesn't even glance his way. She keeps her eyes locked on me as I pull away. "Are you fucking kidding me?"

I shake my head.

"What are you talking about?" Mike asks as he towels the back of his neck. He's a sweat-drenched mess, just like the rest of us, after beating on the drums the way he does. He's the best fucking drummer I've ever seen, and one of the best friends I've ever had, and if Danica Carlisle thinks I'm going to let her crush him again—

"Nothing," Kit and I both say in unison.

Mike raises an eyebrow, stumbling forward when Adam claps him hard on the back. "One more song."

We drag ourselves back onstage, play one final song, and then Adam and I begin walking off, pretending we don't hear Danica shouting, "ADAM! ADAM! IT'S ME, DANICA!"

Even Joel finally notices her, and I have a mini panic attack as I imagine him saying something to Mike before Adam or I get the chance to stop him—but then Kit's arm is hooking around his and she's saying something in his ear. He casts a look at me, and then at Adam, before entering our silent agreement to keep pretending Danica's dead.

And I breathe easy again—too fucking easy, because when we walk out to the buses, there she fucking is.

"MIKE!" she shouts, breaking into a sprint and throwing herself into his arms. Kit takes a step forward, but I catch her by the elbow before she can do anything that would earn her charges and jail time.

Mike's arms hang limp at his sides as Danica hugs him like she never left him—like they're still high school sweethearts. I want him to push her away and tell her to go fuck herself…but that isn't Mike, and eventually, his arms lift to hug her back.

"Aren't you happy to see me?" she squeals, leaving me, Adam, and Joel looking at each other like *what the fuck*.

"What are you doing here?" Mike asks, but Danica is already pulling away to smile wide at Adam. She wraps him in a hug he doesn't return and finally answers Mike.

"I live here now."

Danica hugs Joel next, who pacifies her with a one-fingered tap to her back, and then she moves to me, but I step out of reach. "What are you doing at our show?" I ask, and she pouts at me before giving a bullshit answer.

"I wanted to see Mike."

"Why?" Mike says before any of us can ask the same question, and it's the tiny girl who was standing next to Danica in the crowd who's the next to open her mouth. The girl can only be five foot one at best, with a short auburn bob and big, green eyes.

"Yeah, Dani, why?"

Danica shoots a glare over her shoulder before smiling sweetly up at Mike. "Can we talk?"

Kit gets twitchy with the urge to answer for him, and I hook my arm around her shoulder to keep her from pouncing on anyone. I know how she feels—I want to answer for Mike too, because anything other than "No, you fucking heartless bitch" won't do, but I keep my mouth shut and wait.

"Sure," he says. And then he leads her onto the bus.

"I WANTED TO punch her in her stupid face," Kit says the next day at her parents' place. As usual, her dad is in the bathroom, her mom is in the kitchen, and the rest of us are hanging in the den—me, Kit, Leti, all four of Kit's brothers...I'm still not sure if they like me yet or not, but at least they're not still trying to put me in the hospital.

I'm rubbing the phantom bruises on my side, and Mason is smirking, when Kit furrows her brow at me and says, "Do you think they hooked up?" Her eyes search mine, but I know she already knows the answer.

Yeah, I think they hooked up. When Danica asked him to show her the other bus and Mike agreed, the rest of us sat with her cousin, Hailey, on the double-decker. It was awkward as hell, but Hailey handled it like a champ. As soon as she saw Mike's video game setup, she asked if she could play, and then she and Peach entertained themselves while the rest of us wished the she-devil on the other bus would hurry up and dive back down to hell.

"Yeah, I think he hooked up with her," I answer honestly, and Kit growls.

"Why?"

"Was she hot?" Bryce suggests, and Kit shoots him a deadly look that almost makes me laugh.

"He's *Mike*," she counters, and I know what she means. Mike isn't one for groupies or shallow girls, but…

"He's still a dude," Mason throws in. "When's the last time he got laid?"

"Mike could have girls a lot prettier than her."

It's true, but none of those girls is Danica—his first love, his first lay, his first everything. "He loved her," I say, and Kit's face softens with worry.

"Do you think he still does?"

I know better than to try to sugarcoat it. "Probably."

"I don't like her."

"None of us do."

"I like her cousin though…And she was like…*a gamer*." A mischievous smile curves Kit's troublemaker lips, and I chuckle at the suggestion in her voice.

"So you're playing matchmaker now?"

"I'm just saying."

"You sound like Mom," Ryan says, and as if on cue, Mrs. Larson's voice winds through the house, calling us to the dinner table.

On one side of the table, it's Leti, Kale, Kit, me. On the other, Ryan, Mason, Bryce. Under the table, my fingers twine into the denim threads barely covering Kit's knee, and when I glance over at her, her cheeks are a pretty pink that makes me slide my hand even higher.

"So Shawn," Mrs. Larson says, and I jerk my fingers away from Kit's thigh so fast, Kit almost laughs the spaghetti right out of her mouth. "Do your parents both have dark hair?"

I clear my throat and shift in my chair, making sure that my napkin is positioned where it needs to be. "Yeah. It runs in my family."

Mrs. Larson beams. "Oh, that's perfect." She takes another sip of her water and continues smiling at me. "I always imagined a whole houseful of dark-haired grandbabies."

"MOM!" Kit and Mason bark while Ryan, Leti, and Kale all chuckle and Bryce continues slurping up his spaghetti.

"She's like twelve years old!" Mason adds.

"I'm not saying right now!" Mrs. Larson scolds him with a severe crease between her eyebrows before turning another sweet smile on me. "I'm just saying...I mean, you do want kids someday, right Shawn?"

"Oh my God." Kit's face is a sheet of white when I look over at her, her big eyes and gaping jaw directed at her mom.

"I, um…" I scratch a hand through my hair and almost laugh when Kit's expression swings to me, panic flash-firing in her wide, dark eyes.

"You don't have to answer that," she rushes to say. "Don't answer that."

I'm about to answer that when Leti says, "Personally, I think Kale and I would make the cutest babies." He props his chin on his fist and gazes lovingly at Kale. "Your hair, your eyes, my toes."

"What's wrong with my toes?" Kale asks through a smile.

"Dude," Bryce says, "I know you aren't making fun of Larson toes."

I brace myself for Kit's wrath before I look at her and say, "Is that why you always wear your boots?"

She laughs and swats at me while her dad chuckles and insists they got them from their mom. Mrs. Larson chucks a piece of garlic bread all the way down the table, and my arm drapes around Kit's chair.

"They come in useful!" Bryce insists.

"Like when you're outside weeding but don't feel like bending over?" Leti quips, and Bryce shrugs and nods, which makes even Mason start to laugh.

In the commotion, while everyone else is arguing about the pros and cons of having hands for feet, I lean over and plant a kiss against Kit's temple. She melts into it, and I whisper, "I love you."

"Even my toes?" she whispers back.

"Especially your toes."

THAT NIGHT, AS I turn my ignition off in front of my apartment building, Kit opens her door and slides out of the passenger seat before I can get out and open it for her. "I still can't believe my mom did that," she says over my trunk as we circle behind the car to meet each other halfway.

I think about holding her hand, stop myself, and then reach out and do it anyway. "What, you don't want to give your parents a tour bus full of grandkids?"

Kit's cheeks blush an adorable rose-petal pink as we cross the parking lot to my building, and she turns her chin up to wrinkle her nose at me. "A *tour bus*?"

I grin and thread my calloused fingers with hers. "How many then?"

"Are we seriously talking about this?"

I tug her backward when she reaches out to open the door, opening it for her and smirking at the way she pretends to be irritated, the hint of a smile playing at the corners of her mouth.

"Why not?" I ask.

In truth, I'd never thought about kids or a family or anything else—not before Kit. But now, during nights when she's lying in my arms, sometimes I think of the kind of diamond ring she'd wear, of big weddings with tons of family, of how she'll look with crow's feet, gray hair, and a guitar still molded to her lap. And I fall asleep smiling, breathing in the scent of her hair and holding her tight against my chest.

At the end of the hall, Kit hits the button to the elevator and then stares at the glowing white light while nibbling the inside of her bottom lip between her teeth. "I don't know. Maybe one or two...someday. Not anytime soon." She pauses for a long time before lifting her eyes to mine, and I'm sure my palm starts to sweat at the way those eyes make my heart trip in my chest, but Kit holds on tight. "What about you?"

"Maybe one or two," I say, my answer coming more easily than I thought it would. "Someday." I echo Kit, thinking of what her mom said—of little kids with Kit's dark hair. And maybe with my green eyes. And I can tell Kit knows what I'm thinking, because the pink in her cheeks deepens and her free hand begins fidgeting with her pocket. "Not anytime soon though," I add before our palms get too slick to hold. "I have my hands full with Adam."

She laughs and steps onto the elevator when it opens, dragging me with her. "Want to know something super embarrassing?"

She drops my hand to back up against the wall and brace both of hers on the metal railing lining the elevator. Her knee bends, poking through the gaping hole in her jeans as she plants a combat boot against the wall.

"About you?" I say with a grin as I lean against the wall opposite her. "Do you even need to ask?"

Kit drums her fingers against the railing—and drums and drums—until she blurts, "I may or may not have written 'Kit Scarlett' down in a notebook a few dozen times in junior high."

She immediately covers her face with both hands, and my laughter fills the metal box. "You're kidding."

"I wish."

The elevator dings, and she doesn't wait for me before taking quick steps into the hallway. But I catch her before she can get too far, pulling her back against my chest and pinning my chin in the crook of her neck. "That's adorable," I say, smiling against her skin.

Held tight in my arms, she huffs out a breath and says, "I can't believe I told you that."

"I think Kit Scarlett has a nice ring to it."

When she turns her face to the side to stare at me, her skin is that kissable pink that's quickly becoming one of my favorite colors. "You do?" Her voice is a quiet, timid thing, in complete contrast to the rest of her.

I smile as I press a big kiss against her neck. "I do," I say, when what I'm really thinking is, *someday*.

I let go and lead her the rest of the way to my apartment, unlocking the door while she's still too busy blushing to see that the tips of my ears are as red as her cheeks. And then I head toward my room and stop her before she can follow me in. "Wait out here, okay?"

"Why?"

"Because."

"Because why?"

"Because you want to."

"Since when?"

She narrows her eyes at me as I spin her around and nudge her toward the couch, and then I slip into my room and wipe my clammy palms on my jeans. Adam and Peach are gone for the night, just like they swore they'd be, and I have something special planned—something I've been planning for a while.

The night I took Kit's virginity, I was a half-drunk high school senior who had no idea what he was doing. I gave her a night she couldn't forget instead of a night she'd want to remember. And ever since I found that out, it's bugged the hell out of me. That night should've involved candles and rose petals and...I don't know, at least me giving her her first fucking orgasm. But that guy wasn't me, not back then, and now all I can do is try my hardest to make up for it.

It takes me two tries to light the lighter in my hand, and then I touch it to scented candle after scented candle, setting them on my shelves, my dresser, my nightstand. I pull a bag of red rose petals from a cooler and feel like an idiot as I sprinkle them throughout the room and over my dark green comforter. I grab a sheer red cloth from a plastic shopping bag and drape it over my table lamp. And then I look around the room and take a deep breath.

This is so fucking corny. This is the corniest, nerdiest, lamest shit I've ever done.

Kit had better love it.

When I open the door and call her over, she does exactly what I thought she'd do: she takes it all in and giggles, and that sound makes all my embarrassment worth it.

"Seriously?" she says while I smile like the love-struck teenager I should've been for her six years ago.

"This is what I should've done for your first time."

Kit's rosy grin gives her away—she loves it, just like I knew she would. "You're so corny."

"It's your fault."

"No music?"

I hit a button on the remote to my stereo, and Brand New pours through the speakers. She bursts out laughing.

"This isn't exactly Marvin Gaye, Shawn."

"I know, but it's your favorite."

Her arms wrap around my neck and her fingers curl in the back of my hair. "It is." She lifts onto her tiptoes and kisses me softly. "*You're* my favorite."

"And you're calling *me* corny?" I chide with my heart racing against hers, and she laughs and slaps my shoulder a second before I toss her onto my rose-petaled bed.

She giggles until I crawl on top of her, and then she stops laughing, I stop smiling, and I kiss her—I kiss her like I wouldn't have been able to six years ago even if I wanted to. Because back then, I didn't realize she was my other half. Back then, I didn't realize I *had* another half.

Now, I do, and I wrap her in my arms.

Are you new to Jamie's super-hot rock stars?

Find out how Adam-freakin'-Everest fell hard for
Rowan "Peach" Michaels in

MAYHEM...

And don't miss the wild ride that brought
Joel Gibbon and Dee Dawson together in

RIOT...

Available now in print and e-book from
Avon Impulse.

But the final member of
The Last Ones to Know is still single...
Watch for drummer Mike Madden's story
coming soon!

Acknowledgments

When I wrote the acknowledgments for *Mayhem* and *Riot*, those books hadn't been released yet—which makes this the very first time I'm writing an acknowledgments page as a published author, as an author with *readers*, and it's you I want to thank first.

You are the reason I write. Before I was published, I dreamed of you, of strangers who would read my books and hopefully love them. And I just want to say—you've far exceeded even my greatest expectations. You put a smile on my face every single day—with your emails, your messages, your fangirling over The Last Ones to Know. Thank you for buying my books and loving my rocker boys. You are why I'm able to continue doing what I love—and why I continue loving it.

Big squishy hugs, especially, to all of the amazing readers in my Facebook fan group, Jamie's Rock Stars. You guys *are* freaking rock stars, and you blow me away with your support, your enthusiasm, and your ability to make me laugh. You're the best fans and friends I could ask for, and I hope you know how much I adore you.

And of course, major love to the readers who make it their mission to support books, authors, and this entire community of readers—the bloggers. Thank you for supporting me, my novels, my characters, and my dreams. You are truly some of the most amazing, selfless people I have ever met. Thank you so much for writing your kick-ass reviews, for pimping my books, and for making me cry from laughing so hard when you've fought over Adam, Joel, Shawn, and Mike. You guys rock hard, and I appreciate *all* that you do.

Thanks, too, to all of the authors who have leant me their support while I've learned the ropes of publishing— Jay Crownover, Tiffany King, Wendy Higgins, Megan Erickson, Sophie Jordan, and so, so many more. You have all been so ridiculously encouraging and supportive, with your blurbs and encouragement and advice. I feel so extremely privileged to be a part of this community— and to be able to call you friends.

And finally, to all the people who helped make this book what it is—

My critique partners are my behind-the-scenes crew, who get to know my characters long before they're ever put into print. They're the gals in my corner, squirting water in my mouth when I'm about to pass out, pushing me in the right direction when I begin to lose focus, and assuring me I can kick this book's ass when I begin to feel like it's the other way around. So thank you, thank you, thank you to Kim Mong, Rocky Allinger, Marla Wilson, and my mom, Claudia. Kim, you were Shawn's very first fangirl, and it's for Shawn-groupies like you that I *knew* I had to write his story. Rocky, you keep me sane while I ride the writer rollercoaster, and I have no freaking idea what I'd do without you. Marla, your enthusiasm for these books is the perfect writing fuel, and I'm so glad you joined my Panera dream team. And Mom, thank you for always being my biggest cheerleader. All four of you are incredible critique partners and friends, and I hope you know I'm never letting you go—EVER. I'm sorry, but you're mine now.

Mushy love, too, to my rock star literary agent, Stacey Donaghy, who knew even before I did that each of my boys needed their own story. Stacey, you know how much I adore you, and I can't wait to continue this journey together.

And more mushy love to my editor, Nicole Fischer, for being a freaking *saint* while I wrote this book. Nicole, you went above and beyond the call of duty for me, and well...I'm kind of in love with you for it. Thanks for *always* being in my corner, and for responding to emails when the rest of the world was sleeping. You're seriously the best.

And finally, thanks to my husband, Mike, who loves me even when I don't shower for days, who brings me food when I'm too busy writing to remember to eat, and who I love more than words can say. Everything I know about true love, I know because of you.

Give in to your Impulses . . .
Continue reading for excerpts from
our newest Avon Impulse books.
Available now wherever e-books are sold.

CHASING JILLIAN
A LOVE AND FOOTBALL NOVEL
By Julie Brannagh

EASY TARGET
AN ELITE OPS NOVEL
By Kay Thomas

DIRTY THOUGHTS
A MECHANICS OF LOVE NOVEL
By Megan Erickson

LAST FIRST KISS
A BRIGHTWATER NOVEL
By Lia Riley

An Excerpt from

CHASING JILLIAN
A Love and Football Novel

by Julie Brannagh

The fifth novel in *USA Today* bestselling author Julie Brannagh's Love and Football series! Jillian Miller likes her job working in the front office for the Seattle Sharks, but lately she needs a change, which takes her into foreign territory: the Sharks' workout facility after hours. The last thing she expects is a hot, grumbly god among men to be there as witness.

As Jillian discovers that the new her is about so much more than she sees in the mirror, can she discover that happiness and love are oh-so-much better than perfect?

One dance with him and Jillian was pulling herself out of his arms and getting back into the car. She could dance with him and not get emotional about it. He was just another guy. She was not going to let herself get stupid over someone who was clearly only interested in her as a friend.

His hold on her was gentle. He smelled good. She saw the flash of his smile when she peeked up at him. She'd felt shy with Carlos because she didn't know him. She didn't have that problem with Seth. She wanted to move closer, but she shouldn't.

She tried to remind herself of the fact that Seth probably had more than a few friends with benefits, even if he was between girlfriends at the time. He was a guy. He probably wasn't celibate, and they weren't romantic with each other. There was also the tiny fact that anything that happened between them was not going to end well.

She was in more trouble than she knew how to get out of.

At first, Jillian rested her head against his cheek. A minute or so later, she laid her head on his chest. They swayed together, feet barely moving, and he realized his heart was pounding. He'd never experienced anything as romantic as dancing late at night in a deserted city park to a song playing on his car's sound system. The darkness wrapped them in the softest cocoon. He glanced down at her as he felt her slowly relaxing against him.

It's not the pale moon that excites me
That thrills and delights me
Oh, no
It's just the nearness of you

He took a deep breath of the vanilla scent he'd recognize anywhere as hers. His fingers stroked the small of her back, and he heard her sigh. Slow dancing was even better than he remembered. Then again, he wasn't in junior high anymore, and he held a woman in his arms, not a teenage girl. There was a lot to be said for delayed gratification. Dancing with Jillian was all about the smallest movements, and letting things build. He laid his cheek against hers.

"I shouldn't be doing this," she whispered.

"Why not?" he whispered back.

"It's not a good idea."

"We're just dancing, Jill."

And if things got any hotter between them, they'd be naked. She didn't try to step away from him. If she'd resisted him at all, if she'd shown reluctance or fear or hesitation, he would have let her go, and he would walk away. Her fingers tangled in his hair.

They were just friends. He didn't think he had those kinds of feelings for this woman: the sexual, amorous, bow-chicka-bow-bow feelings, despite the fact his pulse was racing, his fingers itched to touch her, and he knew he should let go of her. It didn't matter that he was still having hotter-than-the-invention-of-fire dreams about Jillian most nights, either. He wasn't going to consider what kind of tricks his subconscious played on him. Instead, he pulled her a fraction of an inch closer. He slid one hand up her back, feeling her long, silky-soft blonde hair cascading over his fingers, and she trembled. He cupped her cheek in his hand. He couldn't take his eyes off her mouth. Just a couple of inches more and he'd kiss her. He moved slowly, but purposefully.

He watched her eyelids flutter closed. He felt her quick intake of breath. He wondered how she tasted. He'd know in a few seconds.

"I want to kiss you," he breathed against her mouth.

The silence was broken by the screaming guitars of Guns n' Roses.

That would teach him to use the "shuffle" function.

An Excerpt from

EASY TARGET
An Elite Ops Novel
by *Kay Thomas*

Award-winning author Kay Thomas continues
her thrilling Elite Ops series. Fighting to clear her
brother of murder, freelance reporter Sassy Smith
is suddenly kidnapped and thrown into a truck
with other women who are about to be sold . . .
or worse. When she sees an opportunity for
escape Sassy takes it, but she may have just
jumped from the frying pan into the fire.

"You're thinking too much." She felt his words vibrate against the inside of her thigh as he kissed her there before easing up beside her on the bed. "Stop that."

She smiled, not at all surprised that he seemed to read her mind. He sat up on the edge of the lower bunk next to her and took his own boots and socks off, then his shirt, jeans, and . . .

She closed her eyes.

He was going to be naked soon, and she had to say something first. He slid up beside her on the mattress and pulled her back to his front, with his back toward the wall. She felt the insistence of his erection against her bottom.

She started to turn in his arms, but he held onto her with an arm clamped around her waist. "Slow down. I just want to enjoy holding you a while. I've thought about this for a very long time."

Really? That came as a complete surprise. It was on the tip of her tongue to ask how long, but when he trailed his fingertips back and forth across her rib cage, she quit thinking. Instead, she sighed in relaxed contentment. "I didn't know it could be like that."

Why had she been nervous about this for so long? She could tell him now. It'd be okay.

He kissed the side of her neck and whispered in her ear, "Well, I promise we're just getting started."

She tensed, and he absolutely noticed but misunderstood the reason.

He gathered her more snugly against his chest. "Don't worry, we can take this as slow as you want."

"You'd do that?" The mixture of relief and disappointment she felt was . . . confusing.

"God, Sassy. What sort of men have you—"

The sound of screeching brakes interrupted whatever else he'd been about to say. Sassy felt the momentum shoving her backward into his chest.

"What's happening?" she gasped.

"I don't know." He tugged his arm from under her body to see his watch. "We're not scheduled to stop for several more hours." The stark change from relaxed lover to alert super soldier was dramatic. "Get dressed. Now."

Bryan hauled himself forward out of bed and started shoving clothes toward her while Sassy was still playing catch-up. Her panties were inside out, but she slid them on at his urging without fixing them.

"C'mon, Sassy."

The horrific screeching continued, intensifying as she pulled her jeans, sweater, socks, and boots on. She was lacing up as a rumbling shuddering started.

"Fuck," Bryan mumbled.

"What is it?" She finished with the boots and looked up from her crouched position as the screeching abruptly stopped.

"Hang on!" He grabbed for her.

The rail car shifted, and she felt like she was in a carnival house ride as the compartment swayed wildly from side to side. The car tilted, and the bed she was sitting on flew up in the air. She hit her head on the bunk above, and the world went black.

An Excerpt from

DIRTY THOUGHTS
A Mechanics of Love Novel
by *Megan Erickson*

Some things are sexier the second time around.

Cal Payton has gruff and grumbly down to an art . . . all the better for keeping people away. And it usually works. Until Jenna Macmillan—his biggest mistake—walks into Payton and Sons mechanic shop all grown up, looking like sunshine, and inspiring more than a few dirty thoughts.

Okay, so admittedly Jenna had known this was a stupid idea. She'd tried to talk herself out of it the whole way, muttering to herself as she sat at a stop light. The elderly man in the car in the lane beside her had been staring at her like she was nuts.

And she was. Totally nuts.

It'd been almost a decade since she'd seen Cal Payton and yet one look at those silvery blue eyes and she was shoved right back to the head-over-heels *in love* eighteen-year-old girl she'd been.

Cal had been hot in high school, but damn, had time been good to him. He'd always been a solid guy, never really hitting that awkward skinny stage some teenage boys went through after a growth spurt.

And now . . . well . . . Cal looked downright sinful standing there in the garage. He'd rolled down the top of his coveralls, revealing a white T-shirt that looked painted on, for God's sake. She could see the ridges of his abs, the outline of his pecs. A large smudge on the sleeve drew her attention to his bulging biceps and muscular, veined forearms. Did he lift these damn cars all day? Thank God it was hot as Hades outside already so she could get by with flushed cheeks.

And he was staring at her, those eyes which hadn't changed one bit. Cal never cared much for social mores. He looked people in the eye and he held it long past comfort. Cal had always needed that, to be able to measure up who he was dealing with before he ever uttered a word.

She wondered how she measured up. It'd been a long time since he'd laid eyes on her, and the last time he had, he'd been furious.

Well, she was the one that came here. She was the one that needed something. She might as well speak up, even though what she needed right now was a drink. A stiff one. "Hi, Cal." She went with a smile that surely looked a little strained.

He stood with his booted feet shoulder-width apart, and at the sound of her voice, he started a bit. He finally stopped doing that staring thing as his gaze shifted to the car by her side, then back to her. "Jenna."

His voice. Well, crap, how could she have forgotten about his voice? It was low and silky with a spicy edge, like Mexican chocolate. It warmed her belly and raised goose bumps on her skin.

She cleared her throat as he began walking toward her, his gaze teetering between her and the car. Brent was off to the side, watching them with his arms crossed over his chest. He winked at her. She hid her grin with pursed lips and rolled her eyes. He was a good-looking bastard, but irritating as hell. Nice to see *some* things never changed. "Hey, Brent."

"Hey there, Jenna. Looking good."

Cal whipped his head toward his brother. "Get back to work."

Brent gave him a sloppy salute and then shot her another

knowing smirk before turning around and retreating back into the garage bay.

When she faced Cal again, she jolted, because he was close now, almost in her personal space. His eyes bored into her. "What're ya doing here, Jenna?"

His question wasn't accusatory. It was conversational, but the intent was in his tone, laying latent until she gave him reason to really put the screws to her. She didn't know if he meant what was she doing here, at his garage, or what he was doing in town. But she went for the easy question first.

She gestured to the car. "I, uh, I think the bearings need to be replaced. I know that I could take it anywhere but . . ." She didn't want to tell him it was Dylan's car, and he was the one who let it go so long that she swore the front tires were going to fall off. As much as her brother loved his car, he was an idiot. An idiot who despised Cal, and she was pretty sure the feeling was vice versa. "I wanted to make sure the job was done right and everyone knows you do the best job here." That part was true. The Paytons had a great reputation in Tory.

But Cal never let anything go. He narrowed his eyes and propped his hands on his hips, drawing attention to the muscles in his arms. "How do you know we still do the best job here if you haven't been back in ten years?"

Well then. Couldn't he just nod and take her keys? She held them in her hand, gripping them so tightly that the edge was digging into her palm. She loosened her grip. "Because when I did live here, your father was the best, and I know *you* don't do anything unless you do it the best." Her voice faded off. Even though the last time she'd seen Cal, his eyes had been snapping in anger, at least they'd been showing some sort of emotion. This steady blank gaze was killing her. Not when she knew how his eyes looked when he smiled, as the skin at the corners crinkled and the silver of his irises flashed.

She thought now that this had been a mistake. She'd offered to get the car fixed for her brother while he was out of town. And while she knew Cal worked with his dad now, she'd still expected to run into Jack. And even though he was a total jerk face, she would have rather dealt with him than endure this uncomfortable situation with Cal right now. "You know, it's fine. Don't worry about it, I'll just—"

He snatched the keys out of her hand. Right. Out. Of. Her. Hand.

"Hey!" She propped a hand on her hip, but he wasn't even looking at her, instead fingering the key ring. "Do you always steal keys from your customers?"

He cocked his head and raised an eyebrow at her. There was the smallest hint of a smile, just a tug at the corner of his lips. "I don't make that a habit, no."

"So I'm special then?" She was flirting. Was this flirting? Oh God, it was. She was flirting with her high school boyfriend, the guy who'd taken her virginity, and the guy whose heart she'd broken when she had to make one of the most difficult decisions of her life.

She'd broken her own heart in the process.

His gaze dropped, just for a second, then snapped back to her face. "Yeah, you're special."

He turned around, checking out the car, while she stood gaping at his back. He'd . . . he'd flirted back, right? Cal wasn't really a flirting kind of guy. He said what he wanted and followed through. But flirting Cal?

She shook her head. It'd been over ten years. Surely he'd lived a lot of life during that time she'd been away, going to college, then grad school, then working in New York. She didn't want to think about what that flirting might mean, now that she was back in Tory for good. Except he didn't know that.

An Excerpt from

LAST FIRST KISS
A Brightwater Novel

by Lia Riley

A kiss is just the beginning . . .

Pinterest Perfect. Or so Annie Carson's life
appears on her popular blog. Reality is . . . messier.
Especially when it lands her back in one-cow
town, Brightwater, California, and back in the
path of the gorgeous six-foot-four reason she left.

"**S**awyer?" All she could do was gape, wide-eyed and breathless—too breathless. Could he tell? Hard to say as he maintained his customary faraway expression, the one that made it look as if he'd stepped out of a black and white photograph.

"Annie."

She jumped. Hearing her name on his tongue plucked something deep in her belly, a sweet aching string, the hint of a chord she only ever found in the dark with her own hand. It was impossible not to stare, and suddenly the long years disappeared, until she was that curious seventeen-year-old girl again, seeing a gorgeous boy watching her from the riverbanks, and wondering if the Earth's magnetic poles had quietly flipped.

Stop. Just say no to unwelcome physical reactions. Her body might turn traitor, but her mind wouldn't let her down. She'd fallen for this guy's good looks before, believed they mirrored a goodness inside—a mistake she wouldn't make twice. No man would ever be allowed to stand by and watch her crash again.

Never would she cry in the shower so no one could hear.

Never would she wait for her child to fall asleep so she could fall apart.

Never would she jump and blindly fall.

Sawyer removed his worn tan Stetson and stood. Treacherous hyperawareness raced along her spine and radiated through her hips in a slow, hot electric pulse. He clocked in over six-feet, with steadfast sagebrush green eyes that gave little away. Flecks of ginger gleamed from the scruff roughing his strong jaw and lightened the dark chestnut of his short-cropped hair.

"Hey." Her cheeks warmed as any better words scampered out of reach. The mile-long "to do" list taped to the fridge didn't include squirming in front of the guy she'd nurtured a secret crush on during her teenage years. A guy who, at the sole party Annie attended in high school, abandoned her in a hallway closet during "Seven Minutes in Heaven" to mothballed jackets, old leather shoes, ruthless taunts, and everlasting shame.

He reset his hat. "Did I wake you?" His voice had always appealed to her, but the subtle rough deepening was something else, as if every syllable dragged over a gravel road.

She checked her robe's tie. "Hammering at sunrise kind of has that effect on people."

He gave her a long look. His steadfast perusal didn't waver an inch below her neck, but still, as he lazily scanned each feature, she felt undressed to bare skin. Guess his old confidence hadn't faded, not a cocky manufactured arrogance, but a guy completely comfortable in his own skin.

And what ruggedly handsome, sun-bronzed skin it was, covering all sorts of interesting new muscles he hadn't sported in high school.

"Heard Grandma paid you a visit," he said at last.

Annie doused the unwelcome glow kindling in her chest with a bucket of ice-cold realism. He wasn't here to see her, merely deal with a mess. *Hear that, hormones? Don't be stupid.* She set a hand on her hip, summoning as much dignity as she could muster with a serious case of bedhead. "Visit? Your grandma killed one of our chickens and baked it in a pie. Not exactly the welcome wagon. More like a medieval, craz—"

"Subtlety isn't one of her strong points. We had words last night. It won't happen again." He dusted his hands on his narrow, denim-clad hips and bent down.

Unf.

The hard-working folks at Wrangler deserved a medal for their service. Nothing—NOTHING—else made a male ass look so fine. "Found this, too." He lifted her forgotten bottle of scotch.

"Oh, weird." She plucked it from his grasp. "Wonder how that got out here?" Crap, too saccharine a tone, sweet but clearly false.

He raised his brows as his hooded gaze dropped a fraction. Not enough to be a leer, but definitely a look.

Her threadbare terrycloth hit mid-thigh. Here stood the hottest guy west of the Mississippi and she hadn't shaved since who-the-hell knows and sported a lop-sided bruise on her knee from yesterday's unfortunate encounter with a gopher hole.

Maybe she failed at keeping up appearances, but God as her witness, she'd maintain her posture. "About your Grandma, I was two seconds from calling the cops on her last night."

"That a fact?" The corner of his wide mouth twitched. "Next time, that's exactly what you should do."

"Next time?" She sputtered, waving the bottle for emphasis. "There sure as heck better not be a next time!"

That little burst of sass earned the full-force of his smile. Laugh lines crinkled at the corners of deep-set eyes that belonged nowhere but the bedroom. As a boy, he was a sight, as a man, he'd become a vision. "Why are you back? I mean, after all this time?"